Pot-Likker

-

Folklore, Fairy Tales and Settler Stories From America

Traditional tales, fables and sagas from the United States of America

Compiled & Edited by Clive Gilson

Tales from the World's Firesides

Book 6 in Part 2 of the series: North America

Pot-Likker,

edited by Clive Gilson, Solitude, Bath, UK

www.clivegilson.com

First published as an eBook in 2020

2nd edition © 2020 Clive Gilson

3rd edition © 2023 Clive Gilson

Printed by IngramSpark

ISBN: 978-1-913500-35-1

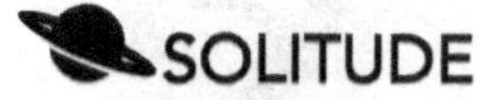

Contents

ORIGINAL FICTION BY CLIVE GILSON

- Songs of Bliss
- Out of the Walled Garden
- The Mechanic's Curse
- The Insomniac Booth
- A Solitude of Stars

AS EDITOR – *FIRESIDE TALES – Part 1, Europe*

- Tales From the Land of Dragons
- Tales From the Land of The Brave
- Tales From the Land of Saints And Scholars
- Tales From the Land of Hope And Glory
- Tales From Lands of Snow and Ice
- Tales From the Viking Isles
- Tales From the Forest Lands
- Tales From the Old Norse
- More Tales About Saints and Scholars
- More Tales About Hope and Glory
- More Tales About Snow and Ice
- Tales From the Land of Rabbits
- Tales Told by Bulls and Wolves
- Tales of Fire and Bronze
- Tales From the Land of the Strigoi
- Tales Told by the Wind Mother
- Tales from Gallia
- Tales from Germania

EDITOR – *FIRESIDE TALES – Part 2, North America*

- Okaraxta - Tales from The Great Plains
- Tibik-Kìzis – Tales from The Great Lakes & Canada
- Jóhonaa'éí –Tales from America's Southwest
- Qugaaĝix̂ - First Nation Tales from Alaska & The Arctic
- Karahkwa - First Nation Tales from America's Eastern States
- Pot-Likker - Folklore, Fairy Tales, and Settler Stories from America

EDITOR – *FIRESIDE TALES – Part 3, Africa*

- Arokin Tales – Folklore & Fairy Tales from West Africa
- Hadithi Tales – Folklore & Fairy Tales from East Africa
- Inkathaso Tales – Folklore & Fairy Tales from Southern Africa
- Tarubadur Tales – Folklore & Fairy Tales from North Africa
- Elephant And Frog – Folklore from Central Africa

Preface

I've been collecting and telling stories for a couple of decades now, having had several of my own works published in recent years. My particular focus is on short story writing in the realms of magical realities and science fiction fantasies.

I've always drawn heavily on traditional folk and fairy tales, and in so doing have amassed a collection of many thousands of these tales from around the world. It has been one of my long-standing ambitions to gather these stories together and to create a library of tales that tell the stories of places and peoples from the four corners of our world.

One of the main motivations for me in undertaking the project is to collect and tell stories that otherwise might be lost or, at best forgotten. Given that a lot of my sources are from early collectors, particularly covering works produced in the late eighteenth century, throughout the nineteenth century, and in the early years of the twentieth century, I do make every effort to adapt stories for a modern reader. Early collectors had a different world view to many of us today, and often expressed views about race and gender, for example, that we find difficult to reconcile in the early years of the twenty-first century. I try, although with varying degrees of success, to update these stories with sensitivity while trying to stay as true to the original spirit of each story as I can.

I also want to assure readers that I try hard not to comment on or appropriate originating cultures. It is almost certainly true that the early collectors of these tales, with their then prevalent world views, have made assumptions about the originating cultures that have given us these tales. I hope that you'll accept my mission to preserve these tales, however and wherever I find them, as just that. I have, therefore, made sure that every story has a full attribution, covering both the original collector / writer and the collection title that this version has been adapted from, as well as having notes about publishers and other relevant and, I hope, interesting source data. Wherever possible I have added a cultural or indigenous attribution as well, although for some of the tiles, the country-based theme is obvious.

The tales in *Pot-Likker* are firmly rooted in the folk traditions that have evolved since Europeans arrived on the continent. Many traditional American stories and tall tales are based on real-life historical figures such as Daniel Boone and Davy Crockett, while others are pure fiction such as Paul Bunyan and the Lone Ranger. Some narratives are born of exaggeration, while others were created to help make sense of aspects of the world not understood at the time, and others to shape the ideals of society.

The founding of the United States is often surrounded by legends and tall tales. Many stories have developed since the founding long ago to become a part of America's folklore and cultural awareness, and non-Native American folklore especially includes any narrative which has contributed to the shaping of American culture and belief systems. These narratives may be true and may be false or may be a little true and a little false; the veracity of the stories is not necessarily a determining factor.

A number of these tales are also examples of early fictional writing in America, combining folklore and social commentary in innovative ways. Kate Chopin in particular embodies this form in her tales set in Louisiana.

The tall tale is also a fundamental element of American folk literature. The tall tale's origins are seen in the bragging contests that often occurred when men of the American frontier gathered. A tall tale is a story with unbelievable elements, related as if it were true and factual. Some such stories are exaggerations of actual events; others are completely fictional tales set in a familiar setting, such as the American Old West, or the beginning of the Industrial Revolution. They are usually humorous or good-natured. The line between myth and tall tale is distinguished primarily by age; many myths exaggerate the exploits of their heroes, but in tall tales the exaggeration looms large, to the extent of becoming the whole of the story.

I feel that we are just touching the tip of the iceberg here, based on those few texts that I've collected so far. There is, I believe a vast weight of storytelling beneath the waters upon which we sail in this collection. I hope that you enjoy these tales as much as I have in their discovery and their mild adaptation.

Clive

Bath, 2023

At His Bedside

This story has been edited and adapted from Henry W. Shoemaker's Allegheny Episodes, first published in 1922 by the Altoona Tribune Company, based out of Altoona, Pennsylvania. This was one of a series of collections forming the Pennsylvania Folk Lore series.

When old Jacob Loy passed away at the age of eighty years, he left a pot of gold to be divided equally among his eight children. It was a pot of such goodly proportions that there was a nice round sum for all, and the pity of it was after the long years of privation which had collected it, that some of the heirs wasted it quickly on organs, fast horses, cheap finery and stock speculations, for it was before the days of player-pianos, victrolas and automobiles.

Yolande, his youngest daughter, was a really attractive girl, even though she had but a small share in the pot of gold, and had many suitors. Though farm raised and inured to hardships she was naturally refined, with wonderful dark eyes and hair, and pallid face – the perfect type of Pennsylvania Mountain loveliness.

Above all her admirers she liked best of all Adam Drumheller, a shrewd young farmer of the neighbourhood, and eventually married him. Three children were born in quick succession, in the small tenant house on his father's farm in Chest Township, where the young couple had gone to live immediately after their wedding.

Shortly after the birth of the last child old Jacob Drumheller died, and the son and his family moved into the big stone farmhouse near the banks of the sulphurous Clearfield Creek. It was not long after this fortuitous move that the young wife began to show signs of the favourite Pennsylvania mountain malady–consumption. Whether it was caused by a deep-seated cold or came about from sleeping in rooms with windows nailed shut, no one could tell, but the beautiful young woman became paler and more wax-like, until she realized that a speedy end was inevitable. Many times she found comfort in her misfortune by having her husband promise that in the event of her death he would never remarry.

"Never, never," he promised. "I could never find your equal again."

He was sincere in some respects; it would be hard to find her counterpart, and she had made a will leaving him everything she possessed, and he imagined that the pot of gold transformed into a bank balance or Government bonds would be found somewhere among her effects.

Before ill health had set in he had quizzed her many times, as openly as he dared, on the whereabouts of her share of the pot.

"It is all safe," she would say. "It will be forthcoming some time when you need it more than you do today," and he was satisfied.

As she grew paler and weaker Adam began to think more of Alvira Hamel, another comely girl whom he had loved when he railroaded out of Johnstown, at Kimmelton, and whom he planned to claim as his own should Yolande pass away.

Perhaps his thoughts dimly reflected on the dying wife's sub-conscious mind, for she became more insistent every day that he promise never to remarry.

"Think of our dear little children," she kept saying, "sentenced to have a stepmother; I will come back and haunt you if you perpetrate such a cruelty to me and mine."

Adam had little faith in a hereafter, and less in ghosts, so he readily promised anything, vowing eternal celibacy cheerfully and profoundly.

When Yolande did finally fade away, she died reasonably happy, and at least died bravely. She never shed a tear, for it is against the code of the Pennsylvania Mountain people to do so – perhaps a survival of the Indian blood possessed by so many of them.

Three days after the funeral Adam hied himself to Ebensburg to "settle up the estate," but also to look up Alvira Hamel, who was now living there. She seemed glad to see him, and when he broached a possible union she acted as if pleased at everything except to go on to that lonely farm on the polluted Clearfield Creek.

By promising to sell out when he could and move to Barnesboro or Spangler, a light came in her dark eyes, and though he did not visit the lawyer in charge of his late wife's affairs, his day in town was successful in arranging for the new alliance with his sweetheart of other days.

In due course of time it was discovered that the equivalent of Yolande's share of the pot of gold left by old Jacob Loy was not to be found. "She may have kept it in coin and buried it in the orchard," was some of the very consoling advice that the lawyer gave.

At any rate it was not located by the time that Adam and Alvira were married, but the bridegroom was well to do and could afford to wait. After a short trip to Pittsburgh and Wheeling the newly married couple took up housekeeping in the big brick farmstead above the creek.

The first night that they were back from the honeymoon – it was just about midnight and Alvira was sleeping peacefully – Adam thought that he heard footsteps on the stairs. He could not be mistaken. Noiselessly the door opened, and the form of Yolande glided into the room; she was in her shroud, all white, and her face was whiter than the shroud, and her long hair never looked blacker.

Along the whitewashed wall by the bedside was a long row of hooks on which hung the dead woman's wardrobe. It had never been disturbed; Alvira was going to cut the things up and make new garments out of them in the Spring. Adam watched the apparition while she moved over to the clothing, counting them, and smoothed and caressed each skirt or waist, as if she regretted having had to abandon them for the steady raiment of the shroud.

Then she came over to the bed and sat on it close to Adam, eyeing him intently and silently. Just then Alvira got awake, but apparently could see nothing of the ghost, although the room was bright as day, bathed in the full moon's light.

Yolande seemed to remain for a space of about ten minutes, then passed through the alcove into the room where the children were sleeping and stood by their bedside. The next night she was back again, repeating the same performance, the next night, and the next, and still the next, each night remaining longer, until at last she stayed until daybreak. In the morning as the hired men were coming up the boardwalk which led to the kitchen door, they would meet Yolande, in her shroud coming from the house, and passing out of the back gate. On one occasion Alvira was pumping water on the porch, but made no move as she passed, being evidently like so many persons, spiritually blind. The hired men had known Yolande all their lives, and were surprised to see her spooking in daylight, but refrained from saying anything to the new wife.

Every day for a week after that she appeared on the kitchen porch, or on the boardwalk, in the yard, on the road, and was seen by her former husband many times, and also her night prowling went on as of yore. The hired men began to complain; it might make them sick if a ghost was around too much; these spooks were supposed to exhale a poison much as copperhead snakes do, and also draw their "life" away, and they threatened to quit if she wasn't "laid." All of them had seen spooks before, on occasion, but a daily visitation of the same ghost was more than they cared about.

Had it not been for the excitable hired men, Adam, whose nerves were like iron, could have stood Yolande's ghost indefinitely. In fact, he thought it rather nice of her to come back and see him and the children "for old time's sake." But the farm hands must be conserved at any cost, even to the extent of laying Yolande's unquiet spirit.

The next night when she appeared, he made bold and spoke to her, "What do you want, Yolande," he said softly, so as not to wake the soundly sleeping Alvira at his side. "Is there anything I can do for you, dear?"

Yolande came very close beside him, and bending down whispered in his ear, "Adam," said she, "how can you ask me why I am here? You surely know. Did you not, time and time again, promise never to marry again, if I died, for the sake of our darling children? Did you not make such a promise, and see how quickly you broke it! Where I am now I can hold no resentments, so I forgive you for all your transgressions, but I hope that Alvira will be good to our children. I have one request to make: After I left you, you were keen to find what I did with my share of daddy's pot of gold. I had it buried in the orchard at my old home, under the Northern Spy, but after we moved here, one time when you went deer hunting to Centre County, I dug it up and brought it over here and buried it in the cellar of this house. It is here now. There are just one hundred and fifty-three twenty-dollar gold pieces; that was my share. The children and the money were on my mind, not your broken promise and rash marriage, which you will repent, and which I tell you again I forgive you for. I want my children to have that money, every one of the one hundred and fifty-three twenty-dollar gold pieces. I buried it a little to the east of the spring in the cellar, about two feet underground, in a tin cartridge box; Dig it up tomorrow morning, and if you find the one hundred and fifty-three coins, and give each and every one of them to the children, and I will never come again and upset your hired men. Why I have Myron Shook about half scared to death already, but if you don't find every single coin I'll have to come back until you do, or if you hold it back from the children, you will not be able to keep a hireling on this place, or any other place to which you move. Many live folks can't see ghosts; your wife is one of these; she will never worry until the hired men quit, then she'll up and have you make sale and move to town. Be square and give the children the money, and I'll not trouble you again."

"Oh, Yolande," answered Adam in gentle tones, "you are no trouble to me, not in the least. I love to have you visit me at night, and look at the children, but you are making the hired help terribly uneasy. That part you must quit."

"That's enough of your drivel, Adam," spoke Yolande, in a sterner tone of voice. "Talk less like a fool, and more like a man. Dig up that money in the morning, count it, and give it to the children and I'll be glad never to see you again."

To be reproached by a ghost was too much for Adam, and he lapsed into silence, while Yolande slipped out of the room, over to the bedside of the sleeping children, where she lingered until daylight.

Adam was soon asleep, but was up bright and early the next morning, starting to dress just as the ghost glided out of the door. By six o'clock he had exhumed Yolande's share of the pot of gold which was buried exactly as her ghost had described.

It was a hard wrench to hand the money over to the children, or rather to take it to Ebensburg and start savings accounts in their names. But he did it without a murmur. The cashier, a horse fancier, gave him a present of a new whip, of a special kind that he had made to order at Pittsburgh, so he came home happy and contented.

Night was upon him, and supper over, he retired early, dozing a bit before the "witching hour." As the old Berks County tall clock in the entry struck twelve, he began to watch for Yolande's accustomed entrance. But not a shadow appeared. The clock struck the quarter, the half, three quarters and one o'clock. No Yolande or anything like her came; she was true to her promise, as true as he had been false. It was an advantage to be a ghost in some ways. They were honourable creatures.

Adam did not know whether to feel pleased or not. His vanity had been not a little appealed to by a dead wife visiting him nightly; now he was sure that it wasn't for love of him or jealousy, she had been coming back, but to see that the children got the money that had been buried in the cellar. And at last she had spoken rather unkindly, so the great change called death had ended her love, and she wasn't grieving over his second marriage at all. However, he fell to consoling himself that she had chided him for breaking his word and marrying again; she must have cared for him or she would not have said those things. Then the thought came to him that she wasn't really peeved at anything concerning his marriage to Alvira except that the children had gotten a stepmother. He wondered if Alvira would continue to be kind to them. Just as he went to sleep he had forgotten both Yolande and Alvira, chuckling over a pretty High School girl he had seen on the street at the 'burg, and whom he had winked at.

The Gray Champion

This story has been edited and adapted from Nathaniel Hawthorne's Twice Told Tales, first published in 1889 by David McKay, Publisher, Philadelphia.

There was once a time when New England groaned under the actual pressure of heavier wrongs than those threatened ones which brought on the Revolution. James II., the bigoted successor of Charles the Voluptuous, had annulled the charters of all the colonies and sent a harsh and unprincipled soldier to take away our liberties and endanger our religion. The administration of Sir Edmund Andros lacked scarcely a single characteristic of tyranny - a governor and council holding office from the king and wholly independent of the country; laws made and taxes levied without concurrence of the people, immediate or by their representatives; the rights of private citizens violated and the titles of all landed property declared void; the voice of complaint stifled by restrictions on the press; and finally, disaffection overawed by the first band of mercenary troops that ever marched on our free soil. For two years our ancestors were kept in sullen submission by that filial love which had invariably secured their allegiance to the mother-country, whether its head chanced to be a Parliament, Protector or popish monarch. Till these evil times, however, such allegiance had been merely nominal, and the colonists had ruled themselves, enjoying far more freedom than is even yet the privilege of the native subjects of Great Britain.

At length a rumour reached our shores that the prince of Orange had ventured on an enterprise the success of which would be the triumph of civil and religious rights and the salvation of New England. It was but a doubtful whisper; it might be false or the attempt might fail, and in either case the man that stirred against King James would lose his head. Still, the intelligence produced a marked effect. The people smiled mysteriously in the streets and threw bold glances at their oppressors, while far and wide there was a subdued and silent agitation, as if the slightest signal would rouse the whole land from its sluggish despondency. Aware of their danger, the rulers resolved to avert it by an imposing display of strength, and perhaps to confirm their despotism by yet harsher measures.

One afternoon in April 1689, Sir Edmund Andros and his favourite councillors, being warm with wine, assembled the red-coats of the governor's guard and made their appearance in the streets of Boston. The sun was near setting when the march commenced. The roll of the drum at that unquiet crisis seemed to go through the streets less as the martial music of the soldiers than as a muster-call to the inhabitants themselves. A multitude by various avenues assembled in King street, which was destined to be the scene, nearly a century afterward, of another encounter between the troops of Britain and a people struggling against her tyranny.

Though more than sixty years had elapsed since the Pilgrims came, this crowd of their descendants still showed the strong and sombre features of their character perhaps more strikingly in such a stern emergency than on happier occasions. There was the sober garb, the general severity of mien, the gloomy but undismayed expression, the scriptural forms of speech and the confidence in Heaven's blessing on a righteous cause which would have marked a band of the original Puritans when threatened by some peril of the wilderness. Indeed, it was not yet time for the old spirit to be extinct, since there were men in the street that day who had worshipped there beneath the trees before a house was reared to the God for whom they had become exiles. Old soldiers of the Parliament were here, too, smiling grimly at the thought that their aged arms might strike another blow against the house of Stuart. Here, also, were the veterans of King Philip's war, who had burned villages and slaughtered young and old with pious fierceness while the godly souls throughout the land were helping them with prayer. Several ministers were scattered among the crowd, which, unlike all other mobs, regarded them with such reverence as if there were sanctity in their very garments. These holy men exerted their influence to quiet the people, but not to disperse them.

Meantime, the purpose of the governor in disturbing the peace of the town at a period when the slightest commotion might throw the country into a ferment was almost the Universal subject of inquiry, and variously explained.

"Satan will strike his master-stroke presently," cried some, "because he knows that his time is short. All our godly pastors are to be dragged to prison. We shall see them at a Smithfield fire in King street."

Hereupon the people of each parish gathered closer round their minister, who looked calmly upward and assumed a more apostolic dignity, as well befitted a candidate for the highest honour of his profession - a crown of martyrdom. It was actually fancied at that period that New England might have a John Rogers of her own to take the place of that worthy in the Primer.

"The pope of Rome has given orders for a new St. Bartholomew," cried others. "We are to be massacred, man and male-child."

Neither was this rumour wholly discredited; although the wiser class believed the governor's object somewhat less atrocious. His predecessor under the old charter, Bradstreet, a venerable companion of the first settlers, was known to be in town. There were grounds for conjecturing that Sir Edmund Andros intended at once to strike terror by a parade of military force and to confound the opposite faction by possessing himself of their chief.

"Stand firm for the old charter-governor!" shouted the crowd, seizing upon the idea - "the good old Governor Bradstreet!"

While this cry was at the loudest the people were surprised by the well-known figure of Governor Bradstreet himself, a patriarch of nearly ninety, who appeared on the elevated steps of a door and with characteristic mildness besought them to submit to the constituted authorities.

"My children," concluded this venerable person, "do nothing rashly. Cry not aloud, but pray for the welfare of New England and expect patiently what the Lord will do in this matter."

The event was soon to be decided. All this time the roll of the drum had been approaching through Cornhill, louder and deeper, till with reverberations from house to house and the regular tramp of martial footsteps it burst into the street. A double rank of soldiers made their appearance, occupying the whole breadth of the passage, with shouldered matchlocks and matches burning, so as to present a row of fires in the dusk. Their steady march was like the progress of a machine that would roll irresistibly over everything in its way. Next, moving slowly, with a confused clatter of hoofs on the pavement, rode a party of mounted gentlemen, the central figure being Sir Edmund Andros, elderly, but erect and soldier-like. Those around him were his favourite councillors and the bitterest foes of New England. At his right hand rode Edward Randolph, our arch-enemy, that "blasted wretch," as Cotton Mather calls him, who achieved the downfall of our ancient government and was followed with a sensible curse - through life and to his grave. On the other side was Bullivant, scattering jests and mockery as he rode along. Dudley came behind with a downcast look, dreading, as well he might, to meet the indignant gaze of the people, who beheld him, their only countryman by birth, among the oppressors of his native land. The captain of a frigate in the harbour and two or three civil officers under the Crown were also there. But the figure which most attracted the public eye and stirred up the deepest feeling was the Episcopal clergyman of King's Chapel riding haughtily among the magistrates in his priestly vestments, the fitting representative of prelacy and persecution, the union of Church and State, and all those abominations which had driven the Puritans to the wilderness. Another guard of soldiers, in double rank, brought up the rear.

The whole scene was a picture of the condition of New England, and its moral, the deformity of any government that does not grow out of the nature of things and the character of the people - on one side the religious multitude with their sad visages and dark attire, and on the other the group of despotic rulers with the high churchman in the midst and here and there a crucifix at their bosoms, all magnificently clad, flushed with wine, proud of unjust authority and scoffing at the universal groan. And the mercenary soldiers, waiting but the word to deluge the street with blood, showed the only means by which obedience could be secured.

"O Lord of hosts," cried a voice among the crowd, "provide a champion for your people!"

This ejaculation was loudly uttered, and served as a herald's cry to introduce a remarkable personage. The crowd had rolled back, and were now huddled together nearly at the extremity of the street, while the soldiers had advanced no more than a third of its length. The intervening space was empty - a paved solitude between lofty edifices which threw almost a twilight shadow over it. Suddenly there was seen the figure of an ancient man who seemed to have emerged from among the people and was walking by himself along the centre of the street to confront the armed band. He wore the old Puritan dress - a dark cloak and a steeple-crowned hat in the fashion of at least fifty years before, with a heavy sword upon his thigh, but a staff in his hand to assist the tremulous gait of age.

When at some distance from the multitude, the old man turned slowly round, displaying a face of antique majesty rendered doubly venerable by the hoary beard that descended on his breast. He made a gesture at once of encouragement and warning, then turned again and resumed his way.

"Who is this grey patriarch?" asked the young men of their sires.

"Who is this venerable brother?" asked the old men among themselves.

But none could make reply. The fathers of the people, those of fourscore years and upward, were disturbed, deeming it strange that they should forget one of such evident authority whom they must have known in their early days, the associate of Winthrop and all the old councillors, giving laws and making prayers and leading them against the savage. The elderly men ought to have remembered him, too, with locks as grey in their youth as their own were now. And the young! How could he have passed so utterly from their memories - that hoary sire, the relic of long-departed times, whose awful benediction had surely been bestowed on their uncovered heads in childhood?

"Where did he come from? What is his purpose? Who can this old man be?" whispered the wondering crowd.

Meanwhile, the venerable stranger, staff in hand, was pursuing his solitary walk along the centre of the street. As he drew near the advancing soldiers, and as the roll of their drum came full upon his ear, the old man raised himself to a loftier mien, while the decrepitude of age seemed to fall from his shoulders, leaving him in grey but unbroken dignity. Now he marched onward with a warrior's step, keeping time to the military music. Thus the aged form advanced on one side and the whole parade of soldiers and magistrates on the other, till, when scarcely twenty yards remained between, the old man grasped his staff by the middle and held it before him like a leader's truncheon.

"Stand!" cried he.

The eye, the face and attitude of command, the solemn yet warlike peal of that voice - fit either to rule a host in the battle-field or be raised to God in prayer - were irresistible. At the old man's word and outstretched arm the roll of the drum was hushed at once and the advancing line stood still. A tremulous enthusiasm seized upon the multitude. That stately form, combining the leader and the saint, so grey, so dimly seen, in such an ancient garb, could only belong to some old champion of the righteous cause whom the oppressor's drum had summoned from his grave. They raised a shout of awe and exultation, and looked for the deliverance of New England.

The governor and the gentlemen of his party, perceiving themselves brought to an unexpected stand, rode hastily forward, as if they would have pressed their snorting and affrighted horses right against the hoary apparition. He, however, blenched not a step, but, glancing his severe eye round the group, which half encompassed him, at last bent it sternly on Sir Edmund Andros. One would have thought that the dark old man was chief ruler there, and that the governor and council with soldiers at their back, representing the whole power and authority of the Crown, had no alternative but obedience.

"What does this old fellow here?" cried Edward Randolph, fiercely. "On, Sir Edmund! Bid the soldiers forward, and give the dotard the same choice that you give all his countrymen - to stand aside or be trampled on."

"Nay, nay! Let us show respect to the good grandsire," said Bullivant, laughing. "See you not he is some old round-headed dignitary who has lain asleep these thirty years and knows nothing of the change of times? Doubtless he thinks to put us down with a proclamation in Old Noll's name."

"Are you mad, old man?" demanded Sir Edmund Andros, in loud and harsh tones. "How dare you stay the march of King James's governor?"

"I have stayed the march of a king himself before now," replied the grey figure, with stern composure. "I am here, Sir Governor, because the cry of an oppressed people has disturbed me in my secret place, and, beseeching this favour earnestly of the Lord, it was vouchsafed me to appear once again on earth in the good old cause of his saints. And what speak you of James? There is no longer a popish tyrant on the throne of England, and by tomorrow noon his name shall be a by-word in this very street, where you would make it a word of terror. Back, you who was a governor, back! With this night your power is ended. Tomorrow, the prison! Back, lest I foretell the scaffold!"

The people had been drawing nearer and nearer and drinking in the words of their champion, who spoke in accents long disused, like one unaccustomed to converse except with the dead of many years ago. But his voice stirred their souls. They confronted the soldiers, not wholly without arms and ready to convert the very stones of the street into deadly weapons. Sir Edmund Andros looked at the old man; then he cast his hard and cruel eye over the multitude and beheld them burning with that lurid wrath so difficult to kindle or to quench, and again he fixed his gaze on the aged form which stood obscurely in an open space where neither friend nor foe had thrust himself. He did not utter a word, but, whether the oppressor was overawed by the Gray Champion's look or perceived his peril in the threatening attitude of the people, it is certain that he gave back and ordered his soldiers to commence a slow and guarded retreat. Before another sunset the governor and all that rode so proudly with him were prisoners, and long before it was known that James had abdicated, King William was proclaimed throughout New England.

But where was the Gray Champion? Some reported that when the troops had gone from King street and the people were thronging tumultuously in their rear, Bradstreet, the aged governor, was seen to embrace a form more aged than his own. Others soberly affirmed that while they marvelled at the venerable grandeur of his aspect the old man had faded from their eyes, melting slowly into the hues of twilight, till where he stood there was an empty space. But all agreed that the hoary shape was gone. The men of that generation watched for his reappearance in sunshine and in twilight, but never saw him more, nor knew when his funeral passed nor where his gravestone was.

And who was the Gray Champion? Perhaps his name might be found in the records of that stern court of justice which passed a sentence too mighty for the age, but glorious in all after-times for its humbling lesson to the monarch and its high example to the subject. I have heard that whenever the descendants of the Puritans are to show the spirit of their sires the old man appears again. When eighty years had passed, he walked once more in King street. Five years later, in the twilight of an April morning, he stood on the green beside the meeting-house at Lexington where now the obelisk of granite with a slab of slate inlaid commemorates the first-fallen of the Revolution. And when our fathers were toiling at the breastwork on Bunker's Hill, all through that night the old warrior walked his rounds. Long, long may it be before he comes again! His hour is one of darkness and adversity and peril. But should domestic tyranny oppress us or the invader's step pollute our soil, still may the Gray Champion come, for he is the type of New England's hereditary spirit, and his shadowy march on the eve of danger must ever be the pledge that New England's sons will vindicate their ancestry.

The Legend Of Monte Del Diablo

This story has been edited and adapted from Bret Harte's Legends And Tales, first published in 1898 by The Jefferson Press, New York.

For many years after Father Junipero Serro first rang his bell in the wilderness of Upper California, the spirit which animated that adventurous priest did not wane. The conversion of the heathen went on rapidly in the establishment of Missions throughout the land. So sedulously did the good Fathers set about their work, that around their isolated chapels there presently arose adobe huts, whose mud-plastered and savage tenants partook regularly of the provisions, and occasionally of the Sacrament, of their pious hosts. Nay, so great was their progress, that one zealous Padre is reported to have administered the Lord's Supper one Sabbath morning to "over three hundred heathen Salvages." It was not to be wondered that the Enemy of Souls, being greatly incensed thereat, and alarmed at his decreasing popularity, should have grievously tempted and embarrassed these Holy Fathers, as we shall presently see.

Yet they were happy, peaceful days for California. The vagrant keels of prying Commerce had not as yet ruffled the lordly gravity of her bays. No torn and ragged gulch betrayed the suspicion of golden treasure. The wild oats drooped idly in the morning heat, or wrestled with the afternoon breezes. Deer and antelope dotted the plain. The watercourses brawled in their familiar channels, nor dreamed of ever shifting their regular tide. The wonders of the Yosemite and Calaveras were as yet unrecorded. The Holy Fathers noted little of the landscape beyond the barbaric prodigality with which the quick soil repaid the sowing. A new conversion, the advent of a Saint's day, or the baptism of a native baby, was at once the chronicle and marvel of their day.

At this blissful epoch there lived at the Mission of San Pablo Father Jose Antonio Haro, a worthy brother of the Society of Jesus. He was of tall and cadaverous aspect. A somewhat romantic history had given a poetic interest to his lugubrious visage. While a youth, pursuing his studies at famous Salamanca, he had become enamoured of the charms of Dona Carmen de Torrencevara, as that lady passed to her matutinal devotions. Untoward circumstances, hastened, perhaps, by a wealthier suitor, brought this amour to a disastrous issue; and Father Jose entered a monastery, taking upon himself the vows of celibacy. It was here that his natural fervour and poetic enthusiasm conceived expression as a missionary. A longing to convert the uncivilized heathen succeeded his frivolous earthly passion, and a desire to explore and develop unknown fastnesses continually possessed him. In his flashing eye and sombre exterior was detected a singular commingling of the discreet Las Casas and the impetuous Balboa.

Fired by this pious zeal, Father Jose went forward in the van of Christian pioneers. On reaching Mexico, he obtained authority to establish the Mission of San Pablo. Like the good Junipero, accompanied only by an acolyte and muleteer, he unsaddled his mules in a dusky canyon, and rang his bell in the wilderness. The savages - a peaceful, inoffensive race - presently flocked around him. The nearest military post was far away, which contributed much to the security of these pious pilgrims, who found their open trustfulness and amiability better fitted to repress hostility than the presence of an armed, suspicious, and brawling soldiery. So the good Father Jose said matins and prime, mass and vespers, in the heart of Sin and Heathenism, taking no heed to himself, but looking only to the welfare of the Holy Church. Conversions soon followed, and, on the 7th of July 1760, the first native baby was baptized, - an event which, as Father Jose piously records, "exceeds the richness of gold or precious jewels or the chancing upon the Ophir of Solomon."

The Mission of San Pablo progressed and prospered until the pious founder thereof, like the infidel Alexander, might have wept that there were no more heathen worlds to conquer. But his ardent and enthusiastic spirit could not long brook an idleness that seemed begotten of sin; and one pleasant August morning, in the year of grace 1770, Father Jose issued from the outer court of the Mission building, equipped to explore the field for new missionary labours.

Nothing could exceed the quiet gravity and unpretentiousness of the little cavalcade. First rode a stout muleteer, leading a pack-mule laden with the provisions of the party, together with a few cheap crucifixes and hawks' bells. After him came the devout Padre Jose, bearing his breviary and cross, with a black serapa thrown around his shoulders; while on either side trotted a dusky convert, anxious to show a proper sense of their regeneration by acting as guides into the wilds of their heathen brethren. Their new condition was agreeably shown by the absence of the usual mud-plaster, which in their unconverted state they assumed to keep away vermin and cold. The morning was bright and propitious. Before their departure, mass had been said in the chapel, and the protection of St. Ignatius invoked against all contingent evils, but especially against bears, which, like the fiery dragons of old, seemed to cherish unconquerable hostility to the Holy Church.

As they wound through the canyon, charming birds disported upon boughs and sprays, and sober quails piped from the alders; the willowy water-courses gave a musical utterance, and the long grass whispered on the hillside. On entering the deeper defiles, above them towered dark green masses of pine, and occasionally the madrono shook its bright scarlet berries. As they toiled up many a steep ascent, Father Jose sometimes picked up fragments of scoria, which spoke to his imagination of direful volcanoes and impending earthquakes. To the less scientific mind of the muleteer Ignacio they had even a more terrifying significance; and he once or twice snuffed the air suspiciously, and declared that it smelt of sulphur. So the first day of their journey wore away, and at night they encamped without having met a single heathen face.

It was on this night that the Enemy of Souls appeared to Ignacio in an appalling form. He had retired to a secluded part of the camp and had sunk upon his knees in prayerful meditation, when he looked up and perceived the Arch-Fiend in the likeness of a monstrous bear. The Evil One was seated on his hind legs immediately before him, with his fore paws joined together just below his black muzzle. Wisely conceiving this remarkable attitude to be in mockery and derision of his devotions, the worthy muleteer was transported with fury. Seizing an arquebuse, he instantly closed his eyes and fired. When he had recovered from the effects of the terrific discharge, the apparition had disappeared. Father Jose, awakened by the report, reached the spot only in time to chide the muleteer for wasting powder and ball in a contest with one whom a single ave would have been sufficient to utterly discomfit. What further reliance he placed on Ignacio's story is not known; but, in commemoration of a worthy Californian custom, the place was called La Canada de la Tentacion del Pio Muletero, or "The Glen of the Temptation of the Pious Muleteer," a name which it retains to this day.

The next morning the party, issuing from a narrow gorge, came upon a long valley, sear and burnt with the shadeless heat. Its lower extremity was lost in a fading line of low hills, which, gathering might and volume toward the upper end of the valley, upheaved a stupendous bulwark against the breezy North. The peak of this awful spur was just touched by a fleecy cloud that shifted to and fro like a banneret. Father Jose gazed at it with mingled awe and admiration. By a singular coincidence, the muleteer Ignacio uttered the simple ejaculation "Diablo!"

As they penetrated the valley, they soon began to miss the agreeable life and companionable echoes of the canyon they had quitted. Huge fissures in the parched soil seemed to gape as with thirsty mouths. A few squirrels darted from the earth, and disappeared as mysteriously before the jingling mules. A grey wolf trotted leisurely along just ahead. But whichever way Father Jose turned, the mountain always asserted itself and arrested his wandering eye. Out of the dry and arid valley, it seemed to spring into cooler and bracing life. Deep cavernous shadows dwelt along its base; rocky fastnesses appeared midway of its elevation; and on either side huge black hills diverged like massy roots from a central trunk. His lively fancy pictured these hills peopled with a majestic and intelligent race of savages; and looking into futurity, he already saw a monstrous cross crowning the dome-like summit. Far different were the sensations of the muleteer, who saw in those awful solitudes only fiery dragons, colossal bears and break-neck trails. The converts, Concepcion and Incarnacion, trotting modestly beside the Padre, recognized, perhaps, some manifestation of their former weird mythology.

At nightfall they reached the base of the mountain. Father Jose unpacked his mules, said vespers, and, formally ringing his bell, called upon the Gentiles within hearing to come and accept the Holy Faith. The echoes of the black frowning hills around him caught up the pious invitation, and repeated it at intervals; but no Gentiles appeared that night. Nor were the devotions of the muleteer again disturbed, although he afterward asserted, that, when the Father's exhortation was ended, a mocking peal of laughter came from the mountain. Nothing daunted by these intimations of the near hostility of the Evil One, Father Jose declared his intention to ascend the mountain at early dawn; and before the sun rose the next morning he was leading the way.

The ascent was in many places difficult and dangerous. Huge fragments of rock often lay across the trail, and after a few hours' climbing they were forced to leave their mules in a little gully, and continue the ascent afoot. Unaccustomed to such exertion, Father Jose often stopped to wipe the perspiration from his thin cheeks. As the day wore on, a strange silence oppressed them. Except the occasional pattering of a squirrel, or a rustling in the chimisal bushes, there were no signs of life. The half-human print of a bear's foot sometimes appeared before them, at which Ignacio always crossed himself piously. The eye was sometimes cheated by a dripping from the rocks, which on closer inspection proved to be a resinous oily liquid with an abominable sulphurous smell. When they were within a short distance of the summit, the discreet Ignacio, selecting a sheltered nook for the camp, slipped aside and busied himself in preparations for the evening, leaving the Holy Father to continue the ascent alone. Never was there a more thoughtless act of prudence, never a more imprudent piece of caution. Without noticing the desertion, buried in pious reflection, Father Jose pushed mechanically on, and, reaching the summit, cast himself down and gazed upon the prospect.

Below him lay a succession of valleys opening into each other like gentle lakes, until they were lost to the southward. Westerly the distant range hid the bosky canada which sheltered the mission of San Pablo. In the farther distance the Pacific Ocean stretched away, bearing a cloud of fog upon its bosom, which crept through the entrance of the bay, and rolled thickly between him and the north-eastward; the same fog hid the base of mountain and the view beyond. Still, from time to time the fleecy veil parted, and timidly disclosed charming glimpses of mighty rivers, mountain defiles, and rolling plains, sear with ripened oats, and bathed in the glow of the setting sun. As Father Jose gazed, he was penetrated with a pious longing. Already his imagination, filled with enthusiastic conceptions, beheld all that vast expanse gathered under the mild sway of the Holy Faith, and peopled with zealous converts. Each little knoll in fancy became crowned with a chapel; from each dark canyon gleamed the white walls of a mission building. Growing bolder in his enthusiasm, and looking farther into futurity, he beheld a new Spain rising on these savage shores. He already saw the spires of stately cathedrals, the domes of palaces, vineyards, gardens, and groves. Convents, half hid among the hills, peeping from plantations of branching limes; and long processions of chanting nuns wound through the defiles. So completely was the good Father's conception of the future confounded with the past, that even in their choral strain the well-remembered accents of Carmen struck his ear. He was busied in these fanciful imaginings, when suddenly over that extended prospect the faint, distant tolling of a bell rang sadly out and died. It was the Angelus. Father Jose listened with superstitious exaltation. The mission of San Pablo was far away, and the sound must have been some miraculous omen. But never before, to his enthusiastic sense, did the sweet seriousness of this angelic symbol come with such strange significance. With the last faint peal, his glowing fancy seemed to cool; the fog closed in below him, and the good Father remembered he had not had his supper. He had risen and was wrapping his serapa around him, when he perceived for the first time that he was not alone.

Nearly opposite, and where should have been the faithless Ignacio, a grave and decorous figure was seated. His appearance was that of an elderly hidalgo, dressed in mourning, with moustaches of iron-grey carefully waxed and twisted around a pair of lantern-jaws. The monstrous hat and prodigious feather, the enormous ruff and exaggerated trunk-hose, contrasted with a frame shrivelled and wizened, all belonged to a century previous. Yet Father Jose was not astonished. His adventurous life and poetic imagination, continually on the lookout for the marvellous, gave him a certain advantage over the practical and material minded. He instantly detected the diabolical quality of his visitant, and was prepared. With equal coolness and courtesy he met the cavalier's obeisance.

"I ask your pardon, Sir Priest," said the stranger, "for disturbing your meditations. Pleasant they must have been, and right fanciful, I imagine, when occasioned by so fair a prospect."

"Worldly, perhaps, Sir Devil, - for such I take you to be," said the Holy Father, as the stranger bowed his black plumes to the ground, "worldly, perhaps; for it has pleased Heaven to retain even in our regenerated state much that pertained to the flesh, yet still, I trust, not without some speculation for the welfare of the Holy Church. In dwelling upon yon fair expanse, my eyes have been graciously opened with prophetic inspiration, and the promise of the heathen as an inheritance has marvellously recurred to me. For there can be none here who lack such diligence in the True Faith, but may see that even the conversion of these pitiful salvages has a meaning. As the blessed St. Ignatius discreetly observes," continued Father Jose, clearing his throat and slightly elevating his voice, "'the heathen is given to the warriors of Christ, even as the pearls of rare discovery which gladden the hearts of shipmen.' Nay, I might say…"

But here the stranger, who had been wrinkling his brows and twisting his moustaches with well-bred patience, took advantage of an oratorical pause. "It grieves me, Sir Priest, to interrupt the current of your eloquence as discourteously as I have already broken your meditations; but the day has already waned to night. I have a matter of serious importance to make with you, so could I entreat your cautious consideration a few moments."

Father Jose hesitated. The temptation was great, and the prospect of acquiring some knowledge of the Great Enemy's plans was not the least trifling object. And if the truth must be told, there was a certain decorum about the stranger that interested the Padre. Though well aware of the Protean shapes the Arch-Fiend could assume, and though free from the weaknesses of the flesh, Father Jose was not above the temptations of the spirit. Had the Devil appeared, as in the case of the pious St. Anthony, in the likeness of a comely damsel, the good Father, with his certain experience of the deceitful sex, would have whisked her away in the saying of a paternoster. But there was, added to the security of age, a grave sadness about the stranger, a thoughtful consciousness as of being at a great moral disadvantage, which at once decided the Padre on a magnanimous course of conduct.

The stranger then proceeded to inform him, that he had been diligently observing the Holy Father's triumphs in the valley. That, far from being greatly exercised thereat, he had been only grieved to see so enthusiastic and chivalrous an antagonist wasting his zeal in a hopeless work. For, he observed, the issue of the great battle of Good and Evil had been otherwise settled, as he would presently show him. "It wants but a few moments of night," he continued, "and over this interval of twilight, as you know, I have been given complete control. Look to the West."

As the Padre turned, the stranger took his enormous hat from his head, and waved it three times before him. At each sweep of the prodigious feather, the fog grew thinner, until it melted impalpably away, and the former landscape returned, yet warm with the glowing sun. As Father Jose gazed, a strain of martial music arose from the valley, and issuing from a deep canyon, the good Father beheld a long cavalcade of gallant cavaliers, habited like his companion. As they swept down the plain, they were joined by like processions, that slowly defiled from every ravine and canyon of the mysterious mountain. From time to time the peal of a trumpet swelled fitfully upon the breeze; the cross of Santiago glittered, and the royal banners of Castile and Aragon waved over the moving column. So they moved on solemnly toward the sea, where, in the distance, Father Jose saw stately caravels, bearing the same familiar banner, awaiting them. The good Padre gazed with conflicting emotions, and the serious voice of the stranger broke the silence.

"You have beheld, Sir Priest, the fading footprints of adventurous Castile. You have seen the declining glory of old Spain, declining as yonder brilliant sun. The sceptre she has wrested from the heathen is fast dropping from her decrepit and fleshless grasp. The children she has fostered shall know her no longer. The soil she has acquired shall be lost to her as irrevocably as she herself has thrust the Moor from her own Granada."

The stranger paused, and his voice seemed broken by emotion; at the same time, Father Jose, whose sympathizing heart yearned toward the departing banners, cried in poignant accents, "Farewell, you gallant cavaliers and Christian soldiers! Farewell, you, Nunes de Balboa! you, Alonzo de Ojeda! and you, most venerable Las Casas! Farewell, and may Heaven prosper still the seed you left behind!"

Then turning to the stranger, Father Jose beheld him gravely draw his pocket-handkerchief from the basket-hilt of his rapier, and apply it decorously to his eyes.

"Pardon this weakness, Sir Priest," said the cavalier, apologetically, "but these worthy gentlemen were ancient friends of mine, and have done me many a delicate service, much more, perchance, than these poor sables may signify," he added, with a grim gesture toward the mourning suit he wore.

Father Jose was too much preoccupied in reflection to notice the equivocal nature of this tribute, and, after a few moments' silence, said, as if continuing his thought, "But the seed they have planted shall thrive and prosper on this fruitful soil."

As if answering the interrogatory, the stranger turned to the opposite direction, and, again waving his hat, said, in the same serious tone, "Look to the East!"

The Father turned, and, as the fog broke away before the waving plume, he saw that the sun was rising. Issuing with its bright beams through the passes of the snowy mountains beyond, appeared a strange and motley crew. Instead of the dark and romantic visages of his last phantom train, the Father beheld with strange concern the blue eyes and flaxen hair of a Saxon race. In place of martial airs and musical utterance, there rose upon the ear a strange din of harsh gutturals and singular sibilation. Instead of the decorous tread and stately mien of the cavaliers of the former vision, they came pushing, bustling, panting, and swaggering. And as they passed, the good Father noticed that giant trees were prostrated as with the breath of a tornado, and the bowels of the earth were torn and rent as with a convulsion. And Father Jose looked in vain for holy cross or Christian symbol; there was but one that seemed an ensign, and he crossed himself with holy horror as he perceived it bore the effigy of a bear.

"Who are these swaggering Ishmaelites?" he asked, with something of asperity in his tone.

The stranger was gravely silent.

"What do they here, with neither cross nor holy symbol?" he again demanded.

"Have you the courage to see, Sir Priest?" responded the stranger, quietly.

Father Jose felt his crucifix, as a lonely traveller might his rapier, and assented.

"Step under the shadow of my plume," said the stranger.

Father Jose stepped beside him, and they instantly sank through the earth.

When he opened his eyes, which had remained closed in prayerful meditation during his rapid descent, he found himself in a vast vault, bespangled overhead with luminous points like the starred firmament. It was also lighted by a yellow glow that seemed to proceed from a mighty sea or lake that occupied the centre of the chamber. Around this subterranean sea dusky figures flitted, bearing ladles filled with the yellow fluid, which they had replenished from its depths. From this lake diverging streams of the same mysterious flood penetrated like mighty rivers the cavernous distance. As they walked by the banks of this glittering Styx, Father Jose perceived how the liquid stream at certain places became solid. The ground was strewn with glittering flakes. One of these the Padre picked up and curiously examined. It was virgin gold.

An expression of discomfiture overcast the good Father's face at this discovery; but there was trace neither of malice nor satisfaction in the stranger's air, which was still of serious and fateful contemplation. When Father Jose recovered his equanimity, he said, bitterly, "This, then, Sir Devil, is your work! This is your deceitful lure for the weak souls of sinful nations! So would you replace the Christian grace of holy Spain!"

"This is what must be," returned the stranger, gloomily. "But listen, Sir Priest. It lies with you to avert the issue for a time. Leave me here in peace. Go back to Castile, and take with you your bells, your images, and your missions. Continue here, and you only precipitate results. Stay! Promise me you will do this, and you shall not lack that which will render your old age an ornament and a blessing," and the stranger motioned significantly to the lake.

It was here that the Devil showed - as he always shows sooner or later - his cloven hoof. The worthy Padre, sorely perplexed by his threefold vision, and, if the truth must be told, a little nettled at this wresting away of the glory of holy Spanish discovery, had shown some hesitation. But the unlucky bribe of the Enemy of Souls touched his Castilian spirit. Starting back in deep disgust, he brandished his crucifix in the face of the unmasked Fiend, and in a voice that made the dusky vault resound, cried, "Avaunt you, Sathanas! Diabolus, I defy you! What! Would you bribe me, me, a brother of the Sacred Society of the Holy Jesus, Licentiate of Cordova and Inquisitor of Guadalaxara? Do you think to buy me with your sordid treasure? Avaunt!"

What might have been the issue of this rupture, and how complete might have been the triumph of the Holy Father over the Arch-Fiend, who was recoiling at hearing these sacred titles and the flourishing symbol, we can never know, for at that moment the crucifix slipped through the Padre's fingers.

Scarcely had it touched the ground before Devil and Holy Father simultaneously cast themselves toward it. In the struggle they clinched, and the pious Jose, who was as much the superior of his antagonist in bodily as in spiritual strength, was about to treat the Great Adversary to a back somersault, when he suddenly felt the long nails of the stranger piercing his flesh. A new fear seized his heart, a numbing chillness crept through his body, and he struggled to free himself, but in vain. A strange roaring was in his ears; the lake and cavern danced before his eyes and vanished; and with a loud cry he sank senseless to the ground.

When he recovered his consciousness he was aware of a gentle swaying motion of his body. He opened his eyes, and saw it was high noon, and that he was being carried in a litter through the valley. He felt stiff, and, looking down, perceived that his arm was tightly bandaged to his side. He closed his eyes and after a few words of thankful prayer, thought how miraculously he had been preserved, and made a vow of candlesticks to the blessed Saint Jose. He then called in a faint voice, and presently the penitent Ignacio stood beside him.

The joy the poor fellow felt at his patron's returning consciousness for some time choked his utterance. He could only ejaculate, "A miracle! Blessed Saint Jose, he lives!" and kiss the Padre's bandaged hand. Father Jose, more intent on his last night's experience, waited for his emotion to subside, and asked where he had been found.

"On the mountain, your Reverence, but a few varas from where he attacked you."

"How? You saw him then?" asked the Padre, in unfeigned astonishment.

"Saw him, your Reverence! Mother of God, I should think I did! And your Reverence shall see him too, if he ever comes again within range of Ignacio's arquebuse."

"What do you mean, Ignacio?" said the Padre, sitting bolt-upright in his litter.

"Why, the bear, your Reverence, the bear, Holy Father, who attacked your worshipful person while you were meditating on the top of yonder mountain."

"Ah!" said the Holy Father, lying down again. "Chut, child! I would be at peace."

When he reached the Mission, he was tenderly cared for, and in a few weeks was enabled to resume those duties from which, as will be seen, not even the machinations of the Evil One could divert him. The news of his physical disaster spread over the country; and a letter to the Bishop of Guadalaxara contained a confidential and detailed account of the good Father's spiritual temptation. But in some way the story leaked out; and long after Jose was gathered to his fathers, his mysterious encounter formed the theme of thrilling and whispered narrative. The mountain was generally shunned. It is true that Senor Joaquin Pedrillo afterward located a grant near the base of the mountain; but as Senora Pedrillo was known to be a termagant half-breed, the Senor was not supposed to be over-fastidious.

The Wedding-Knell

This story has been edited and adapted from Nathaniel Hawthorne's Twice Told Tales, first published in 1889 by David McKay, Publisher, Philadelphia.

There is a certain church, in the city of New York which I have always regarded with peculiar interest on account of a marriage there solemnized under very singular circumstances in my grandmother's girlhood. That venerable lady chanced to be a spectator of the scene, and ever after made it her favourite narrative. Whether the edifice now standing on the same site is identical to the one to which she referred I am not antiquarian enough to know, nor would it be worthwhile to correct myself, perhaps, of an agreeable error by reading the date of its erection on the tablet over the door. It is a stately church surrounded by an enclosure of the loveliest green, within which appear urns, pillars, obelisks, and other forms of monumental marble, the tributes of private affection or more splendid memorials of historic dust. With such a place, though the tumult of the city rolls beneath its tower, one would be willing to connect some legendary interest.

The marriage might be considered as the result of an early engagement, though there had been two intermediate weddings on the lady's part and forty years of celibacy on that of the gentleman. At sixty-five Mr. Ellenwood was a shy but not quite a secluded man; selfish, like all men who brood over their own hearts, yet manifesting on rare occasions a vein of generous sentiment; a scholar throughout life, though always an indolent one, because his studies had no definite object either of public advantage or personal ambition; a gentleman, high-bred and fastidiously delicate, yet sometimes requiring a considerable relaxation in his behalf of the common rules of society. In truth, there were so many anomalies in his character, and, though shrinking with diseased sensibility from public notice, it had been his fatality so often to become the topic of the day by some wild eccentricity of conduct, that people searched his lineage for a hereditary taint of insanity. But there was no need of this. His caprices had their origin in a mind that lacked the support of an engrossing purpose, and in feelings that preyed upon themselves for want of other food. If he were mad, it was the consequence, and not the cause, of an aimless and abortive life.

The widow was as complete a contrast to her third bridegroom in everything but age as can well be conceived. Compelled to relinquish her first engagement, she had been united to a man of twice her own years, to whom she became an exemplary wife, and by whose death she was left in possession of a splendid fortune. A Southern gentleman considerably younger than herself succeeded to her hand and carried her to Charleston, where after many uncomfortable years she found herself again a widow. It would have been singular if any uncommon delicacy of feeling had survived through such a life as Mrs. Dabney's; it could not but be crushed and killed by her early disappointment, the cold duty of her first marriage, the dislocation of the heart's principles consequent on a second union, and the unkindness of her Southern husband, which had inevitably driven her to connect the idea of his death with that of her comfort. To be brief, she was that wisest but unloveliest variety of woman, a philosopher, bearing troubles of the heart with equanimity, dispensing with all that should have been her happiness and making the best of what remained. Sage in most matters, the widow was perhaps the more amiable for the one frailty that made her ridiculous. Being childless, she could not remain beautiful by proxy in the person of a daughter; she therefore refused to grow old and ugly on any consideration; she struggled with Time, and held fast her roses in spite of him, till the venerable thief appeared to have relinquished the spoil as not worth the trouble of acquiring it.

The approaching marriage of this woman of the world with such an unworldly man as Mr. Ellenwood was announced soon after Mrs. Dabney's return to her native city. Superficial observers, and deeper ones, seemed to concur in supposing that the lady must have borne no inactive part in arranging the affair; there were considerations of expediency which she would be far more likely to appreciate than Mr. Ellenwood, and there was just the specious phantom of sentiment and romance in this late union of two early lovers which sometimes makes a fool of a woman who has lost her true feelings among the accidents of life. All the wonder was how the gentleman, with his lack of worldly wisdom and agonizing consciousness of ridicule, could have been induced to take a measure at once so prudent and so laughable. But while people talked the wedding-day arrived. The ceremony was to be solemnized according to the Episcopalian forms and in open church, with a degree of publicity that attracted many spectators, who occupied the front seats of the galleries and the pews near the altar and along the broad aisle. It had been arranged, or possibly it was the custom of the day, that the parties should proceed separately to church. By some accident the bridegroom was a little less punctual than the widow and her bridal attendants, with whose arrival, after this tedious but necessary preface, the action of our tale may be said to commence.

The clumsy wheels of several old-fashioned coaches were heard, and the gentlemen and ladies composing the bridal-party came through the church door with the sudden and gladsome effect of a burst of sunshine. The whole group, except the principal figure, was made up of youth and gayety. As they streamed up the broad aisle, while the pews and pillars seemed to brighten on either side, their steps were as buoyant as if they mistook the church for a ball-room and were ready to dance hand in hand to the altar. So brilliant was the spectacle that few took notice of a singular phenomenon that had marked its entrance. At the moment when the bride's foot touched the threshold the bell swung heavily in the tower above her and sent forth its deepest knell. The vibrations died away, and returned with prolonged solemnity as she entered the body of the church.

"Good heavens! What an omen!" whispered a young lady to her lover.

"On my honour," replied the gentleman, "I believe the bell has the good taste to toll of its own accord. What has she to do with weddings? If you, dearest Julia, were approaching the altar, the bell would ring out its merriest peal. It has only a funeral-knell for her."

The bride and most of her company had been too much occupied with the bustle of entrance to hear the first boding stroke of the bell or, at least, to reflect on the singularity of such a welcome to the altar. They therefore continued to advance with undiminished gayety. The gorgeous dresses of the time - the crimson velvet coats, the gold-laced hats, the hoop-petticoats, the silk, satin, brocade and embroidery, the buckles, canes and swords, all displayed to the best advantage on persons suited to such finery - made the group appear more like a bright-coloured picture than anything real. But by what perversity of taste had the artist represented his principal figure as so wrinkled and decayed, while yet he had decked her out in the brightest splendour of attire, as if the loveliest maiden had suddenly withered into age and become a moral to the beautiful around her? On they went, however, and had glittered along about a third of the aisle, when another stroke of the bell seemed to fill the church with a visible gloom, dimming and obscuring the bright-pageant till it shone forth again as from a mist.

This time the party wavered, stopped and huddled closer together, while a slight scream was heard from some of the ladies and a confused whispering among the gentlemen. Thus tossing to and fro, they might have been fancifully compared to a splendid bunch of flowers suddenly shaken by a puff of wind which threatened to scatter the leaves of an old brown, withered rose on the same stalk with two dewy buds, such being the emblem of the widow between her fair young bridesmaids. But her heroism was admirable. She had started with an irrepressible shudder, as if the stroke of the bell had fallen directly on her heart; then, recovering herself, while her attendants were yet in dismay, she took the lead and paced calmly up the aisle. The bell continued to swing, strike and vibrate with the same doleful regularity as when a corpse is on its way to the tomb.

"My young friends here have their nerves a little shaken," said the widow, with a smile, to the clergyman at the altar. "But so many weddings have been ushered in with the merriest peal of the bells, and yet turned out unhappily, that I shall hope for better fortune under such different auspices."

"Madam," answered the rector, in great perplexity, "this strange occurrence brings to my mind a marriage-sermon of the famous Bishop Taylor wherein he mingles so many thoughts of mortality and future woe that, to speak somewhat after his own rich style, he seems to hang the bridal-chamber in black and cut the wedding-garment out of a coffin-pall. And it has been the custom of divers nations to infuse something of sadness into their marriage ceremonies, so to keep death in mind while contracting that engagement which is life's chiefest business. Thus we may draw a sad but profitable moral from this funeral-knell."

But, though the clergyman might have given his moral even a keener point, he did not fail to despatch an attendant to inquire into the mystery and stop those sounds so dismally appropriate to such a marriage. A brief space elapsed, during which the silence was broken only by whispers and a few suppressed titterings among the wedding-party and the spectators, who after the first shock were disposed to draw an ill-natured merriment from the affair. The young have less charity for aged follies than the old for those of youth. The widow's glance was observed to wander for an instant toward a window of the church, as if searching for the time-worn marble that she had dedicated to her first husband; then her eyelids dropped over their faded orbs and her thoughts were drawn irresistibly to another grave. Two buried men with a voice at her ear and a cry afar off were calling her to lie down beside them. Perhaps, with momentary truth of feeling, she thought how much happier her fate had been if, after years of bliss, the bell were now tolling for her funeral and she were followed to the grave by the old affection of her earliest lover, long her husband. But why had she returned to him when their cold hearts shrank from each other's embrace?

Still the death-bell tolled so mournfully that the sunshine seemed to fade in the air. A whisper, communicated from those who stood nearest the windows, now spread through the church: a hearse with a train of several coaches was creeping along the street, conveying some dead man to the churchyard, while the bride awaited a living one at the altar. Immediately after, the footsteps of the bridegroom and his friends were heard at the door. The widow looked down the aisle and clenched the arm of one of her bridesmaids in her bony hand with such unconscious violence that the fair girl trembled.

"You frighten me, my dear madam," cried she. "For heaven's sake, what is the matter?"

"Nothing, my dear, nothing," said the widow; then, whispering close to her ear, "There is a foolish fancy that I cannot get rid of. I am expecting my bridegroom to come into the church with my two first husbands for groomsmen."

"Look! Look!" screamed the bridemaid. "What is here? The funeral!"

As she spoke a dark procession paced into the church. First came an old man and woman, like chief mourners at a funeral, attired from head to foot in the deepest black, all but their pale features and hoary hair, he leaning on a staff and supporting her decrepit form with his nerveless arm. Behind appeared another and another pair, as aged, as black and mournful as the first. As they drew near the widow recognized in every face some trait of former friends long forgotten, but now returning as if from their old graves to warn her to prepare a shroud, or, with purpose almost as unwelcome, to exhibit their wrinkles and infirmity and claim her as their companion by the tokens of her own decay. Many a merry night had she danced with them in youth, and now in joyless age she felt that some withered partner should request her hand and all unite in a dance of death to the music of the funeral-bell.

While these aged mourners were passing up the aisle it was observed that from pew to pew the spectators shuddered with irrepressible awe as some object hereto concealed by the intervening figures came full in sight. Many turned their faces away; others kept a fixed and rigid stare, and a young girl giggled hysterically and fainted with the laughter on her lips. When the spectral procession approached the altar, each couple separated and slowly diverged, till in the centre appeared a form that had been worthily ushered in with all this gloomy pomp, the death-knell and the funeral. It was the bridegroom in his shroud.

No garb but that of the grave could have befitted such a death-like aspect. The eyes, indeed, had the wild gleam of a sepulchral lamp; all else was fixed in the stern calmness which old men wear in the coffin. The corpse stood motionless, but addressed the widow in accents that seemed to melt into the clang of the bell, which fell heavily on the air while he spoke.

"Come, my bride!" said those pale lips. "The hearse is ready; the sexton stands waiting for us at the door of the tomb. Let us be married, and then to our coffins!"

How shall the widow's horror be represented? It gave her the ghastliness of a dead man's bride. Her youthful friends stood apart, shuddering at the mourners, the shrouded bridegroom and herself; the whole scene expressed by the strongest imagery of the vain struggle of the gilded vanities of this world when opposed to age, infirmity, sorrow and death.

The awestruck silence was first broken by the clergyman. "Mr. Ellenwood," said he, soothingly, yet with somewhat of authority, "you are not well. Your mind has been agitated by the unusual circumstances in which you are placed. The ceremony must be deferred. As an old friend, let me entreat you to return home."

"Home? Yes, but not without my bride," answered he, in the same hollow accents. "You deem this mockery - perhaps madness. Had I bedecked my aged and broken frame with scarlet and embroidery, had I forced my withered lips to smile at my dead heart, that might have been mockery or madness; but now let young and old declare which of us has come here without a wedding-garment - the bridegroom or the bride."

He stepped forward at a ghostly pace and stood beside the widow, contrasting the awful simplicity of his shroud with the glare and glitter in which she had arrayed herself for this unhappy scene. None that beheld them could deny the terrible strength of the moral which his disordered intellect had contrived to draw.

"Cruel! cruel!" groaned the heart-stricken bride.

"Cruel?" repeated he. Then, losing his deathlike composure in a wild bitterness, he said, "Heaven judge which of us has been cruel to the other! In youth you deprived me of my happiness, my hopes, my aims; you took away all the substance of my life and made it a dream without reality enough even to grieve at, with only a pervading gloom, through which I walked wearily and cared not where. But after forty years, when I have built my tomb and would not give up the thought of resting there - no, not for such a life as we once pictured - you call me to the altar. At your summons I am here. But other husbands have enjoyed your youth, your beauty, your warmth of heart and all that could be termed your life. What is there for me but your decay and death? And therefore I have bidden these funeral-friends, and asked for the sexton's deepest knell, and am come in my shroud to wed you as with a burial-service, that we may join our hands at the door of the sepulchre and enter it together."

It was not frenzy, it was not merely the drunkenness of strong emotion in a heart unused to it, that now worked upon the bride. The stern lesson of the day had done its work; her worldliness was gone. She seized the bridegroom's hand.

"Yes!" cried she, "let us wed even at the door of the sepulchre. My life is gone in vanity and emptiness, but at its close there is one true feeling. It has made me what I was in youth: it makes me worthy of you. Time is no more for both of us. Let us wed for eternity."

With a long and deep regard the bridegroom looked into her eyes, while a tear was gathering in his own. How strange that gush of human feeling from the frozen bosom of a corpse! He wiped away the tear, even with his shroud.

"Beloved of my youth," said he, "I have been wild. The despair of my whole lifetime had returned at once and maddened me. Forgive and be forgiven. Yes; it is evening with us now, and we have realized none of our morning dreams of happiness. But let us join our hands before the altar as lovers whom adverse circumstances have separated through life, yet who meet again as they are leaving it and find their earthly affection changed into something holy as religion. And what is time to the married of eternity?"

Amid the tears of many and a swell of exalted sentiment in those who felt aright the union of two immortal souls was solemnized. The train of withered mourners, the hoary bridegroom in his shroud, the pale features of the aged bride and the death-bell tolling through the whole till its deep voice overpowered the marriage-words, all marked the funeral of earthly hopes. But as the ceremony proceeded, the organ, as if stirred by the sympathies of this impressive scene, poured forth an anthem, first mingling with the dismal knell, then rising to a loftier strain, till the soul looked down upon its woe. And when the awful rite was finished and with cold hand in cold hand the married of eternity withdrew, then the organ's peal of solemn triumph drowned the wedding-knell.

The Enchanted Burro

This story has been edited and adapted from Charles F. Lummis's The Enchanted Burro And Other Stories As I Have Known Them From Maine To Chile And California, first published in 1912 by A. C. McClurg & Co., Chicago.

Lelo dropped the point of his heavy irrigating hoe and stood with chin dented upon the rude handle, looking intently to the east. Around his bare ankles the rill from the acéquia eddied a moment and then sucked through the gap in the little ridge of earth which bounded the irrigating bed. The early sun was yellow as gold upon the crags of the mesa - that league-long front of ragged cliffs whose sandstones, black-capped by the lava of the immemorial Year of Fire, here wall the valley of the Rio Grande on the west. Where a spur of the frowning Kú-mai runs out is a little bay in the cliffs; and here the outermost fields of Isleta were turning green with spring. The young wheat swayed and whispered to the water, whose scouts stole about amid the stalks, and came back and called their fellows forward, and spread here and yon, till every green blade was drinking and the tide began to creep up the low boundaries at either side. Up at the sluice gate a small but eager stream was tumbling from the big, placid ditch, and on it came till it struck the tiny dam which closed the furrow just beyond Lelo, and, turning, stole past him again to join the rest amid the wheat. The irrigating bed, twenty feet square, filled and filled, and suddenly the gathered puddle broke down a barrier and came romping into the next bed without so much as saying "By your leave." And here it was not so friendly; for, forgetting that it had come only to bring a drink, it went stampeding about, knocking down the tender blades and half covering them with mud. At the sound of this, Lelo seemed suddenly to waken, and lifting with his hoe the few clods which dammed the furrow, he dropped them into the first gap, and jumping into the second bed repaired its barrier also with a few strokes. Then he let in a gentler stream from the furrow.

"Poco, and I should have lost a bed," he said to himself, good-naturedly.

He always took things easy, and I presume that is the reason no one ever called him anything but Lelo, which means "Slow-poke", for native boys are as given to nicknames as are any others, and the mote had stuck to him ever since its invention. He was rather slow, this big, powerful boy, with a round, heavy chin and a face less clear-cut than was common in the pueblo. Old 'Lipe had taken to wife a Navajo captive, and all could see that the boy carried upon his father's strong frame the flatter, more stolid features of his mother's nomad people.

But now the face seemed not quite so heavy; for again he was looking toward the pueblo and bending his head as one who listens for a far whisper. There it came again, a faint, faint air which not one of us could have heard, but to this boy it told of shouts and mingled wails.

"What will be?" cried Lelo, stamping his hoe upon the barrier, and with unwonted fire in his eyes. "For surely I hear the voice of women lamenting, and there are men's shouts as in anger. Something heavy it will be, and perhaps I am needed."

Splashing up to the ditch, he shut the gate and threw down his hoe, and a moment later was running toward Isleta with the long, heavy, tireless stride that was the jest of the other boys in the rabbit hunt, but left Lelo not so very far behind them after all.

In the pueblo was, indeed, excitement enough. Little knots of the swart people stood here and there, talking earnestly but low; in the broad, flat plaza were many hurrying to and fro; and in the street beyond was a great crowd about a house from which arose the long, wild wails of mourners.

"What is, tio Diego?" asked Lelo, stopping where a number of men stood in gloomy silence. "What has happened? For even in the milpa I heard the cries, and came running to see."

"It is ill," answered the old man he had addressed as uncle. "It seems that Those Above are angry with us! For this morning the captain of war finds himself dead in bed - and scalped! And no tracks of man were about his door."

"Ay, all is ill!" groaned a short, heavy-set man, in a frayed blanket. "For yesterday, coming from the llano with my burro, I met a stranger, a bárbaro. And, blowing upon Paloma, he bewitched the poor beast so that it sprang off the trail and was killed at the bottom of the cliff. It lacked only that! Last month it was the raid of the Comanche; and, though we followed and slew many of the robbers and got back many animals, yet mine were not found, and this was the very last that remained to me."

"Pero, Don 'Colás!" cried Lelo, "I saw your burro this very morning as I went to the field before the sun. Paloma it was, with the white face and the white hind foot, for do I not know him well? He was passing through the bushes under the cliffs at the point, and turned to look at me as I crossed the fields below."

"Vaya!" cried Nicolás, angrily. "Did I not see him, with these my eyes, jump the cliff of two hundred feet yesterday, and with these my hands feel him at the foot that he was dead? Go, with your stories of a stupid, for…"

But here the alguazil, who was one of the group, interrupted, "Lelo has no fool's eyes, and this thing I shall look into. Since this morning, many things look suspicious. Come, show me where your burro fell, for to me all these doings are cousins one to another."

Nicolás, with angry confidence, accompanied the broad-shouldered native sheriff, and their companions followed silently. Across the adobe-walled gardens they trudged, and into the sandy "draw," whose trail led along the cliff and up among the jumble of fallen crags at one side.

"Yonder he jumped off," said 'Colás, "and fell…" But even then he rubbed his eyes and turned pale. For where he had left the limp, bleeding carcass of poor Paloma only twenty-four hours before, there was now nothing to be seen. Only, upon a rock, were a few red blotches.

"What is this!" demanded the alguazil, sternly. "Have you hidden him away? It is clear that something fell here, for there is blood and a tuft of hair upon yon stone. But where is the burro?"

"How should I hide him since he was as dead as the rocks? It is witchcraft, I tell you. Look! There are no tracks of him going away, even where the earth is soft. And for the coyotes and wildcats, they would have left his bones. The Gentile I met, he is the witch. First he gave the evil eye to my poor beast, that it killed itself; and now he has flown away in its shape to do other ills."

"It can be so," mused the sheriff, gravely, "but in the meantime there is no remedy. I have to answer to the Fathers of Medicine for you who bring such stories of dead burros, but cannot show them. For, I tell you, this has something to say for the deed that was done in the pueblo this morning. Al calaboz!"

Half an hour later, poor Nicolás was squatted disconsolately upon the bare floor of the adobe jail, that simple prison from which no one of the simple prisoners ever thinks to dig out. It is not so much the clay wall that holds them, as the authority of law, which no Pueblo ever yet questioned.

"'Colás's burro" was soon in every mouth. The strange story of its death and its reappearance to Lelo were not to be mocked at. So it used to be, that the animals were as people; and everyone knew that there were witches still who took the forms of brutes and flew by night to work mischief. Perhaps it was some wizard of the Comanche who thus, by the aid of the evil ones, was avenging the long-haired horse-thieves who had fallen at Tajique. And now Pascual, returning from a ranch across the river, made known that, sitting upon his roof all night to think of the year, he had been aware of a burro that passed down the street even to the house of the war captain; after which he had noticed it no more. Clearly, then!

Some even thought that Lelo should be imprisoned, since he had seen the burro in the morning. And when, searching anew, they found in a splinter of the captain's door a long, coarse, grey hair, every man looked about him suspiciously. But there was no other clue, save that Francisco, the cleverest of hunters, called the officials to a little corner of the street, where the people had not crowded, and pointed to some dim marks in the sand.

"Que importa?" said the grey haired governor, shrugging his shoulders, as he leaned on his staff of office and looked closely. "In Isleta there are two thousand burros, and their paths are everywhere."

"But see!" persisted the trailer. "Are they like this? For this brute was lame in all the legs, so that his feet fell over to the inside a little, instead of coming flatly down. It will be the Enchanted Burro!"

"Ahu!" cried Lelo, who stood close by. "And this morning when I passed the burro of Don 'Colás in the bushes, I saw that it was laming along as if its legs were stiff."

By now no one doubted that there was witchcraft afoot, and the officials whose place it is were taking active measures to preserve the pueblo. The cacique sat in his closed house fasting and praying, with ashes upon his head. The Cum-pa-huit-la-wen were running here and there with their sacred bows and arrows, prying into every corner, if haply they might find a witch. In the house of mourning the Shamans were blinding the eyes of the ghosts, that none might follow the trail of the dead captain and do him harm before he should reach the safe other world. And in the medicine house the Father of All Medicine was blowing the slow smoke across the sacred bowl, to read in that magic mirror the secrets of the whole world.

But in spite of everything, a curse seemed to have fallen upon the peaceful town. Lucero, the third assistant war captain, did not return with his flock, and when searchers went to the llano, they found him lying by a chapparo bush dead, and his sheep gone. But worst of all, he was scalped, and all the wisdom of that cunning head had been carried away to enrich the mysterious foe, for the soul and talents of a man go with his hair, according to common belief.

And in a day or two came running Antonio Peralta to the pueblo, grey as the dead and without his blanket. Herding his father's horses back of the Accursed Hill, he sat upon a block of lava to watch them. As they grazed, a lame burro came around the hill grazing toward them. And when it was among them, they suddenly raised their heads in fear and snorted and turned to run; but the burro, rising like a mountain lion, sprang upon one of them and fastened on its neck, and all the herd stampeded to the west, the accursed burro still perched upon its victim and tearing it. Ay! A grey burro, jovero, and with a white foot behind. Antonio had his musket, but he dared not fire after this witch beast. And here were twelve more good horses gone from those that the Comanche robbers had left.

By now the whole pueblo was wrought to the highest tension. That frightful doubt which seizes a people oppressed by supernatural fears brooded everywhere. No man but was sure that the man he hated was mixed up in the witchcraft; no man who was disliked by anyone but felt the finger of suspicion pointing at him. People grew dumb and moody, and looked at each other from the corner of the eye as they passed without even a kindly "Hina-kú-p'wiu, neighbour." As for work, that was almost forgotten, though the fields cried out for care. No one dared take a flock to the llano, and few went even to their gardens. There were medicine makings every night to exorcise the evil spirits, and the Shamans worked wonders, and the medicine guards prowled high and low for witches. The cacique sat always in his house, seeing no one, nor eating, but torturing his flesh for the safety of his people.

And still there was no salvation. Not a night went by but some new outrage befell. Now it was a swooping away of herds, now some man of the wisest and bravest was slain and scalped in his bed. And always there were no more tracks than those of a burro, stiff-kneed, whose hoofs did not strike squarely upon the ground. Many, also, caught glimpses of the Enchanted Burro as they peered at midnight from their dark windows. Sometimes he plodded mournfully along the uncertain streets, as burros do; but some vowed that he came down suddenly from the sky, as alighting from a long flight. Without a doubt, old Melo had seen the brute walk up the ladder of Ambrósio's house the very night Ambrósio was found dead in the little lookout room upon his own roof. And a burro which could climb a ladder could certainly fly.

On the fourth day Lelo could stand it no longer. "I am going to the field," he said, "before the wheat dies. For it is as well to be eaten by the witches now as that we should starve to death next winter, when there will be nothing to eat."

"What folly is this?" cried the neighbours. "Does Lelo think he is stronger than the ghosts? Let him stay behind those who are more men."

But Lelo had another trait, quite as marked as his slowness and good nature. When his deliberate mind was made up there was no turning him; and, though he was as terrified as anyone by the awful happenings of the week, he had decided to attend to his field. So he only answered the taunts with a stolid, respectful, "No, I do not put myself against the ghosts. But perhaps they will let me alone, knowing that my mother has now no one else to feed her."

His mother brought him two tortillas for lunch; and putting her hands upon his shoulders, looked at him a moment from wet eyes, saying not a word. And slinging over his shoulder the bow-case and quiver, Lelo trudged away.

He plodded along the crooked meadow road, white-patched here and there with crystals of alkali; jumped the main irrigating ditch with a great bound, and took "across lots" over the adobe fences and through the vineyards and the orchards of apple, peach and apricot.

In the farther edge of the last orchard stood a tiny adobe house, where old Reyes had lived in the summer-time to guard her ripening fruits. Since her death it had been abandoned, with the garden, and next summer the local congress could allot it to anyone who asked, since it would have been left untilled for five years. The house was half hidden from sight, overshadowed on one side by ancient pear trees and on the other by the black cliffs of an advance guard of the lava flow.

As he passed the ruined hut Lelo suddenly stooped and began looking anxiously at a footprint in the soft earth. "That was from no moccasin of the Tee-wahn," he muttered to himself, "for the sole is flatter than ours. And it comes out of the house, where no one ever goes now that Grandmother Reyes is dead. But this! For in three steps it is no more the foot of a man, but of a beast, going even to the bushes where I saw the Enchanted Burro that morning".

All of a tremble, Lelo leaned up against the wall of the house. It was all he could do to keep from turning and bolting for home, and you need not laugh at him. The bow-case at his side was from the tawny mountain lion Lelo had slain with his own hands in the cañons of the Tetilla; and when Refúgio, the youngest medicine-man, fell wounded in the fore-front of the fight at Tajique, it was Lelo who had lumbered forward and brought him away in his arms, saving his life and hair from the Comanche knife. But it takes a braver man to stand against his own superstitions than to face wild beast or wilder warrior; and now, though Lelo did not flee, his knees smote together and the blood seemed to have left his head dry and over-light. He sat down, so weak was he; and, with back against the wall, he tried to gather his scattered thoughts.

At that very moment, if Lelo had turned his head a very little more to the left and looked at one particular rift in the thorny greasewoods that choked the foot of the cliff, he might have seen two dark, hungry eyes fixed upon him; but Lelo was not looking that way so much as to the corner of the cliff. There he would have to pass to the field; and it was just around that corner that he had seen the Enchanted Burro.

"And there also I have seen the mouth of a cave, where they say the ogres used to live and where no one dares to enter".

He shivered again, like one half frozen. Then he did look back to the left, but saw nothing, for the eyes were no longer there. Only, a few rods farther to the left, and where Lelo could not see for the wall at his back, the tall, white ears of a burro were moving quietly along in the bushes, which hid the rest of its body. Now and then the animal stopped and cocked up its ears, as if to listen; and its eyes rose over the bush, shining with a deep, strange light. Just beyond was the low adobe wall which separated Reyes's garden from the next, running from the foot of the cliff down past the old house.

To go on to the field needed even more courage than to keep from fleeing for home; and stubborn as he was, Lelo was trying to muster up legs and heart to proceed. He even rose to his feet and drew back his elbows fiercely, straining the muscles of his chest, where there seemed to be such a weight. Just around the corner of the house, at that same moment, a burro's head, with white ears and a blazed face, rose noiselessly above the adobe fence, and seeing nothing, a pair of black hoofs came up, and in a swift bound the animal was over the wall, so lightly that even the sharp lad's ears not fifteen feet away heard nothing of it.

But if Lelo did not notice, a sharper watcher did. "Kay-eé-w'yoo!" cried a complaining voice, and a brown bird with broad wings and a big, round head went fluttering from its perch on the roof. Lelo started violently, and then smiled at himself. "It is only tecolóte," he muttered, "the little owl that lives with the túsas, and they say he is very wise. To see where he went."

The boy stole around the corner of the house, but the owl was nowhere to be seen, and he started back. As he turned the angle again, he caught sight of a burro's head just peeping from around the other corner; and Lelo felt the blood sinking from his face. The beast gave a little start and then dropped its head to a bunch of alfalfa that was green at the corner. But this did not relieve Lelo's terror. It was Paloma, dead Paloma, now the Witch Burro. There was no mistaking that jovero face. And plain it was, too, that this was no longer burro-true, but one of the accursed spirits in burro shape.

Those eyes! They seemed, in that swift flash in which they had met Lelo's, to be sunk far, far into the skull; and he was sure that deep in them he saw a dull gleam of red. And the ears and head, they were touched with death, too! Their skin seemed hard and as ridged as a rawhide, instead of fitting as the skin does in life. So, also, was the neck; but no more was to be seen for the angle of the wall.

There are men who die at seventy without having lived so long or suffered so much as Lelo lived and suffered in those few seconds. His breath refused to come, and his muscles seemed paralyzed. This, then, was the Enchanted Burro, the witch that had slain the captain of war, and his lieutenants, and many more. And now he was come for Lelo, for though he nosed the alfalfa, one grim eye was always on the boy. So, no doubt, he had watched his other victims, but from behind, for not one of them had ever moved. And with that thought a sudden rush of blood came pricking like needles in Lelo's head.

"Not one of them saw him, else they had surely fought! And shall I give myself to him like a sheep? Not if he were ten witches!"

And with the one swift motion of all his life, the lad dropped on one knee, even as hand and hand clapped notch to bowstring, and, in a mighty tug, drew the arrow to the head. Lightning-like as was his move, the burro understood, and hastily reared back, but a hair too late. The agate-tipped shaft struck midway of its neck with a loud tap as upon a drum, and bored through and through till the feathers touched the skin. The animal sprang high in air, with so wild and hideous a scream as never came from a burro's throat before, and fell back amid the alfalfa, floundering and pawing at its neck.

But Lelo had waited for no more. Already he was over the wall and running like a scared mustang, the bow gripped in his left hand, his right clutching the bow-case, whose tawny tail leaped and fluttered behind him. One-Eyed Quico could have made it to the pueblo no faster than the town slow-poke, who burst into the plaza and the porch of the governor's house, gasping, "The Enchanted Burro! I have…killed…him!"

Fifteen minutes later the new war captain, the medicine men, the governor, and half the rest of the men of the pueblo were entering Reyes's garden, and Lelo was allowed to walk with the principals. All were very grave, and some a little pale, for it was no laughing matter to meddle with the fiend, even after he was dead. There lay the burro, motionless. No pool of blood was around the corpse; but the white feathers of the arrow had turned red. Cautiously they approached till suddenly Francisco, the sharpest eyed of trailers, dashed forward and caught up the two hind legs from amid the alfalfa, crying, "Said I not that he tipped the hoofs? With reason!"

For from each ankle five dark, naked toes projected through a slit in the hide.

"Ay, well bewitched!" exclaimed the war captain. "Pull me the other side!" And at their tug the belly of the burro parted lengthwise, showing only a stiff, dried skin, and inside the cavity a swart body stripped to the breech-clout. Alongside lay arrows and a strong bow of buffalo horn, with a light copper hatchet and a keen scalping knife.

"Sácalo!" ordered the war captain; but it was easier said than done. They bent the stubborn rawhide well apart; but not until one had run his knife up the neck of the skin and cut both ends of Lelo's arrow could they haul out the masquerader. The shaft had passed through his throat from side to side, pinning it to the rawhide, and there he had died.

When the slippery form was at last dragged forth, and they saw its face, there was a startled murmur through the crowd; for even without the long scalp lock and the vermilion face-paint, there were many there who would have known the Comanche medicine man, whose brother was the chief that fell at Tajique. He, too, had been taken prisoner, and had taunted his captors and promised to pay them, and in the night had escaped, leaving one sentinel dead and another wounded.

The Enchanted Burro was all very plain now. The plains conjurer, knowing well by habit how to play on superstitious fears, had used poor Paloma as the instrument of his revenge, hiding the carcass and drying the skin quickly on a frame with hot ashes, so that it stood perfectly in shape by itself. The bones of the fore legs he had left in, to be managed with his hands; and in the dark or amid grass, no one would have noticed the peculiarity of the hind legs. He had only to pry open the slit in the belly and crawl in, and the stiff hide closed after him. Thus he had wreaked the vengeance for which, uncompanioned, he had followed the Pueblos back to their village. In the cave behind the greasewoods were the scalps of his victims, drying on little willow hoops; but instead of going to deck a Comanche lodge in the great plains, they were tenderly buried in the old church-yard, restored to their proper owners.

After all these years there still are in the pueblo many tales of the Enchanted Burro, nothing lost by the re-telling. As for the skin itself, it lies moth-eaten in the dark storeroom of the man who has been first assistant war captain for twenty years, beginning his novitiate the very day he finished a witch and a Comanche with a single arrow.

The Vision Of The Fountain

This story has been edited and adapted from Nathaniel Hawthorne's Twice Told Tales, first published in 1889 by David McKay, Publisher, Philadelphia.

At fifteen I became a resident in a country village more than a hundred miles from home. The morning after my arrival - a September morning, but warm and bright as any in July - I rambled into a wood of oaks with a few walnut trees intermixed, forming the closest shade above my head. The ground was rocky, uneven, overgrown with bushes and clumps of young saplings and traversed only by cattle-paths. The track which I chanced to follow led me to a crystal spring with a border of grass as freshly green as on a May morning, and overshadowed by the limb of a great oak. One solitary sunbeam found its way down and played like a goldfish in the water.

From my childhood I have loved to gaze into a spring. The water filled a circular basin, small but deep and set round with stones, some of which were covered with slimy moss, the others naked and of variegated hue - reddish, white and brown. The bottom was covered with coarse sand, which sparkled in the lonely sunbeam and seemed to illuminate the spring with an unborrowed light. In one spot the gush of the water violently agitated the sand, but without obscuring the fountain or breaking the glassiness of its surface. It appeared as if some living creature were about to emerge - the naiad of the spring, perhaps, in the shape of a beautiful young woman with a gown of filmy water-moss, a belt of rainbow-drops and a cold, pure, passionless countenance. How would the beholder shiver, pleasantly yet fearfully, to see her sitting on one of the stones, paddling her white feet in the ripples and throwing up water to sparkle in the sun! Wherever she laid her hands on grass and flowers, they would immediately be moist, as with morning dew. Then would she set about her labours, like a careful housewife, to clear the fountain of withered leaves, and bits of slimy wood, and old acorns from the oaks above, and grains of corn left by cattle in drinking, till the bright sand in the bright water were like a treasury of diamonds. But, should the intruder approach too near, he would find only the drops of a summer shower glistening about the spot where he had seen her.

Reclining on the border of grass where the dewy goddess should have been, I bent forward, and a pair of eyes met mine within the watery mirror. They were the reflection of my own. I looked again, and, lo, another face, deeper in the fountain than my own image, more distinct in all the features, yet faint as thought. The vision had the aspect of a fair young girl with locks of pale gold. A mirthful expression laughed in the eyes and dimpled over the whole shadowy countenance, till it seemed just what a fountain would be if, while dancing merrily into the sunshine, it should assume the shape of woman. Through the dim rosiness of the cheeks I could see the brown leaves, the slimy twigs, the acorns and the sparkling sand. The solitary sunbeam was diffused among the golden hair, which melted into its faint brightness and became a glory round that head so beautiful.

My description can give no idea how suddenly the fountain was thus tenanted and how soon it was left desolate. I breathed, and there was the face; I held my breath, and it was gone. Had it passed away or faded into nothing? I doubted whether it had ever been.

My sweet readers, what a dreamy and delicious hour did I spend where that vision found and left me! For a long time I sat perfectly still, waiting till it should reappear, and fearful that the slightest motion, or even the flutter of my breath, might frighten it away. Thus have I often started from a pleasant dream, and then kept quiet in hopes to wile it back. Deep were my musings as to the race and attributes of that ethereal being. Had I created her? Was she the daughter of my fancy, akin to those strange shapes which peep under the lids of children's eyes? And did her beauty gladden me for that one moment and then die? Or was she a water-nymph within the fountain, or fairy or woodland goddess peeping over my shoulder, or the ghost of some forsaken maid who had drowned herself for love? Or, in good truth, had a lovely girl with a warm heart and lips that would bear pressure stolen softly behind me and thrown her image into the spring?

I watched and waited, but no vision came again. I departed, but with a spell upon me which drew me back that same afternoon to the haunted spring. There was the water gushing, the sand sparkling and the sunbeam glimmering. There the vision was not, but only a great frog, the hermit of that solitude, who immediately withdrew his speckled snout and made himself invisible - all except a pair of long legs - beneath a stone. I thought he had a devilish look. I could have slain him as an enchanter who kept the mysterious beauty imprisoned in the fountain.

Sad and heavy, I was returning to the village. Between me and the church-spire rose a little hill, and on its summit a group of trees insulated from all the rest of the wood, with their own share of radiance hovering on them from the west and their own solitary shadow falling to the east. The afternoon being far declined, the sunshine was almost pensive and the shade almost cheerful; glory and gloom were mingled in the placid light, as if the spirits of the Day and Evening had met in friendship under those trees and found themselves akin. I was admiring the picture when the shape of a young girl emerged from behind the clump of oaks. My heart knew her: it was the vision, but so distant and ethereal did she seem, so unmixed with earth, so imbued with the pensive glory of the spot where she was standing, that my spirit sunk within me, sadder than before. How could I ever reach her?

While I gazed a sudden shower came pattering down upon the leaves. In a moment the air was full of brightness, each raindrop catching a portion of sunlight as it fell, and the whole gentle shower appearing like a mist, just substantial enough to bear the burden of radiance. A rainbow vivid as Niagara's was painted in the air. Its southern limb came down before the group of trees and enveloped the fair vision as if the hues of heaven were the only garment for her beauty. When the rainbow vanished, she who had seemed a part of it was no longer there. Was her existence absorbed in nature's loveliest phenomenon, and did her pure frame dissolve away in the varied light? Yet I would not despair of her return, for, robed in the rainbow, she was the emblem of Hope.

Thus did the vision leave me, and many a doleful day succeeded to the parting moment. By the spring and in the wood and on the hill and through the village, at dewy sunrise, burning noon, and at that magic hour of sunset, when she had vanished from my sight, I sought her, but in vain. Weeks came and went, months rolled away, and she appeared not in them. I imparted my mystery to none, but wandered to and fro or sat in solitude like one that had caught a glimpse of heaven and could take no more joy on earth. I withdrew into an inner world where my thoughts lived and breathed, and the vision in the midst of them. Without intending it, I became at once the author and hero of a romance, conjuring up rivals, imagining events, the actions of others and my own, and experiencing every change of passion, till jealousy and despair had their end in bliss. Oh, if I had the burning fancy of my early youth mixed with manhood's colder gift, then the power of expression, my sweet ladies, should make your hearts flutter at my tale.

In the middle of January I was summoned home. The day before my departure, visiting the spots which had been hallowed by the vision, I found that the spring had a frozen bosom, and nothing but the snow and a glare of winter sunshine on the hill of the rainbow.

"Let me hope," thought I, "or my heart will be as icy as the fountain and the whole world as desolate as this snowy hill."

Most of the day was spent in preparing for the journey, which was to commence at four o'clock the next morning. About an hour after supper, when all was in readiness, I descended from my chamber to the sitting-room to take leave of the old clergyman and his family with whom I had been an inmate. A gust of wind blew out my lamp as I passed through the entry.

According to their invariable custom - so pleasant a one when the fire blazes cheerfully - the family were sitting in the parlour with no other light than what came from the hearth. As the good clergyman's scanty stipend compelled him to use all sorts of economy, the foundation of his fires was always a large heap of tan, or ground bark, which would smoulder away from morning till night with a dull warmth and no flame. This evening the heap of tan was newly put on and surmounted with three sticks of red oak full of moisture, and a few pieces of dry pine that had not yet kindled. There was no light except the little that came sullenly from two half-burnt brands, without even glimmering on the andirons. But I knew the position of the old minister's arm-chair, and also where his wife sat with her knitting-work, and how to avoid his two daughters - one a stout country lass, and the other a consumptive girl. Groping through the gloom, I found my own place next to that of the son, a learned collegian who had come home to keep school in the village during the winter vacation. I noticed that there was less room than usual tonight between the collegian's chair and mine.

As people are always taciturn in the dark, not a word was said for some time after my entrance. Nothing broke the stillness but the regular click of the matron's knitting-needles. At times the fire threw out a brief and dusky gleam which twinkled on the old man's glasses and hovered doubtfully round our circle, but was far too faint to portray the individuals who composed it. Were we not like ghosts? Dreamy as the scene was, might it not be a type of the mode in which departed people who had known and loved each other here would hold communion in eternity? We were aware of each other's presence, not by sight nor sound nor touch, but by an inward consciousness. Would it not be so among the dead?

The silence was interrupted by the consumptive daughter addressing a remark to someone in the circle whom she called Rachel. Her tremulous and decayed accents were answered by a single word, but in a voice that made me start and bend toward the spot from where it had proceeded. Had I ever heard that sweet, low tone? If not, why did it rouse up so many old recollections, or mockeries of such, the shadows of things familiar yet unknown, and fill my mind with confused images of her features who had spoken, though buried in the gloom of the parlour? Whom had my heart recognized, that it throbbed so? I listened to catch her gentle breathing, and strove by the intensity of my gaze to picture forth a shape where none was visible.

Suddenly the dry pine caught; the fire blazed up with a ruddy glow, and where the darkness had been, there was she - the vision of the fountain. A spirit of radiance only, she had vanished with the rainbow and appeared again in the firelight, perhaps to flicker with the blaze and be gone. Yet her cheek was rosy and lifelike, and her features, in the bright warmth of the room, were even sweeter and more tender than my recollection of them. She knew me. The mirthful expression that had laughed in her eyes and dimpled over her countenance when I beheld her faint beauty in the fountain was laughing and dimpling there now. One moment our glance mingled; the next, down rolled the heap of tan upon the kindled wood, and darkness snatched away that daughter of the light, and gave her back to me no more!

Fair ladies, there is nothing more to tell. Must the simple mystery be revealed, then, that Rachel was the daughter of the village squire and had left home for a boarding-school the morning after I arrived and returned the day before my departure? If I transformed her to an angel, it is what every youthful lover does for his mistress. Therein consists the essence of my story. But slight the change, sweet maids, to make angels of yourselves.

The Strong Man Of Santa Barbara

This story has been edited and adapted from May Wentworth's Fairy Tales From Gold Lands, first published in 1868 by A. Roman and Company.

Many years ago, in the old Spanish mission of Santa Barbara, lived an old Mexican, named Joza Silva, with his wife and child, in a little adobe house, containing but one room. There was a small window, rudely latticed with unplaned laths, and a door opening upon a pleasant view of the golden-sanded beach and the restless waves of the ocean. At that time, the Spaniards, Mexicans, and native peoples were the only inhabitants of the country.

Over these people, the padres, who established the mission, had acquired a most unlimited sway, ruling them more completely than even the Pope and his subjects of the Holy See of Rome.

The Mexicans are an indolent race. The luxurious climate of Santa Barbara is not favourable to the development of latent energy in any people, least of all to the inert Mexicans; yet the padres, by awakening their superstitious fears, made them work until the wilderness became a vineyard, and the golden orange glowed amid the leaves of the fragrant trees.

Poor Joza disliked any exertion, and, if left to his own inclination, would have lived on the spontaneous productions of that almost tropical climate, and been happy after his oyster fashion. Often he obeyed very reluctantly, those whom he thought had power, not only over the body, but could doom his soul to unnumbered years of suffering, in the fearful fires of purgatory.

The padres lived in great ease and comfort; though so far from the elegances of the great world, their own ingenuity and the rapid growth of the country, furnished them with many luxuries. Their quaint adobe houses were very pleasant, built after the Spanish style, in the form of a square with an open court in the centre. Beautiful gardens flourished around them, in which grew the fragrant citron, the lemon, with its shining leaves, and nearly all the rare fruits and flowers of the tropics.

For some years, Joza laboured in the vineyards and gardens; but the ambitious padres were planning a greater work. A new church was to be built, and elaborately ornamented; a convent and college was planned; extensive grounds to be laid out and cultivated, and all to be surrounded by the enduring adobe wall of mud and stones.

One evening, after a weary day in the vineyard, just as Joza was about starting for home, padre Antonio called him. "On the morrow," he said, "we will begin to lay the foundation of the new church, the Grand San Pedro; you shall be permitted to aid in the blessed work, by carrying stones and mortar, for which great mercy thank the holy Mother and all the saints, especially the blessed San Pedro, who is the patron saint of this great enterprise." Then the padre blessed him, and wandered off into the delicious shade of the garden.

In the gathering gloom of the twilight, Joza returned to his cottage, more disheartened than ever, wondering how much more torturing the fires of purgatory could be, than carrying stones under the burning sun of Santa Barbara.

As he approached his cottage, he saw his wife sitting before the door with a stranger, both smoking, with the greatest apparent enjoyment.

His son, and a large dog, were rolling about on the soft earth, near them, raising a cloud of dust, and making a great noise, which seemed to disturb no one, and to afford them much pleasure.

When Joza came up, his wife introduced the stranger as his old playmate, and her brother Schio, who, many years before, had gone away, and, until that evening, had never been heard from.

Joza welcomed his old friend in the cordial Spanish way, placing his house at his disposal.

For a short time, in pleasant memories of their boyhood, he forgot the weary present. After they had eaten their frugal supper, and were again seated in the vine-clad doorway, Joza looked out upon the great ocean, dusky with the shadows of evening, growing sad and silent.

"What ails you, brother," said Schio, in his clear, ringing voice, that sounded like the strong notes of a clarinet. "You are changed; you are growing old, but see me, I am as young in heart as your boy, and strong as a bullock."

He lifted a great stone that lay near him, and held it at arms' length, laughing loudly, till the caves of the ocean sent back a hundred echoes.

With many sighs, Joza told the story of his troubles; how, for years, till his back had grown old and stiff, he had worked in the vineyard of the padre, but the purple harvest had brought no blessing to him. Now a harder task was to be laid upon him. He was to hew and carry the heavy foundation-stones of the Grand San Pedro, and even at the thought of so great a labour, the beaded sweat rolled down his forehead.

His sympathizing wife sobbed aloud, but the brother only laughed, till again he woke the mysterious voices of the ocean caves.

Half angry, Joza turned to Schio, saying, "'Tis all very well for you, Schio, to laugh; you who roam at will in the cool of the evening, and rest in the delightful shade, while the scorching sunshine is burning my life out."

Poor Joza buried his face in his hands and sighed wearily.

"Cheer up, brother," said Schio, pleasantly. "Listen to me. Go in the morning, to padre Antonio, and tell him you are getting old and feeble, and cannot work through the heat of the day, but if he appoints your task, you will accomplish it after the burning sun has gone down. Tell him if you carry those large stones in the day, your life will be consumed like the burning candles before the altar; but that in the cool of the evening, your strength returns as in the days of youth."

"And what, then?" said Joza, wearily.

"I will see that the morning finds your task accomplished," replied Schio.

That night Joza dreamed that his tasks were ended, and that all day long he luxuriated in most delicious ease, under the shade of olive trees, and, when he woke, his heart grew sad, that it was only a dream. He rose in haste to go to his task, for he had overslept; then he thought of Schio's advice. "I will do as he told me, though I fear 'twill do no good," thought he. "I can but fail, and who knows what may come. Schio is such a strange fellow; when he's talking, it seems as though a hundred voices rung changes on his words. God grant he's not in league with the devil."

Joza crossed himself, and muttered prayers most devoutly until he reached the house of the padre Antonio. After he had told the padre all Schio had directed, his task was appointed, and he returned home, all day long resting in the shade of his favourite lime-tree, smoking his cigarettes, and was happy as only a carefree Mexican could be, enjoying the luxury of complete repose.

Toward evening he began to be a little uneasy, but with the dewy twilight, came Schio, waking the mysterious echoes with his ringing laughter, and, as the darkness deepened, he placed a lantern in Joza's hand, saying, "Now, brother, we will go to the task you complain of so bitterly."

Silently they pursued their way, until they arrived at the huge pile, upon which the padre had appointed Joza to begin his work. Many days would have passed before he could have hewn the rock as the padre desired, but, with one blow of an immense drill in Schio's powerful hand, the rock was cleft in twain. As he reduced it to its proper size and shape, Joza stood by, trembling with fear; then pointed out the chosen spot, and, in silence and darkness, the first stone of the Grand San Pedro was laid.

When the full moon arose, clear and bright, shedding its floods of golden light over the mission of Santa Barbara, and the blue waves that washed its sanded shore, the labourers had gone, Joza, to sleep peacefully in his little cottage, and Schio, down to the echoing caverns by the sounding sea.

Morning came, gorgeous with sunshine and beauty, and the padre walked out to inspect the site of his ambitious dreams. He was an avaricious and unscrupulous man. In building this new church, he hoped to erect a tower of strength and greatness for himself, more than an edifice in which to worship the blessed Christ, the immaculate Virgin, and the holy saints.

When he saw the huge foundation-stone that Schio had laid, he was greatly amazed. Even the hewing of it, he knew to be the work of days, and there it was, cleanly cleft, and in its proper place.

"There is a mystery here," he said, "the people will believe it a miracle; be it as it will, I must make the most of it."

He called Joza, who came to him smiling and happy.

"You have done well for the beginning," said the padre, "but tonight, you must lay two stones like this."

"Holy San Pedro, help me!" exclaimed Joza. "It is impossible!" and he turned away, very sorrowful.

At night he told Schio what the padre had said. Schio frowned, and answered, "The padre should not ask too much; but this shall be as he desires."

Again they went out in the twilight, and before the rising of the golden moon, two more foundation-stones were laid.

At daybreak the padre arose, and hastened to see if the task had been accomplished, and before his wondering eyes, lay the three immense foundation-stones, smooth, and in their proper places.

"Holy Virgin! I will give him enough tonight," exclaimed the amazed padre, and again the task was doubled.

Thus it went on, night after night, and week after week, till the Grand San Pedro began to rise up like Aladdin's wonderful palace, but, Schio, the man of iron, grew very angry, as the full moon arose upon him, bending over his unfinished task.

"Joza," said he, "the padre may go too far for even Schio to bear; bid him beware! If the morning sun finds me here, I will not answer for the result; too much pressure will burst open the hidden recesses of earth, and cause the caverns of ocean to resound with fearful echoes of mystery. Can he think San Pedro will bless avarice and oppression, even in the padre Antonio?"

In the morning Joza went to the padre, and entreated him to lessen the task, but he only laughed, and said, "You are getting fat and lazy. I will not double your work tonight, but you shall do four times as much as ever, and I will be there to see it accomplished."

Joza departed with a heavy heart, dreading to meet Schio; and when he told him in the evening, Schio made no reply, but a black frown covered his whole face, and his eyes shot fire.

That night the padre Antonio went out to watch Joza, and when he saw Schio cleaving the huge stones with one blow of his wonderful drill, he thought he had not imposed task enough, and resolved he would command him to finish the Grand San Pedro in one night.

Just after midnight the moon arose, and the startled Joza heard, at every blow of the drill, a hundred echoes ring out from the ocean caverns. But Schio worked steadily on.

"Schio," said Joza, suddenly, "what is it makes these mournings from the sea caves?" But Schio only answered by a heavier blow from his hammer, and under their feet the ground shook violently, then opened, and, where the Grand San Pedro should have stood, yawned a great gulf, that closed upon the labour of many nights; and together with the great foundation-stones down went the ambitious padre.

The morning sun rose on a scene of great desolation, but only Joza was there, with trembling voice, to tell the tale of the padre Antonio and the Grand San Pedro. When others spoke of the great earthquake, he said, "'Twas all Schio's doings. The padre would never be satisfied, and the man of iron grew so angry, that he struck the great stone from the heart of the mountain, and then the earth shook, opened, and swallowed up the padre Antonio and the Grand San Pedro."

Schio was never afterward seen at the mission of Santa Barbara, but often, at evening, his ringing voice was wafted along the shore, from the cave of echoes, down by the sea.

Wayside Destiny

This story has been edited and adapted from Henry W. Shoemaker's Allegheny Episodes, first published in 1922 by the Altoona Tribune Company, based out of Altoona, Pennsylvania. This was one of a series of collections forming the Pennsylvania Folk Lore series.

Like many natives of the Pennsylvania Mountains, Ammon Tatnall was a believer in dreams and ghosts. Even in his less prosperous days, when life was considerable of a struggle, he had time to ponder over the limitless possibilities of the unseen world. Probably his faith in the so-called supernatural was founded on a dream he had while clerking in a hotel at Port Allegheny, during the active days of the lumber business in that part of the Black Forest.

It seemed that his mother was lying at the point of death, and wanted him to come to her, but as she did not know his whereabouts, was suffering much mental anguish. Just in the midst of the dream the alarm clock went off, but he awoke and got up with the impression that his vision had been real. In the office he informed the landlord of his dream. Like a true mountain man, the proprietor merely asked him to come back as soon as he could, such occurrences being not unusual in his range of experience.

At home, in the Wyoming Valley, he found conditions exactly as reproduced in the dream. His sudden coming proved the turning point in his mother's illness; she rallied and got well. During her convalescence, for Tatnall remained longer than he had expected, she told him of a story which her mother had told her of the straight dreaming of some of their ancestors, pioneers of the North Branch.

The woman in question, who lived many years before, dreamed one night that her daughter who lived in Connecticut, and who had married just as they left for Wyoming, appeared to her with a baby in her arms. She said she herself was dead and she desired the baby to be given to the grandmother. As a sign of the reality of the vision, she placed her hand on the wrist of the grandmother, leaving a mark on it that could never be effaced.

The grandmother took the long journey to Connecticut and found that everything had happened as told in the dream. The child grew up, and became the wife of a well-known Methodist preacher, and was famed throughout Northern Pennsylvania for her good deeds.

Tatnall gradually advanced in life, and became agent or traveling salesman for several wholesale lumber concerns. He had gotten his start by being polite to the manager of one of the companies who came up from Pittsburgh every week and stopped at the hotel. He made a success as a salesman, and it was a matter of quiet satisfaction to him that in ten years he had sold 160,000,000 feet of lumber. But he had been too busy to marry, too busy to have a home; he was a driving, pushing machine in the interests of his employers. Sometimes on the trains he met with intelligent people, but generally his associates were like himself, human dynamos, but without his interest in the supernatural.

There was one railway journey which he took frequently, and on fast trains. His westbound trips carried him through the most mountainous part of the country in the late afternoon, but there was generally light enough to show the various aspects of the wild, rugged landscape. There was a little abandoned graveyard, all overgrown, with an uneven stone wall around it, near where the tracks crossed the river bridge. Standing among the lop-sided and battered tombstones, the tips of some of the older ones of brownstone being barely visible, looking as if they were sinking into the earth, he would always see the figure of a young woman attired completely in grey. The train was always traveling so fast that he counted a different number of stones every time he went by - there were probably a "Baker's Dozen."

For a long time he thought that she must be some particularly devoted mourner, a recently bereaved widow, but it did seem a strange coincidence that she should be there on the same days and hour that he passed by in the fast train. Once he called his seat-mate's attention to the figure, but the companion could see nothing, and laughingly said, "Why, you must be seeing a ghost."

The word ghost sent a thrill through Tatnall, and after that he said no more to anyone, but conceded to himself that the girl in grey was a wraith of some kind. Though the train did not pass close to the graveyard, and was always moving rapidly, he fancied that he could discern the ghost's type of feature, or imagined he did; at any rate he had an exact mental picture of what he thought she looked like, and would pick her out in a crowd if he ever saw her in hailing distance.

This had kept up for five years, and he began to feel that it was getting on his nerves; he must either abandon that particular train or go to the graveyard and investigate. He chose the latter course, and one afternoon arrived at the nearest station, via a local train. The graveyard was on the opposite side of the river, and there seemed to be very little hurry on the part of the boatman, who lived on the far shore, to carry him across. It was late in the fall, after Thanksgiving, and the trees were bare of leaves, and shook and rattled their bare branches in the gusts of wind that came out of the east.

He sat down on an old rotting shell of a dugout by the bank, watching the cold, grey current, for the river was high after many days of fall rains. It was a dreary, but imposing scene, the wide, swollen river, the wooded banks and hills beyond, and back of him, high rocky mountains, partly covered with scrubby growth and dead pines.

Finally, in response to frequent calling, he could see the boat launched; it looked like a black speck at first, and gradually drew nearer to him and beached. The boatman was a tiny man, with a long drooping moustache and goatee, wearing a Grand Army button; he was pleasant, but inquisitive, though he "allowed" Tatnall could have no other business than to be a "drummer" bound for the crossroads store on the opposite bank.

Tatnall had remembered a small, dingy store in a hamlet, about half mile from the little cemetery; he had intended going there as he wanted information concerning the families who were buried there. Perhaps he could learn all he wanted to know from the riverman, and save the walk down the track to the store, but for some reason held his tongue.

The boatman's final remark was that it was strange for anyone to be willing to pay a dollar to be ferried across the river, when most people walked the railroad bridge. It was trespassing on railroad property, and dangerous to do it, but it was worth the risk, many travellers thought.

Arriving safely across the roily current, Tatnall paid and thanked the boatman, and started in the direction of the little country store. In front of the store was a row of mature Ailanthus trees, which seemed like sturdy guards over the old stone structure, which had once been a tavern stand. The porch was filled with packing cases and barrels.

As Tatnall opened the door, he could see a number of habitues seated about on crates and barrels. One of them, a white bearded Civil War Veteran, rose up, leaning heavily on his cane, and bid the stranger welcome. Almost before he had a chance to engage in conversation with the regulars, he glanced behind the counter, where he beheld a young woman, who had just emerged from an inner apartment behind the storeroom.

In the dim half-light, the dark aquiline face and meagre figure seemed strangely familiar. She was more Oriental than Native American in type, with that curly hair and wonderful nose, those thin lips, and complexion, the deep pink tone of a wild pigeon's breast. Where had they met before? For a moment his mind refused to correlate, then like a flash, he realized that she was the counterpart of the girl in grey who haunted the little disused cemetery so regularly. And the way she looked at him was as if they had seen one another before, for on her face was a look of mild surprise.

Addressing some pleasantries to her, they were soon engaged in conversation, as if they had known each other for years. It was getting late, time to light lamps and fires at home, so the long-winded dissertations of the habitues were left off, to be continued after supper. One by one they filed out of the store; if they had any opinion of the stranger conversing with Elma Hacker, the store-keeper's niece, it was that he was probably some traveling man, "talking up" his line of goods.

When the last one had gone, and the acquaintance had progressed far enough, Tatnall, leaning over the counter, confided bravely the purpose of his visit to the remote neighbourhood. For five years he had been seeing a figure in grey, in the late afternoons, while passing by the little graveyard in the western express. No one else could see it, yet he was certain that his senses were not deceiving him. Did she know anything of this, and could she help him fathom the mystery?

The dark girl dropped her eyes and was silent for a moment. She was hesitating as to whether to disclaim all knowledge, or to be frank and divulge a story which concerned her soul.

"Yes, I do know all about it, how very funny! I, too, have had the power of seeing that figure in grey, though very few others have ever been able to, and many's the time I've been called crazy when I mentioned it. 'The girl in grey,' as you call her, strangely enough was an ancestress of mine, or rather belonged to my father's family, and while I have the same name, Elma Hacker, I don't know whether I was named for her or not, as my parents died when I was a little girl.

"It used to make me feel terrible when I was a little girl and told about seeing the figure. I hated to be regarded as untruthful or 'dull,' but at last my uncle, hearing of it, came to the rescue and told me not to mind what anyone said, that, from the description, he was sure I had seen the ghost. He had never had the power to see her, but his father, my grandfather had, and other members of the family.

"It was a sad and curious story. It all happened in the days of the very first white settlers in these mountains, when my ancestors kept the first stopping place for travellers, a Stone fortress-like house, in Black Wolf Gap; the ruins of the foundations are still visible, and folks call it 'The Indian Fort.' The Hackers were friendly with the native peoples, who often came for square meals, and other favours from the genial pioneer landlord and his wife. The Elma Hacker of those days had a sweetheart who lived alone on the other side of the Gap; his name was Ammon Quicksall, and from all accounts, he was a fine, manly fellow, a great hunter and fighter.

"He would often drop in on his beloved on his way home from his hunting trips, at all hours of the day. On one occasion four warriors appeared at the tavern, intimating that they were hungry, as native folk generally were. Elma carried a pewter dish containing all the viands the house afforded to each, which they sat eating on a long bench outside the door.

"One of the warriors was a peculiar, half-witted young wretch who went by the name of Chansops. He came to the public house quite often, being suspected of having a fondness for Elma and for hard cider. She always treated him pleasantly, but kept him at a distance, and never felt fear of any kind in his presence. No doubt his feelings were of a volcanic order, and under his stoical exterior burned a consuming passion. He was munching his lunch, apparently most interested in his food, when Ammon Quicksall and his hunting dogs hove in sight.

"Their barking and yelping were a signal to Elma, who rushed out of the house to greet her lover, perhaps showing her feelings a trifle too much; though she had no reason to imagine she should restrain herself in the presence of the native warriors. All the while Chansops was eyeing her with gathering rage and fury. When Elma took her lover's arm, for she must have been a very impulsive girl, and rested her head against his shoulder, it was too much for the irate man.

"He jumped up, firing his pewter dish into the creek which flowed near the house, and danced up and down in sheer fury. His companions tried hard to calm him, as they wanted to keep on good terms with the innkeeper's family, but he was beyond all control. Quicksall and Elma were walking on the path which led along the creek; their backs were turned, and they little dreamed of the drama being enacted behind them. The other warrior folk, realizing that Chansops meant trouble, lay hold of him, but he wrenched himself free with a superhuman strength, threatening to kill anyone who laid hands on him again.

"Old Adam Hacker, Elma's father, finally heard the commotion and came out, and asked in Dutch what the trouble was all about. One of the men, the oldest and most sensible, replied that it was only Chansops having a jealous fit because he saw Elma walking off with Quicksall. While these words were being said, Chansops was edging further away, and looking around furtively, saw that he had a chance to get away, and sprang after the retreating couple. Bounding like a deer, he was a few paces behind Quicksall in a twinkling of an eye. He had a heavy old flint-lock pistol with him, which he drew and fired point blank into the young lover's back at two or three paces. With a groan, Quicksall sank down on the ground, dying before Elma could comfort him.

"Before Adam Hacker or the friendly braves could reach the scene of the horrid tragedy, Chansops had escaped into the forests, followed by Quicksall's hounds yelping at his heels. He was seen no more. The dogs, tired and dejected, re-appeared the next day; evidently they had been outraced by the fleet fugitive runner.

"It was a blow from which the bereaved girl could not react. She was brave enough at the time, but she was never the same again. She gradually pined away, until she was about my age, she died, and was buried not in the little graveyard, but in her father's yard. That was done because it was feared that the crazy Chansops might return and dig up her body, and carry it away to his lodge in the heart of the forest. Quicksall was buried in the pioneer cemetery, and that is the place where Elma Hacker of those days evidently frequents, trying to be near her sweetheart's last resting place, and to reason out the tragedy of her unfulfilled existence.

"It is a very strange story, but odder still, to me, that you, a stranger, should have seen the apparition so frequently, when others do not, and been interested enough to have come here to unravel the mystery."

"It is a strange story," said Tatnall, after a pause. He was figuring out just what he could say, and not say too much. "The strangest part is that the figure I have been seeing is the image of yourself, bears the same name, and my name, Ammon Tatnall, has a somewhat similar sound, in fact is cousin-german to 'Ammon Quicksall.'"

In the gloom Elma Hacker hung her pretty head still further. She was glad that there was no light as she did not want Tatnall to see the hot purple flush which she felt was suffusing her dark cheeks.

"The minute I came into the store," Tatnall continued, "you looked familiar; it did not take me a minute to identify you as the grey lady."

"And you," broke in Elma, "appear just as I always supposed Ammon Quicksall looked."

How much more intimate the talk would have become, there is no telling, but just then the door was swung open, and in came old Mrs. Becker, a neighbour woman, to buy some bread.

"You must be getting moonstruck, Elma," she said, "to be here and not light the lamps. Why, it is as dark as Egypt in this room, and you were always so prompt to light them."

Elma bestirred herself to find the matches, and soon the swinging lamps were lit, and the store aglow.

Again the door was thrown open, and Elma's uncle came in. He was Adam Hacker, namesake of the old-time landlord, and proprietor of the store. Mrs. Becker got her bread and departed, and Elma introduced Tatnall to the storekeeper. Soon she explained to him the stranger's business, to which the uncle listened sympathetically. At the conclusion he said, "It is really curious, after all these years, to have an Adam Hacker, an Elma Hacker and an Ammon Tatnall – almost Quicksall – here together; if Chansops was here it would be as if the past had risen again."

"Let us hope there'll be no Chansops this time," said Tatnall. "Let us feel that everything that was unfulfilled and went wrong in those old days is to be righted now."

It was a bold statement, but somehow it went unchallenged. "I believe in destiny, the destiny of wayside cemeteries, of chance and opportunity," he resumed. "It can be the only road to true happiness after all."

"How happy we'd all be," said Elma demurely, "if through all this we could only lay the ghost of my poor ancestress, the grey lady."

"Nothing that is started is ever left unfinished," answered Tatnall. "And we of this generation become unconscious actors in the final scenes of a drama that began a couple of centuries ago. In that way the cycle of existence is carried out harmoniously, else this world could not go on if it was merely a jumble of odds and ends, and starts without finishes; as it is, everything that is good, that is worthwhile, sometimes comes to a rounded out and completed fulfilment."

The moon, which had come out clear, was three parts full, and shed a glowing radiance over the rugged landscape. After supper Ammon and Elma strolled out along the white, moon-bathed road. Coming to a cornfield the girl pointed to a great white oak with a plume-like crest which stood on a knoll, facing the valley, the river, and the hills beyond; they climbed the high rail fence, and slipping along quietly, seated themselves beneath the giant tree. Of the many chapters of human life and destiny enacted beneath the oak's spreading branches, none was stranger than this one. There until the flaming orb had commenced to wane in the west, they sat, perfectly content. "Oh, how I like to rest on the earth," said she.

"How I love to be here, and look at your wonderful face," he whispered, as he stroked the perfect lines of her nose, lips, chin and throat.

The Two Churches Of 'Quawket

This story has been edited and adapted from H.C. Bunner's Short Sixes - Stories to be Read While the Candle Burns, first published in 1891 by Puck, Keppler & Schwarzmann, New York.

The Reverend Colton M. Pursly, of Aquawket, (commonly pronounced 'Quawket,) looked out of his study window over a remarkably pretty New England prospect, stroked his thin, greyish side–whiskers, and sighed deeply. He was a pale, sober, ill–dressed Congregationalist minister of forty–two or three. He had eyes of willow–pattern blue, a large nose, and a large mouth, with a smile of forced amiability in the corners. He was amiable, perfectly amiable and innocuous, but that smile sometimes made people with a strong sense of humour want to kill him. The smile lingered even while he sighed.

Mr. Pursly's house was set upon a hill, although it was a modest abode. From his window he looked down one of those splendid streets that are the pride and glory of old towns in New England, a street fifty yards wide, arched with grand Gothic elms, bordered with houses of pale yellow and white, some in the homelike, simple yet dignified colonial style, some with great Doric porticos at the street end. And above the billowy green of the tree–tops rose two shapely spires, one to the right, of granite, one to the left, of sand–stone. It was the sight of these two spires that made the Reverend Mr. Pursly sigh.

With a population of four thousand five hundred, 'Quawket had an Episcopal Church, a Roman Catholic Church, a Presbyterian Church, a Methodist Church, a Universalist Church, (very small,) a Baptist Church, a Hall for the "Seventh–Day Baptists," (used for secular purposes every day but Saturday,) a Bethel, and "The Two Churches" as everyone called the First and Second Congregational Churches. Fifteen years before, there had been but one Congregational Church, where a prosperous and contented congregation worshiped in a plain little old–fashioned red brick church on a side–street. Then, out of this very prosperity, came the idea of building a fine new free–stone church on Main Street.

When the new church was half–built, the congregation split on the question of putting a "rain–box" in the new organ. It is quite unnecessary to detail how this quarrel over a handful of peas grew into a church war, with ramifications and interlacements and entanglements and side–issues and under–currents and embroilments of all sorts and conditions. In three years there was a First Congregational Church, in free–stone, solid, substantial, plain, and a Second Congregational Church in granite, something gingerbready, but showy and modish, for there are fashions in architecture as there are in millinery, and we cut our houses this way this year and that way the next.

These two churches had half a congregation apiece, and a full–sized debt, and they lived together in a spirit of Christian unity, on Capulet and Montague terms. The people of the First Church called the people of the Second Church the "Sadduceeceders," because there was no future for them, and the people of the Second Church called the people of the First Church the "Pharisee–mes". And this went on year after year, through the Winters when the foxes hugged their holes in the ground within the woods about 'Quawket, and through the Summers when the birds of the air twittered in their nests in the great elms of Main Street.

If the First Church had a revival, the Second Church had a fair. If the pastor of the First Church exchanged with a distinguished preacher from Philadelphia, the organist of the Second Church got a celebrated tenor from Boston and had a service of song. This system after a time created a class in both churches known as "the floats," in contradistinction to the "pillars." The floats went from one church to the other according to the attractions offered. There were, in the end, more floats than pillars.

The Reverend Mr. Pursly inherited this contest from his predecessor. He had carried it on for three years. Finally, being a man of logical and precise mental processes, he called the head men of his congregation together, and told them what in worldly language might be set down as follows:

There was room for one Congregational Church in 'Quawket, and for one only. The flock must be reunited in the parent fold. To do this a master stroke was necessary. They must build a Parish House. All of which was true beyond question, and yet the church had a debt of $20,000 and a Parish House would cost $15,000.

And now the Reverend Mr. Pursly was sitting at his study window, wondering why all the rich men would join the Episcopal Church. He cast down his eyes, and saw a rich man coming up his path who could readily have given $15,000 for a Parish House, and who might safely be expected to give $1.50, if he were rightly approached. A shade of bitterness crept over Mr. Pursly's professional smile. Then a look of puzzled wonder took possession of his face. Brother Joash Hitt was regular in his attendance at church and at prayer–meeting; but he kept office–hours in his religion, as in everything else, and never before had he called upon his pastor.

Two minutes later, the minister was nervously shaking hands with Brother Joash Hitt. "I'm very glad to see you, Mr. Hitt," he stammered, "very glad…I'm…I'm…"

"S'prised?" suggested Mr. Hitt, grimly.

"Won't you sit down?" asked Mr. Pursly.

Mr. Hitt sat down in the darkest corner of the room, and glared at his embarrassed host. He was a huge old man, bent, heavily–built, with grizzled dark hair, black eyes, skin tanned to a mahogany brown, a heavy square under–jaw, and big leathery dew–laps on each side of it that looked as hard as the jaw itself. Brother Joash had been all things in his long life, sea–captain, commission merchant, speculator, slave–dealer even, people said, and all things to his profit. Of late years he had turned over his capital in money–lending, and people said that his great claw–like fingers had grown crooked with holding the tails of his mortgages.

A silence ensued. The pastor looked up and saw that Brother Joash had no intention of breaking it. "Can I do anything for you, Mr. Hitt?" inquired Mr. Pursly.

"Ya–as," said the old man. "You can. I believe you generally get something over and above your salary when you preach a funeral sermon?"

"Well, Mr. Hitt, it…yes…it is customary."

"How much?"

"The usual honorarium is…h'm…ten dollars."

"The…what?"

"The…the fee."

"Will you write me one for ten dollars?"

"Why…why…" said the minister, nervously, "I didn't know that anyone had…had died… "

"There ain't no one died, as far as I know. It's my funeral sermon I want."

"But, my dear Mr. Hitt, I trust you are not…that you won't…that… "

"Life's a rope of sand, parson, you'd ought to know that, nor we don't none of us know when it's goin' to fetch loose. I'm most ninety now, and I don't calculate to get no younger."

"Well," said Mr. Pursly, faintly smiling, "when the time does come… "

"No, sir!" interrupted Mr. Hitt, with emphasis, "when the time does come, I won't have no use for it. There ain't no sense in the way most folks is buried. What's the use of puttin' a man into a mahogany coffin, with a silver plate as big as a dishpan, and preachin' a funeral sermon over him, and costin' his estate good money, when he's only a poor deaf, dumb, blind fool corpse, and don't get no good of it? Now, I've been to the undertaker's, and had my coffin made under my own supervision. Good wood, straight grain, no knots. Nuthin' fancy, but durable. I've had my tombstone cut, and chose my text to put onto it - 'we bring nuthin' into the world, and it is certain we can take nuthin' out' - and now

I want my funeral sermon, just as the other folks is goin' to hear it who don't pay nuthin' for it. Can you have it ready for me this day week?"

"I suppose so," said Mr. Pursly, weakly.

"I'll call for it," said the old man. "Heard some talk about a Parrish House, didn't I?"

"Yes," began Mr. Pursly, his face lighting up.

"Ain't no such a bad idea," remarked Brother Joash. "Well, good day." And he walked off before the minister could say anything more.

One week later, Mr. Pursly again sat in his study, looking at Brother Joash, who had a second time settled himself in the dark corner.

It had been a terrible week for Mr. Pursly. He and his conscience, and his dream of the Parish House, had been shut up together working over that sermon, and waging a war of compromises. The casualties in this war were all on the side of the conscience.

"Read it!" commanded Brother Joash. The minister grew pale. This was more than he had expected. He grew pale and then red and then pale again.

"Go ahead!" said Brother Joash.

"Brethren," began Mr. Pursly, and then he stopped short. His pulpit voice sounded strange in his little study.

"Go ahead!" said Brother Joash.

"We are gathered together here today to pay a last tribute of respect and affection..."

"Clk!" There was a sound like the report of a small pistol. Mr. Pursly looked up. Brother Joash regarded him with stern intentness.

"...to one of the oldest and most prominent citizens of our town, a pillar of our church, and a monument of the civic virtues of probity, industry and wisdom, a man in whom we all took pride, and..."

"Clk!" Mr. Pursly looked up more quickly this time, and a faint suggestion of an expression just vanishing from Mr. Hitt's lips awakened in his unsuspicious breast a horrible suspicion that Brother Joash had chuckled.

"...whose like we shall not soon again see in our midst. The children on the streets will miss his familiar face..."

"Say!" broke in Brother Joash, "how'd it be for a delegation of children to follow the remains, with flowers or somethin'? They'd volunteer if you give 'em the hint, wouldn't they?"

"It would be...unusual," said the minister.

"All right," assented Mr. Hitt, "only an idea of mine. Thought they might like it. Go ahead!"

Mr. Pursly went ahead, haunted by an agonizing fear of that awful chuckle, if chuckle it was. But he got along without interruption until he reached a casual and guarded allusion to the widows and orphans without whom no funeral oration is complete. Here the metallic voice of Brother Joash rang out again.

"Say! If the widders and orphans send a wreath, or a Gates–Ajar, if they do, mind you, you'll have it put a–top the coffin, where folks will see it, won't you?"

"Certainly," said the Reverend Mr. Pursly, hastily, "his charities were unostentatious, as was the whole tenor of his life. In these days of spendthrift extravagance, our young men may well…"

"Say!" Brother Joash broke in once more. "If anyone was to get up right there, an' say that I was the darndest meanest, miserly, penurious, parsimonious old hunks in 'Quawket, you wouldn't let him talk like that, would you?"

"Unquestionably not, Mr. Hitt!" said the minister, in horror.

"Thought not. Only that's what I heard one of your deacons say about me the other day. Didn't know I heard him, but I did. I thought you wouldn't allow no such talk as that. Go ahead!"

"I must ask you, Mr. Hitt," Mr. Pursly said, perspiring at every pore, "to refrain from interruptions…or I…I really…cannot continue."

"All right," returned Mr. Hitt, with perfect calmness. "Continue."

Mr. Pursly continued to the bitter end, with no further interruption that called for remonstrance. There were soft inarticulate sounds that seemed to him to come from Brother Joash's dark corner. But it might have been the birds in the Ampelopsis Veitchii that covered the house.

Brother Joash expressed no opinion, good or ill, of the address. He paid his ten dollars, in one–dollar bills, and took his receipt. But as the anxious minister followed him to the door, he turned suddenly and said, "You was talkin' about a Parish House?"

"Yes…"

"Can you keep a secret?"

"I hope so…yes, certainly, Mr. Hitt."

"There'll be one."

The Summer days had begun to grow chill, and the great elms of 'Quawket were flecked with patches and spots of yellow, when, early one morning, the meagre little charity–boy whose duty it was to black Mr. Hitt's boots every day, it being a luxury he allowed himself in his old age, rushed, pale and frightened, into a neighbouring grocery, and cried, "Mist' Hitt's dead!"

"Guess not," said the grocer, doubtfully. "Brother Hitt's got Old Nick's agency for 'Quawket, and I ain't heard that he's been discharged for inattention to duty."

"He's layin' there smilin'," said the boy.

"Smilin'?" repeated the grocer. "Guess I'd better go see."

In very truth, Brother Joash lay there in his bed, dead and cold, with a smile on his hard old lips, the first he had ever worn. And a most sardonic and discomforting smile it was.

The Reverend Mr. Pursly read Mr. Hitt's funeral address for the second time, in the First Congregational Church of 'Quawket. Every seat was filled; every ear was attentive. He stood on the platform, and below him, supported on decorously covered trestles, stood the coffin that enclosed all that was mortal of Brother Joash Hitt. Mr. Pursly read with his face immovably set on the line of the clock in the middle of the choir–gallery railing. He did not dare to look down at the sardonic smile in the coffin below him; he did not dare to let his eye wander to the dark left–hand corner of the church, remembering the dark left–hand corner of his own study.

And as he repeated each complimentary, obsequious, flattering platitude, a hideous, hysterical fear grew stronger and stronger within him that suddenly he would be struck dumb by the "clk!" of that mirthless chuckle that had sounded so much like a pistol–shot. His voice was hardly audible in the benediction.

The streets of 'Quawket were at their gayest and brightest when the mourners drove home from the cemetery at the close of the noontide hour. The mourners were principally the deacons and elders of the First Church. The Reverend Mr. Pursly lay back in his seat with a pleasing yet fatigued consciousness of duty performed and martyrdom achieved. He was exhausted, but humbly happy. As they drove along, he looked with a speculative eye on one or two eligible sites for the Parish House. His companion in the carriage was Mr. Uriel Hankinson, Brother Joash's lawyer, whose entire character had been aptly summed up by one of his fellow–citizens in conferring on him the designation of "a little Joash for one cent."

"Parson," said Mr. Hankinson, breaking a long silence, "that was a first–rate oration you made."

"I'm glad to hear you say so," replied Mr. Pursly, his chronic smile broadening.

"You treated the deceased right handsome, considerin'," went on the lawyer Hankinson.

"Considering what?" inquired Mr. Pursly, in surprise.

"Considerin'…well, considerin'… " replied Mr. Hankinson, with a wave of his hand. "You must feel to be real disappointed about the Parish House, I should s'pose."

"The Parish House?" repeated the Reverend Mr. Pursly, with a cold chill at his heart, but with dignity in his voice. "You may not be aware, Mr. Hankinson, that I have Mr. Hitt's promise that we should have a Parish House. And Mr. Hitt was…was…a man of his word." This conclusion sounded to his own ears a trifle lame and impotent.

"Guess you had his promise that there should be a Parish House," corrected the lawyer, with a chuckle that might have been a faint echo of Brother Joash's.

"Well?"

"Well…the Second Church gets it. I draw'd his will. Good day, parson, I'll alight here. Air's kind of cold, ain't it?"

A Very Fine Fiddle

This story has been edited and adapted from Kate Chopin's Bayou Folk, first published in 1894 by the Houghton Mifflin Company of Boston and New York.

When the half dozen little ones were hungry, old Cléophas would take the fiddle from its flannel bag and play a tune upon it. Perhaps it was to drown their cries, or their hunger, or his conscience, or all three. One day Fifine, in a rage, stamped her small foot and clinched her little hands, and declared, "It's no two way'! I'm goin' smash it, that fiddle, some day in a t'ousan' piece'!"

"You mustn't do that, Fifine," expostulated her father. "That fiddle been older than you an' me three times put together. You done yaird me tell often enough about that Italian what give it to me when he die along yonder before the war. And he say, 'Cléophas, that fiddle, that one part my life, what goin' to live when I be dead...Dieu merci! You talkin' too fast, Fifine."

"Well, I'm goin' do somethin' wid that fiddle, va!" returned the daughter, only half mollified. "Mine what I say."

So once when there were great carryings-on up at the big plantation, no end of ladies and gentlemen from the city, riding, driving, dancing, and making music upon all manner of instruments, Fifine, with the fiddle in its flannel bag, stole away and up to the big house where these festivities were in progress.

No one noticed at first the little barefoot girl seated upon a step of the veranda and watching, lynx-eyed, for her opportunity.

"It's one fiddle I got for sale," she announced, resolutely, to the first who questioned her.

It was very funny to have a shabby little girl sitting there wanting to sell a fiddle, and the child was soon surrounded.

The lustreless instrument was brought forth and examined, first with amusement, but soon very seriously, especially by three gentlemen: one with very long hair that hung down, another with equally long hair that stood up, the third with no hair worth mentioning.

These three turned the fiddle upside down and almost inside out. They thumped upon it, and listened. They scraped upon it, and listened. They walked into the house with it, and out of the house with it, and into remote corners with it. All this with much putting of heads together, and talking together in familiar and unfamiliar languages. And, finally, they sent Fifine away with a fiddle twice as beautiful as the one she had brought, and a roll of money besides!

The child was dumb with astonishment, and away she flew. But when she stopped beneath a big chinaberry-tree, to further scan the roll of money, her wonder was redoubled. There was far more than she could count, more than she had ever dreamed of possessing. Certainly enough to top the old cabin with new shingles; to put shoes on all the little bare feet and food into the hungry mouths. Maybe enough, and Fifine's heart fairly jumped into her throat at the vision, maybe enough to buy Blanchette and her tiny calf that Unc' Siméon wanted to sell!

"It's just like you say, Fifine," murmured old Cléophas, huskily, when he had played upon the new fiddle that night. "It's one fine fiddle; and like you say, it shine' like satin. But some way or other it ain't the same. Yair, Fifine, take it, put it outside. I believe, me, I ain't goin' play the fiddle no more."

The Ghost Flower, Or The White Blackbird

*This story has been edited and adapted from Jane Pentzer Myers'
Stories Of Enchantment, first published in 1901 by A. C. McClurg
& Co., Chicago.*

There is a region of our own land, far to the westward, where great
mountains lift their serene heads into the eternal calm of the upper
air. Sunrise and sunset paint them with unearthly beauties; and
night, with its myriads of flashing stars or its splendid moon,
shines down on their white foreheads, and bids them dream on
through the coming ages, as they have done in the past.

Among their barren valleys one sometimes lights upon a small
oasis. A little mountain stream, fed by the melting snows of the
peaks, leaps and sings and flashes to its grave in the desert sand. Its
banks are fringed with cottonwood trees, and the short grass and
underbrush flourish in their shade.

Usually, some energetic person is ranching it there, and claiming
all the valley; but far away from the towns and the mines one may
sometimes come upon a band of Native Americans, living their
own lives separate and alone in their secluded valley.

A generation ago, a fierce war raged between the whites and the native folks; and during its progress a train of emigrants, passing near a native village, was attacked by the warriors of the tribe. All the whites were killed, except one little child, who crept away into the sagebrush, and, worn out with fear and fatigue, dropped asleep. There the wife of the chief medicine man of the tribe found her; and when the little one opened her eyes, and, putting up a piteous lip, began to sob, the woman gathered her into her arms with tender "No, no's" and soft guttural cooings, that soothed and quieted the child. For the Great Spirit had lately called her own baby "far over the terrible mountains" to the spirit land. And this little one crept into the bereaved heart of the grieving mother.

She took the child to her husband, and received permission to keep her. And so the little girl, with her lint-white hair and blue eyes, grew up among the other children of the valley. Soon after the massacre of the wagon train, the tribe withdrew from the vengeance of the white soldiers to a fertile, wooded valley, hidden in the heart of the mountains. Here little "Snow-flower," as she was named, lived happy with her foster parents. Her mother was very proud of her childish beauty, and took excellent care of her. She bathed her often, in the clear water of the little river that ran through the valley; for, contrary to the popular belief, the people of the mountain are cleanly in their habits, and bathe their persons and wash their garments frequently, if water is plentiful. She braided her fair hair, and made for her pretty little dresses of pink or red calico, bought at the trader's store at the agency, many weary miles away.

In the winter, she wore over her dress a warm fur coat reaching to the ankles, with a hood at the back to draw over her head. This was made of the skins of jack rabbits. Warm leggings and moccasins helped to keep her warm, and she was usually very comfortable.

Sometimes the supply of pine nuts would give out, the fish refuse to bite, or the jack rabbits become scarce and shy. Then the only alternative was to go to the hated agency.

At such times little Snow-flower was hidden in some secure place and warned to remain quiet; for her mother was haunted by the fear of separation from the child. She knew that inquiries had been set afloat at the agency for a little one, said to have been saved from the massacre, and her heart told her that the child's kindred would claim her, sooner or later. So, for many years little Snow-flower never saw a white person.

When she asked her father or mother why she was so different from the other children, they told her The Great Spirit had made her so, and she was content.

"Perhaps it's because I am the great Medicine Chief's daughter," she said to her father; and he gravely nodded.

She was very fond of both of her foster parents; but her love for the medicine man was mingled with awe. When she saw him dressed for some religious dance or yearly festival, in his strange medicine dress, with his face painted in grotesque and horrible pattern, she fled to her mother and hid her face in her lap. She loved her mother devotedly, and her love was returned. The woman was like all mothers, very gentle and kind to her little daughter. The little girl was never punished, and was always spoken to in the soft, low voice peculiar to women. "Little daughter," "Little Starlight," "Little Singing-bird," were the fond names bestowed on her.

The years passed quietly by, until Snow-flower was ten years old, when, one summer day, the medicine man came into the tepee looking very ill. He threw himself down on the pallet on the floor and soon was unconscious. He lingered so nine days, anxiously watched and cared for by his wife and Snow-flower. On the tenth day he opened his eyes and beckoned his wife to him.

"I must go far over the terrible mountains, into the heart of the sunset, into the spirit land. You will come soon; watch for the token I will send you."

Then, closing his eyes, he was quickly gone. And the tepee was very desolate and lonely to the wife and little Snow-flower.

All through the long days and the bright starlit nights the wife watched for the token he would send her, until her knees grew weak, and her head drooped, and she could not walk. Then little Snow-flower fed her, and waited on her, and also watched for the token that was to be sent. One day she crept into the hut and knelt by her mother.

"Mother," she whispered, "I have seen a strange sight: a flock of blackbirds lit close to our home. I thought to snare some for your food; but as I approached them, I saw that one of them was shaped like the rest, but, mother, he was pure white; and he lit on the ridgepole of our home."

Then the pale wife raised herself on her elbow, her eyes shining with joy.

"It is the spirit-bird, dear little one; it is the token. Go now, quickly, up the dark ravine; follow to its source the spring that runs past our door. I have never allowed you to go there, for a dark spirit lives in that dread place; but now, do not fear; the spirit-bird will protect you. Go into the deep wood that grows around the fountain head. You will come to a fallen log. Watch closely; and come and tell me what you see."

So little Snow-flower, shaken with fear and grief, for she knew that her mother must soon leave her, followed the little rill, up the dark ravine, to its source. The white blackbird flitted ahead, and wherever he rested, the sunlight broke through the thick leaves overhead, so that she walked in light all the way. Presently she came in sight of the fallen log, and her heart stood still with fear; for, sitting on the log, wrapped in his blanket, and smoking a long-stemmed, strange-looking pipe, was the medicine man, her foster father. As she came toward him, he arose and fixed on her his bright eyes; and then he spoke in a soft voice that seemed to come from a long distance.

"Little pale-face daughter, take this pipe to my wife. It is a token that you have seen me. Tell her I am lonely without her; that she must be ready when the sun is setting to go with me, through the sunset gates, into the spirit world. As for you, my daughter, your path lies there," pointing toward the east, "follow it to your own nation and your own kindred," and, laying his pipe on the log, he was gone in an instant.

Little Snow-flower, almost overcome with fear, ran quickly to the log. She picked up the pipe, which changed in her hands into a strange flower; the leaves, the stem, and the blossoms were all white. It was the Ghost flower.

Hurrying back down the ravine, she ran with flying feet into the tepee. Her mother snatched the flower from the child's hand and kissed it, then listened anxiously to her story.

"Yes, little one, I must go. I had hoped that you might go with me; but the Great Spirit does not will it so. And before I go, you must leave me; I must see you started on your journey." And then she told her of her rescue, and of her parentage.

"This was tied fast round your neck. I hid it, and told no one." She showed the little girl the case of a gold locket, with a scrap of closely written paper within. "Take this to the agency. The paper talks; but do not fear, it is not bewitched. The agent will speak for it, and I believe it will tell you where to find your kindred. Now hasten, dear child; the sun will soon reach the cleft in the mountain, and then I must go. I will see you again; my husband's power is great; he will let me come to you whenever you find a flower like this, the Ghost flower."

Then, with tears and sobs, they separated. And when the sun was setting, a great flock of blackbirds flew straight into its splendour; and among them were two white ones: the souls of the medicine chief and his wife. And poor little Snow-flower had begun her long journey to the agency. She left the valley secretly, crept away without bidding anyone in the tribe farewell, for her mother feared that they might detain her. The medicine chief's home stood apart from the rest of the village, and was approached by the villagers with fear. When it was known that he was dead, the tribe buried him and mourned for him. But the mother and the daughter were unmolested in their grief.

A few days after Snow-flower had left, a kind-hearted woman ventured near. Great was her surprise to find the tepee empty; and it was believed by all that the medicine man had come for his wife and daughter, and had conveyed them to the spirit world.

Little Snow-flower followed the path as far as she had gone in the old days with her foster mother; but when she came to the cave where she had been concealed, she was at a loss to know which way to go. She wandered on, frightened and weary. The food she had brought with her was almost gone. One night she lay down beside a strange-looking trail. There were short logs laid across it, and on these were long slim logs or poles made of iron. It was in a valley between two great mountains. She wondered at it greatly. It was either a trail made by some wizard or medicine man, or it was made by that strange tribe to which she belonged, and of which she had heard for the first time that day, the "pale-faces."

But at least there was companionship in it, after the horrible loneliness of the mountains. So she snuggled down near the trail, and went to sleep. She was awakened by a terrible rumble and roar that shook the earth around her. Something all fire and flashing eyes went shrieking and hissing past her. She screamed with fear, and tried to run, but her feet refused to carry her. The monster went a little way, and then stopped. Some men sprang from its back and came toward her, carrying a light. She saw that they were fair, like herself, and then she fainted.

The men came hurrying on. It was a special train, carrying the superintendent of the road, and a friend. "Did you say the massacre was just here?" said the gentleman.

"Right about here…perhaps a few feet farther north."

The gentleman sighed. "And has nothing been heard of the child?"

"The tribes-folk positively declare that she is living somewhere in the mountains, and that she is well cared for, but refuse to tell anything more."

"Well, I must have the child, if she is to be found on… Why, what is this?" he exclaimed, as his foot struck against the soft little body of Snow-flower. She shivered and moaned.

"What in this world! A little white girl, dressed like a little native!" cried the superintendent.

"Let me see the child. She looks like my sister Mary did at that age. What if this is her child, the little one I am searching for? Here, let me carry her into the car; she is mine; I am sure of it," said the gentleman.

And so little Snow-flower awoke from her swoon to a new and wonderful life. It almost seemed in later years, as she looked back to that time, that she had entered another world; for she found love, riches, education, all awaiting her.

Once or twice since, in lonely walks, she has found the Ghost flower; and always then appears the vague, misty outline of her medicine mother.

A few days ago, her little son (for she is a woman and a mother now) came into the house crying, "Mother, I saw a white blackbird. It was with a great flock of black ones; it was just like them, only it was white."

She hurried out of the house hoping to find the spirit-bird; but it had visited her, found her happy, and hastened back to the spirit land.

Girty's Notch

This story has been edited and adapted from Henry W. Shoemaker's Allegheny Episodes, first published in 1922 by the Altoona Tribune Company, based out of Altoona, Pennsylvania. This was one of a series of collections forming the Pennsylvania Folk Lore series.

The career of Simon Girty, otherwise spelled Girtee and Gerdes, has become of sufficient interest to cause the only authoritative biography to sell at a prohibitive figure, and outlaw or renegade as he is called, there are post offices, hotels, streams, caves and rocks which perpetuate his name throughout Pennsylvania.

Simon Gerdes was born in the Cumberland Valley on Yellow Breeches Creek, the son of a Swiss-German father and an Irish mother. This origin guaranteed him no high social position, for in the old days, in the Cumberland Valley, in particular, persons of those racial beginnings were never accepted at par by the proud descendants of Quakers, Virginia Cavaliers, and above all, by the Ulster Scots. After the world war similar beginnings have correspondingly lowered in the markets of prestige, and a century or more of gradual family aggrandizement has gone for nil, the social stratification of pre-Revolutionary days having completely re-established itself.

Unfortunately for Simon Gerdes, or Girty, as he was generally called, he was possessed of lofty ambitions. He aimed to be a military hero and a man of quality, like the dignified and exclusive gentry who rode about the valley on their long-tailed white horses and carried swords, and were accompanied by retainers with long rifles. There must have been decent blood in him somewhere to have brought forth such aspirations, but personally he was never fitted to attain them. He had no chance for an education off there in the rude foothills of the Kittochtinnies; he was undersized, swarthy and bushy headed; his hands were hairy, and his face almost impossible to keep free of black beard. If analysed his features were not unpleasant; he had deep set, piercing black eyes, a prominent aquiline nose, a firm mouth and jaw, and his manner was quick, alert and decisive.

Such was Simon Girty when his martial dreams caused him to leave home and proceed to Virginia to enlist in the Rifle Regiment. A half century of Quaker rule in Pennsylvania had failed to disturb the tranquillity of the relations between whites and native folk, but in the Old Dominion, there was a constant bickering with the tribes along the western frontier.

As Girty was a sure shot, he was eagerly accepted, and in a short time was raised to the grade of Corporal. Accompanied by a young Captain-lieutenant named Claypoole, he was sent to the Greenbrier River country to convey a supply train, but owing to the indifference of the officer, the train became strung out, and the vanguard was cut off by a war party, and captured, and the rear-guard completely routed.

As Girty happened to be the vidette, the Captain-lieutenant, who was in the rear and should have come up and seen that his train travelled more compactly, had a splendid opportunity to shift the blame. An investigation was held at Spotsylvania, presided over by a board of officers recently arrived from England, who knew nothing of border warfare, and were sticklers for caste above everything else.

Someone had to be disciplined, and if a fellow could be punished and a gentleman exculpated, why then of course, punish the fellow. This was speedily done, and Girty was taken out before the regiment, stripped of his chevrons, denounced by the Colonel, forced to run the gauntlet, native style, and drummed out of camp.

Girty, though humiliated and shamed, felt glad that he was not shot; he would have been had he been actually guilty of neglect; he was punished as badly as an innocent man dare be punished to shield a guilty superior. After receiving his dishonourable discharge, Girty sorrowfully wended his way back to the parental home on the Yellow Breeches, his visions of glory shattered. He did not tell his parents what had happened, but they knew that something had gone wrong, and pitied him, as only poor, lowly people can pity another.

Henry Fielding, a gentleman born and bred, has said, "Why is it that the only really kindly people are the poor," and again, "Why is it that persons in high places are always so hard?"

About this time Simon Girty found work breaking colts on the estate of an eccentric character named Gaspar, known in the Cumberland Valley as "French Louis," who resided near the mouth of Dublin Gap, on the same side of the trail, but nearer the valley than the present Sulphur Springs Hotel.

"French Louis" Gaspar was a Huguenot, a Gascon, and prided himself on a resemblance to Henry of Navarre, and wore the same kind of fan-shaped, carefully brushed beard. His wife was also of French origin, a member of the well-known Le Tort family, and a woman of some education and character. They had several daughters, all of whom married well, and at the time of Girty's taking employment, but one was at home, the youngest, Eulalie.

She was a slim, dark girl, with hair and eyes as black as Girty's, a perfect mate in type and disposition. It is a curious thing while unravelling these stories of old time Pennsylvania, that in seeking descriptions of the personal appearance (which is always the most interesting part) of the persons figuring in them at an early day, scarcely any blondes are recorded; the black, swarthy visages so noticeable to strangers traveling through Pennsylvania today, were also prevalent, commonly met with types of our Colonial period.

Eulalie Gaspar could see that there was something on Girty's mind, and tried to be kind to him and encourage him, but she asked no questions, and he volunteered no information. If he had not received such a complete social setback at Spotsylvania, the youth might have aspired to the girl's hand, but he now was keenly aware of the planes of caste, realizing that he stood very low on the ladder of quality.

He seemed to be improving in spirits under the warm sun of encouragement at Chateau Gaspar, as "French Louis" liked to call his huge house of logs and stone, for the Huguenot adventurer was much of a Don Quixote, and lived largely in a world of his own creation. Eulalie, hot-blooded and impulsive, often praised his prowess as a horseman, and otherwise smiled on him.

There was a great sale of Virginia bred horses being held in the marketplace at Carlisle, and, of course, "French Louis", mounted on a superbly caparisoned, ambling horse, and wearing a hat with a plume, and attended by Simon Girty, was among those present.

The animals ranged from packers and palfreys to fancy saddlers of the high school type, and although Gaspar had every stall full at home, and some wandering, hobbled about the old fields, he bought six more at fancy prices, and it would be an extensive task to return them safely to the stables at the "Chateau".

It was near the close of the sale when a young Virginian named Conrad Gist or Geist, one of the sellers of horses, who had been a sergeant in Girty's regiment, and witnessed his degradation at Spotsylvania, came up, and in the presence of the crowd, taunted young Simon on being court-martialled and kicked out of camp.

Girty, though the humiliating words were said among divers of his friends, bit his lips and said nothing at the time. Later in the tap room, when "French Louis" was having a final jorum before starting homeward, the Virginian repeated his taunts, and Girty, though half his size, slapped his face. Gist quickly drew a horse pistol from one of the deep pockets of his long riding coat, and tried to shoot the affronted youth. Girty was too quick for him, and in wresting the pistol from his hand, it went off, and shot the Virginian through the stomach. He fell to the sanded floor, and was soon dead.

Other Virginians present raised an outcry, in which they were upheld by those of similar social status in the fraternity of "gentlemen horse dealers" residing at Carlisle. Threats were made to hang Girty to a tree and fill him full of bullets. He felt that he was lucky to escape in the melee, and make for the mountains.

Public opinion was against him, and a reward placed on his head. Armed posses searched for him for weeks, eventually learning that he was being harboured by a band of escaped redemptioners, slaves, and gaol breakers, who had a cabin or shack in the wilds along Shireman's Creek. It was vacated when the pursuers reached it, but they burnt it to the ground, as well as every other roof in the wilds that it could be proved he had ever slept under.

By 1750 he became known as the most notorious outlaw in the Juniata country, and pursuit becoming too "hot", he decided to migrate west, which he did, allying himself with the Wyandot tribes He lived with them as a foe to the whites, crueller and more relentless, the Colonial Records state, than his adopted people.

Some of his marauding expeditions took him back to the Susquehanna country, and he made several daring visits to his parents, on one of which he learned to his horror and disgust, that Eulalie Gaspar, while staying with one of her married sisters at Carlisle, had met and married the now Captain Claypoole, the author of his degradation, who had come there in connection with the mustering of Colonial troops.

During these visits Girty occupied at times a cave facing the Susquehanna River, in the Half Fall Hills, directly opposite to Fort Halifax, which he could watch from the top of the mountain. The narrow, deep channel of the river, at the end of the Half Fall Hills, so long the terror of the "up river" raftsmen, became known as Girty's Notch. The sinister reputation of the locality was borne out in later years in a resort for rivermen called Girty's Notch Hotel, now a pleasant, homelike retreat for tired and thirsty autoists who draw birch beer through straws, and gaze at the impressive scenery of river and mountain from the cool, breeze swept verandas.

But the most imposing of all is the stone face on the mountain side, looking down on the state road and the river, which clearly shows the rugged outlines of the features of the notorious borderer. An excellent photograph of "Girty's Face" can be seen in the collection of stereoscopic views possessed by the genial "Charley Mitchell" proprietor of the Owens House, formerly the old Susquehanna House, at Liverpool.

It was after General Braddock's defeat in 1755 that Captain, now Major Claypoole, decided to settle on one of his parental estates on the Redstone River, (now Fayette County) in Western Pennsylvania. Being newly wedded and immensely wealthy for his day, he caused to be erected a manor house of the showy native red stone, elaborately stuccoed, on a bluff overlooking this picturesque winding river. He cleared much land, being aided by Negro slaves, and a horde of German redemptioners.

When General Forbes' campaign against Fort Duquesne was announced in 1757, he decided to again try for actual military laurels, though his promotion in rank had been rapid for one of his desultory service; so he journeyed to Carlisle, and was reassigned to the Virginia Riflemen, with the rank of Lieutenant Colonel of Staff.

He was undecided what to do with his young wife in his absences, but as she had become interested in improving "Red Clay Hall," as the new estate was called, he decided to leave her there, well-guarded by his armed Virginia overseers. The native peoples had been cleared out of the valley for several years, and were even looked upon as curiosities when they passed through the country, so consequently all seemed safe on that score.

However, while Lieutenant-Colonel Claypoole was at Carlisle, before the Forbes-Bouquet Army had started westward, a native warrior with face blackened and painted, in the full regalia of a chief, appeared at the door of "Red Clay Hall" and asked to see the lady of the manor, with whom he said he was acquainted, and that she would know him by the name of Suckaweek.

This was considered peculiar, and he was told to wait outside, until "her ladyship" could be informed of his presence. Eulalie Gaspar Claypoole, clad in a gown of rose brocade, was in her living room on the second story of the mansion, an apartment with high ceilings and large windows, which commanded a view of the Red Stone Valley, clear to its point of confluence with the lordly Monongahela. She was seated at an inlaid rosewood desk, writing a letter to her husband, when the German chief steward entered to inform her of the strange visitor waiting on the lawn, whom she would know by the name of Suckaweek.

Taking the quill pen from her lips, for she had been trying to think of something to write, the dark beauty directed the steward to admit the visitor at once, and show him into the library. Hurrying to a pier glass, she adjusted her elaborate apparel, and taking a rose from a vase, placed it carefully in her sable hair before she descended the winding stairway.

"Suckaweek" (Black Fish), which was a pet name she used to call Girty in the old days, was waiting in the great hall, and the greeting between the ill-assorted pair seemed dignified, yet cordial. They spent the balance of the afternoon between the library and strolling over the grounds, admiring the extensive views, dined together in the state dining room, and the last the stewards and servants saw of them, when informed their presence would be no longer required, was the pair sitting in easy chairs on either side of the great fireplace, both smoking long pipes of fragrant Virginia tobacco.

In the morning the warrior-chief and Madame Claypoole were missing, and an express was sent at once to Carlisle to acquaint the Colonel with this daring abduction of a lady of quality. The news came as a great shock to the young officer, who obtained a leave of absence and a platoon of riflemen to engage in the search for his vanished spouse.

The marriage had seemed a happy one, but in discussing the case with his father-in-law, "French Louis," indiscreetly admitted that his daughter had once seemed a little sweet on Simon Girty, the outlaw. All was clear now, the motive revealed. It was the truth, the lovely "Lady" Claypoole, as she was styled by the mountain folks, had gone off with the seemingly uncouth renegade, Simon Girty.

Why she had done so, she could never tell, but doubtless it was a spark of love lain dormant since the old days at Chateau Gaspar, when she had seen the young outlaw breaking her father's unmanageable colts, that furnished the motive for the elopement.

In the glade, where at an early hour in the morning, Girty and his fair companion joined his entourage of outlaws, Simon, in the presence of all, unsheathed his formidable hunting knife, a relic of his first campaign against the native tribes when he belonged to the Virginia "Long Knives," and cut a notch on the stock of his trusty rifle, which was handed to him by his favourite bodyguard, a half Jew, half native, named Mamolen, a native of Heidelberg in Berks County.

Although during the past eight years he had personally killed and scalped over a hundred people, Girty had never, as the other frontiersmen always did, "nicked" his rifle stock.

Turning to Lady Claypoole with a smile, he said, "Someday I will tell you why I have cut this notch; it is a long and curious story."

In order to have her safe from capture or molestation, Girty took the woman on a lengthy and perilous journey to Kentucky, "the dark and bloody ground." To the country of the mysterious Green River, in what is now Edmonson County, land of caves, and sinks, and knobs, and subterranean lakes and streams, amid hardwood groves and limestone, he built a substantial log house, where he left her, protected only by the faithful Mamolen, while he returned to fight along the banks of the Ohe-yu, "The Beautiful River."

The defeat of the allied forces by the British, and the abandonment of Fort Duquesne, were sore blows to Simon Girty's plans and hopes, but his position and prestige among the native tribes remained undimmed.

Claypoole, though promoted to full Colonel, did not take part in any of the battles, being intermittently off on leave, hunting for his recreant wife, and spluttering vengeance against "that snake, that dog, Girty," as he alternately called him. It seemed as if the earth had swallowed up the lovely object of the outlaw's wiles, for though Girty himself was heard of everywhere, being linked with the most hideous atrocities and ambushes, no prisoner, even under the most dreadful torture, could reveal the Lady Claypoole's whereabouts. The reason for that was only two persons in the service knew, one was Mamolen, the other Girty, and Mamolen remained behind with the fair runaway.

It was not until after the final collapse of the French power in 1764, and the western country was becoming opened for settlement, that Colonel Claypoole received an inkling of Eulalie's whereabouts. It did not excite his curiosity to see her again, or bring her back, but merely fired his determination the more to even his score with Girty. When he was sober and in the sedate atmosphere of his correctly appointed library on Grant's Hill, in the new town of Pittsburgh, he realized how foolish it would be to journey to the wilds to kill "a scum of the earth," he a gentleman of many generations of refined ancestry, all for a "skirt" as he contemptuously alluded to his wife.

But when in his cups, and that was often, he vowed vengeance against the despoiler of his home, and the things he planned to do when once he had him in his clutches would have won the grand prize at a Spanish Inquisition.

If it was Girty's destiny to notch his rifle once, Nemesis provided that Colonel Claypoole should also have that rare privilege. At a military muster on the Kentucky side of Big Sandy, during the Revolutionary War, Simon Girty boldly ventured to the outskirts of the encampment, to spy on the strength and armament of the patriot forces, as he had done a hundred times before. Colonel Claypoole, riding on the field on his showy, jet black charger, noticed a low-brewed face, whiskered like a Bolshevik, peering out through a clump of bushes. Recognizing him after a lapse of over a quarter of a century, he rode at him rashly, parrying with the flat blade of his sabre, the well-directed bullet which Girty sent at him. Springing from his mount, which he turned loose, and which ran snorting over the field, with pistol in one hand, sabre in the other, he rushed into the thicket, and engaged his foe in deadly combat. He was soon on top of the surprised Girty, and stamping on him, like most persons do with a venomous snake, at the same time shooting and stabbing him.

When his frightened orderly, leading the recaptured charger, rode up, followed by a number of excited officers and men, and drew near to the thicket, they were just in time to see Colonel Claypoole emerging from it, red-faced but calm, carrying a long rifle.

"I see you have put a notch in it already," said one of his companions, as he eagerly wrung his hand.

"So I perceive," replied the Colonel, "but it was hardly necessary, for I have only killed a snake."

There are some who say that Colonel Claypoole's victim was not Simon Girty at all, but merely a drunken settler who was coming out of the bushes after a mid-day nap, and a coincidence that the fellow was armed with a rifle on which there was a single nick. Yet for all intents and purposes Colonel Claypoole had killed a good enough Simon Girty, and had his rifle to prove it.

Other reports have it that Simon Girty survived the Revolution, where he played such a reprehensive part, to marry Catharine Malott, a former captive among the native tribes, in 1784, and was killed in the Battle of the Thames, in the War of 1812.

C. W. Butterworth in his biography of the Girty family, says that Simon, in later life, became totally blind, dying near Amlerstburg, Canada, February 18, 1818, was buried on his farm, and a troop of British soldiers from Fort Malden fired a volley at his grave.

Old Aunt Peggy

This story has been edited and adapted from Kate Chopin's Bayou Folk, first published in 1894 by the Houghton Mifflin Company of Boston and New York.

When the war was over, old Aunt Peggy went to Monsieur, and said, "Master, I ain't never goin to quit you. I'm gettin' old and feeble, and my days is few in this land o' sorrow and sin. All I axes is a little corner where I can set down and wait peaceful for the end."

Monsieur and Madame were very much touched at this mark of affection and fidelity from Aunt Peggy. So, in the general reconstruction of the plantation which immediately followed the surrender, a nice cabin, pleasantly appointed, was set apart for the old woman. Madame did not even forget the very comfortable rocking-chair in which Aunt Peggy might "set down," as she herself feelingly expressed it, "and wait for the end."

She has been rocking ever since.

At intervals of about two years Aunt Peggy hobbles up to the house, and delivers the stereotyped address which has become more than familiar, "Mistress, I've come to take a last look at you all. Let me look at you good. Let me look at the chillun,—the big chillun an' the little chillun. Let me look at the pictures and the photygraphs an' the piano and everything before it's too late. One eye is done gone, and the other's a-goin' fast. Any mornin' your poor ole Aunt Peggy goin' wake up and find herself stone-blind."

After such a visit Aunt Peggy invariably returns to her cabin with a generously filled apron.

The scruple which Monsieur one time felt in supporting a woman for so many years in idleness has entirely disappeared. Of late his attitude towards Aunt Peggy is simply one of profound astonishment and wonder at the surprising age which an old woman may attain when she sets her mind to it, for Aunt Peggy is a hundred and twenty-five, so she says.

It may not be true, however. Possibly she is older.

The Hampshire Hills

This story has been edited and adapted from Eugene Field's book A Little Book of Profitable Tales, first published in 1891 in New York.

One afternoon many years ago two little brothers named Seth and Abner were playing in the orchard. They were not troubled with the heat of the August day, for a soft, cool wind came up from the river in the valley over yonder and fanned their red cheeks and played all kinds of pranks with their tangled curls. All about them was the hum of bees, the song of birds, the smell of clover, and the merry music of the crickets. Their little dog Fido chased them through the high, waving grass, and rolled with them under the trees, and barked himself hoarse in his attempt to keep pace with their laughter. Wearied at length, they lay beneath the bellflower-tree and looked off at the Hampshire hills, and wondered if the time ever would come when they should go out into the world beyond those hills and be great, noisy men. Fido did not understand it at all. He lolled in the grass, cooling his tongue on the clover bloom, and puzzling his brain to know why his little masters were so quiet all at once.

"I wish I were a man," said Abner, ruefully. "I want to be somebody and do something. It is very hard to be a little boy so long and to have no companions but little boys and girls, to see nothing but these same old trees and this same high grass, and to hear nothing but the same bird-songs from one day to another."

"That is true," said Seth. "I, too, am very tired of being a little boy, and I long to go out into the world and be a man like my gran'pa or my father or my uncles. With nothing to look at but those distant hills and the river in the valley, my eyes are wearied; and I shall be very happy when I am big enough to leave this stupid place."

Had Fido understood their words he would have chided them, for the little dog loved his home and had no thought of any other pleasure than romping through the orchard and playing with his little masters all day. But Fido did not understand them.

The clover bloom heard them with sadness. Had they but listened in turn they would have heard the clover saying softly, "Stay with me while you may, little boys; trample me with your merry feet; let me feel the imprint of your curly heads and kiss the sunburn on your little cheeks. Love me while you may, for when you go away you never will come back."

The bellflower-tree heard them, too, and she waved her great, strong branches as if she would caress the impatient little lads, and she whispered, "Do not think of leaving me: you are children, and you know nothing of the world beyond those distant hills. It is full of trouble and care and sorrow; abide here in this quiet spot till you are prepared to meet the vexations of that outer world. We are for you, we trees and grass and birds and bees and flowers. Abide with us, and learn the wisdom we teach."

The cricket in the raspberry-hedge heard them, and she chirped, oh! so sadly, "You will go out into the world and leave us and never think of us again till it is too late to return. Open your ears, little boys, and hear my song of contentment."

So spoke the clover bloom and the bellflower-tree and the cricket; and in like manner the robin that nested in the linden over yonder, and the big bumblebee that lived in the hole under the pasture gate, and the butterfly and the wild rose pleaded with them, each in his own way; but the little boys did not heed them, so eager were their desires to go into and mingle with the great world beyond those distant hills.

Many years went by; and at last Seth and Abner grew to manhood, and the time was come when they were to go into the world and be brave, strong men. Fido had been dead a long time. They had made him a grave under the bellflower-tree, yes, just where he had romped with the two little boys that August afternoon Fido lay sleeping amid the humming of the bees and the perfume of the clover. But Seth and Abner did not think of Fido now, nor did they give even a passing thought to any of their old friends, the bellflower-tree, the clover, the cricket, and the robin. Their hearts beat with exultation. They were men, and they were going beyond the hills to know and try the world.

They were equipped for that struggle, not in a vain, frivolous way, but as good and brave young men should be. A gentle mother had counselled them, a prudent father had advised them, and they had gathered from the sweet things of Nature much of that wisdom before which all knowledge is as nothing. So they were fortified. They went beyond the hills and came into the West. How great and busy was the world, how great and busy it was here in the West! What a rush and noise and turmoil and seething and surging, and how keenly did the brothers have to watch and struggle for vantage ground. Withal, they prospered; the counsel of the mother, the advice of the father, the wisdom of the grass and flowers and trees, were much to them, and they prospered. Honour and riches came to them, and they were happy. But amid it all, how seldom they thought of the little home among the circling hills where they had learned the first sweet lessons of life!

And now they were old and grey. They lived in splendid mansions, and all people paid them honour.

One August day a grim messenger stood in Seth's presence and beckoned to him.

"Who are you?" cried Seth. "What strange power have you over me that the very sight of you chills my blood and stays the beating of my heart?"

Then the messenger threw aside his mask, and Seth saw that he was Death. Seth made no outcry; he knew what the summons meant, and he was content. But he sent for Abner.

And when Abner came, Seth was stretched upon his bed, and there was a strange look in his eyes and a flush upon his cheeks, as though a fatal fever had laid hold on him.

"You shall not die!" cried Abner, and he threw himself about his brother's neck and wept.

But Seth bade Abner cease his outcry. "Sit here by my bedside and talk with me," said he, "and let us speak of the Hampshire hills."

A great wonder overcame Abner. With reverence he listened, and as he listened a sweet peace seemed to steal into his soul.

"I am prepared for Death," said Seth, "and I will go with Death this day. Let us talk of our childhood now, for, after all the battle with this great world, it is pleasant to think and speak of our boyhood among the Hampshire hills."

"Say on, dear brother," said Abner.

"I am thinking of an August day long ago," said Seth, solemnly and softly. "It was so very long ago, and yet it seems only yesterday. We were in the orchard together, under the bellflower-tree, and our little dog…"

"Fido," said Abner, remembering it all, as the years came back.

"Fido and you and I, under the bellflower-tree," said Seth. "How we had played, and how weary we were, and how cool the grass was, and how sweet was the fragrance of the flowers! Can you remember it, brother?"

"Oh, yes," replied Abner, "and I remember how we lay among the clover and looked off at the distant hills and wondered of the world beyond."

"And amid our wonderings and longings," said Seth, "how the old bellflower-tree seemed to stretch her kind arms down to us as if she would hold us away from that world beyond the hills."

"And now I can remember that the clover whispered to us, and the cricket in the raspberry-hedge sang to us of contentment," said Abner.

"The robin, too, carolled in the linden."

"It is very sweet to remember it now," said Seth. "How blue and hazy the hills looked; how cool the breeze blew up from the river; how like a silver lake the old pickerel pond sweltered under the summer sun over beyond the pasture and broomcorn, and how merry was the music of the birds and bees!"

So these old men, who had been little boys together, talked of the August afternoon when with Fido they had romped in the orchard and rested beneath the bell-flower-tree. And Seth's voice grew fainter, and his eyes were, oh so dim; but to the very last he spoke of the dear old days and the orchard and the clover and the Hampshire hills. And when Seth fell asleep forever, Abner kissed his brother's lips and knelt at the bedside and said the prayer his mother had taught him.

In the street without there was the noise of passing carts, the cries of tradespeople, and all the bustle of a great and busy city; but, looking upon Seth's dear, dead face, Abner could hear only the music voices of birds and crickets and summer winds as he had heard them with Seth when they were little boys together, back among the Hampshire hills.

The Ambitious Guest

This story has been edited and adapted from Nathaniel Hawthorne's Twice Told Tales, first published in 1889 by David McKay, Publisher, Philadelphia.

One September night a family had gathered round their hearth and piled it high with the driftwood of mountain-streams, the dry cones of the pine, and the splintered ruins of great trees that had come crashing down the precipice. Up the chimney roared the fire, and brightened the room with its broad blaze. The faces of the father and mother had a sober gladness; the children laughed. The eldest daughter was the image of Happiness at seventeen, and the aged grandmother, who sat knitting in the warmest place, was the image of Happiness grown old. They had found the "herb heart's-ease" in the bleakest spot of all New England. This family were situated in the Notch of the White Hills, where the wind was sharp throughout the year and pitilessly cold in the winter, giving their cottage all its fresh inclemency before it descended on the valley of the Saco. They dwelt in a cold spot and a dangerous one, for a mountain towered above their heads so steep that the stones would often rumble down its sides and startle them at midnight.

The daughter had just uttered some simple jest that filled them all with mirth, when the wind came through the Notch and seemed to pause before their cottage, rattling the door with a sound of wailing and lamentation before it passed into the valley. For a moment it saddened them, though there was nothing unusual in the tones. But the family were glad again when they perceived that the latch was lifted by some traveller whose footsteps had been unheard amid the dreary blast which heralded his approach and wailed as he was entering and went moaning away from the door.

Though they dwelt in such a solitude, these people held daily converse with the world. The romantic pass of the Notch is a great artery through which the life-blood of internal commerce is continually throbbing between Maine on one side and the Green Mountains and the shores of the St. Lawrence on the other. The stage-coach always drew up before the door of the cottage. The wayfarer with no companion but his staff paused here to exchange a word, that the sense of loneliness might not utterly overcome him before he could pass through the cleft of the mountain or reach the first house in the valley. And here the teamster on his way to Portland market would put up for the night, and, if a bachelor, might sit an hour beyond the usual bedtime and steal a kiss from the mountain-maid at parting. It was one of those primitive taverns where the traveller pays only for food and lodging, but meets with a homely kindness beyond all price. When the footsteps were heard, therefore, between the outer door and the inner one, the whole family rose up, grandmother, children and all, as if about to welcome someone who belonged to them, and whose fate was linked with theirs.

The door was opened by a young man. His face at first wore the melancholy expression, almost despondency, of one who travels a wild and bleak road at nightfall and alone, but soon brightened up when he saw the kindly warmth of his reception. He felt his heart spring forward to meet them all, from the old woman who wiped a chair with her apron to the little child that held out its arms to him. One glance and smile placed the stranger on a footing of innocent familiarity with the eldest daughter.

"Ah! This fire is the right thing," cried he, "especially when there is such a pleasant circle round it. I am quite benumbed, for the Notch is just like the pipe of a great pair of bellows; it has blown a terrible blast in my face all the way from Bartlett."

"Then you are going toward Vermont?" said the master of the house as he helped to take a light knapsack off the young man's shoulders.

"Yes, to Burlington, and far enough beyond," replied he. "I meant to have been at Ethan Crawford's tonight, but a pedestrian lingers along such a road as this. It is no matter; for when I saw this good fire and all your cheerful faces, I felt as if you had kindled it on purpose for me and were waiting my arrival. So I shall sit down among you and make myself at home."

The frank-hearted stranger had just drawn his chair to the fire when something like a heavy footstep was heard without, rushing down the steep side of the mountain as with long and rapid strides, and taking such a leap in passing the cottage as to strike the opposite precipice. The family held their breath, because they knew the sound, and their guest held his by instinct.

"The old mountain has thrown a stone at us for fear we should forget him," said the landlord, recovering himself. "He sometimes nods his head and threatens to come down, but we are old neighbours, and agree together pretty well, upon the whole.

Besides, we have a sure place of refuge hard by if he should be coming in good earnest."

Let us now suppose the stranger to have finished his supper of bear's meat, and by his natural felicity of manner to have placed himself on a footing of kindness with the whole family; so that they talked as freely together as if he belonged to their mountain-brood. He was of a proud yet gentle spirit, haughty and reserved among the rich and great, but ever ready to stoop his head to the lowly cottage door and be like a brother or a son at the poor man's fireside. In the household of the Notch he found warmth and simplicity of feeling, the pervading intelligence of New England, and a poetry of native growth which they had gathered when they little thought of it from the mountain-peaks and chasms, and at the very threshold of their romantic and dangerous abode. He had travelled far and alone; his whole life, indeed, had been a solitary path, for, with the lofty caution of his nature, he had kept himself apart from those who might otherwise have been his companions. The family, too, though so kind and hospitable, had that consciousness of unity among themselves and separation from the world at large which in every domestic circle should still keep a holy place where no stranger may intrude. But this evening a prophetic sympathy impelled the refined and educated youth to pour out his heart before the simple mountaineers, and constrained them to answer him with the same free confidence. And thus it should have been. Is not the kindred of a common fate a closer tie than that of birth?

The secret of the young man's character was a high and abstracted ambition. He could have borne to live an undistinguished life, but not to be forgotten in the grave. Yearning desire had been transformed to hope, and hope, long cherished, had become like certainty that, obscurely as he journeyed now, a glory was to beam on all his pathway, though not, perhaps, while he was treading it. But when posterity should gaze back into the gloom of what was now the present, they would trace the brightness of his footsteps, brightening as meaner glories faded, and confess that a gifted one had passed from his cradle to his tomb with none to recognize him.

"As yet," cried the stranger, his cheek glowing and his eye flashing with enthusiasm - "as yet I have done nothing. Were I to vanish from the earth tomorrow, none would know so much of me as you - that a nameless youth came up at nightfall from the valley of the Saco, and opened his heart to you in the evening, and passed through the Notch by sunrise, and was seen no more. Not a soul would ask, 'Who was he? Where did the wanderer go?' But I cannot die till I have achieved my destiny. Then let Death come, for I shall have built my monument."

There was a continual flow of natural emotion gushing forth amid abstracted reverie which enabled the family to understand this young man's sentiments, though so foreign from their own. With quick sensibility of the ludicrous, he blushed at the ardour into which he had been betrayed.

"You laugh at me," said he, taking the eldest daughter's hand and laughing himself. "You think my ambition as nonsensical as if I were to freeze myself to death on the top of Mount Washington only that people might spy at me from the country roundabout. And truly that would be a noble pedestal for a man's statue."

"It is better to sit here by this fire," answered the girl, blushing, "and be comfortable and contented, though nobody thinks about us."

"I suppose," said her father, after a fit of musing, "there is something natural in what the young man says; and if my mind had been turned that way, I might have felt just the same. It is strange, wife, how his talk has set my head running on things that are pretty certain never to come to pass."

"Perhaps they may," observed the wife. "Is the man thinking what he will do when he is a widower?"

"No, no!" cried he, repelling the idea with reproachful kindness. "When I think of your death, Esther, I think of mine too. But I was wishing we had a good farm in Bartlett or Bethlehem or Littleton, or some other township round the White Mountains, but not where they could tumble on our heads. I should want to stand well with my neighbours and be called squire and sent to General Court for a term or two; for a plain, honest man may do as much good there as a lawyer. And when I should be grown quite an old man, and you an old woman, so as not to be long apart, I might die happy enough in my bed, and leave you all crying around me. A slate gravestone would suit me as well as a marble one, with just my name and age, and a verse of a hymn, and something to let people know that I lived an honest man and died a Christian."

"There, now!" exclaimed the stranger, "it is our nature to desire a monument, be it slate or marble, or a pillar of granite, or a glorious memory in the universal heart of man."

"We're in a strange way tonight," said the wife, with tears in her eyes. "They say it's a sign of something when folks' minds go a-wandering so. Hark to the children!"

They listened accordingly. The younger children had been put to bed in another room, but with an open door between; so that they could be heard talking busily among themselves. One and all seemed to have caught the infection from the fireside circle, and were outvying each other in wild wishes and childish projects of what they would do when they came to be men and women. At length a little boy, instead of addressing his brothers and sisters, called out to his mother.

"I'll tell you what I wish, mother," cried he, "I want you and father and grandma'm, and all of us, and the stranger too, to start right away and go and take a drink out of the basin of the Flume."

Nobody could help laughing at the child's notion of leaving a warm bed and dragging them from a cheerful fire to visit the basin of the Flume, a brook which tumbles over the precipice deep within the Notch.

The boy had hardly spoken, when a wagon rattled along the road and stopped a moment before the door. It appeared to contain two or three men who were cheering their hearts with the rough chorus of a song which resounded in broken notes between the cliffs, while the singers hesitated whether to continue their journey or put up here for the night.

"Father," said the girl, "they are calling you by name."

But the good man doubted whether they had really called him, and was unwilling to show himself too solicitous of gain by inviting people to patronize his house. He therefore did not hurry to the door, and, the lash being soon applied, the travellers plunged into the Notch, still singing and laughing, though their music and mirth came back drearily from the heart of the mountain.

"There, mother!" cried the boy, again, "they'd have given us a ride to the Flume."

Again they laughed at the child's pertinacious fancy for a night-ramble. But it happened that a light cloud passed over the daughter's spirit; she looked gravely into the fire and drew a breath that was almost a sigh. It forced its way, in spite of a little struggle to repress it. Then, starting and blushing, she looked quickly around the circle, as if they had caught a glimpse into her bosom.

The stranger asked what she had been thinking of. "Nothing," answered she, with a downcast smile, "only I felt lonesome just then."

"Oh, I have always had a gift of feeling what is in other people's hearts," said he, half seriously. "Shall I tell the secrets of yours? For I know what to think when a young girl shivers by a warm hearth and complains of lonesomeness at her mother's side. Shall I put these feelings into words?"

"They would not be a girl's feelings any longer if they could be put into words," replied the mountain-nymph, laughing, but avoiding his eye.

All this was said apart. Perhaps a germ of love was springing in their hearts so pure that it might blossom in Paradise, since it could not be matured on earth; for women worship such gentle dignity as his, and the proud, contemplative, yet kindly, soul is oftenest captivated by simplicity like hers. But while they spoke softly, and he was watching the happy sadness, the lightsome shadows, the shy yearnings, of a maiden's nature, the wind through the Notch took a deeper and drearier sound. It seemed, as the fanciful stranger said, like the choral strain of the spirits of the blast who in old times had their dwelling among these mountains and made their heights and recesses a sacred region. There was a wail along the road as if a funeral were passing. To chase away the gloom, the family threw pine-branches on their fire till the dry leaves crackled and the flame arose, discovering once again a scene of peace and humble happiness. The light hovered about them fondly and caressed them all. There were the little faces of the children peeping from their bed apart, and here the father's frame of strength, the mother's subdued and careful mien, the high-browed youth, the budding girl and the good old grandam, still knitting in the warmest place.

The aged woman looked up from her task, and with fingers ever busy was the next to speak. "Old folks have their notions," said she, "as well as young ones. You've been wishing and planning and letting your heads run on one thing and another till you've set my mind a-wandering too. Now, what should an old woman wish for, when she can go but a step or two before she comes to her grave? Children, it will haunt me night and day till I tell you."

"What is it, mother?" cried the husband and wife at once.

Then the old woman, with an air of mystery which drew the circle closer round the fire, informed them that she had provided her grave-clothes some years before, being a nice linen shroud, a cap with a muslin ruff, and everything of a finer sort than she had worn since her wedding-day. But this evening an old superstition had strangely recurred to her. It used to be said in her younger days that if anything were amiss with a corpse, if only the ruff were not smooth or the cap did not set right, then the corpse, in the coffin and beneath the clods, would strive to put up its cold hands and arrange it. The bare thought made her nervous.

"Don't talk so, grandmother," said the girl, shuddering.

"Now," continued the old woman, with singular earnestness, yet smiling strangely at her own folly, "I want one of you, my children, when your mother is dressed and in the coffin, I want one of you to hold a looking-glass over my face. Who knows but I may take a glimpse at myself and see whether all's right?"

"Old and young, we dream of graves and monuments," murmured the stranger-youth. "I wonder how mariners feel when the ship is sinking and they, unknown and undistinguished, are to be buried together in the ocean, that wide and nameless sepulchre?"

For a moment the old woman's ghastly conception so engrossed the minds of her hearers that a sound abroad in the night, rising like the roar of a blast, had grown broad, deep and terrible before the fated group were conscious of it. The house and all within it trembled; the foundations of the earth seemed to be shaken, as if this awful sound were the peal of the last trump. Young and old exchanged one wild glance and remained an instant pale, affrighted, without utterance or power to move. Then the same shriek burst simultaneously from all their lips:

"The slide! The slide!"

The simplest words must intimate, but not portray, the unutterable horror of the catastrophe. The victims rushed from their cottage and sought refuge in what they deemed a safer spot, where, in contemplation of such an emergency, a sort of barrier had been reared. Alas! they had quitted their security and fled right into the pathway of destruction. Down came the whole side of the mountain in a cataract of ruin. Just before it reached the house the stream broke into two branches, shivered not a window there, but overwhelmed the whole vicinity, blocked up the road and annihilated everything in its dreadful course. Long before the thunder of that great slide had ceased to roar among the mountains the mortal agony had been endured and the victims were at peace. Their bodies were never found.

The next morning the light smoke was seen stealing from the cottage chimney up the mountain-side. Within, the fire was yet smouldering on the hearth, and the chairs in a circle round it, as if the inhabitants had but gone forth to view the devastation of the slide and would shortly return to thank Heaven for their miraculous escape. All had left separate tokens by which those who had known the family were made to shed a tear for each. Who has not heard their name? The story has been told far and wide, and will for ever be a legend of these mountains. Poets have sung their fate.

There were circumstances which led some to suppose that a stranger had been received into the cottage on this awful night, and had shared the catastrophe of all its inmates; others denied that there were sufficient grounds for such a conjecture. Woe for the high-souled youth with his dream of earthly immortality! His name and person utterly unknown, his history, his way of life, his plans, a mystery never to be solved, his death and his existence equally a doubt... Whose was the agony of that death-moment?

Black Alice Dunbar

This story has been edited and adapted from Henry W. Shoemaker's Allegheny Episodes, first published in 1922 by the Altoona Tribune Company, based out of Altoona, Pennsylvania. This was one of a series of collections forming the Pennsylvania Folk Lore series.

Down in the wilds of the Fourth Gap, latterly used as an artery of travel between Sugar Valley and White Deer Hole Valley, commonly known as "White Deer Valley," a forest ranger's cabin stands on the site of an ancient encampment, the only clearing in the now dreary drive from the "Dutch End" to the famous Stone Church. Until a dozen years ago much of the primeval forest remained, clumps of huge, original white pines stood here and there, in the hollows were hemlock and rhododendron jungles, while in the fall the flickers chased one another among the gorgeous red foliage of the gum trees.

Now much is changed; between "Tom" Harter and "Charley" Steele, and other lumbermen, including some gum tree contractors, little remains but brush and slash; forest fires have sacrificed the remaining timber, and only among the rocks, near the mouth of the gap, can be seen a few original yellow pines, shaggy topped in isolated grandeur. Someday the tragic history of White Deer Hole Valley will come to its own, and present one of the most tragic pages in the narrative of the passing of the native American man.

It was into this isolated valley, that terminates in Black Hole Valley, and the Susquehanna River, near Montgomery, that numbers of the Monsey Tribe of the Lenni-Lenape, called by some the Delaware, retreated after events subsequent to the Walking Purchase, made them outcasts on the face of the earth. It was not long afterwards that warlike parties of their cruel Nemesis, the Senecas, appeared on the scene, informing the Monseys that they had sold the country to the whites, and if they stayed, it was at their peril.

Even at that early day white men were not wholly absent; they came in great numbers after the Senecas had sold the lands of the Lenni-Lenape to the "Wunnux," but even coincident with the arrival of the Delawares, a few white traders and adventurers inhabited the most inaccessible valleys.

Alexander Dunbar, a Scotchman, married to a Monsey woman, arrived in White Deer Hole Valley with the first contingent of his wife's tribes-people, settling near the confluence of White Deer Hole Creek and South Creek. Whether he was any relation to the Dunbar family, who have long been so prominent in this valley is unknown, as his family moved further west, and the last heard of them was when his widow died and was buried in the vicinity of Dark Shade Creek, Somerset County.

Dunbar was a dark, swarthy complexioned man, more like a native than a Celt, and dressed in the tribal garb, could easily have passed off as one of the tribesmen. At one time he evidently intended to remain in the Fourth Gap, as in the centre of the greensward which contained the native encampment, he erected a log fortress, with four bastions, the most permanent looking structure west of Fort Augusta. In it he aimed to live like a Scottish Laird, with his great hall, the earthen floor, covered with the skins of panthers, wolves and bears, elk and deer antlers hanging about, and a huge, open fireplace that burned logs of colossal size, and would have delighted an outlaw like Rob Roy MacGregor.

When the Seneca penetrated into the valley they were at a loss at first to ascertain Alexander Dunbar's true status. If he was related to the prominent Scotch families identified with the Penn Government, he would be let alone, but if a mere friendless adventurer, he would be driven out the same as any one of the "Original People."

Dunbar was a silent man, and by his taciturnity won toleration for a time, as he never revealed his true position. When the Senecas became reasonably convinced that, no matter who he had been in the Highlands of Scotland, he was a person of no importance in the mountains of Pennsylvania, they began a series of prosecutions that finally ended with his murder. This took its first form by capturing all members of the Lenni-Lenape tribe who ventured into the lower end of the valley, for those who had settled further down, and on the banks of the Susquehanna and Monsey Creek had moved westward when they learned that they had been "sold out." However, the residents of Dunbar's encampment occasionally ventured down South Creek on hunting and fishing expeditions. When the heads of half a dozen families, and several squaws, young girls and children had been captured, over a dozen in all, and put into a stockade near the present village of Spring Garden, and rumour had it that they were being ill-treated, Alexander

Dunbar, carrying a flag of truce, set off to treat with the Seneca Council, at what is now Allenwood, with a view to having them paroled.

The unfortunate man never reached the Senecas' headquarters, being shot from ambush, and left to die like a dog on the trail, not far from the Panther Spring.

While the surviving, able bodied Monseys could have risen and started a warfare, they deemed it prudence to remain where they were, and to make Sugar Valley, and the valleys adjacent to White Deer Creek, their principal hunting grounds.

While Dunbar had lived, squaw man, though he was, he was the leader of the native people among whom he resided, else they would never have permitted his erecting a pretentious fortress in the midst of their humble tepees of hides and poorly constructed log cabins. At his death the leadership devolved on his eighteen-year-old daughter, "Black Agnes", his widow being a poor, inoffensive creature, a typical drudge.

Black Agnes was even darker complexioned than her father, but was better looking, having fine, clear cut features, expressive dark eyes which flashed fire, although she was much below medium height, in fact, no bigger than a twelve-year-old child. She wore her hair in such a tangled way that her eyes, lean cheeks and white throat were half hidden by the masses of her sable tresses. She usually attired herself in a blue coat and cape, a short tan skirt trimmed with grey squirrel tails, and long native stockings. She was in miniature a counterpart of Miriam Donsdebes, the beautiful heroine of one of the chapters in this writer's book *South Mountain Sketches*.

While it may have given the Senecas added cause to repeat their jibe of "old women" at the Lenni-Lenapes, for not avenging Dunbar's death, it was a case of living on sufferance anyway, and foolish to have attacked superior numbers. The Senecas always had white allies to call on for arms and ammunition, while from the first, the Delawares were a proscribed people, slated to be run off the earth and exterminated.

During this lull, following the Scotchman's murder, which the Senecas would doubtless have disavowed, an embassy appeared at the Dunbar stronghold to ask Black Agnes' hand in marriage with a young Seneca warrior named Shingaegundin, whom the intrepid young girl had never seen. While it would have been extremely politic for Black Agnes to have accepted, and allied herself with the powerful tribe that had wronged her people, she sent back word firmly declining.

After the emissaries departed through the gate of the stockade, she turned to her warriors, saying, in the metaphorical language of her race, "The sky is overcast with dark, blustering clouds," which means that troublesome times were coming, that they would have war.

The embassy returned crestfallen to Shingaegundin, who was angry enough to have slain them all. Instead, he rallied his braves, and told them that if he could not have Black Agnes willingly, he would take her by force, and if she would not be a happy and complaisant bride, he would tie her to a tree and starve her until she ceased to be recalcitrant.

The bulk of the Monseys having departed from the valleys on both sides of the Susquehanna, to join others of their tribe at the headwaters of the Ohe-yu, left the Dunbar clan in the midst of an enemy's country, so that it would look like an easy victory for Shingaegundin's punitive expedition.

Black Agnes had that splendid military quality of knowing ahead of time what her adversaries planned to do, whether "second sight" from her Scotch blood, or merely a highly developed sense of strategy, matters not. At any rate, she was ready to deal a blow at her unkind enemies. Therefore she posted her best marksmen along the rocky face of the South Mountains, on either side of Fourth Gap. Behind these grey-yellow, pulpit-shaped rocks, the tribesmen crouched, ready for the oncoming Senecas. Black Agnes herself was in personal command inside the stockade, where she was surrounded by a courageous bodyguard twice her size. The women, old men and children, were sent to the top of the mountain, to about where Zimmerman's Run heads at the now famous Zimmerman Mountain-top Hospice. At a signal, consisting of a shot fired in the air by Black Agnes herself, the fusillade from the riflemen concealed among the rocks was to begin, to make the Fourth Gap a prototype of Killiecrankie.

In turn the entrance of the Senecas into the defile was to be announced by arrow shot into the air by a Monsey scout who was concealed behind the Raven's Rock, the most extensive point of vantage overlooking the "Gap."

When Black Agnes saw the graceful arrow speed up into space, she again spoke metaphorically, "The path is already shut up!" which meant that hostilities had commenced, the war begun.

The little war sprite timed her plot to a nicety. When the Senecas were well up in the pass, and surrounded on all sides by the Monseys, whom they imagined all crowded into the stockade, Black Agnes fired her shot, and the slaughter began. The Senecas began falling on all sides, thanks to the unerring aim of the Monsey riflemen, but they were too inured to warfare to break and run, especially when caught in a trap.

Shingaegundin, enraged beyond all expression at again being flouted by a woman, and a member of the tribe of "old women," determined to die gamely, and within the stockade which harboured Black Agnes. He seemed to bear a charmed life, for while his cohorts fell about him, he plunged on unhurt. The gate of the stockade was open, and Black Agnes stood just within it, directing her warriors, a quaint but captivating little figure, more like a sprite or fairy than one of flesh and blood.

Shingaegundin espied her, and knew at a glance that this must be the woman who the wise men of his tribe had selected to be his bride, and the cause of this senseless battle. His was a case of love at first sight, the very drollness of her tiny form adding to his passion, and he ran forward, determined to be killed holding her in his arms and pressing kisses on her dusky cheeks.

Such thoughts enhanced his ambition and courage, and he shouted again and again to his braves to pick themselves up and come on as he was doing. Dazed with love, he imagined in a blissful moment that he would yet have the victory and carry Black Agnes home under his arm like a naughty child.

Just outside the palisade he was met by three of Agnes' bodyguard, armed with stone hatchets. None of his warriors were near him; shot and bleeding, they were writhing on the grass, while some were already in the hands of the Monsey braves, who had come down from their eyries, and were dexterously plying the scalping knives. Few of the mutilated Senecas uttered cries, although as the scalps were jerked off, it was hard to suppress involuntary sobs of pain.

Black Agnes saw nothing in the long, lank form of Shingaegundin to awaken any love; she detested him as belonging to the race that had sold her birth right and foully murdered her father, and she called to her warriors, "Suffer no grass to grow on the war-path," signifying to carry on the fight with vigour.

Shingaegundin was soon down, his skull battered and cracked in a dozen places. Even when down, his ugly spirit failed to capitulate. Biting and scratching and clawing with his nails like a beast, he had to have his skull beaten like a copperhead before he stretched out a lifeless, misshapen corpse. As he gave his last convulsive kick the Monsey warriors began streaming through the gates, some holding aloft scalps dripping with blood, while others waved about by the scalp locks, the severed heads of their defeated foemen.

Never had such a rout been inflicted on the Senecas; perhaps Black Agnes would be a second Jeanne d'Arc, and lead the Lenni-Lenape back to their former glories and possessions!

The victorious Monseys became very hilarious. Hoisting the scalps on poles, they shimmied around Black Agnes, yelling and singing their ancient war songs, the proudest moment of their bellicose lives.

Black Agnes was calm in triumph, for she knew how transitory life or fame is. Biting her thin lips, she drew her scalping knife and bent down over the lifeless form of Shingaegundin, to remove his scalp in as business-like a manner as if she was skinning a rabbit. Addressing the grinning corpse, she said, "Bury it deep in the earth," meaning that the Seneca's injury would be consigned to oblivion. Then, with rare dexterity, she removed the scalp, a difficult task when the skull has been broken in, in so many places.

Holding aloft the ugly hirsute trophy, she almost allowed herself to smile in her supreme moment of success. Her career was now made; she would rally the widely scattered remnants of the Delawares, and fight her way to some part of Pennsylvania where prestige would insure peace and uninterrupted happiness. But in these elevated moments comes the bolt from the blue.

One of the panic-stricken Senecas, bolting from the ignominious ambush of his fellows, had scrambled up the boulder-strewn side of the mountain, taking refuge behind the Raven's Rock, lately occupied by the chief lookout of the Monseys – he who had shot the warning arrow into the air. Crouching abject and trembling at first, he began to peer about him as the fusillade ceased and the smoke of battle cleared. He saw his slain and scalped clansmen lying about the greensward, and in the creek, and the awful ignominy meted out to his lion-hearted sachem, Shingaegundin. At his feet lay the bow and quiver full of arrows abandoned by the scout when he rushed down pell mell to join in the bloody scalping bee.

The sight of Black Agnes holding aloft his chieftain's scalp, the horribly mutilated condition of Shingaegundin's corpse, the shimmying, singing Monseys, waving scalps and the severed heads of his brothers and friends, all drew back to his heart what red blood ran in his veins.

Black Agnes stood there so erect and self-confident, like a little robin red-breast, ready for a potpie, and he would lay her low and end her pretensions. Taking careful aim, for he was a noted archer, the Seneca let go the arrow, which sped with the swiftness of a passenger pigeon, finding a place in the heart of the brave girl. The tip came out near her backbone, her slender form was pierced through and through. The slight flush on her dark cheeks gave way to a deadly pallor, and, facing her unseen slayer, Black Agnes Dunbar tumbled to the earth dead.

The dancing, singing Monseys suddenly became a lodge of sorrow, weeping and wailing as if their hearts would break. The Seneca archer could have killed more of them, they were so bewildered, but he decided to run no further risks, and made off towards his encampment to tell his news, good and bad, to his astounded tribesmen.

When it was seen that Black Agnes was no more, and could not be revived, the sorrowful Monseys dug a grave within the stockade. It was a double death for them, as they knew that they would be hunted to the end like the Wolf Tribe that they were, and they had lost an intrepid and beloved leader.

According to the custom, before the interment, Black Agnes' clothing was removed, the braves deciding to take it as a present to the dead girl's mother, to show how bravely she died. They walled up the grave and covered the corpse with rocks so that wolves could not dig it up, graded a nice mound of sod over the top, and, like the white soldiers at Fort Augusta, fired a volley over her grave.

That night there was a sorrowing scene enacted at the campground near the big spring at Zimmerman's Run. The grief-stricken mother wanted to run away into the forest, to let the wild beasts devour her, and was restrained with great difficulty by her tribesmen, who had also lost all in life that was worth caring for, peace and security.

With heavy hearts they started on a long journey for the west, carrying the heart-broken mother Karendonah in a hammock, to the asylum offered to them by the Wyandots on the Muskingum. The bereaved woman carried the blood-stained, heart-pierced raiment of her heroic daughter as a priceless relic, and it was in her arms when she died suddenly on the way, in Somerset County, and was buried beside the trail, on the old Forbes Road. The Monseys, however, took the costume with them as a fetich, and for years missionaries and others interested in the tragic story of Black Agnes Dunbar were shown her blue jacket with the hole in the breast where the arrow entered.

That arrow pierced the hearts of all the Monseys, for they became a dejected and beaten people in their Ohio sanctuary.

While it is true that most of the very old people who lived in the vicinity of the Fourth Gap have passed away, it may yet be possible to learn the exact location of the cairn containing the remains of Black Agnes and place a suitable marker over it. One thing seems certain, if the tradition of the Lenni-Lenape that persons dying bravely in battle reach a higher spiritual plane once their souls are released, her ghost will not have to hunt the hideous, burnt-over slashings that were once the wildly romantic Fourth Gap; it has gone to a realm beyond the destructive commercialism of this dollar-mad age, where beauty finds a perpetual reward and recognition.

Désirée's Baby

This story has been edited and adapted from Kate Chopin's Bayou Folk, first published in 1894 by the Houghton Mifflin Company of Boston and New York.

As the day was pleasant, Madame Valmondé drove over to L'Abri to see Désirée and the baby. It made her laugh to think of Désirée with a baby. Why, it seemed but yesterday that Désirée was little more than a baby herself; when Monsieur in riding through the gateway of Valmondé had found her lying asleep in the shadow of the big stone pillar.

The little one awoke in his arms and began to cry for "Dada." That was as much as she could do or say. Some people thought she might have strayed there of her own accord, for she was of the toddling age. The prevailing belief was that she had been purposely left by a party of Texans, whose canvas-covered wagon, late in the day, had crossed the ferry that Coton Maïs kept, just below the plantation. In time Madame Valmondé abandoned every speculation but the one that Désirée had been sent to her by a beneficent Providence to be the child of her affection, seeing that she was without child of the flesh. The girl grew to be beautiful and gentle, affectionate and sincere, the idol of Valmondé.

It was no wonder, when she stood one day against the stone pillar in whose shadow she had lain asleep, eighteen years before, that Armand Aubigny riding by and seeing her there, had fallen in love with her. That was the way all the Aubignys fell in love, as if struck by a pistol shot. The wonder was that he had not loved her before; for he had known her since his father brought him home from Paris, a boy of eight, after his mother died there. The passion that awoke in him that day, when he saw her at the gate, swept along like an avalanche, or like a prairie fire, or like anything that drives headlong over all obstacles.

Monsieur Valmondé grew practical and wanted things well considered: that is, the girl's obscure origin. Armand looked into her eyes and did not care. He was reminded that she was nameless. What did it matter about a name when he could give her one of the oldest and proudest in Louisiana? He ordered the corbeille from Paris, and contained himself with what patience he could until it arrived; then they were married.

Madame Valmondé had not seen Désirée and the baby for four weeks. When she reached L'Abri she shuddered at the first sight of it, as she always did. It was a sad looking place, which for many years had not known the gentle presence of a mistress, old Monsieur Aubigny having married and buried his wife in France, and she having loved her own land too well ever to leave it. The roof came down steep and black like a cowl, reaching out beyond the wide galleries that encircled the yellow stuccoed house. Big, solemn oaks grew close to it, and their thick-leaved, far-reaching branches shadowed it like a pall. Young Aubigny's rule was a strict one, too, and under it his negroes had forgotten how to be gay, as they had been during the old master's easy-going and indulgent lifetime.

The young mother was recovering slowly, and lay full length, in her soft white muslins and laces, upon a couch. The baby was beside her, upon her arm, where he had fallen asleep, at her breast. The yellow nurse woman sat beside a window fanning herself.

Madame Valmondé bent her portly figure over Désirée and kissed her, holding her an instant tenderly in her arms. Then she turned to the child.

"This is not the baby!" she exclaimed, in startled tones. French was the language spoken at Valmondé in those days.

"I knew you would be astonished," laughed Désirée, "at the way he has grown. The little cochon de lait! Look at his legs, mamma, and his hands and finger-nails, real finger-nails. Zandrine had to cut them this morning. Is not that true, Zandrine?"

The woman bowed her turbaned head majestically, "Mais si, Madame."

"And the way he cries," went on Désirée, "is deafening. Armand heard him the other day as far away as La Blanche's cabin."

Madame Valmondé had never removed her eyes from the child. She lifted it and walked with it over to the window that was lightest. She scanned the baby narrowly, then looked as searchingly at Zandrine, whose face was burned to gaze across the fields.

"Yes, the child has grown, has changed," said Madame Valmondé, slowly, as she replaced it beside its mother. "What does Armand say?"

Désirée's face became suffused with a glow that was happiness itself. "Oh, Armand is the proudest father in the parish, I believe, chiefly because it is a boy, to bear his name; though he says not, and that he would have loved a girl as well. But I know it is not true. I know he says that to please me. And mamma," she added, drawing Madame Valmondé's head down to her, and speaking in a whisper, "he has not punished one of them. not one of them since baby is born. Even Négrillon, who pretended to have burnt his leg that he might rest from work - he only, laughed, and said Négrillon was a great scamp. Oh, mamma, I'm so happy; it frightens me."

What Désirée said was true. Marriage, and later the birth of his son, had softened Armand Aubigny's imperious and exacting nature greatly. This was what made the gentle Désirée so happy, for she loved him desperately. When he frowned she trembled, but loved him. When he smiled, she asked no greater blessing of God. But Armand's dark, handsome face had not often been disfigured by frowns since the day he fell in love with her.

When the baby was about three months old, Désirée awoke one day to the conviction that there was something in the air menacing her peace. It was at first too subtle to grasp. It had only been a disquieting suggestion; an air of mystery among the workers; unexpected visits from far-off neighbours who could hardly account for their coming. Then there was a strange, an awful change in her husband's manner, which she dared not ask him to explain. When he spoke to her, it was with averted eyes, from which the old love-light seemed to have gone out. He absented himself from home; and when there, avoided her presence and that of her child, without excuse. And the very spirit of Satan seemed suddenly to take hold of him in his dealings with the slaves. Désirée was miserable enough to die.

She sat in her room, one hot afternoon, in her peignoir, listlessly drawing through her fingers the strands of her long, silky brown hair that hung about her shoulders. The baby, half naked, lay asleep upon her own great mahogany bed, that was like a sumptuous throne, with its satin-lined half-canopy. One of La Blanche's little quadroon boys, half naked too, stood fanning the child slowly with a fan of peacock feathers. Désirée's eyes had been fixed absently and sadly upon the baby, while she was striving to penetrate the threatening mist that she felt closing about her. She looked from her child to the boy who stood beside him, and back again; over and over. "Ah!" It was a cry that she could not help; which she was not conscious of having uttered. The blood turned like ice in her veins, and a clammy moisture gathered upon her face.

She tried to speak to the little quadroon boy; but no sound would come, at first. When he heard his name uttered, he looked up, and his mistress was pointing to the door. He laid aside the great, soft fan, and obediently stole away, over the polished floor, on his bare tiptoes.

She stayed motionless, with gaze riveted upon her child, and her face the picture of fright.

Presently her husband entered the room, and without noticing her, went to a table and began to search among some papers which covered it.

"Armand," she called to him, in a voice which must have stabbed him, if he was human. But he did not notice. "Armand," she said again. Then she rose and tottered towards him. "Armand," she panted once more, clutching his arm, "look at our child. What does it mean? tell me."

He coldly but gently loosened her fingers from about his arm and thrust the hand away from him. "Tell me what it means!" she cried despairingly.

"It means," he answered lightly, "that the child is not white; it means that you are not white."

A quick conception of all that this accusation meant for her nerved her with unwonted courage to deny it. "It is a lie; it is not true, I am white! Look at my hair, it is brown; and my eyes are grey, Armand, you know they are grey. And my skin is fair," seizing his wrist. "Look at my hand; whiter than yours, Armand," she laughed hysterically.

"As white as La Blanche's," he returned cruelly; and went away leaving her alone with their child.

When she could hold a pen in her hand, she sent a despairing letter to Madame Valmondé.

"My mother, they tell me I am not white. Armand has told me I am not white. For God's sake tell them it is not true. You must know it is not true. I shall die. I must die. I cannot be so unhappy, and live.".

The answer that came was as brief: "My own Désirée: Come home to Valmondé; back to your mother who loves you. Come with your child."

When the letter reached Désirée she went with it to her husband's study, and laid it open upon the desk before which he sat. She was like a stone image: silent, white, motionless after she placed it there.

In silence he ran his cold eyes over the written words. He said nothing. "Shall I go, Armand?" she asked in tones sharp with agonized suspense.

"Yes, go."

"Do you want me to go?"

"Yes, I want you to go."

He thought Almighty God had dealt cruelly and unjustly with him; and felt, somehow, that he was paying Him back in kind when he stabbed thus into his wife's soul. Moreover he no longer loved her, because of the unconscious injury she had brought upon his home and his name.

She turned away like one stunned by a blow, and walked slowly towards the door, hoping he would call her back.

"Good-by, Armand," she moaned.

He did not answer her. That was his last blow at fate.

Désirée went in search of her child. Zandrine was pacing the sombre gallery with it. She took the little one from the nurse's arms with no word of explanation, and descending the steps, walked away, under the live-oak branches.

It was an October afternoon; the sun was just sinking. Out in the still fields the negroes were picking cotton.

Désirée had not changed the thin white garment nor the slippers which she wore. Her hair was uncovered and the sun's rays brought a golden gleam from its brown meshes. She did not take the broad, beaten road which led to the far-off plantation of Valmondé. She walked across a deserted field, where the stubble bruised her tender feet, so delicately shod, and tore her thin gown to shreds.

She disappeared among the reeds and willows that grew thick along the banks of the deep, sluggish bayou; and she did not come back again.

Some weeks later there was a curious scene enacted at L'Abri. In the centre of the smoothly swept back yard was a great bonfire. Armand Aubigny sat in the wide hall-way that commanded a view of the spectacle; and it was he who dealt out to a half dozen negroes the material which kept this fire ablaze.

A graceful cradle of willow, with all its dainty furnishings, was laid upon the pyre, which had already been fed with the richness of a priceless layette. Then there were silk gowns, and velvet and satin ones added to these; laces, too, and embroideries; bonnets and gloves; for the corbeille had been of rare quality.

The last thing to go was a tiny bundle of letters; innocent little scribblings that Désirée had sent to him during the days of their espousal. There was the remnant of one back in the drawer from which he took them. But it was not Désirée's; it was part of an old letter from his mother to his father. He read it. She was thanking God for the blessing of her husband's love.

"But, above all," she wrote, "night and day, I thank the good God for having so arranged our lives that our dear Armand will never know that his mother, who adores him, belongs to the race that is cursed with the brand of slavery."

Juanetta, Or, The Treasure Of The Lake Of The Tulies

This story has been edited and adapted from May Wentworth's Fairy Tales From Gold Lands, first published in 1868 by A. Roman and Company.

A great many years ago, before the discovery of the wonderful gold mines of California, there lived in Los Angelos an old Spanish family of pure Castilian blood.

Don Carlos De Strada was very rich. Far as the eye could reach his broad acres were spread out to his admiring view, and his flocks and herds almost literally fed upon a thousand hills.

His house was large and commodious, built after the Spanish fashion, an adobe house, surrounded on all sides by a wide piazza, and in the centre an open courtyard. The windows were guarded by latticed bars of iron, and all the gates and doors were opened by massive keys. Bolts and bars belong as much to a Spanish house, as light elegancies to the hotel of a Parisian.

When Don Carlos left the banks of the Guadalquivir for the wild Lake of the Tulies, he brought with him a beautiful young wife, who loved him with all the passionate ardour of a Spanish woman.

It was a great change for the dainty lady, from the stately halls of castellated Spain to the wilderness of Los Angelos, although it was a wilderness of sweets, and the most enchanting climate in the world. Though the Don was a thorough-bred aristocrat, he was a shrewd businessman, and so intent was he on becoming a great lord of the soil in the new country, that he did not notice the roses fading from the olive cheeks of his wife, and the soft mellow light of the woman's eye giving place to the more ethereal brightness of spiritual fire.

Spanish women seldom work, but in their hours of apparent listlessness they indulge in wild and ardent imaginings; and thus she would sit on the vine-clad piazza of the inner court, looking up to the clear sky, unrivalled even in Italy, until she would almost fancy, from the heavens above, she heard the rippling of the blue waters of the Guadalquivir.

There was one great hunger of her heart the Don seldom satisfied. She was his wife, and beautiful; as such, he loved her; but he never lavished the thousand little endearments upon her that is the natural food of woman's heart.

As the evening drew near, she would go to the barred window and look out upon the luxurious landscape, thinking only of the coming of her lord; and when she saw him, she would go timidly out to meet him, and hold her beautiful oval face up for a kiss, longing for him to throw his arms around her, and, if only for a moment, hold her to his heart.

He would kiss her lightly, saying, coldly, "There, that will do; be a woman now, not a baby." Then she would call up a quiet dignity, until she could steal for a few moments away, unobserved, and press her hands tightly upon her heart, saying, "If he would only love me! If he would only love me, I could live away from home, away from Spain, from everything, for him! I must learn to be a woman, and then, at least he'll respect me.

"Oh, dear! I wish he didn't think it so foolish in me to want to be loved! But I must go to him. I'll try and talk like a woman, but I don't know anything about the business that occupies his thoughts and time. He never tells me anything because he thinks I'm such a baby. If he'd only love me, and let me be a baby sometimes, I think I'd be more of a woman."

Then the young wife would try to call up from her weakness new strength, and wiping away the traces of her emotion, would go out to be what pleased her lord, only a little paler, but with heart-strings quivering like an Æolian harp in a cold north wind.

One year passed in the strange, new country, and a beautiful babe was born to the ancient house of De Strada, but the mother died, and was buried by the clear Lake of the Tulies.

Don Carlos wept for his beautiful young wife, whose heart had been a sealed book, "Love, the Secret of Happiness," written for him in an unknown tongue.

His days of mourning were few. The rain fell upon the new-made grave as he gave the infant in charge of a native nurse who had just lost her own little baby. The mother took the child to her bosom, while the polished father turned away and looked out upon the green hills rich in verdure, counting the probable increase of his flocks and herds in the coming year, and, in the pleasant prospect, forgot his sorrow.

The little Juanetta grew to be a beautiful, healthy child, under the care of her indulgent nurse. She knew where all the wildflowers grew, could shoot an arrow very well, or climb a tree, and, in many of the curious arts of the tribe, was quite skilful.

She was well versed in all the local traditions, and believed them with childish credulity. She seemed to have drawn the wildness, of the indigenous nature from the dusky bosom of her nurse, and with her little bow and arrow would roam the woods for whole days.

At times her father would ask the nurse, "How is Juanetta?" and, at the reply, "The child is well," he would forget that every day she was growing less and less an infant, and needed more and more a mother's care.

Thus things went on until she was eleven years old. She was very tall of her age, with her long black hair hanging over her graceful shoulders, her rich olive complexion deepened by the glowing sun, and her dark eyes, fawn-like in their softness and timidity, she looked like a beautiful child of the wild wood.

Her father would look at her, and say, "The girl is a perfect savage; she must be placed at a convent; the Sisters would soon make a lady of her, for the De Strada blood is rich in her veins," and then he would smile proudly at her rare beauty.

The summer following brought a change to Don Carlos. Till then he had been prosperous; but there had been no rain, and the grass withered and dried up until the famished cattle died by thousands, and the hills, once covered with animal life, were left bare and desolate. Don Carlos, who lost heavily, became more than ever absorbed in business cares, and again the child was forgotten.

Juanetta saw that her father was greatly troubled, and she thought if she could only find some of the treasures hidden so many years ago by the great Chief of the Tulies, she could make him rich again, and he would smile upon her as he sometimes used to before the cattle died. Since then, his dark frowning face had frightened her.

She had often listened to her old nurse, sitting by the clear lake, as she told her how, years ago, a great ship came to Los Angelos filled with fair men, with long flowing beards, golden in the sunshine, and eyes like the blue summer sky, and how there was one among them, taller and nobler than all the rest, who was their Chief.

For days they rode about the country, making their camp by the Lake of the Tulies, and tradition said they brought beautiful shining stones, that glistened like the stars of night, and great sacks of yellow gold to the lake, and buried them there at midnight; then went away in the great ship over the water.

They were seen by an old woman, who was gathering magic herbs, but from that moment it seemed as though a fearful spell had fallen upon her, for when she tried to tell the story, just as she was about to speak of the place where the treasure was hidden, her tongue would cleave to the roof of her mouth, and she could not utter a word; and when she attempted to go to the spot where it was buried, her feet would fasten themselves to the ground, and she could not move. From that night she seemed bewitched, and she soon died, taking the secret of the buried treasure with her to the unknown spirit land.

Juanetta had nothing to do but listen to the wild native lore, and roam through the woods and down by the Lake of the Tulies; and it was not strange that with her poetic temperament, she revelled in the marvellous, till it seemed to her the natural and the real.

She longed for the magic talisman to point her to the hidden treasure, and show her the wonders of the deep, until she felt sure that one day she should discover it. She told all these fancies to her nurse, who was almost her only companion, and who encouraged her, believing her, in her fond love, to be one of the Great Spirit's chosen children.

The winter came on with rare beauty. The rain, so long withheld, fell copiously, until the hills were covered with luxurious verdure and gorgeous flowers. Don Carlos's heart grew lighter; he might hope to recover his losses in time. The orange orchard was laden with fruit, and the lemons fell to the ground from the bending trees. Juanetta loved the green grass, the fragrant flowers, and the golden fruit, and her wild nature expanded into the poetry of the year.

One morning she rose with the crimson dawning, and, stealing away while her old nurse slept, she ran softly to the Lake of the Tulies, and bathed her face in the clear water till the brightness of youth and morning seemed united in her radiant beauty.

Suddenly Juanetta stopped, her tiny hand dripping with water, half raised to her glowing face, and her soft, dark eyes sparkling with strange excitement. Upon the brow of the distant hill, still covered with the mist of the morning, she saw the Chief of the Lake of the Tulies. She knew it was him by the soft, purple light that gathered around him; by the glow of perpetual youth that enveloped him, and by the crimson clouds that dropped their fleece so near, and yet could not conceal his noble bearing.

To her eye, there seemed a shining glory about his bronze beard, and his brow and cheeks glowing in the early sunlight, were fairer than any she had ever seen among the dusky tribes or olive Spaniards.

Down the hill he came, a light straw hat in his hand, and the air playing with the light waves of his abundant hair. On he came to the lake, and to the spot where the little maiden sat, full of wonder and admiration.

He, too, seemed a little surprised when he saw her, but in the soft Spanish tongue, bade her "Good morning," and asked whose little girl she was, and what had brought her so early to the charmed lake.

"I am Don Carlos's daughter, Juanetta," said the child, "and you, the Chief of the Lake of the Tulies?"

A smile gathered around the lips of the Chief, and filled his blue eye with a light so pleasant that the child drew near him, and placed her little brown hand confidingly in his. He drew her to him, saying, kindly, "You know me, then? I am the Chief of the Lake of the Tulies, and what can I do for the little Juanetta?"

"Tell me," said the child, "of all the wonderful treasures hidden by the lake, and of the palaces of the sea, and the coral groves under the great waters!"

The Chief led her to a rock that overhung the lake, and told her to look over into the waters, and she saw them clear and sparkling in the morning sun, and it seemed as though the light of a thousand brilliants was stealing through the shining waves.

He told her of glittering diamonds beneath the sea, richer far than all the hills and valleys of Los Angelos, covered with flocks and herds; and how the coral trees outshone the trees of earth, in beauty, and of the crystal palaces of the deep, and of the maidens of the sea, whose, purple hair like sea-weed, sometimes floated above the waves.

Juanetta told him she had often found locks of their silken hair upon the beach, and how beautiful it was. He told her of the sounding shells, and ocean harps breathing their rich, deep-toned melody, and the thousand mysteries of the wild sea lore, till the delighted Juanetta begged him to take her with him down, down to the crystal caves, and let her become a sea-maiden, and gather pearls under the blue waters of the deep.

But he replied, "You are a child of the woods, not of the wave; you may become an immortal spirit in the sky, but never in the deep, deep sea."

Tears gathered in her eyes, and she said, "You are cruel to Juanetta, Chief of the Lake of the Tulies. You of all your wealth of beauty, will grant Juanetta nothing. Juanetta must live alone, in the woods and fields, with only the old nurse and the father who always forgets her."

He soothed the little maiden gently, and told her he would grant her greater treasures than those of the deep, if she would obey him; and she kissed his hand and promised.

Then he took from his bosom, a talisman, and gave it to her, saying, "Juanetta, this cross will guard you from evil spirits. When you are troubled or angry, take it from your bosom, and ask the great Father above to bless you and help you. Do this earnestly five minutes, and the evil spirits will leave you." And Juanetta kissed the cross and promised.

"I have yet another talisman" he continued, "and very powerful. It opens a new world of delight and beauty, to those who are willing to give their time, care, and diligent attention to the study of it. Would you like it, Juanetta? You could no longer wander all day through the woods, hunting wild-flowers, or dream away your life by the Lake of the Tulies. Could you give up the wild pleasures of your present life, for the gifts of the talisman I have promised?"

Juanetta's face was glowing with wonder and delight; she longed to enter the unknown promised land. "I will do anything, I will give up any thing you tell me, she cried, with enthusiasm."

She was enchanted with the unseen gifts that left so much to her fervid imagination to picture, and she was delighted with the giver, the handsome young Chief of the Lake of the Tulies, whose pleasant smile, and pleasing words, made morning's golden sunshine in her heart.

"But won't you show me where the treasure of the Lake of the Tulies lies hidden?" she said, blushingly. "All those rare gems, crimson, purple, golden, and diamonds sparkling like the morning dew. What can be more beautiful than these?"

All her life, Juanetta had heard of the matchless lustre of these hidden jewels, and now to be so near them, with the Chief of the Lake of the Tulies by her side, she felt that her daydreams of beauty might, with one word of his, or a touch of his magic wand, be realized.

"Do not ask for too much in one morning, Juanetta," he replied, laughing. "Now for talisman number two," and he took a book from his pocket, and until the sun had risen high in the heavens, they sat bending over it together with mutual pleasure.

Then the Chief of the Lake of the Tulies arose, taking her little bronzed hand in his, saying, "I must go, my little Juanetta. Keep the talisman, and study it well. The new morning is dawning for you now; what a queen of light 'twill make you?" And he passed his hand over the thick waves of tangled hair that fell in long masses over the shoulders of the beautiful child.

Tears gathered in the dark eyes of the maiden. "Are you going now, Chief of the Lake of the Tulies?" said she, sadly, "Going to the crystal palaces of the sea? And shall you take the treasure of the lake with you? Take the talisman, I can do nothing without you! Here alone! Only the old nurse, and the father who never thinks, never thinks of Juanetta! And you, too, will forget Juanetta!"

"No! No, Juanetta, I will not forget you, but will come again tomorrow. I will not go to the sea, since you cannot go, but will stay and teach you the use of the talisman, and the treasure of the lake shall rest till we can find it together! So now goodbye today."

And then they parted, and Juanetta was very happy in the light of the new dawning. All day long she studied, and many successive days, and the Chief of the Lake of the Tulies always came, either at morning or at evening, to hear her lesson.

Sometimes she would ask him about the hidden treasure, as they walked by the lake; he would smile and say, "I have found a treasure by the Lake of the Tulies richer than all the gems of the ocean," and when Juanetta begged him to show it to her, he would tell, her to look into the water; but she could see only the reflection of her own sweet face, full of wondering happiness.

Then he would laugh again, and say, he could not tell her now of his treasure by the Lake of the Tulies, but he would describe the rich gold mine he had discovered in the cañon, and tell her there was gold enough in it almost to fill up the lake.

Thus weeks and months passed by. Juanetta was twelve years old. She had improved rapidly in her studies, and had learned to call her young teacher by another name, not so long or high sounding, but very pleasant to them both, and often they would laugh at their first strange meeting by the charmed Lake of the Tulies.

At last her father was aroused to the sense of her increasing beauty. He saw, that the years of childhood were fast passing away, and that she stood upon the threshold of dawning womanhood. He was greatly surprised, and delighted to find her proficient in studies of which he supposed she knew nothing, and he made all possible haste to have her placed at a convent, where she could enjoy every advantage of culture and refinement.

The young stranger who had been her teacher, became a great favourite with Don Carlos. He was engaged in developing a mine, in the San Francisco cañon, in which he succeeded in amassing great wealth, though in after years the mine failed to yield its store of golden treasure.

Four years passed away, and Juanetta returned to her father's house, an accomplished, and beautiful lady. Again by the Lake of the Tulies, she met the Chief of her childhood's dreams, and there together, they found the treasure greater than all the wealth of land or sea, the pure and earnest love of their youthful hearts. They were married, and Don Carlos's heart swelled proudly, as he thought of the great wealth their union had brought into his family, while they blessed God for the lifelong treasure He had given them, by the charmed Lake of the Tulies.

Do You Believe In Ghosts?

This story has been edited and adapted from Henry W. Shoemaker's Allegheny Episodes, first published in 1922 by the Altoona Tribune Company, based out of Altoona, Pennsylvania. This was one of a series of collections forming the Pennsylvania Folk Lore series.

A. D. Karstetter, painstaking local historian, tells us that there was no more noteworthy spot in the annals of mountainous Pennsylvania than the old Washington Inn at Logansville. Built after the fashion of an ancient English hostelry, with its inn-yard surrounded by sheds and horse stables, it presented a most picturesque appearance to discerning travellers. The passage of time had obliterated it, long before the great fire on June 24, 1918, swept the town, removing even the landmarks which would have showed where the old-time inn was situated.

Many are the tales, grave or gay, clustered about its memory, far more, says Mr. Karstetter, than were connected with the Logan Hotel, run by the Coles, which was erected at a much later day, just when the old coaching days were passing out, and the new era coming in. All of the history that grew up about the Washington

Inn ante-dated the Civil War, while that of the Logan Hotel was of the period of that war and later. This gives one a good mental picture of the type of legend interwoven with the annals of the ancient Washington Inn.

A winter rain had set in, just at dusk, as the great lumbering five-horse coach (three wheelers and two leaders) from Hightown entered the straggling outskirts of Logansville. The post boy on the boot blew his long horn vociferously, waking the echoes up Summer Creek, then back again, clear to the "Grandfather Pine" at Chadwick's Gap.

A whimsical old German, who worked at Jacob Eilert's pottery, picked up his old tin horn that he used to blow as a boy when wolves or native folks were about, and answered the clarion in cracked, uncertain notes. Lights glimmered in cabin windows, and many a tallow dip, fat lamp or rushlight was held aloft to get a good view of the coach as it swirled along through the mud, and its crowded company. Everybody was standing up, buttoning their coats and gathering together their luggage, as the big, clumsy vehicle checked up under the swinging sign, on which was painted the well-loved features of the Father of His Country.

The old landlord, his wife and the hostelers and stable boys and household help were outside to assist the travellers to alight and show them into the comfortable glow of the lobby.

"When do you start out in the morning?" all were asking of the rosy-cheeked driver, although the hour for continuing the journey west from Logansville was printed in big letters on the rate card at the posting office at Hightown, as "Sharp, 6.00 A. M."

In the candle-lit lobby, by a blazing fire of maple logs, the travellers surveyed one another, the landlord and their surroundings. They were an even dozen in number, nine men and three women. Some of the men were hunters and had their Lancaster rifles with them; the others commercial travellers. The women were also engaged in business pursuits.

The stage was the sole means of penetrating into the back country, and the canals and the Pennsylvania Central Railroad (now known as the Main Line) the only methods of crossing the Keystone State in those early days.

A good supper was served, that being hickory smoked ham and eggs, hot cakes and native grown maple syrup, and plentiful libations of original Murray "Sugar Valley" whiskey, which put the huntsmen and the drummers in capital humour. After the meal they brought out their pipes and sat in groups about the fire in the great, low-ceilinged room. The three women, who were middle-aged and of stolid appearance, sat together, talking in undertones.

All at once, when the fire suddenly spluttered up, one of the drummers, a big, black-bearded fellow, said loudly enough so that all could hear – he was evidently trying to make the conversation general – "In the mountains they say that it's a sign of a storm when the fire jumps up like that."

"And I guess we're having it," said another of the travellers dryly, a little man with grey side whiskers.

Then, as wide shadows fell across the floor, another of the men, a hunter, ventured the remark, "Do you believe in ghosts?"

There was a pause, as if no one wanted to take up such a very personal topic before strangers. It was in the days when the Fox sisters were electrifying all of Pennsylvania, including the celebrated Dr. Elisha Kane, with their mediumship, so that it was as popular a topic then as now, in the days of Sir Oliver Lodge and Mrs. Herbine.

At length one of the men, also a hunter, from Berks County, broke the silence by asking if any one present had heard the story of the Levan ghost of Oley Township, in Berks; if not, he would tell it. None had ever heard it, so he told of the young Levan girl who had lost her father, to whom she was particularly attached.

One evening, while milking, she was seized with a very strong feeling that her father was near, which feeling kept up for a week, growing stronger daily. At last one evening she went into her room, the house being built all on one floor, and she saw her father, as natural as life, seated on an old chest that had come from France, for the Levans were Huguenot refugees.

The girl did not seem to be afraid to see her father, about whom a light seemed to radiate, and they conversed some time together, mostly on religious topics. Her mother and sisters, who were in another room, heard her talking, and the voice which sounded like that of the departed, and came to the door, which was ajar.

"Who are you talking to?" the mother inquired.

"To father. He is here. Come in and see him," replied the girl, calmly.

The family was afraid to enter, remaining outside until the conversation had finished and the ghost vanished. When the girl re-joined them, the side of her face that had been turned to her father was slightly scorched or reddened, as if she had been close to a fire. And that tenderness of skin remained as long as she lived.

While other versions of the story have appeared, this is the way it was told that stormy night in the Washington Inn in the long ago.

The ice having been broken, one of the women spoke up, saying that the part of the story which told of the girl's face being burned by the aura from the ghost interested her most, that over in the Nittany Valley there was a case in the old Carroll family of a woman who had an only child which she loved to distraction, but which unfortunately died. The mother took on terribly, and during the night when she was sitting up with the little corpse, besought it to prove to her that the dead lived, if only for just one minute.

In the midst of her weeping and wailing, and romping about the cold, dimly-lit room, the dead child rose up in its little pine box and motioned its sorrowing mother to come to it. The woman ran to the coffin and the little one touched her forehead with its finger, which burned her like a red-hot poker. Then it sank back with a gasp and a groan, and was dead again. Ever afterwards there was a sore, tender spot on the woman's forehead where the corpse had touched it.

Then another of the women told how she had been selling Bibles in the Great Smoky Mountains in Tennessee, and one of the wheels of her carriage became dished from the bad roads. She had tried to put up with a mountaineer who would not take her in, and gave her the choice of sleeping in the barn with the team and the driver, or to occupy a room in a deserted Negro "quarters" across the road.

All night long she had been annoyed by her candles being blown out and the door blowing open, though she locked it time and again.

It was a commonplace sort of a ghost story, and one of the hunters yawned at its conclusion. The evening's reminiscences might have ended then and there if the third woman traveller, the youngest and sturdiest of the lot, who thus far had been the quietest, turned to the landlord, who sat smoking in the settle, with a couple of his guests, asking him if he remembered the Big Calf.

"What do you know about the Big Calf?" he said, quizzically, looking at the woman in order to see if he could recognize her.

"I know as much as you do, I reckon," she said. "I lived here for a year learning millinery with Emilie Knecht."

"You know, I think I remember you…" said the landlord.

"You surely do," responded the woman, "and I knew you well, Jakey Kleckner, in those days." "said the bonny face, sitting up very straight.

"Long years ago," began the businesswoman, "when this public house was first opened, the landlord's cow gave birth to an unusual calf. At six weeks it was as big as most heifers of six months, and it was handsome and intelligent, a brown-grey colour, 'Brown Swiss' they called the breed. All the drovers and cattle buyers in the mountains wanted that calf for a show, and her fame spread all over the 'five counties.'

"There were two buyers from out about Greensburg that came in all the ways to get her, but the price was too steep. They hung around all day, drinking with the landlord in the tap room, and though he took too much in this drunken bout, kept enough of his wits with him to refuse to lower the price one shilling. The next morning he had to go away on important business, and in the afternoon the drovers returned, telling the landlord's wife that they had met her husband on the road, and he had consented to accept a lower figure.

"The woman replied that while she was sorry her 'man' had shown such weakness to change his mind so quickly, when on leaving he had told her that he had been sickened by the importunities of the two strangers the day before, yet she claimed, the calf as hers and it would not leave the premises for any price, and except over her dead body. She prized it especially since she had also raised the mother, which had recently been killed by a wandering panther.

"The men departed in an ugly mood. When the man returned in the evening he was indignant at what his wife told him; he had not met the drovers on the road, and if he had, the calf was not for sale.

"Shortly after his arrival a German Gypsy, one of the Einsicks, appeared in the inn-yard with a big she-bear, a brown one, which he took about the mountains to dance and amuse the crowds at public houses, fairs and political meetings. The stables were full, but after some arguing the landlord consented to let the bear occupy the box stall where he kept the Big Calf, which he removed to the smoke house.

"During the night, which was very dark, the covetous drovers returned, and, not knowing of the Big Calf's changed quarters, one of them went into steal it. In the darkness the bear seized him and hugged him almost to death. His companion, vexed at his slowness in fetching out the Big Calf, called to him, and he made known his predicament.

"There was no way to free the captive but to begin clubbing the bear, which set up such a loud growling that it aroused the owner and the landlord, who ran out with pistols, just in time to see the two would-be cattle thieves decamping from the inn-yard. They both fired after them, but the scoundrels got off scot free. They never returned.

"The Big Calf grew into a very handsome cow, and was the pride of the mountain community. It was always brought in from pasture at night and milked, lest it share its mother's fate and be pulled down by a Pennsylvania lion.

"One evening, while the landlord's only daughter, a very pretty, graceful girl, was driving the cow home, she was joined by a handsome, dark-complexioned young man, mounted on a superb black horse. He accompanied her to the stables, where he watched her milk, and then put up for the night at the inn. Next day he became very sick, and several doctors were called in, who bled him, but could not diagnose his ailment.

"Meanwhile he proposed marriage to the landlord's daughter, who nursed him, pretending that he was a young man of quality from Pittsburgh, which flattered the innkeeper and his daughter mightily.

"All this while he was trying to learn if the landlord kept any large sum of money in the house. It was not long until the girl confided to him that her father had gone into debt buying a farm in Nippenose Bottom, as he wanted to retire from the tavern business. It was there where he was when the two dishonest drovers from Greensburg had returned and tried to euchre his wife out of the Big Calf.

"Satisfied that there was no booty in the house, the fellow rose one morning before daybreak, dressed quietly, although the girl was in the room, wrote a note to her which he left on the clothes press, and made his escape. The wording of the letter ran about as follows:

"'Dearest Love, I am sorry to have left without saying goodbye, but my intentions were not sincere, for while I admired your beauty and good sense, which none can deny, I was only here to find out where your father kept his money. But since he has none, and has gone into debt, I need remain no longer. I thank you for all the information you gave me, and for your kind attentions. Gratefully yours, David Lewis.'

"The poor girl had been one of the dupes of the celebrated 'Lewis the Robber,' or someone impersonating him, as he had many alter egos, some more daring than himself, and understudies. If half the stories told of his exploits were true, he would have had to be a hundred years old to do them, and get to so many places.

"At any rate, the pretty girl was frightfully cut up by her misfortune, and took to the bed lately vacated by 'Lewis.' She had told all of her friends that she was to marry in a fortnight, and go to live in a big house on Grant's Hill, Pittsburgh, and it was all terrible and humiliating. Rather than let the real story get out, the girl's parents connived with her to say that word had been brought that the young gentleman, while riding near Standing Stone Town, had been thrown from his horse and killed. Hence when the girl was able to reappear, she was dressed in black, as if in mourning for her dashing sweetheart.

"The first time she came out of doors she went for a walk alone just about dusk, so that not many people would be abroad, towards the lower part of the village. She was never seen or heard of again. There was no stream or pool big enough for her to drown herself in; a panther could hardly have dragged her off and not left signs of a struggle; she might have fallen in a cave or sink, it is true. At all events, it seemed as if the earth had swallowed her up. Perhaps Lewis, or whoever he was, came back after her.

"When I came to Logansville to learn millinery with Emilie Knecht, I lived in her house over the store, just across the way from this hotel; the building was burned down afterwards. How such a gifted milliner came to settle off here in the mountains I could never tell, but I suppose mountain ladies must have nice hats just like those in the valleys.

"We became good friends, and very confidential, though at that time she was over thirty years of age and I was at least a dozen years younger. She would never tell where she came from, except that it was down country, and there seemed to be something on her mind which weighed on her terribly. Though I think she was the loveliest looking woman I have ever seen, she cared absolutely nothing for the men. As she believed in ghosts, and so did I, we compared experiences.

"I told her of a ghostly episode which left a deep impression on my childish nature, which happened when I was six years old. My father worked in the mines, and was on 'night shift.' Mother locked the doors and we all went to bed. Mother's room adjoined mine and my sister's. After we were in bed for some time, but not yet asleep, a man, he seemed to be black, came to the door which led from mother's room to ours, and smiled at us. He drew back, re-appeared and smiled again, or rather grinned, showing his white teeth; it was a peculiar smile.

"I wanted to call mother, but sister, who was eight, said I must not speak, I must keep very still.

"Next morning we asked father what time he came home, and he said, 'not until morning.' We told our experience, but father and mother seemed to think we had only imagined it.

"But two persons do not imagine the same thing at the same time. Besides, we were not afraid. I have often wondered what it was. My sister died shortly after that. Could it have been a 'warning,' I wonder?

"The pretty milliner's story was even more startling and unusual. She declared that her grandmother's ghost had come to her bedside every night since she was a small child. She said that she never feared it, but took it as a matter of course. I think that these nightly visitations took a whole lot out of her. I can see her yet running down the steep, narrow stairs in the mornings to the shop where I was working - I was always an early riser – her face looking as if it had been whitewashed, more so perhaps because her hair and eyes were so dark.

"She was often nervous and irritable, and I laid it all to the vital force which the ghost must be drawing out of her to materialize, but she said it was only her liver which made her so dauncy. I begged her to let me sleep with her, that I did not think that the ghost would come if I was present, and if it did it could draw on some of my vitality, as I was a big, strong, hearty girl. She would not let me sleep with her, saying that she had gotten used to the ghost.

"One evening Miss Knecht and I were invited to a chicken and waffle supper at the home of old Mrs. Eilert, wife of the potter, whose house was the last one in town. In those days there was quite a distance not built up between the potter's home and the rest of the village. The holidays were approaching, and we were getting ready for the Christmas trade, consequently stayed later in the shop than we had expected.

"As I said before, Mrs. Eilert lived at the extreme end of town. When we were a few squares from home we noticed a woman dressed in mourning who seemed to be following us, or at least going in our direction. She was an entire stranger to us, and we wondered where she could be going; so each house we came to I would look back to see whether she entered. When we were half a square from where we were going, we passed a house which stood back pretty far from the road. There was considerable ground to the place, and a high board fence all around. After we passed the gate I turned, as before, to see whether this woman would enter. She did not. I watched her until she was past the gate quite a ways. I turned and told my companion she had not entered, and immediately turned to look at her again, and she was gone!

"Where could she have gone in those few seconds in which I was not looking at her? Everywhere there was open space, nowhere for her to hide. Had she jumped the fence she could not have gotten out of sight in those few seconds. I have often wondered since what it was.

"When we reached the Eilert home I noticed that Miss Knecht was in a highly unstrung condition, more so than I had ever seen her before. We told the story, and the old potter smiled grimly, saying, 'You surely have seen the ghost of the landlord's daughter who disappeared, all dressed in black, after being jilted by the robber.'

"Emilie shook her pretty dark curls, muttering that she feared it was something worse. She was afraid to go home that night, and we spent the night with our friends; yet she would not remain unless given a room by herself. In the morning she was in a most despondent mood; she had not seen her grandmother, and she feared as to what it could mean?

"The woman in black must have been her 'familiar' leaving her, warning her to that effect, and not the ghost of the landlord's daughter after all, she maintained. I tried to reassure her that she would see her grandmother once she was in her own room, but next morning brought the tidings that the faithful spirit was again absent. This continued for a week, my friend becoming more nervous and despondent.

"One morning she did not come downstairs, so at eight o'clock I went up after her, to see if she were ill. The bed was empty, and had not been slept in. I searched the house and found her lying beautiful in death on a miserable cot in the cellar, which an elderly Dutchman sometimes occupied when cutting wood and taking care of the garden for us. She had drunk a potion of arsenic that she had bought some months before to poison rats which infested the cellar, but her lovely face was not marked.

"I left town shortly afterwards, and have never been back until tonight."

The burly commercial traveller who had started the general conversation stroked his long black beard. "I guess it is time for all of us to retire. I don't think we need to ask this lady again, 'Do you believe in ghosts?'"

The Shaker Bridal

This story has been edited and adapted from Nathaniel Hawthorne's Twice Told Tales, first published in 1889 by David McKay, Publisher, Philadelphia.

One day, in the sick-chamber of Father Ephraim, who had been forty years the presiding elder over the Shaker settlement at Goshen, there was an assemblage of several of the chief men of the sect. Individuals had come from the rich establishment at Lebanon, from Canterbury, Harvard and Alfred, and from all the other localities where this strange people have fertilized the rugged hills of New England by their systematic industry. An elder was likewise there who had made a pilgrimage of a thousand miles from a village of the faithful in Kentucky to visit his spiritual kindred the children of the sainted Mother Ann. He had partaken of the homely abundance of their tables, had quaffed the far-famed Shaker cider, and had joined in the sacred dance every step of which is believed to alienate the enthusiast from earth and bear him onward to heavenly purity and bliss. His brethren of the North had now courteously invited him to be present on an occasion when the concurrence of every eminent member of their community was peculiarly desirable.

The venerable Father Ephraim sat in his easy-chair, not only hoary-headed and infirm with age, but worn down by a lingering disease which it was evident would very soon transfer his patriarchal staff to other hands. At his footstool stood a man and woman, both clad in the Shaker garb.

"My brethren," said Father Ephraim to the surrounding elders, feebly exerting himself to utter these few words, "here are the son and daughter to whom I would commit the trust of which Providence is about to lighten my weary shoulders. Read their faces, I pray you, and say whether the inward movement of the spirit has guided my choice aright."

Accordingly, each elder looked at the two candidates with a most scrutinizing gaze. The man, whose name was Adam Colburn, had a face sunburnt with labour in the fields, yet intelligent, thoughtful and traced with cares enough for a whole lifetime, though he had barely reached middle age. There was something severe in his aspect and a rigidity throughout his person, characteristics that caused him generally to be taken for a schoolmaster; which vocation, in fact, he had formerly exercised for several years. The woman, Martha Pierson, was somewhat above thirty, thin and pale, as a Shaker sister almost invariably is, and not entirely free from that corpse-like appearance which the garb of the sisterhood is so well calculated to impart.

"This pair are still in the summer of their years," observed the elder from Harvard, a shrewd old man. "I would like better to see the hoar-frost of autumn on their heads. I think, also, they will be exposed to peculiar temptations on account of the carnal desires which have heretofore subsisted between them."

"Nay, brother," said the elder from Canterbury, "the hoar-frost and the black frost has done its work on Brother Adam and Sister Martha, even as we sometimes discern its traces in our cornfields while they are yet green. And why should we question the wisdom of our venerable Father's purpose, although this pair in their early youth have loved one another as the world's people love? Are there not many brethren and sisters among us who have lived long together in wedlock, yet, adopting our faith, find their hearts purified from all but spiritual affection?"

Whether or not the early loves of Adam and Martha had rendered it inexpedient that they should now preside together over a Shaker village, it was certainly most singular that such should be the final result of many warm and tender hopes. Children of neighbouring families, their affection was older even than their school-days; it seemed an innate principle interfused among all their sentiments and feelings, and not so much a distinct remembrance as connected with their whole volume of remembrances. But just as they reached a proper age for their union misfortunes had fallen heavily on both and made it necessary that they should resort to personal labour for a bare subsistence. Even under these circumstances Martha Pierson would probably have consented to unite her fate with Adam Colburn's, and, secure of the bliss of mutual love, would patiently have awaited the less important gifts of Fortune. But Adam, being of a calm and cautious character, was loth to relinquish the advantages which a single man possesses for raising himself in the world. Year after year, therefore, their marriage had been deferred.

Adam Colburn had followed many vocations, had travelled far and seen much of the world and of life. Martha had earned her bread sometimes as a sempstress, sometimes as help to a farmer's wife, sometimes as schoolmistress of the village children, sometimes as a nurse or watcher of the sick, thus acquiring a varied experience the ultimate use of which she little anticipated. But nothing had gone prosperously with either of the lovers; at no subsequent moment would matrimony have been so prudent a measure as when they had first parted, in the opening bloom of life, to seek a better fortune. Still, they had held fast their mutual faith. Martha might have been the wife of a man who sat among the senators of his native State, and Adam could have won the hand, as he had unintentionally won the heart, of a rich and comely widow. But neither of them desired good-fortune save to share it with the other.

At length that calm despair which occurs only in a strong and somewhat stubborn character and yields to no second spring of hope settled down on the spirit of Adam Colburn. He sought an interview with Martha and proposed that they should join the Society of Shakers. The converts of this sect are oftener driven within its hospitable gates by worldly misfortune than drawn there by fanaticism, and are received without inquisition as to their motives. Martha, faithful still, had placed her hand in that of her lover and accompanied him to the Shaker village. Here the natural capacity of each, cultivated and strengthened by the difficulties of their previous lives, had soon gained them an important rank in the society, whose members are generally below the ordinary standard of intelligence. Their faith and feelings had in some degree become assimilated to those of their fellow-worshippers. Adam Colburn gradually acquired reputation not only in the management of the temporal affairs of the society, but as a clear and efficient preacher of their doctrines. Martha was not less distinguished in the duties proper to her sex. Finally, when the infirmities of Father Ephraim had admonished him to seek a successor in his patriarchal office, he thought of Adam and Martha, and proposed to renew in their persons the primitive form of Shaker government as established by Mother Ann. They were to be the father and mother of the village. The simple ceremony which would constitute them such was now to be performed.

"Son Adam and daughter Martha," said the venerable Father Ephraim, fixing his aged eyes piercingly upon them, "if you can conscientiously undertake this charge, speak, that the brethren may not doubt of your fitness."

"Father," replied Adam, speaking with the calmness of his character, "I came to your village a disappointed man, weary of the world, worn out with continual trouble, seeking only a security against evil fortune, as I had no hope of good. Even my wishes of worldly success were almost dead within me. I came here as a man might come to a tomb willing to lie down in its gloom and coldness for the sake of its peace and quiet. There was but one earthly affection in my breast, and it had grown calmer since my youth; so that I was satisfied to bring Martha to be my sister in our new abode. We are brother and sister, nor would I have it otherwise. And in this peaceful village I have found all that I hope for, all that I desire. I will strive with my best strength for the spiritual and temporal good of our community. My conscience is not doubtful in this matter. I am ready to receive the trust."

"You have spoken well, son Adam," said the father. "God will bless you in the office which I am about to resign."

"But our sister," observed the elder from Harvard. "Has she not likewise a gift to declare her sentiments?"

Martha started and moved her lips as if she would have made a formal reply to this appeal. But, had she attempted it, perhaps the old recollections, the long-repressed feelings of childhood, youth and womanhood, might have gushed from her heart in words that it would have been profanation to utter there. "Adam has spoken," said she, hurriedly, "his sentiments are likewise mine."

But while speaking these few words Martha grew so pale that she looked fitter to be laid in her coffin than to stand in the presence of Father Ephraim and the elders; she shuddered, also, as if there were something awful or horrible in her situation and destiny. It required, indeed, a more than feminine strength of nerve to sustain the fixed observance of men so exalted and famous throughout the sect as these were. They had overcome their natural sympathy with human frailties and affections. One, when he joined the society, had brought with him his wife and children, but never from that hour had spoken a fond word to the former or taken his best-loved child upon his knee. Another, whose family refused to follow him, had been enabled, such was his gift of holy fortitude, to leave them to the mercy of the world. The youngest of the elders, a man of about fifty, had been bred from infancy in a Shaker village, and was said never to have clasped a woman's hand in his own, and to have no conception of a closer tie than the cold fraternal one of the sect. Old Father Ephraim was the most awful character of all. In his youth he had been a dissolute libertine, but was converted by Mother Ann herself, and had partaken of the wild fanaticism of the early Shakers. Tradition whispered at the firesides of the village that Mother Ann had been compelled to sear his heart of flesh with a red-hot iron before it could be purified from earthly passions.

However that might be, poor Martha had a woman's heart, and a tender one, and it quailed within her as she looked round at those strange old men, and from them to the calm features of Adam Colburn. But, perceiving that the elders eyed her doubtfully, she gasped for breath and again spoke.

"With what strength is left me by my many troubles," said she, "I am ready to undertake this charge, and to do my best in it."

"My children, join your hands," said Father Ephraim.

They did so. The elders stood up around, and the father feebly raised himself to a more erect position, but continued sitting in his great chair.

"I have bidden you to join your hands," said he, "not in earthly affection, for you have cast off its chains for ever, but as brother and sister in spiritual love and helpers of one another in your allotted task. Teach unto others the faith which you have received. Open wide your gates. I deliver you the keys thereof. Open them wide to all who will give up the iniquities of the world and come here to lead lives of purity and peace. Receive the weary ones who have known the vanity of earth; receive the little children, that they may never learn that miserable lesson. And a blessing be upon your labours; so that the time may hasten on when the mission of Mother Ann shall have wrought its full effect, when children shall no more be born and die, and the last survivor of mortal race, some old and weary man like me, shall see the sun go down nevermore to rise on a world of sin and sorrow."

The aged father sank back exhausted, and the surrounding elders deemed, with good reason, that the hour was come when the new heads of the village must enter on their patriarchal duties. In their attention to Father Ephraim their eyes were turned from Martha

Pierson, who grew paler and paler, unnoticed even by Adam Colburn. He, indeed, had withdrawn his hand from hers and folded his arms with a sense of satisfied ambition. But paler and paler grew Martha by his side, till, like a corpse in its burial-clothes, she sank down at the feet of her early lover; for, after many trials firmly borne, her heart could endure the weight of its desolate agony no longer.

Boulôt And Boulotte

This story has been edited and adapted from Kate Chopin's Bayou Folk, first published in 1894 by the Houghton Mifflin Company of Boston and New York.

When Boulôt and Boulotte, the little piny-wood twins, had reached the dignified age of twelve, it was decided in family council that the time had come for them to put their little naked feet into shoes. They were two brown-skinned, black-eyed 'Cadian roly-polies, who lived with father and mother and a troop of brothers and sisters halfway up the hill, in a neat log cabin that had a substantial mud chimney at one end. They could well afford shoes now, for they had saved many a picayune through their industry of selling wild grapes, blackberries, and "socoes" to ladies in the village who "put up" such things.

Boulôt and Boulotte were to buy the shoes themselves, and they selected a Saturday afternoon for the important transaction, for that is the great shopping time in Natchitoches Parish. So upon a bright Saturday afternoon Boulôt and Boulotte, hand in hand, with their quarters, their dimes, and their picayunes tied carefully in a

Sunday handkerchief, descended the hill, and disappeared from the gaze of the eager group that had assembled to see them go.

Long before it was time for their return, this same small band, with ten year old Seraphine at their head, holding a tiny Seraphin in her arms, had stationed themselves before the cabin at a convenient point from which to make quick and careful observation.

Even before the two could be caught sight of, their chattering voices were heard down by the spring, where they had doubtless stopped to drink. The voices grew more and more audible. Then, through the branches of the young pines, Boulotte's blue sun-bonnet appeared, and Boulôt's straw hat. Finally the twins, hand in hand, stepped into the clearing in full view.

Consternation seized the band. "You both crazy donc, Boulôt and Boulotte," screamed Seraphine. "You go buy shoes, and come home barefoot like you was go!"

Boulôt flushed crimson. He silently hung his head, and looked sheepishly down at his bare feet, then at the fine stout brogans that he carried in his hand. He had not thought of it.

Boulotte also carried shoes, but of the glossiest, with the highest of heels and brightest of buttons. But she was not one to be disconcerted or to look sheepish; far from it.

"You 'spec' Boulôt and me we got money for waste... us?" she retorted, with withering condescension. "You think we go buy shoes for ruin them in the dust? Comment!"

And they all walked into the house crest-fallen; all but Boulotte, who was mistress of the situation, and Seraphin, who did not care one way or the other.

The Rebel Double Runner

This story has been edited and adapted from Charles F. Lummis's The Enchanted Burro And Other Stories As I Have Known Them From Maine To Chile And California, first published in 1912 by A. C. McClurg & Co., Chicago.

When I was a lad in a lonely New Hampshire village, in the memorable year of 1863, a great many fathers and uncles and older brothers were off at some fearful and dimly-comprehended distance, dressed in blue, and, as we reckoned it, fighting battles daily.

How brave they had looked one morning, as they left town, marching with fife and drum along the crazy sidewalk, and off down the "Depot Hill!"

After that, the games at school and after school took a decidedly warlike tinge. Wooden swords and muskets largely usurped the place of top and ball; and proud was the small boy whose grand-dad would lend him a real sword of 1812, or an ancient militia shako.

When the stern New Hampshire winter came on, with its sleighing and coasting and skating, military evolutions were somewhat curtailed, but not altogether. There were snow forts and snow battles; white-blocked Sumters that defied the assault of the enemy.

Patriotic feeling ran riot; and when one young school-fellow, named Tip, espoused the Southern cause for fun, and began to press our ramparts sore, gaining recruits every day by his sheer audacity, there came to be snow-balls slightly thawed and then left out over night to turn to ice, and, as a result, some dangerous casualties on the battle-field.

The very opposite of Tip in many ways was Mat Marks. Tip was restless, sometimes reckless, always full of mischief, but one of the squarest and least self-conscious of boys. His sudden "turning Rebel," when he could hardly draft rebels enough to make the holding of our forts against them half-way interesting, was from no lack of as good patriotism as ours.

But Tip liked excitement, and was less vain than most of us; and without a second thought of any prejudice that he might excite because of this boyish enterprise, he abandoned the fort and took command of the enemy, "just to make it interesting."

And, though he was always overwhelmingly outnumbered, interesting enough he made it for "Us Unions" before he finished.

Mat, on the other hand, while in a way as active and enterprising as Tip, was much bound to the traditions, not from any principle or understanding of them, but because he liked to be on the popular side, and at the head of it, too; for he had a remarkably good opinion of himself.

Thanks to his diplomacy, he counted more followers than any other lad in town, and was fully satisfied of the justice of his preëminence. He liked to deem himself "a born leader of men," such as he read of; and I have often wondered, since, that we so long and so unquestioningly obeyed his smooth dictatorship. He was always "organizing", and the snow-ball battles were the outcome of his genius, and we carried out his orders with remarkable fidelity.

With the twentieth of December came a three-foot fall of snow, and in a few days it was hard packed on every highway, like a squeaky, white pavement. No more skating now—the sled was to be king for the next two months. For a few days everybody coasted, hit or miss; and the long slide swarmed like an ant-hill going crazy. But then the administrative mind of Mat began to work. Everyone sliding down hill on his own hook and straggling back at will, this was altogether too puerile and unorganized!

So Mat called a council of war. "Say, boys," he said, "I'll tell you what let's do! Instead of going higgledy-piggledy at it, like a lot of girls, let's organize the coasting in good shape. We'll have our rules and signals and right of way, just like a railroad, and a switch at the tannery corner so the small boys can go on to the toll-bridge, carrying supplies for the army, and the express-trains can turn off to the depot and take troops to the front.

"Then, too, I think father'll let me have old Nell, and we can make her haul back all the sleds in a string, and let fellows have turns riding her down to meet us again. So that'll get rid of the meanest part of it, the pulling our sleds up hill. Besides, we're all the time having trouble with teams now; but if they all knew we were coming down in a steady string, they'd keep out of the way, and do their sledding only when the coast was clear. What do you fellows think?"

"Good enough!" "That's the way!" "All right!" cried the crowd, in various voices, but with one mind. But when the exclamations were over, Tip tilted his sharp face a bit and said, "Well, what are you going to do while Nell is getting downhill? Sit in the snow-drift there at the depot and rub your ears? Strikes me it's better to turn around and climb back, and keep warm, 'stead of waiting there half an hour to freeze. And s'posing some team that didn't know about our all comin' down together was to get in the way? Then we'd be apt to get tangled up with each other and go to smash."

"Huh!" retorted Mat, sharply, "I guess you're scared. But you don't have to join us. If the rest say to go in, I guess we can get along without you. What do you say, fellows? Shall we do it?"

"Course we will!" was the chorus; and Mat looked triumphantly at his rival, for there was no denying that Mat reckoned as a rival, and therefore a foe, anyone who didn't agree with him, as Tip generally did not.

Tip returned the glance coolly and answered, "Why, you fellows do as you like, of course. I ain't bossing you. But you can count me out from any such goose-tag as that."

"We wouldn't have you anyhow!" cried Mat, nettled at this comparing them to a flock of geese waddling one after the other. "We don't care to have any traitors in our crowd."

"Yah, you old Rebel!" piped little Bill Burpee, taking his cue as usual; and several others echoed what was then the most dreadful word in our vocabulary.

"I ain't a Rebel, and you know it!" Tip answered, warmly. "I guess my father's fighting as hard as any of yours. and he ain't staying home to tend grocery stores, like Mat's!", with which parting shot he walked off scornfully and quite alone.

I can hardly understand now why we were so unjust to Tip. He had more in him than any other boy among us, was less selfish, more trustworthy and a better friend than ten Mats, and had done each of us no end of boy-kindnesses, instead of using us as cat's-paws for his own ambition.

But just because he had "played Rebel" for a few days solely to put a little life into the war, the boys were "down on" him. His followers in that campaign we made no note of and harboured no grudge against.

Perhaps there was wounded vanity in the recollection how nearly his superior generalship had routed our superior forces. So unreasoning are early prejudices that I presume a few of us never did quite get the last grain of grudge out of our heads, unless, perhaps, fifteen years later, when Mat was clerking in his father's store, and word came of the death of Captain Tip in Arizona. He was slain by the Apaches after a heroic fight which saved an immigrant party till the arrival of troops enough to scatter the Apache war band.

Well, Mat's plan progressed famously. A small army of us, with brooms and shovels, worked over that mile and a half of road till the coast was in such good shape as no one ever dreamed of before.

The weather stayed obstinately cold; so, under Mat's direction, we brought water by the bucketful and wet down the safer parts of the slide. There was some friction about this, for the older people objected to so much glare ice; but Mat compromised by not wetting the street crossings, and only a narrow track at the side of the road, so that sleighs had plenty of room without encroaching on our slide.

At the tannery corner we made a crescent of hard-packed snow, with sloping concavity, which rendered it rather easier to turn that dangerous angle. It was like the raised rail on the outside of the railway curve, or the "saucer-edge" of an automobile race-track.

And then came the marshalling of the clans. Our embryo Napoleon, of course, was commander-in-chief, and his pride, the double-runner sled "Avalanche," led the line. There were in those days but half a dozen other double-runners in town. These were owned by young men. Mat's was the only one in "our crowd." It was a very fancy affair for then and there.

Right-hand-man Hunt was privileged to manage the rear, and the coveted remaining seats were occupied by guests of passing invitation. It was no small social power to control a double-runner, and Mat made the most of it, giving rides to all his friends with great princeliness. But I remember that we never saw on Mat's "traverse" any of the urchins from the lower end of the village, for they had no "influence."

Behind the "Avalanche" came sleds of all sorts and sizes. As for Tip, no one had seen him for several days. He lived up on the other hill, a hill even steeper than Dolloff's, but coming in with such an ugly turn at the engine-house that no one coasted there since big Ned Green broke his neck on a wood-pile around the bend.

The great Saturday came for the formal inauguration of the Cannonball Railroad. Sixty-odd boys were gathered at the top of Dolloff's Hill. Some girls were there, too, with their high, flatrunnered sleds, upon which we looked with supreme scorn. Kitty White and Annie Waters and May Thurston were comfortably tucked up on the cushioned seat behind Mat on his double-runner; and Hunt was holding back on the tail-board till the signal.

"All ready… Go!" yelled Mat. Hunt sprang to his seat, and the sled slipped away, gaining momentum swiftly. Charlie White flung himself on his long cutter and was at its heels; and one after another, in continuous line, the whole array of boys on their sleds went sweeping down the hill.

Just as the last of us were whizzing by the engine-house, there was a shrill yell, and a dark flash from the other arm of the "Y" of the roads shot alongside in a swirl of snow-flower, and was past almost before anyone could crack a wink.

All we were sure of was that Tip and a party had gone by us, but how, or on what, no one knew. Anyhow, it was just like him. No one but Tip could have turned that lopsided corner in that way, and grazed safely within two feet of us. And one after another of the brown line ahead, we could see this astounding meteor picking up and passing them all.

Mat was right on the town bridge, steering his grandest to cut a fine curve through the square, when he caught that odd singing of tempered runners. Before he could turn his head, Tip streaked by without a glance, doubled the corner with a beautiful swing, and was out of sight on the next pitch when the "Avalanche" turned into the square.

Tip was on a double-runner, and one with wings, too, to judge by its speed! And Lou Berry and Kate Morris and Amy Belle and that pauper Okey boy with him, and that big Brown behind. It was altogether too much! When we got to the bottom of Depot Hill, Tip and his party were starting back, dragging the new craft. It was a very heavy double-runner, with a long, springy plank of ash, set rather low. There was no paint on runners or deck, but everything about the sandpapered wood had a clipper look, and the runners were shod with steel rods of an odd spring.

"Where'd you get it, Tip?" "Ain't it a whaler?" "Lemme go down once with you, Tip!" cried such of the boys as could catch up, which was not so difficult, as old Nell was dragging our sleds.

Tip trudged on, answering composedly, "Oh, Mr. Brown and I got it fixed up. Course you can go, one at a time, we've got room for just one more."

But just then Mat, whose heavy sled went farther than our light ones, overtook us. No doubt he felt pretty sore over being so egregiously beaten at his own game; and his look was anything but amiable as he observed, loudly and in his most scornful tone, "Huh! We feel pretty smart with a Rebel double-runner, don't we?"

Kate and Lou flushed up, and Brown stuck out his lip contemptuously, but Tip only answered, drily, "No-o, not so awful smart, just smart enough for what we need."

This was fuel to the fire. Mat, who was much the heavier of the two, stepped forward; and very likely there would have been a scene, except that the good old minister just then stopped his sleigh for a chat with some friends, the boys. But Mat had clinched a nickname, and Tip's turnout became in every mouth "The Rebel Double-runner."

Nor did it stop there. An organized movement, in which Mat was far too shrewd to let himself be seen, leaving it to his younger followers, was made to cut (boycott, as we would say nowadays) everyone who had anything to do with Tip.

Brown evidently didn't borrow much trouble about the scorn of boys so much younger than himself; and whatever Tip may have felt, he said nothing.

But Kate and Lou felt it keenly, for even the sisters of the camp were enlisted to make things unpleasant for "all who gave aid and comfort to Rebels." But, as they were loyal and plucky girls, they stuck to their friend in a fashion that was rather heroic, considering the heat and the meanness of youthful partisanship. I trust that for the many shabby turns done them they found some recompense in the regularity with which, day after day and many times a day, they whizzed past their envious persecutors. For Tip had left no gap in his plans. The Rebel double-runner was safe to win every time, thanks partly to its superior construction, partly to the dangerous hill on which it got its headway, and partly to the tremendous send-off given it by that hatefully muscular Brown.

Besides, Tip had a perfect genius as a steerer, the genius of effort and fixity, which counts oftener than any other kind. He seemed afraid of nothing because he really "saw his way through." He had studied that slide in every inch, and knew how to give his sled every advantage of it.

It was an aggravation almost beyond endurance to have them flash by us so easily every time; but for all Mat's efforts and schemes and our wild jockeying, they continued to do it. If the continued triumph of the Rebel double-runner was aggravating to us, it was gall and wormwood to Mat. The thing became a town joke; and older folks, who did not share our grudge against Tip nor our awe of our "Napoleon," poked all manner of fun.

Suave, self-satisfied, Mat grew glum and snappish. Those of us who ventured to ride with Tip, and it must be confessed that our patriotism was not always proof against the temptation, were made to feel the weight of Mat's displeasure. Our "leader of men" had not quite learned to lead himself.

As we trudged up with our sleds from the depot one afternoon, we caught sight of Tip's outfit whisking around the tannery corner and bearing down like a streak of dark lightning.

Mat was ahead, talking hard to young Burpee, who had a long red-bark switch in his hand. Just as the flying traverse was close, the young imp flung his stick down across the road.

Quick as thought we saw the act, and that Tip saw it, too. He slid back, with feet braced hard on the crosspiece, and swung the sled a trifle to the right.

He was pale, but not half so white as Mat, who stood glaring at him like one fascinated. It was right on the last bridge, over the big fall, that old wooden bridge with its crazy railing!

We were too horror-struck even to cry out, and there was no sound from the white faces on the sled. I can remember yet how the great falls roared, as out of a dead hush; how Tip's teeth showed, and that the steering-rope was sunk deep in his wrists. How many things made themselves seen and felt in that instant!

The sled struck the slender switch exactly square. We looked to see its occupants fly off into space; but, though Tip was snapped forward until his knees bruised his face, those wiry legs saved him and the rest, who were half piled upon him.

The flying ends of the switch told the story. Tip had steered upon the slenderer end, and the swift, high-tempered runners had chopped it in two, as was his hope, and without too great a shock.

Had the switch resisted never so little! It seemed to us, and does to me yet, almost a miracle of escape. But for Tip's instant wit, the whole party would have broken their necks on the hill, or crashed through the rail to the falls.

That day broke the back of the Cannonball Railroad. No one would so much as look at Burpee; but we felt that the responsibility rested further back.

Of course, Mat had not told him to throw the switch, and doubtless made himself believe that he had no blame in the matter. But the rest of us, well, even boys sometimes know how to read between the lines.

Tip never opened his mouth about the matter, and promptly stopped any attempted reference to it. He had plenty of companions now, and treated them in his square-toed boy way, as though nothing had ever happened.

A week after the switch episode, the crowd, including Tip, was straggling up the hill as Mat and his few remaining satellites came down on the "Avalanche." Just as they reached the grist-mill, a loaded wood-sledge stalled at the tannery corner—the snow was soft that day. The sled was, for the same reason, not going half so fast as usual, but quite fast enough. Seeing the dangerous passage thus blockaded, Mat began to get panicky, and the sled wobbled.

"He's going to jump!" exclaimed someone. "Don't!"

Tip flung his sled-rope to me. "Hold to her, Mat!" he yelled, standing at the very edge of the slide and balanced, catlike. But

Mat did not hold on. The "Avalanche" slewed to one side, and he leaped and went ploughing and rolling fifty feet in the slush. Almost as he struck the road, Tip had flung himself headlong upon the steering-seat and caught the lines.

He was just in time to "snub" the front sled before it could "turn cross" and make a wreck; and, steering through the narrow space between the wood-sledge and the bridge-rail, he fetched up safely with the traverse and its four frightened boys on the grade that climbs to Water Street.

That settled the business. From that day out, I think no one was ever heard to mention anything that sounded like "Rebel double-runner." It was "Tip's Tornado," and there wasn't a boy in town, except one, but was glad to ride on it, or to follow Tip in anything. It was the quietest of victories, but complete.

Emperor Norton

This story has been edited and adapted from May Wentworth's Fairy Tales From Gold Lands, first published in 1868 by A. Roman and Company.

Once upon a time there lived near a small village on the shore of the Atlantic, an honest farmer named Norton, who had three sons.

The two elder were smart, active lads, but the youngest was quiet, and so much given to dreaming that his brothers ridiculed and often slighted him.

"He is so stupid," they would say, "he will be a disgrace to the family," but what annoyed him most, they gave him the unpleasant sobriquet of Dumpy, on account of his fat, rosy cheeks.

As the boys grew up, the eldest took the farm, and was to take care of the father and mother, the second became clerk to a merchant in a neighbouring city, but poor Dumpy, in the indolence of his disposition, did nothing. He was always hoping some impossible thing would "turn up," but he had no rich relations, indeed no one seemed to take much interest in him but the mother, who would always say, "Poor Dumpy, he is a good-hearted boy," then she would sigh heavily, as though there was nothing more to be said.

At last the father became quite out of patience, and calling the boy to him one day, he said, "You are now twenty years old, and never have earned so much as your salt, and it is quite time for you to do something for yourself. Your brother, who has taken the farm, complains that he is obliged to support you in idleness, which certainly is not right."

"For the farm he will take care of your mother and me, but you and your other brother must look out for yourselves."

"Give me," answered Dumpy, "what money you can spare, I ask nothing more, I will go and seek my fortune, and you shall hear of me when I become a rich man."

The father gave him what money he could, and he went away, no one at home knew where, leaving only the mother to weep for him.

When Dumpy left the farm-house he walked on to the village, feeling that he was going into the great world full of promise, but he never dreamed of disappointment.

When he arrived at the village inn the stage was standing at the door. "I will go," he said, "where fortune leads me." So he took his seat in the stage, and paid his fare to the end of the route, which happened to be the great city of New York.

All day long he was very happy looking out of the windows upon the changing landscape, and indulging in day-dreams. Sometimes he would come to a pretty village nestling among the hills. "I would like," he would think, "of all things to stop here, 'tis so very pleasant, but I have paid my money, and I must go on."

It was night when the stage entered the city, its heavy wheels rumbling over the paved streets, and crowding along past carts, omnibuses, and carriages, till poor Dumpy, who had never been in the city before, began to feel very much bewildered and confused.

"Where shall I go," said Dumpy to the driver when the stage stopped. "'Tis so noisy I can't hear myself think. Oh, dear! I don't know what to do," and he looked so pitiably helpless that the driver was sorry for him, though he could not help laughing. "Come with me, my boy," he said, so he went with the driver to the cheap lodging-house, where he stopped when in town.

To enumerate all poor Dumpy's adventures while in New York would be impossible. Enough to say it was not long before his money was gone, and he shipped before the mast in a merchant vessel for California.

Poor Dumpy! Now came woeful experiences, for a time he was wretchedly seasick, and he soon found that to go before the mast was no joke, but in his way he was quite a philosopher, and after a few weeks became a very good sailor.

As he was pleasant and obliging he became a favourite with all on board, but he loved most of all when off duty, to sit by himself in the soft starlit evenings as the good ship sailed over the tropic seas, and dream of the land of gold to which he was going.

He possessed a vivid imagination, and his visions of the wealth of the new Eldorado were most glowing.

He would picture to himself how like a prince he would luxuriate in riches, how great and generous he would be, even to the brothers who had despised him. It is a happiness to be able to revel in dreams as he did, for the pleasures of anticipation are but too often greater than the reality.

He loved his mother, she at least had always been kind and gentle to him. "My dear mother," he would say to himself, with a bright tear in his eye, "she shall yet live in a palace. God bless her, dear mother."

Then he would sigh till a bright thought drove away the sad one. "Oh, 'tis so delightful to be rich," he would say. Then he would rub his hands as complacently as though the wealth of the Indies lay at his feet.

"I shall give the father everything he wishes of course," he would continue, "and I will make the brothers rich men, for to be generous and forgive is the attribute of true greatness, and for myself I will marry the prettiest woman in the world, and I will give her everything she can possibly desire."

Often the sharp quick bell, for change of watch, would call him to duty, and scatter his gorgeous dreams, leaving only the dull, hard present in his mind and heart.

At length the good ship arrived in San Francisco, and there again Dumpy found all the wild bustle and confusion of the early days. Gold was plenty in dust and bars. When a man bought anything he would take out of his bag of gold dust as much dust as he was to pay for the article, and he would be off.

The highest price was paid for labour, and Dumpy soon engaged to drive a cart for two hundred and fifty dollars per month, but he determined to make this arrangement only for a short time, till he could get money enough to go out prospecting in the mining districts.

This he soon accomplished, but he found a life in the mines even harder than before the mast, but the golden future was before him, and he persevered.

He and another young adventurer built a cabin together by a little spring of clear, bubbling water. They worked early and late, with the wearisome pick and shovel for the precious gold that was to pave the pathway of their lives with happiness, but often night found them disappointed and weary, and they would return to their lonely cabins, cook and eat their coarse supper, and lie down upon the hard floor, wrap their blankets around them, with heavy and hopeless hearts. But thank God, sunshine and the fresh morning brings renewed life and hope to young hearts.

One morning when Dumpy awoke he found his companion had risen and gone out before him, so he went out alone, thinking, "who knows what will turn up before night, I may become a millionaire. I'll try my luck alone today," so he did not go to the ledge they had been prospecting the day before, but started off in a new direction.

All day long he worked diligently, but the sunset found him as poor as the dawning, and quite worn out, he threw himself down upon the ledge to rest a little before going home. "Ah, me!" thought he, sadly, "how long the poor mother will have to wait for her palace."

As the sunset deepened into twilight, he rose, and shouldering his pick and shovel, started for the cabin. "I cannot call it home," he said to himself, "there is no mother there."

He had not gone far, before a little shrill voice arrested him, and looking down, he saw a little old man, sitting among the loose stones, rubbing his foot and ankle, and groaning piteously.

He was very quaintly dressed, in a little red jacket, and wore a Spanish hat with little gold bells around it, and his long grey beard swept the ground, as he sat dismally among the rocks.

"Oh, dear! I cannot move," said the little man, "I have sprained my foot, will not you help me home? Oh dear! Oh dear!" and he moaned so piteously that Dumpy, who was kind-hearted, was very sorry for him; so he took the old man up in his arms as tenderly as if he had been an infant.

The old man pointed out the way, and Dumpy trudged wearily on, for though he was no bigger than a child of eight years old, he seemed quite heavy to Dumpy. After working all day with the pick and shovel, and finding nothing, his heart was heavy with hope deferred. "If I had found gold today," thought he, "a light heart would have made a light burden; but thank God I am well, and this poor man suffers fearfully."

Poor Dumpy! He went on, down the cañon, then up the mountain, it seemed to him for miles; at last the little man pointed to a crevice in the rock, through which Dumpy managed with some difficulty to creep; but as he went on it widened, and suddenly opened into a large cavern.

"Go on," said the old man, sharply, as Dumpy stopped and gazed around with astonishment. So he went on till they came to a large hall sparkling with crystal, and glowing with precious stones.

A large chandelier hung from the roof, and cast a flood of softened light through the whole cavern, and Dumpy could see in the stone floor large masses of pure yellow gold.

He saw in the huge irregular pillars that rose to the dome of the cavern, great veins of the precious ore, and everywhere it was scattered about with the most lavish profusion.

Curious golden figures, carved with strange devices, stood in the niches, and there were couches with golden frames, and tables of gold, so that the light, reflected from the clear crystal dome, glittering with shining pendants, by the softening yellow tinge, was mellow and pleasant.

Poor Dumpy had been so long in the twilight and darkness, that he was dazzled by the brilliant scene, and for a few moments was obliged to close his eyes, and when he opened them, he saw that he was surrounded by a large crowd of the little people, who were full of anxious fears about the old man he held in his arms, but he assured them he was suffering only from a sprain, which, though very painful, was not dangerous. They gathered anxiously around the little man as he laid him upon a couch.

He soon discovered that the man he had assisted was king over the little people who guard the mountain treasures, covering the rich places with unpromising stones and earth, and often misleading the honest miner by scattering grains of the precious metal in waste places; thus it is we hear so often of disappointed hopes, and abandoned mines.

After they had in some measure relieved the suffering of their chief, they turned to Dumpy, who stood in the most profound astonishment, drinking in all he saw or heard.

"You have done me a great kindness," said the chief, "and, though it is our business to mislead miners, we can be grateful, and you may now claim any reward you desire."

"I have saved your ruler," said Dumpy, looking at the crowd of little people, and trying to think of something great to ask as a reward.

"Our chief! Our king!" cried all the little people, together. "Ask what you will and it shall be granted."

"I would be great as well as rich," thought Dumpy, so he said aloud, "Make me emperor of all the mines, and let all the miners pay tribute to me."

"It shall be so," said the king. Then he called one of his servants to bring the golden crown and sceptre, and bidding Dumpy kneel before him, he placed the sceptre in his hand and the crown upon his head, and striking him a sharp blow upon his shoulder, he said, "Arise, Emperor Norton.

"As long as you preserve this crown and sceptre from moth or rust, dew or fog, you shall be the true emperor of all the mines in California and Nevada, and all the miners shall pay you yearly tribute, but if you lose either crown or sceptre, or moth, rust, midnight dews and damps fall upon them, they will fade away, and you will be emperor in name only, and the miners shall pay you no yearly tribute."

"So let it be," said the newly-made emperor; and they all sat down to a table spread with every delicacy, and feasted till the noon of the following day.

When the emperor bade the knights of the mountain adieu, the little grey king said, "Beware of the dews and damps of the night," and he started for his cabin.

"I will first visit my old comrade," he said, "though he is now one of my subjects, I will not be proud and haughty."

One of the little men ran before him, and led the way out of the cave into the sunlight, which was so bright that the emperor shaded his eyes with his hand, and when he had removed it the little man had disappeared.

The emperor looked around, but could see no trace of him; even the crevice through which he had passed, was nowhere to be seen.

"It is a wonderful dream," said he; but no! There was the golden crown upon his head, and the sceptre in his hand.

"I will find that cave," thought he; so he began to look for it very eagerly, till the lengthening shadows told of the coming of evening, and he thought of the grey king's warning, "Beware of the dews and damps of night."

"Oh dear! If I should lose the tribute money," he said, in great distress, "I should be emperor but could build no palace for the mother, nor could I marry the prettiest woman in the world, and supply her innumerable wants," so he started in great haste for the camp, always keeping fast hold of the crown and sceptre.

On he rushed till the shades of twilight filled the deep cañon, through which he was obliged to pass, then he broke into a run, crying, "Oh me! If I should be too late! Too late! Now that my hopes are crowned with success. Too late! Too late!"

"Haste makes waste," and so the emperor found it. He lost the path and became entangled in brush and rocks, until he became almost wild with despair. The night came on with a heavy mist that near morning deepened into rain.

With the grey twilight of the dawning, weary and worn, he reached his cabin door, but the golden crown and sceptre had passed away into the mists of night.

The poor emperor told of his wanderings to his comrades, and mourned over the night in which his crown and sceptre had departed from him, but they only laughed, saying, "You have been dreaming again, Emperor Norton."

He never took the pick and shovel again. "Shall an emperor work," he would say, "while thousands of his subjects roll in luxury?"

An emperor, he thought, should reside in the chief city of his realm, so he left the mines and came to San Francisco. Here for years he has lived, always wearing a well-worn suit of blue, with epaulettes upon the shoulders, which, perhaps, might have been an unmentioned gift of the grey king of the mountains.

At the table of all restaurants and hotels he is a free and welcome guest, and all places of amusement are open to him; in fact, wherever you go in San Francisco, you are almost sure to meet the Emperor Norton.

A Stone's Throw

This story has been edited and adapted from Henry W. Shoemaker's Allegheny Episodes, first published in 1922 by the Altoona Tribune Company, based out of Altoona, Pennsylvania. This was one of a series of collections forming the Pennsylvania Folk Lore series.

When land warrants were allotted to Jacob Marshall and Jacob Mintges, of the Hebrew colony at Schaefferstown, there were elaborate preparations made by these two lifelong friends to migrate to the new country of the Christunn. That the warrants were laid side by side made the situation doubly pleasant, a compensation in a measure for any regrets at leaving the banks of the beautiful Milbach. The country was becoming too closely settled, opportunities were circumscribed, and the liberality of the Proprietary Government should be taken advantage of.

When the two groups of pioneers were ready to start for the new home, it was like some scene from the patriarchal days of the Old Testament. The long, lean, gaunt, black-bearded Jews, black-capped, cloaked to their heels, and carrying big staffs, led the way, followed by their families and possessions of livestock, farming and household utensils. Each head of a family had a servant or two, which added to the picturesqueness of the caravans. Dogs, part wolf, herded the flocks of sheep, goats and young cattle, while the women rode on mares, the foals of which trotted along unsteadily at their sides.

Rachel, Jacob Marshall's handsome daughter, was mounted on a piebald filly; on her back was slung her violin, a genuine Joseph Guarnerius, with which she discoursed sacred music around the campfire in the evenings, just as her ancestors may have done on some harp or cruit in remote days in Palestine or in the Arabian highlands.

These German Jews, who came to Pennsylvania in 1702 to re-convert the Native Americans, whom they believed to be the lost tribe of Israel, back to the ancient faith of Moses, while destined to fail as proselyters, became one of the potent root sources of the so-called Pennsylvania Dutch, "The Black Dutch" of the Christunn, Philadelphia, New York and the World.

The Pennsylvania Dutch are the most adaptable race in the world, altering the spelling of their names, their genealogies and traditions with every generation. They find success in all callings and in all walks of life like the true Nomads that they are. A Pennsylvania Dutchman's lineage is kaleidoscopic any way, possibly German, Jewish, probably Native American, with sure admixtures of Dutch, Quaker, Swiss, Scotch-Irish, Greek, Bohemian, Spanish or Huguenot. And there were some propagandists shallow enough to try to line them up with Kaiserism in the days just anterior to the World War, and call them "Pennsylvania Germans."

Their very swarthiness and leanness, the intenseness of their black eyes, gave the lie to any Teutonic affiliations, despite the jargon that they speak. And what a race of giants they have produced, Pershing, Hoover, Gorgas, Schwab, Replogle, Sproul, the Wanamakers, Newton Diehl Baker, Jane Addams, a group as potent as any other in the sublime effort of making the world "safe for democracy."

When the pilgrims reached the Karoondinha, they were met by the local agents and surveyors of the Proprietors, who escorted them to their new estates, which were bounded on the south by the Christunn, now renamed "Middle Creek," and on the north by the craggy heights of the culminating pinnacle of Jack's Mountain, the famed "High Top," climbed by the Pennsylvania Alpine Club, August 24, 1919.

A large grey fox, or Colishay, having led Mintges' dogs away from the camp, caused this "Father in Israel" to be absent during the critical moments when the line between his property and that of Marshall was being confirmed by the Proprietary surveyors. When he returned, exultingly swinging the fox's pelt above his head and looking all the world like a lower Fifth Avenue fur jobber, the day was almost spent and the surveyors were gathering up their instruments.

Marshall, who was a kindly and just man, tried to explain to his friend, before the sun went down, just where the line was blazed. It seemed fair enough at the time to Mintges. Later on, when alone one day, he walked over the line, comparing it with the warrant, and it did not seem to satisfy him as much. He believed that the surveyors had deviated a rod or two all along, to his disadvantage. Doubtless if such was the case, it had been due to their haste to get through, for they had a daily grind of similar cases, but Marshall, he thought, should have compelled them to follow the parchment drafts, and not uncertain instruments.

Nevertheless, he decided to say nothing to his friend; they had always been good intimates, why should their relations be jeopardized for a paltry rod or two. Mintges confided the mistake to his wife, and later on to his children. It was unfortunate, but where there were so few neighbours it was hardly worth a fight.

As Mintges grew older the matter began to prey on his mind, to obsess him. It worried him until his head ached, and he could not drive it away. Marshall and his heirs were profiting at his expense; it should not be allowed to rest that way.

The surveyors had placed a great stone at the upper corner of the line, at the slope of the mountain, and there Jacob Mintges repaired one moonlight night, armed with a crowbar, and reset the stone two rods on the alleged domain of Jacob Marshall. Mintges was an old man at the time, rabbinical in appearance, and he chuckled and "washed his hands" as he stood and viewed the fruits of his labour. A wrong had been quietly righted; why hadn't he done it twenty years ago?

It so happened that Jacob Marshall went out for chestnuts a week or so after Mintges' performance, and saw the altered position of the stone. Instead of hastening to his friend's house and asking him for a frank explanation, he, not being conscious of any wrong-doing, moved the stone back to its original position, to rebuke the presumptuous Mintges. Then he stood admiring his work, while he stroked his long black beard.

A few weeks later Mintges and his sons went to the mountain to brush out a road on which to haul logs with their ox teams in the winter-time. One of the boys, named Lazarus, called his father's attention to the stone's position. It made the old man "see red," and he would not rest until, with the aid of his sons, it was again set where he felt it should rightfully be.

All this produced a coolness, almost a feud, between the two families, which kept up until Jacob Mintges died at the age of eighty years. Jacob Marshall, friend of his youth and companion of his "trek" to the wilderness, did not attend the obsequies.

It was not many nights afterwards when reports were made on all sides that Mintges' spook was abroad, walking about the fields and lanes adjacent to Jacob Marshall's home, his arms holding aloft a great block of stone. Marshall saw the apparition several times, but shunned it as he had the living Mintges the last years of his life.

What he wanted was very plain, for sometimes the night wind wafted the mournful words down Marshall's bedroom chimney (for he always kept his windows nailed shut), "Where shall I put it; oh, where shall I put it?"

The ghost began his hauntings in the spring, kept it up all summer, fall, winter, then another spring and summer. He had affixed himself to the family, Marshall thought, as he racked his brain to lay the troublesome night prowler.

It was during the fall of the second year that a big party of moonlight 'coon hunters went up the lane which led between the Marshall and Mintges farms, headed for the rocky heights of Jack's Mountain. In the party was Otto Gleim, the half-witted drunkard of Selin's Grove, little, dumpy, long-armed High German, high-shouldered Otto Gleim, who was left at the foot of the mountain to hold one of the lanterns.

Gleim was half full on this occasion, as it was in the cider season, and he staggered about under the aged chestnut trees, while his wits revolved in his head with the speed of an electric fan. He felt lonesome, sick and uncomfortable. It was a relief to see a great, tall figure, with a long, black beard, approaching him, holding aloft a huge stone. It looked like "Uncle Jake" Marshall at first; no, it wasn't…it was no one else but the late "Uncle Jake" Mintges, his neighbour.

As the gaunt figure drew nearer, it began groaning and wailing, "Where shall I put it; oh, where shall I put it?" in tones as melancholy as those of the Great Horned Owl on a New Year's Eve.

"Put it where it belongs," spluttered Otto Gleim, the drunkard, with a gleam of super-human prescience, and lo and behold, the ghost set the stone where it had been for twenty years after the surveyors had placed it there. Then the apparition vanished, and Gleim, in a matter-of-fact way, sat down on the cornerstone, where he waited until the 'coon hunters returned.

Jake Mintges' ghost ceased to wander and lament, but instead allied itself closely with Jake Marshall's family as private stock banshee, warning, token or familiar. Whenever a disaster was due to any member he would show his grinning tusks, as much as to say, "Now, make the best of what is coming; life is short anyway."

No doubt his visits of forewarning strengthened the nerves of the family to face trouble with a greater degree of equanimity; in all events the poor old fellow meant it that way. Old and young, rich and poor, in cities or in the wilds, wherever the blood of Jacob Marshall flowed, the ghost of Mintges was in evidence at the climacteric moments of their lives. They were all used to him, and never resented his visits or tried in any way to lay him.

The scene shifts to one of the last to encounter this strange old ghost. It is in a great city, in a high-ceilinged, yet gloomy room, furnished in the plush and mahogany of the middle eighties of the last century but one. A very dark girl, with full pouting lips and black eyes, half closed and sullen, yet beautiful in the first flush of youth withal, is seated on one of the upholstered easy chairs. Standing in the bay window facing her is a very tall man, equally dark, his drooping black moustache and long Prince Albert coat making him appear at least ten years older than the twenty-eight which was his correct age.

On a centre table, with a top of brown onyx, on which were also several bisque ornaments, lay an ancient violin and bow, a veritable Joseph Guarnerius. It was made of a curious piece of spruce which, when growing in some remote forest of Northern Italy, had been punctured by a "Gran Pico" or large green woodpecker, and the wood stained, giving a unique and picturesque touch to this specimen of the skill of the old master of Cremona.

"I have determined to go home tonight," said the dark girl, with decision, "and nothing can stop me. When any of our family see the face of Jacob Mintges, it means disaster to someone near to us; my mother and her old parents, whom I left so suddenly, may be grieving to death; I will go to them tonight."

The tall man fumbled with his long fingers among the tassels on the back of a chair in front of him, as if trying to frame up a decisive answer. "This is what I call base ingratitude," he faltered at length, in high, almost feminine tones. "Just when I have had your musical talent developed, turning you from a common fiddler to a finished artiste, and having you almost ready to make your stage debut as a popular juvenile, you leave me in the lurch, and all because you imagined you saw a ghost, imagined, I say, for there are no such things."

The dark girl sat perfectly still, biting her full red lips, her immobile face as if made of ivory.

"What are you, anyway?" she finally responded, "nothing but what my father called a mountebank; he hated them, an actor, and I owe you nothing but contempt for having brought me here to be your plaything while my youth and good looks last."

Then, as she got up and started towards a door, the tall man darted after her. "I'll not let you make a fool of yourself," he hissed, theatrically. Catching her by the wrists, he attempted to detain her. "Sit down; we must have this out."

She was almost as tall as he, and very muscular, and the Jewish strain in her blood was hot. The pair struggled about the room, until the man in his anger seized the old violin and hit her a heavy blow over the head. She sank down on the floor in a limp mass, and the man, picking up his brown Fedora, ran out of the room and down the long flight of stairs and out into the street. The girl was not badly hurt, only stunned, and came to herself in about fifteen minutes. She saw that she was alone, and the Guarnerius was around her neck.

Gathering herself up, her first thought was for the violin, and tying the smallest chips in her handkerchief she went to the inner room and began to pack a large portmanteau. Then she put on her hat, veil and cloak and, locking the apartment door and slipping the key in her grip, she left the house and hurried down town towards the railroad depot.

It was dark when she reached there, and she quickly boarded a local, to wait in the suburbs until the night sleeping car train for

Derrstown made its stop there. All went well, and by midnight she was boarding the sleeper and was soon afterwards undressed and under the sooty-smelling blankets in a lower berth.

She did not know how long she had been sleeping when the train suddenly stopped with a jerk and she was awake. Looking around, she saw a face peering through the curtains. It was not the porter, but the leering, open mouth, old Jacob Mintges himself, tusks and all. Twice now in twenty-four hours he had come to her, for the night previous she had waked just in the grey half-light before dawn, and had seen him standing grinning by her bedside.

An inexperienced person might have screamed, but not so Eugenie Carlevan, the great-great-granddaughter of Jacob Marshall. When their eyes met, Mintges quickly withdrew, and the girl, wide awake, began thinking over the past years of her life, as the train again started to roll on into the night. She had always been fond of music and theatres. The violin given to her on her sixth birthday by her grandfather Marshall had become the evil genius of her destiny. Her father had died and her mother was too much of a drudge to control her. She had attended every circus, burlesque, minstrel show or dramatic performance that had come to the town where she had lived, since she was thirteen years old.

When the young Thespian who called himself Derment Catesby had come with the "Lights O'London" Company to Swinefordstown, where she was visiting an aunt, she had fallen violently in love with him, had made his acquaintance, and he, struck by her imperious beauty and musical predilections, had asked her to go away with him.

She had joined him a few days later in Sunbury, bringing her precious violin, and travelled with him to the great city. There the actor soon signed up to play in repertoire at a stock company. She liked him well enough, despite his vanity and selfishness, for he was very handsome. It was before the days when actors were clean-shaven like every servant, and looked much like other people. However much she had loved him, Jacob Mintges' ghost had revealed a more pressing duty twice, and she was on her way home.

Soon she fell asleep again, and did not wake until the porter's face appeared to notify her that the train was leaving Sunbury. Her mother lived with her aged parents out near Hartley Hall, among the high mountains; it would be a relief to see those lofty peaks and wide expanse of vision once more, after the cramped outlook of the city. How peculiarly sweet the air seemed, with the sun coming up behind the fringe of old yellow pines and oaks along the river! What refreshing zephyrs were wafted from those newly-ploughed fields. The bluebirds and robins were singing in the maple trees about the station. On a side-track stood the little wood-burner engine, with its bulbous stack, puffing black smoke, ready to pull its train of tiny cars out to the wonderful, wild mountain country, the land of Lick Run Gap, the Lost Valley, the High Head, Big Buffalo, Winklebleck and Shreiner!

How well she remembered the first time she had seen that wood-burner, as a little tot, going on a visit with her father and mother. It was in the golden hour, and deep purple shadows fell from the station roof athwart the golden light on the platform!

All these thoughts were crowding through her head until the bell on the little engine reminded her that the L. & T. train was soon to depart.

She reached home in time for dinner, was received with no enthusiasm, for her mother and grandparents were true mountaineers, and their swarthy faces masked their feelings, yet she was made to feel perfectly welcome.

Nobody had died, no one was sick, the house hadn't burned down, so evidently the trials foretold by Jake Mintges were yet to come.

That afternoon she showed the broken violin to her grandfather, who took it to his workbench in an out-house to repair it, undaunted by the seeming endlessness of the reconstruction.

Eugenie seemed perfectly contented to be at home, She had had enough of the bizarre, and revelled again in the humdrum. Five or six days after her return the weekly county paper appeared at the house, with its boiler plate front page and patent insides. Some instinct made her open the wrapper as it lay on the kitchen table. On the front page she saw the likeness of a familiar face, the well-known full eyes, oval cheeks, rounded chin and drooping moustache of Derment Catesby. Then the headlines caught her eyes, "Handsome Actor Shot to Death by Insanely Jealous Husband at Stage Door." Then she glanced at the date and the hour. It was the night that she had taken the train, the very moment, perhaps, that Jacob Mintges' grinning face had looked through the curtains of her berth. Yes, the murderer had waited a long time, as the victim had tarried in the green-room.

Eugenie sucked her full lips a moment, then looked hard at the picture and the whole article again. Then she turned to her mother and grandparents, who were seated about the stove.

"Say, folks," she said, coldly, "there's the fine gent I went away with from Swinefordstown. I got out in time, the very night he was murdered."

The mother and the old people half rose in their chairs to look at the wood cut.

"How did you know he was playing you false?" said the old grandfather.

"How did I know, gran'pap?" she replied. "Why, the night before, Jake Mintges came to me, and I knew something was due to go wrong, and home was the place for little me. You see I missed it all by a stone's throw."

"You're right, 'Genie'," said the old mountaineer. "Mintges never comes to us unless he means business."

Endicott And The Red Cross

This story has been edited and adapted from Nathaniel Hawthorne's Twice Told Tales, first published in 1889 by David McKay, Publisher, Philadelphia.

At noon of an autumnal day more than two centuries ago the English colours were displayed by the standard bearer of the Salem train-band, which had mustered for martial exercise under the orders of John Endicott. It was a period when the religious exiles were accustomed often to buckle on their armour and practise the handling of their weapons of war. Since the first settlement of New England its prospects had never been so dismal. The dissensions between Charles I. and his subjects were then, and for several years afterward, confined to the floor of Parliament. The measures of the king and ministry were rendered more tyrannically violent by an opposition which had not yet acquired sufficient confidence in its own strength to resist royal injustice with the sword. The bigoted and haughty primate Laud, archbishop of Canterbury, controlled the religious affairs of the realm, and was consequently invested with powers which might have wrought the utter ruin of the two Puritan colonies, Plymouth and Massachusetts. There is evidence on record that our forefathers perceived their danger, but were resolved that their infant country should not fall without a struggle, even beneath the giant strength of the king's right arm.

Such was the aspect of the times when the folds of the English banner with the red cross in its field were flung out over a company of Puritans. Their leader, the famous Endicott, was a man of stern and resolute countenance, the effect of which was heightened by a grizzled beard that swept the upper portion of his breastplate. This piece of armour was so highly polished that the whole surrounding scene had its image in the glittering steel. The central object in the mirrored picture was an edifice of humble architecture with neither steeple nor bell to proclaim it - what, nevertheless, it was - the house of prayer. A token of the perils of the wilderness was seen in the grim head of a wolf which had just been slain within the precincts of the town, and, according to the regular mode of claiming the bounty, was nailed on the porch of the meeting-house. The blood was still splashing on the doorstep. There happened to be visible at the same noontide hour so many other characteristics of the times and manners of the Puritans that we must endeavour to represent them in a sketch, though far less vividly than they were reflected in the polished breastplate of John Endicott.

In close vicinity to the sacred edifice appeared that important engine of Puritanic authority the whipping-post, with the soil around it well-trodden by the feet of evil-doers who had there been disciplined. At one corner of the meeting-house was the pillory and at the other the stocks, and, by a singular good fortune for our sketch, the head of an Episcopalian and suspected Catholic was grotesquely encased in the former machine, while a fellow-criminal who had boisterously quaffed a health to the king was confined by the legs in the latter. Side by side on the meeting-house steps stood a male and a female figure. The man was a tall, lean, haggard personification of fanaticism, bearing on his breast this label, "A WANTON GOSPELLER," which betokened that he had dared to give interpretations of Holy Writ unsanctioned by the infallible judgment of the civil and religious rulers. His aspect showed no lack of zeal to maintain his heterodoxies even at the stake. The woman wore a cleft stick on her tongue, in appropriate retribution for having wagged that unruly member against the elders of the church, and her countenance and gestures gave much cause to apprehend that the moment the stick should be removed a repetition of the offence would demand new ingenuity in chastising it.

The above-mentioned individuals had been sentenced to undergo their various modes of ignominy for the space of one hour at noonday. But among the crowd were several whose punishment would be lifelong - some whose ears had been cropped like those of puppy-dogs, others whose cheeks had been branded with the initials of their misdemeanours; one with his nostrils slit and seared, and another with a halter about his neck, which he was forbidden ever to take off or to conceal beneath his garments. I think he must have been grievously tempted to affix the other end of the rope to some convenient beam or bough. There was likewise a young woman with no mean share of beauty whose doom it was to wear the letter A on the breast of her gown in the eyes of all the world and her own children. And even her own children knew what that initial signified. Sporting with her infamy, the lost and desperate creature had embroidered the fatal token in scarlet cloth with golden thread and the nicest art of needlework; so that the capital A might have been thought to mean "Admirable," or anything rather than "Adulteress."

Let not the reader argue from any of these evidences of iniquity that the times of the Puritans were more vicious than our own, when as we pass along the very street of this sketch we discern no badge of infamy on man or woman. It was the policy of our ancestors to search out even the most secret sins and expose them to shame, without fear or favour, in the broadest light of the noonday sun. Were such the custom now, perchance we might find materials for a no less piquant sketch than the above.

Except the malefactors whom we have described and the diseased or infirm persons, the whole male population of the town, between sixteen years and sixty were seen in the ranks of the train-band. A few stately natives in all the pomp and dignity of the primeval warrior stood gazing at the spectacle. Their flint-headed arrows were but childish weapons, compared with the matchlocks of the Puritans, and would have rattled harmlessly against the steel caps and hammered iron breastplates which enclosed each soldier in an individual fortress. The valiant John Endicott glanced with an eye of pride at his sturdy followers, and prepared to renew the martial toils of the day.

"Come, my stout hearts!" said he, drawing his sword. "Let us show these poor heathen that we can handle our weapons like men of might. Well for them if we do not have to prove it in earnest!"

The iron-breasted company straightened their line, and each man drew the heavy butt of his matchlock close to his left foot, thus awaiting the orders of the captain. But as Endicott glanced right and left along the front he discovered a personage at some little distance with whom it behoved him to hold a parley. It was an elderly gentleman wearing a black cloak and band and a high-crowned hat beneath which was a velvet skull-cap, the whole being the garb of a Puritan minister. This reverend person bore a staff which seemed to have been recently cut in the forest, and his shoes were bemired, as if he had been travelling on foot through the swamps of the wilderness. His aspect was perfectly that of a pilgrim, heightened also by an apostolic dignity. Just as Endicott perceived him he laid aside his staff and stooped to drink at a bubbling fountain which gushed into the sunshine about a score of yards from the corner of the meeting-house. But before the good man drank he turned his face heavenward in thankfulness, and then, holding back his grey beard with one hand, he scooped up his simple draught in the hollow of the other.

"What ho, good Mr. Williams!" shouted Endicott. "You are welcome back again to our town of peace. How does our worthy Governor Winthrop? And what news from Boston?"

"The governor has his health, worshipful sir," answered Roger Williams, now resuming his staff and drawing near. "And, for the news, here is a letter which, knowing I was to travel here today, His Excellency committed to my charge. It probably contains tidings of much import, for a ship arrived yesterday from England."

Mr. Williams, the minister of Salem, and of course known to all the spectators, had now reached the spot where Endicott was standing under the banner of his company, and put the governor's epistle into his hand. The broad seal was impressed with Winthrop's coat-of-arms. Endicott hastily unclosed the letter and began to read, while, as his eye passed down the page, a wrathful change came over his manly countenance. The blood glowed through it till it seemed to be kindling with an internal heat, nor was it unnatural to suppose that his breastplate would likewise become red hot with the angry fire of the bosom which it covered.

Arriving at the conclusion, he shook the letter fiercely in his hand, so that it rustled as loud as the flag above his head.

"Black tidings these, Mr. Williams," said he, "blacker never came to New England. Doubtless you know their purport?"

"Yea, truly," replied Roger Williams, "for the governor consulted respecting this matter with my brethren in the ministry at Boston, and my opinion was likewise asked. And His Excellency entreats you by me that the news be not suddenly noised abroad, lest the people be stirred up unto some outbreak, and thereby give the king and the archbishop a handle against us."

"The governor is a wise man - a wise man, and a meek and moderate," said Endicott, setting his teeth grimly. "Nevertheless, I must do according to my own best judgment. There is neither man, woman nor child in New England but has a concern as dear as life in these tidings; and if John Endicott's voice be loud enough, man, woman and child shall hear them. Soldiers, wheel into a hollow square. Ho, good people! Here are news for one and all of you."

The soldiers closed in around their captain, and he and Roger Williams stood together under the banner of the red cross, while the women and the aged men pressed forward and the mothers held up their children to look Endicott in the face. A few taps of the drum gave signal for silence and attention.

"Fellow-soldiers, fellow-exiles," began Endicott, speaking under strong excitement, yet powerfully restraining it, "why did you leave your native country? Why, I say, have we left the green and fertile fields, the cottages, or, perchance, the old grey halls, where we were born and bred, the churchyards where our forefathers lie buried? Why have we come here to set up our own tombstones in a wilderness? A howling wilderness it is. The wolf and the bear meet us within halloo of our dwellings. The natives lie in wait for us in the dismal shadow of the woods. The stubborn roots of the trees break our ploughshares when we would till the earth. Our children cry for bread, and we must dig in the sands of the seashore to satisfy them. Why, I say again, have we sought this country of a rugged soil and wintry sky? Was it not for the enjoyment of our civil rights? Was it not for liberty to worship God according to our conscience?"

"Do you call this liberty of conscience?" interrupted a voice on the steps of the meeting-house. It was the wanton gospeller. A sad and quiet smile flitted across the mild visage of Roger Williams, but Endicott, in the excitement of the moment, shook his sword wrathfully at the culprit - an ominous gesture from a man like him.

"What have you to do with conscience, you knave?" cried he. "I said liberty to worship God, not license to profane and ridicule him. Break not in upon my speech, or I will lay you neck and heels till this time tomorrow. Hearken to me, friends, nor heed that accursed rhapsodist. As I was saying, we have sacrificed all things, and have come to a land of which the Old World has scarcely heard, that we might make a new world for ourselves and painfully seek a path from here to heaven. But what do you think now? This son of a Scotch tyrant, this grandson of a papistical and adulterous Scotch woman whose death proved that a golden crown does not always save an anointed head from the block…"

"Nay, brother, nay," interposed Mr. Williams, "your words are not meet for a secret chamber, far less for a public street."

"Hold your peace, Roger Williams!" answered Endicott, imperiously. "My spirit is wiser than yours for the business now in hand. I tell you, fellow-exiles, that Charles of England and Laud, our bitterest persecutor, arch-priest of Canterbury, are resolute to pursue us even here. They are taking counsel, says this letter, to send over a governor-general in whose breast shall be deposited all the law and equity of the land. They are minded, also, to establish the idolatrous forms of English episcopacy; so that when Laud shall kiss the pope's toe as cardinal of Rome he may deliver New England, bound hand and foot, into the power of his master."

A deep groan from the auditors, a sound of wrath as well as fear and sorrow, responded to this intelligence.

"Look to it, brethren," resumed Endicott, with increasing energy. "If this king and this arch-prelate have their will, we shall briefly behold a cross on the spire of this tabernacle which we have built, and a high altar within its walls, with wax tapers burning round it at noon-day. We shall hear the sacring-bell and the voices of the Romish priests saying the mass. But think, Christian men, that these abominations may be suffered without a sword drawn, without a shot fired, without blood spilt, even on the very stairs of the pulpit? No! Be strong of hand and stout of heart. Here we stand on our own soil, which we have bought with our goods, which we have won with our swords, which we have cleared with our axes, which we have tilled with the sweat of our brows, which we have sanctified with our prayers to the God that brought us here! Who shall enslave us here? What have we to do with this mitred prelate and with this crowned king? What have we to do with England?"

Endicott gazed round at the excited countenances of the people, now full of his own spirit, and then turned suddenly to the standard-bearer, who stood close behind him. "Officer, lower your banner," said he.

The officer obeyed, and, brandishing his sword, Endicott thrust it through the cloth and with his left hand rent the red cross completely out of the banner. He then waved the tattered ensign above his head.

"Sacrilegious wretch!" cried the high-churchman in the pillory, unable to restrain himself any longer, "you have rejected the symbol of our holy religion."

"Treason! Treason!" roared the royalist in the stocks. "He has defaced the king's banner!"

"Before God and man I will avouch the deed," answered Endicott. "Beat a flourish, drummer. Shout, soldiers and people in honour of the ensign of New England. Neither pope nor tyrant has part in it now."

With a cry of triumph the people gave their sanction to one of the boldest exploits which our history records. And for ever honoured be the name of Endicott! We look back through the mist of ages, and recognize in the rending of the red cross from New England's banner the first omen of that deliverance which our fathers consummated after the bones of the stern Puritan had lain more than a century in the dust.

Where The River Hides Its Pearls

This story has been edited and adapted from Jane Pentzer Myers' Stories Of Enchantment, first published in 1901 by A. C. McClurg & Co., Chicago.

Just where the river bends on its course stands a high point or headland. It is covered with short, sweet grass and white clover, and partly shaded with trees. From its highest point there is a beautiful view of the river, which you may watch sparkling in the sun or dreaming in the moonlight. To the north the path of the river is almost straight for a mile or more; to the south the wooded hills on its farther side confront you, for here it turns and for at least a half mile flows to the west before it turns southward again.

On this headland a company of friends and neighbours were camping; and on the highest point was built the campfire. It was the children's daily task (or pleasure) to collect sticks and bark to keep this fire going from dusk until bedtime. Around it the hammocks were swung, and here the company assembled each night.

But one night, when the moon was very bright and sent its path of silver far across the water, all were on the river, except two children and one who loved them. The children nestled close to their friend, and listened to the soft voices calling or singing across the water. The summer breeze broke it into a thousand little ripples of light.

"How the river shines tonight! It seems full of pearls," one child said, softly.

The other one asked, "Are there pearls in this river as there are in the Mississippi?"

"Oh, quantities of them; but the river hides them safely," answered their friend.

"Can you tell us where it hides them? Please tell us," they pleaded; and their friend softly told the following legend:

Years ago, before there were any white men beside this river, there lived in a village just around the bend a native boy. He was not uncommonly handsome, brave, or good, but very much the reverse; and he spent all of his days and most of his nights idling in his canoe on the river. He did not fish or set traps or do any of the work that the other boys did, but allowed his father and mother to furnish him with food and clothing. His grandfather would shake his head and tell him that someday he would displease the spirit who dwelt in the river, and that harm would befall him. But he was wilful, and laughed at the mention of the spirit. He did not believe there was one; he had never seen it.

One night when he had been far up the river in his canoe, he came floating down in the moonlight, just as that boat is floating there. Do you see that tree that stands out on that point by itself? Yes; just there was once a sand-bar. The moon shone on it, and the yellow sand was like gold, as the boy neared it; he idly gazed at it, for he was half asleep; but his attention was suddenly attracted by a wonderful sight. He lay down in the canoe and let his eyes come just above its rim, and this is what he saw as he slowly drifted past.

An immense mussel shell lay just on the edge of the bar, half in and half out of the water. It was wide open, and was so large that the half of it formed a beautiful seat or throne. The upper valve curved over like a canopy, and seemed to protect a beautiful girl who was reclining in the hollow of the shell. Her face, a soft bronze in colour, stood out in relief against the mother-of-pearl lining of her throne. Her hair waved round her in shining curves. Her hands were clasped above her head. Her dress was of some shining white material, soft and lustrous as silk; she was gazing up into the moonlit sky, and seemed lost in thought. But it was not her beauty or her strange appearance that attracted the boy; his eyes had caught the shine of a wonderful belt she wore around her waist. It seemed to catch and hold the moonbeams and the sparkle of the water. It was made of many strings of what appeared to be the most beautiful wampum the boy had ever seen. But it was not wampum; the beads were pearls. The boy had never seen or heard of pearls, so he naturally decided that it was a belt of glorified wampum, and his heart went out to it; he longed exceedingly to possess it, for he was covetous.

He floated down past the bar, and left the beautiful vision behind him; but all night long he dreamed of the belt, and vowed to himself that he would possess it, if the girl ever returned; so he set his wits to work and devised a plan. He determined to capture her and demand the belt for her ransom. He secured a stout deerskin, and concealing it in his canoe, he entered and paddled a long distance up the river. He spent the day in making out of the skin a strong noose, and practised throwing it until he was perfect in the art. Then, when night came and the moon was rising, he drifted as before down to the sand-bar. The beautiful girl in the great shell was there, and around her waist shone the pearls. Fortune favoured him tonight, for she was asleep. He ventured near her, his feet making no sound on the sands. When close enough he sprang toward her, like a young panther on his prey. She jumped to her feet with a cry, and the noose fell over her head, slipped down past her shoulders, and pinioned her arms to her side. She tried to break away from it, but it held her securely.

Turning, she saw her captor; her eyes flashed. "Cruel wretch!" she cried. "Why do you treat me thus? Have I not allowed you the freedom of the waters, and because I thought that you loved them, have I not guarded you from many dangers? Do you know who I am?"

The boy answered, "I do not know, nor do I care. You must go with me to the village; you shall be adopted into the tribe."

In vain she implored him to set her at liberty; he would not listen. But pretending finally to melt under her prayers and tears, he said, "I will release you if you give me that belt of wampum you wear around your waist."

The girl looked at him sternly. "Can I give away what is not mine? These pearls belong to the river; and because I am the Spirit of the Waters, I am allowed to wear them. I will loan them to you, but there are conditions. You must promise that while you wear them you will refrain from cruel or cowardly deeds, and, because your heart is evil, you must spend today (for day is breaking) in the deep woods, fasting and alone, praying to the Great Spirit for a heart pure enough to wear these pearls. If when the moon has waned and grown bright again, the pearls are not dimmed and you have refrained from evil, the belt may be given to you. But I know that you will not keep it; I shall have it soon again."

So saying, after he had loosed her hands a little, she unclasped her belt and held it out to him.

He snatched it rudely, and said boastfully, "What I get, I keep."

Then he hastened to loosen the thong, for he saw that daylight was coming, and he feared that someone would find him there and compel him to return the belt.

The girl sprang into the shell; it closed, and sank with her into the water, while the boy, overjoyed, made off with his prize.

The pearls were very large, and seemed to shed a soft light around him. He bound the belt around his waist; it was too short, but he lengthened it out with strings.

He entered at once into the deep wood to fast and pray to the Great Spirit, as he had been told to do. But his mind was so fixed upon the belt that he forgot to ask for a heart pure enough to wear it. When evening came, he entered the village. It was the hour of rest after the toils of the day, and men, women, and children were in front of their tepees. Very haughtily he strode past his neighbours. Exclamations of wonder and delight, and questions as to where he had obtained the belt, assailed him. He answered that he had "found" it, but would not tell where.

His grandfather shook his head mysteriously; he did not believe that he had found it. "The River Spirit is weaving her enchantments for the boy; I fear for him greatly," he said.

This made the boy very angry with the old man, and he treated him rudely.

Each day that he wore the belt he grew more insolent and vainer. He spent all his time in admiring himself and the belt. And each day the pearls grew dimmer. He saw that they were fading, and he tried to brighten them. He bathed them in the river and polished them with care, but they did not regain their lustre.

One night when the moon had waned and come again, he was out in his canoe on the river. He had asked a younger boy to go with him, for he feared that, if alone, the spirit would meet him. The child asked him repeatedly where he had found the belt; finally becoming enraged at his questions, the boy raised his paddle and struck him. He fell backward into the water. The boy did not attempt to help him, but turned his back upon him, and paddled swiftly away.

The Spirit of the River saw it all, and hastening to the child, she bore him safe to the shore. The boy hastened up the river until he saw with alarm that he was near the sand-bar where he had secured the belt; and when he felt a hand steadily drawing him to the bar, he was frantic with fear. He resisted with all his might, but the canoe kept steadily on. When it reached the bar, he was thrown violently out on to the sand, and the boat drifted away bottom upward. He sprang to his feet, and was confronted by the spirit; but now she was no delicate girl, but a woman, strong and terrible.

"Give me the pearls," she said, "and the river shall hide them henceforth from the greed of mortals." The boy sullenly returned the belt; and, at a word from the spirit, there came up through the sand and from the river thousands of mussels. Each shell was gaping wide, and into each she dropped a pearl. When all were gone, the shells closed with a snap, and disappeared as quickly as they had come.

The spirit turned to the boy. "Since you know the secret that the river would keep, your lips must be always closed. Stay by these waters forever, and search in vain for the pearls."

So saying, she changed him into a sand-hill crane, and he may still be seen, standing on the sand-bars, looking intently into the water for the pearls.

"We have seen him," cried the children. "He was over on that sand-bar, on the other side of the river, this afternoon."

By and by the smallest child said, softly, "I am sorry for that poor, naughty, sandhill crane."

A Visit To Avoyelles

This story has been edited and adapted from Kate Chopin's Bayou Folk, first published in 1894 by the Houghton Mifflin Company of Boston and New York.

Everyone who came up from Avoyelles had the same story to tell of Mentine. Cher Maître! but she was changed. And there were babies, more than she could well manage; as good as four already. Jules, her husband, was not kind except to himself. They seldom went to church, and never anywhere upon a visit. They lived as poorly as pine-woods people. Doudouce had heard the story often, the last time no later than that morning.

"Ho-a!" he shouted to his mule plumb in the middle of the cotton row. He had staggered along behind the plough since early morning, and of a sudden he felt he had had enough of it. He mounted the mule and rode away to the stable, leaving the plough with its polished blade thrust deep in the red Cane River soil. His head felt like a windmill with the recollections and sudden intentions that had crowded it and were whirling through his brain since he had heard the last story about Mentine.

He knew well enough Mentine would have married him seven years ago had not Jules Trodon come up from Avoyelles and captivated her with his handsome eyes and pleasant speech. Doudouce was resigned then, for he held Mentine's happiness above his own. But now she was suffering in a hopeless, common, exasperating way for the small comforts of life. People had told him so. And somehow, today, he could not stand the knowledge passively. He felt he must see those things they spoke of with his own eyes. He must strive to help her and her children if it were possible.

Doudouce could not sleep that night. He lay with wakeful eyes watching the moonlight creep across the bare floor of his room; listening to sounds that seemed unfamiliar and weird down among the rushes along the bayou. But towards morning he saw Mentine as he had seen her last in her white wedding gown and veil. She looked at him with appealing eyes and held out her arms for protection, for, rescue, it seemed to him. That dream determined him. The following day Doudouce started for Avoyelles.

Jules Trodon's home lay a mile or two from Marksville. It consisted of three rooms strung in a row and opening upon a narrow gallery. The whole wore an aspect of poverty and dilapidation that summer day, towards noon, when Doudouce approached it. His presence outside the gate aroused the frantic barking of dogs that dashed down the steps as if to attack him. Two little brown barefooted children, a boy and girl, stood upon the gallery staring stupidly at him. "Call off you' dogs," he requested; but they only continued to stare.

"Down, Pluto! down, Achille!" cried the shrill voice of a woman who emerged from the house, holding upon her arm a delicate baby of a year or two. There was only an instant of unrecognition.

"Mais Doudouce, that ain't you, comment! Well, if anyone would tole me this mornin'! Get a chair, 'Tit Jules. That's Mista Doudouce, f'om 'way yonder Natchitoches where your maman used to live. Mais, you ain't changed; you're lookin' well, Doudouce."

He shook hands in a slow, undemonstrative way, and seated himself clumsily upon the hide-bottomed chair, laying his broad-rimmed felt hat upon the floor beside him. He was very uncomfortable in the cloth Sunday coat which he wore.

"I had business that call' me to Marksville," he began, "an' I say to myse'f, 'Tiens, you can't pass by without tell' 'em all howdy.'"

"Par example! w'at Jules would said to that! Mais, you' lookin' well; you ain't change', Doudouce."

"An' you' lookin' well, Mentine, Jis' the same Mentine." He regretted that he lacked talent to make the lie bolder.

She moved a little uneasily, and felt upon her shoulder for a pin with which to fasten the front of her old gown where it lacked a button. She had kept the baby in her lap. Doudouce was wondering miserably if he would have known her outside her home. He would have known her sweet, cheerful brown eyes, that were not changed; but her figure, that had looked so trim in the wedding gown, was sadly misshapen. She was brown, with skin like parchment, and piteously thin. There were lines, some deep as if old age had cut them, about the eyes and mouth.

"An' how you left 'em all, yonder?" she asked, in a high voice that had grown shrill from screaming at children and dogs.

"They all well. It's mighty li'le sickness in the country this year. But they been lookin' for you up yonder, straight along, Mentine."

"Don't talk, Doudouce, it's no chance; with that poor worn out piece o' land w'at Jules got. He say, another year like that, he's goin' sell out, him."

The children were clutching her on either side, their persistent gaze always fastened upon Doudouce. He tried without avail to make friends with them. Then Jules came home from the field, riding the mule with which he had worked, and which he fastened outside the gate.

"Here's Doudouce f'om Natchitoches, Jules," called out Mentine, "he stop' to tell us howdy, en passant." The husband mounted to the gallery and the two men shook hands; Doudouce listlessly, as he had done with Mentine; Jules with some bluster and show of cordiality.

"Well, you're a lucky man, you," he exclaimed with his swagger air, "able to broad like that, encore! You could not do that if you had half a dozen mouth' to feed, allez!"

"Non, j'te garantis!" agreed Mentine, with a loud laugh. Doudouce winced, as he had done the instant before at Jules's heartless implication. This husband of Mentine surely had not changed during the seven years, except to grow broader, stronger, handsomer. But Doudouce did not tell him so.

After the mid-day dinner of boiled salt pork, corn bread and molasses, there was nothing for Doudouce but to take his leave when Jules did.

At the gate, the little boy was discovered in dangerous proximity to the mule's heels, and was properly screamed at and rebuked.

"I reckon he likes hosses," Doudouce remarked. "He take' after you, Mentine. I got a li'le pony yonder home," he said, addressing the child, "w'at ain't no use to me. I'm goin' send 'im down to you. He's a good, tough li'le mustang. You jis can let 'im eat grass an' feed 'im a hatful 'o corn, once a while. An' he's gentle, yes. You an' your ma can ride 'im to church, Sundays. Hein! you want?"

"W'at you say, Jules?" demanded Doudouce.

"W'at you say?" echoed Mentine, who was balancing the baby across the gate.

"'Tit sauvage, va!"

Doudouce shook hands all around, even with the baby, and walked off in the opposite direction to Jules, who had mounted the mule. He was bewildered. He stumbled over the rough ground because of tears that were blinding him, and that he had held in check for the past hour.

He had loved Mentine long ago, when she was young and attractive, and he found that he loved her still. He had tried to put all disturbing thought of her away, on that wedding-day, and he supposed he had succeeded. But he loved her now as he never had. Because she was no longer beautiful, he loved her. Because the delicate bloom of her existence had been rudely brushed away; because she was in a manner fallen; because she was Mentine, he loved her; fiercely, as a mother loves an afflicted child. He would have liked to thrust that man aside, and gather up her and her children, and hold them and keep them as long as life lasted.

After a moment or two Doudouce looked back at Mentine, standing at the gate with her baby. But her face was turned away from him. She was gazing after her husband, who went in the direction of the field.

The Little Postmistress

This story has been edited and adapted from Henry W. Shoemaker's Allegheny Episodes, first published in 1922 by the Altoona Tribune Company, based out of Altoona, Pennsylvania. This was one of a series of collections forming the Pennsylvania Folk Lore series.

It was long past dark when Mifflin Sargeant, of the Snow Shoe Land Company, came within sight of the welcoming lights of Stover's. For fourteen miles, through the foothills on the Narrows, he had not seen a sign of human habitation, except one deserted hunter's cabin at Yankee Gap. There was an air of cheerfulness and life about the building he had arrived at. Several doors opened simultaneously at the signal of his approach, given by a faithful watchdog, throwing the rich glow of the fat-lamps and tallow candles across the road.

The structure, which was very long and two stories high, housed under its accommodating roofs a tavern, a boarding house, a farmstead, a lumber camp, a general store, and a post office. It was the last outpost of civilization in the east end of Brush Valley; beyond were mountains and wilderness almost to

Youngmanstown. Tom Tunis had not yet erected the substantial structure on the verge of the forest later known as "The Forest House."

A dark-complexioned lad, who later proved to be Reuben Stover, the son of the landlord, took the horse by the bridle, assisting the young stranger to dismount. He also helped him to unstrap his saddle-bags, carrying them into the house. Sargeant noticed, as he passed across the porch, that the walls were closely hung with stags' horns, which showed the prevalence of these noble animals in the neighbourhood.

Old Daddy and Mammy Stover, who ran the quaint caravansary, quickly made the visitor feel at home. It was after the regular supper-time, but a fresh repast of bear's meat and corn bread was cheerfully prepared in the huge stone chimney.

The young man explained to his hosts that he had ridden that day from New Berlin; he had come from Philadelphia to Harrisburg by train, to Liverpool by packet boat, at which last named place his horse had been sent on to meet him. He added that he was on his way into the Alleghenies, where he had recently purchased an interest in the Snow Shoe development.

After supper he strolled along the porch to the far end, to the post office, thinking he would send a letter home. A mail had been brought in from Rebersburg during the afternoon, consequently the post office, and not the tavern stand, was the attraction of the crowd this night.

The narrow room was poorly lighted by fat-lamps, which cast great, fitful shadows, making grotesques out of the oddly-costumed, bearded wolf hunters present, who were the principal inhabitants of the surrounding ridges. A few women, hooded and shawled, were noticeable in the throng. In a far corner, leaning against the water bench, was young Reuben, the hosteler, tuning up his wheezy fiddle. As many persons as possible hung over the rude counter, across which the mail was being delivered, and where many letters were written in reply. Above this counter were suspended three fat-lamps, attached to grooved poles, which, by cleverly-devised pulleys, could be lifted to any height desired.

The young Philadelphian edged his way through the good-humoured concourse to ask permission to use the ink; he had brought his favourite quill pen and the paper with him. This brought him face to face, across the counter, with the postmistress. He had not been able to see her before, as her trim little figure had been wholly obscured by the ponderous forms that lined the counter.

Instantly he was charmed by her appearance, for it was unusual, by her look of neatness and alertness. Their eyes met, and it was almost with a smile of mutual recognition. When he asked her if he could borrow the ink, which was kept in a large earthen pot of famous Sugar Valley make, she smiled on him again, and he absorbed the charm of her personality anew.

Though she was below the middle height, her figure was so lithe and erect that it fully compensated for the lack of inches. She wore a blue homespun dress, with a neat, checked apron over it, the material for which constituted a luxury, and must have come all the way from Youngmanstown or Sunbury. Her profuse masses of soft, wavy, light brown hair, on which the hanging lamps above brought out a glint of gold, was worn low on her head. Her deep-set eyes were a transparent blue, her features well developed, and when she turned her face in profile, the high arch of the nose showed at once mental stability and energy. Her complexion was pink and white. There seemed to be always that kindly smile playing about the eyes and lips.

When she pushed the heavy inkwell towards him he noticed that her hands were very white, the fingers tapering; they were the hands of innate refinement.

Almost imperceptibly the young man found himself in conversation with the little postmistress. Doubtless she was interested to meet an attractive stranger, one from such a distant city as Philadelphia. While they talked, the letter was gradually written, sealed, weighed and paid for. It was before the days of postage stamps, and the postmistress politely waited on her customers.

He had told her his name, Mifflin Sargeant, and she had given him hers, Caroline Hager, and that she was eighteen years of age. He had told her about his prospective trip into the wilds of Centre County, of the fierce beasts which he had heard still abounded there. The girl informed him that he would not have to go farther west to meet wild animals; that wolf hides by the dozen were brought to Stover's each winter, where they were traded in; that old Stover, a justice of the peace, attested to the bounty warrants, and in fact, the wolves howled from the hill across the road on cold nights when the dogs were particularly restless.

Her father was a wolf hunter, and would never allow her to go home alone; consequently, when he could not accompany her she remained overnight in the dwelling which housed the post office. Panthers, too, were occasionally met with in the locality, and in the original surveys this region was referred to as "Catland". There were also huge red bears and the somewhat smaller black ones.

If he was going West, she continued in her pretty way, he must not fail to visit the great limestone cave near where the Brush Mountains ended. She had a sister married and living not far from it, from whom she had heard wonderful tales, though she had never been there herself. It was a cave so vast it had not as yet been fully explored; one could travel for miles in it in a boat; the Karoondinha, or John Penn's Creek, had its source in it; native folks had formerly lived in the dry parts, and wild beasts. Then she lowered her voice to say that it was now haunted by the natives' spirits.

And so they talked until a very late hour, the crowd in the post office melting away, until Jared Hager, the girl's father, in his wolfskin coat, appeared to escort her home, to the cabin beyond the waterfall near the trail to Dolly Hope's Valley. She was to have a holiday until the next afternoon.

The wolf hunter was a courageous-looking man, much darker than his daughter, with a heavy black beard and bushy eyebrows; in fact, she was the only brown-haired, blue-eyed one in the entire family connection. He spoke pleasantly with the young stranger, and then they all said good night.

"Don't forget to visit the great cavern," Caroline called to the youth.

"I surely will," he answered, "and stop here on my way east to tell you all about it."

"That's good; we want to see you again," said the girl, as she disappeared into the gloomy shadows which the shaggy white pines cast across the road.

Young Stover was playing "Green Grows the Rushes" on his fiddle in the tap-room, and Sargeant sat there listening to him, dreaming and musing all the while, his consciousness singularly alert, until the closing hour came.

That night, in the old, stained four-poster, in his tiny, cold room, he slept not at all. "Yet he feared to dream." Though his thoughts carried him all over the world, the little postmistress was uppermost in every fancy. Among the other things, he wished that he had asked her to ride with him to the cave. They could have visited the subterranean marvels together. He got out of bed and managed to light the fat lamp. By its sputtering gleams he wrote her a letter, which came to an abrupt end as the small supply of ink which he carried with him was exhausted. But as he repented of the intense sentences penned to a person who knew him so slightly, he arose again before morning and tore it to bits.

There was a white frost on the buildings and ground when he came downstairs. The autumn air was cold, the atmosphere was a hazy, melancholy grey. There seemed to be a cessation of all the living forces of nature, as if waiting for the summons of winter. From the chimney of the old inn came purple smoke, charged with the pungent odour of burning pine wood.

With a strange sadness he saddled his horse and resumed his ride towards the west. He thought constantly of Caroline, so much so that after he had travelled ten miles he wanted to turn back; he felt miserable without her. If only she were riding beside him, the two bound for Penn's Valley Cave, he could be supremely happy. Without her, he did not care to visit the cavern, or anything else; so at Jacobsburg he crossed the Nittany Mountains, leaving the southerly valleys behind.

He rode up Nittany Valley to Bellefonte, where he met the agent of the Snow Shoe Company. With this gentleman he visited the vast tract being opened up to lumbering, mining and colonization. But his thoughts were elsewhere; they were across the mountains with the little postmistress of Stover's.

Satisfied that his investment would prove remunerative, he left the development company's cosy lodge-house, and, with a heart growing lighter with each mile, started for the east. It was wonderful how differently, how vastly more beautiful the country seemed on this return journey. He fully appreciated the wistful loveliness of the fast-fading autumn foliage, the crispness of the air, the beauty of each stray tuft of asters, the last survivors of the wildflowers along the trail. The world was full of joy, everything was in harmony.

Again it was after nightfall when he reined his horse in front of Stover's long, rambling public house. This time two doors opened simultaneously, sending forth golden lights and shadows. One was from the tap-room, where the hosteler emerged; the other from the post office, bringing little Caroline. There was no mail that night, consequently the office was practically deserted; she had time to come out and greet her much-admired friend. And let it be said that ever since she had seen him her heart was agog with the image of Mifflin Sargeant. She was canny enough to appreciate such a man; besides, he was a good-looking youth though perhaps of a less robust type than those most admired in the Red Hills.

After cordial greetings the young man ate supper, after which he repaired to the post office. By that time the last straggler was gone; he had a blissful evening with his fair Caroline. She anticipated his coming, being somewhat of a psychic, and had arranged to spend the night with the Stovers. There was no hurry to retire; when they went out on the porch, preparatory to locking up, the hunter's moon was sinking behind the western knobs, which rose like the pyramids of Egypt against the skyline.

Sargeant lingered around the old house for three days, and when he departed it was with extreme reluctance. Seeing Caroline again in the future appeared like something too good to be true, so down-hearted was he at the parting. But he had arranged to come back the following autumn, bringing an extra horse with him, and the two would ride to the wonderful cavern in Penn's Valley and explore to the ends its stygian depths. Meanwhile they would make most of their separation through a regular correspondence.

Despite glances, pressure of hands, chance caresses, and evident happiness in one another's society, not a word of love had passed between the pair. That was why the pain of parting was so intense. If Caroline could have remembered one loving phrase, then she would have felt that she had something tangible on which to hang her hopes. If the young Philadelphian had unburdened his heart by telling her that he loved her, and her alone, and heard her words of affirmation, the world out into which he was riding would have seemed less blank.

But underneath his love, burning like a hot branding iron, was his consciousness of class, his fear of the consequences if he took to the great city a bride from another sphere. As an only son, he could not picture himself deserting his widowed mother and sisters, and living at Snow Shoe; there he was sure that Caroline would be happy. Neither could he see permanent peace of mind if he married her and brought her into his exclusive circles in the Quaker City.

As he was an honourable young man, and his love was real, making her truly and always happy was the solitary consideration. These thoughts marred the parting; they blistered and ravaged his spirit on the whole dreary way back to Liverpool. There his servant was waiting at the old Susquehanna House to ride the horse to Philadelphia.

The young man boarded the packet, riding on it to Harrisburg, where he took the steam train for home. In one way he was happier than ever before in his life, for he had found love; in another he was the most dejected of men, for his beloved might never be his own.

He seemed gayer and stronger to his family; evidently the trip into the wilderness had done him good. He had begun his letter-writing to Caroline promptly. It was his great solace in his heart perplexity. She wrote a very good letter, very tender and sympathetic; the handwriting was clear, almost masculine, denoting the bravery of her spirit.

During the winter he was called upon through his sisters to mingle much with the society of the city. He met many beautiful and attractive young women, but for him the die of love had been cast. He was Caroline's irretrievably. Absence made his love firmer, yet the solution of it all the more enigmatical.

The time passed on apace. Another autumn set in, but on account of important business matters it was not until December that Sargeant departed for the wilds of mountainous Pennsylvania. But he could spend Christmas with his love.

This time he sent two horses ahead to Liverpool. When he reached the queer old river town he dropped into an old saddlery shop, where the canal-boat drivers had their harness mended, and purchased a neat side saddle, all studded with brass-headed nails. This he tied on behind his servant's saddle.

The two horsemen started up the beautiful West Mahantango, crossing the Shade Mountain to Swinefordstown, from there along the edge of Jack's Mountain, by the gently flowing Karoondinha, to Hartley Hall and the Narrows, through the Fox Gap and Minnick's Gap, a slightly shorter route to Stover's.

On his previous trip he had ridden along the river to Selin's Grove, across Chestnut Ridge to New Berlin, over Shamokin Ridge to Youngmanstown, and from there to the Narrows; he was in no hurry; no dearly loved girl was waiting for him in those days.

Caroline, looking prettier than ever, she was a trifle plumper and redder cheeked, was at the post office steps to greet him. Despite his avoidance of words of love, she was certain of his inmost feelings, and opined that somehow the ultimate result would be well.

Sargeant had arranged to arrive on a Saturday evening, so that they could begin their ride to the cave that night after the post office closed, and be there bright and early Sunday morning. For this reason he had travelled by very easy stages from Hartley Hall, that the horses might be fresh for their added journey.

Sargeant's devoted factotum was taken somewhat aback when he saw how attentive the young man was to the girl, and marvelled at the mountain maid's rare beauty. Upon instructions from his master, he set about to changing the saddles, placing the brand new lady's saddle on the horse he had been riding.

It was not long until the tiny post office was closed for the night, and Caroline emerged, wearing a many-caped red riding coat, the hood of which she threw over her head to keep the wavy, chestnut hair in place. She climbed into the saddle gracefully, for she seemed a natural horse-woman, and soon the loving pair were cantering up the road towards Wolfe's Store, Rebersburg and the cave.

It was not quite daybreak when they passed the home of old Jacob Harshbarger, the tenant of the "cave farm". A Creeley rooster was crowing lustily in the barnyard, the unmilked cattle of the ancient black breed shook their shaggy heads lazily; no one was up.

The young couple had planned to visit the cave, breakfast, and spend the day with Caroline's sister, who lived not far away at Centre Hill, and ride leisurely back to Stover's in the late afternoon. It had been a very cold all-night ride, but they had been so happy that it seemed brief and free from all disagreeable physical sensations.

In those days there was no boat in the cave, and no guides; consequently all intending visitors had to bring their own torches. This Caroline had seen to, and in her leisure moments for weeks before her lover's coming, had been arranging a supply of rich pine lights that would see them safely through the gloomy labyrinths.

They fed their horses and then tied them to the fence of the orchard which surrounded the entrance to the "dry" cave, which had been recently set out. Several big original white pines grew along the road, and would give the horses shelter in case it turned out to be a windy day. The young couple strolled through the orchard, and down the steep path to the mouth of the "watery" cave, where they gazed for some minutes at the expanse of greenish water, the high span of the arched roof, the general impressiveness of the scene, so like the stage setting of some elfin drama.

They sat on the dead grass, near this entrance, eating a light breakfast with relish. Then they wended their way up the hill to the circular "hole in the ground" which formed the doorway to the "dry" cave. The torches were carefully lit, the supply of fresh ones was tied in a bundle about Sargeant's waist. The burning pine gave forth an aromatic odour and a mellow light. They descended through the narrow opening, the young man going ahead and helping his sweetheart after him. Down the spiral passageway they went, until at length they came into a larger chamber. Here the torches cast unearthly shadows, bats flitted about; some small animal ran past them into an aperture at a far corner. Sargeant declared that he believed the elusive creature a fox, and he followed in the direction in which it had gone.

When he came to this opening he peered through it, finding that it led to an inner chamber of impressive proportions. He went back, taking Caroline by the hand, and led her to the narrow chamber, into which they both entered. Once in the interior room, they were amazed by its size, the height of its roof, the beauty of the stalactite formations. They sat down on a fallen stalagmite, holding aloft their torches, absorbed by the beauty of the scene.

In the midst of their musing, a sudden gust of wind blew out their lights. They were in utter darkness. The young lover bade his sweetheart be unafraid, while he reached his hand in his pocket for the matches. They were primitive affairs, the few he had, and he could not make them light. He had not counted on the use of the matches, as he thought one torch could be lit from another; consequently had brought so few with him. Finally he lit a match, but the dampness extinguished it before he could ignite his torch.

When the last match failed, it seemed as if the couple were in a serious predicament. They first shouted at the top of their voices but only empty echoes answered them. They fumbled about in the chamber, stumbling over rocks and stalagmites, their eyes refusing to become accustomed to the profound blackness. Try as they would, they could not locate the passage that led from the room they were in to the outer apartment.

Caroline, little heroine that she was, made no complaint. If she had any secret fears, her lover effectually quenched them by telling her that the presence of the two saddle horses tied to the orchard fence would acquaint the Harshbarger family of their presence in the cave.

"Surely," he went on, "we will be rescued in a few hours. There's bound to be some member of the household or some hunter see those horses."

But the hours passed, and with them came no intimations of rescue. But the two "prisoners" loved one another, time was nothing to them. In the outer world, both thought, but neither made bold to say, that they might have to separate, but in the cave they were one in purpose, one in love. How gloriously happy they were! But they did get a trifle hungry, but that was appeased at first by the remnants of the breakfast provisions, which they luckily still had in a little bundle.

When sufficient time had elapsed for night to set in, they fell asleep, and in each other's arms. Caroline's last conscious moment was to feel her lover's kisses. When they awoke, many hours afterwards, they were hungrier than ever, and thirsty. Sargeant fumbled about, locating a small pool of water, where the two quenched their thirsts. But still they were happy, come what may.

They would be rescued, that was certain, unless the horses had broken loose and run away, but there was small chance of that. They had been securely tied. It was strange that no one had seen the steeds in so long a time, with the farmhouse less than a quarter of a mile away, but it was at the foot of the hill.

Hunger grew apace with every hour. After a while drinking water could not sate it. It throbbed and ached, it became a dull pain that only love could triumph over. Again enough hours elapsed to bring sleep, but it was harder to find repose, though Sargeant's kisses were marvellous recompense. Caroline never whimpered from lack of food. To be with her lover was all she asked. She had prayed for over a year to be with him again. She would be glad to die at his side, even of starvation.

The young man was content; hunger was less a pain to him than had been the past fourteen months' separation.

Again came what they supposed to be morning. They knew that there must be some way out near at hand, as the air was so pure. They shouted, but the dull echoes were their only reward. Strangely enough, they had never felt another cold gust like the one which had blown out their torches. Could the shade of one of the old-time folk who had fought for possession of the cave been perpetrator of the trick? That was lovely Caroline's supposition. If so, she thought to herself, he had helped her, not harmed her, for could there be in the world a sensation half so sweet as sinking to rest in her lover's arms?

Meanwhile the world outside the cavern had been going its way. Shortly after the young equestrian passed the Harshbarger dwelling, all the family had come out, and, after attending to their farm duties, driven off to the Seven Mountains, where the sons of the family maintained a hunting camp on Cherry Run, on the other side of High Valley.

The boys had killed an elk, consequently the guests remained longer than expected, to partake of a grand Christmas feast. They tarried at the camp all of that day, all of the next; it was not until early on the morning of the third day that they started back to the Penn's Creek farm.

They had arranged with a neighbour's boy, Mosey Scull, who lived further along the creek below the farmhouse, to do the feeding in their absence; it was winter, there was no need to hurry home.

When they got home they found Mosey in the act of watering two very dejected and dirty looking horses with saddles on their backs.

"Where did they come from?" shouted the big freight-wagon load in unison.

"I found them tied to the fence up at the orchard. By the way they act I'd think they hadn't been watered or fed for several days," replied the boy.

"You dummy!" said old Harshbarger, in Dutch. "Somebody's in that cave, and got lost, and can't get out."

He jumped from the heavy wagon and ran to a corner of the corncrib, where he kept a stock of torches. Then he hurried up the steep hill towards the entrance to the "dry" cave. The big man was panting when he reached the opening, where he paused a moment to kindle a torch with his flints. Then he lowered himself into the aperture, shouting at the top of his voice, "Hello! Hello! Hello!"

It was not until he had gotten into the first chamber that the captives in the inner room could hear him. Sargeant had been sitting with his back propped against the cavern wall, while

Caroline, very pale and white-lipped, was lying across his knees, gazing up into the darkness, imagining that she could see his face.

When they heard the cheery shouts of their deliverer they did not instantly attempt to scramble to their feet. Instead the young lover bent over; his lips touched Caroline's, who instinctively had raised her face to meet his. As his lips touched hers, he whispered, "I love you, darling, with all my heart. We will be married when we get out of here."

Caroline had time to say, "You are my only love," before their lips came together.

They were in that position when the flare of Farmer Harshbarger's torch lit up their hiding place. Pretty soon they were on their feet and, with their rescuer, figuring out just how long they had been in their prison, their prison of love.

They had gone into the cave on the morning of December 24th; it was now the morning of the 27th; in fact almost noon. Christmas had come and gone.

Caroline still had enough strength in reserve to enable her to climb up the tortuous passage, though her lover did help her some, as all lovers should.

The farmer's wife had some coffee and buckwheat cakes ready when they arrived at the mansion; which the erstwhile captives of Penn's Cave sat down to enjoy.

As they were eating, another of Harshbarger's sons rode up on horseback. He had been to the post office at Earlysburg. He handed Sargeant a tiny, roughly typed newspaper published in Millheim. Across the front page, in letters larger than usual, were the words, "Mexico Declares War on the United States."

Sargeant scanned the headline intently, then laid the paper on the table. "Our country has been drawn into a war with Mexico," he said, his voice trembling with emotion. "I had hoped it might be avoided. I am First Lieutenant of the Lafayette Greys; I fear I'll have to go."

Caroline lost the colour which had come back to her pretty cheeks since emerging from the underground dungeon. She reached over, grasping her lover's now clammy hand. Then, noticing that no one was listening, she said, faintly, "It is terrible to have you leave me now; but won't you marry me before you go? I do love you."

Sargeant replied with enthusiasm. "I will have more to fight for, with you at home bearing my name."

Love had broken the bonds of caste.

A Wizard From Gettysburg

This story has been edited and adapted from Kate Chopin's Bayou Folk, first published in 1894 by the Houghton Mifflin Company of Boston and New York.

It was one afternoon in April, not long ago, only the other day, and the shadows had already begun to lengthen. Bertrand Delmandé, a fine, bright-looking boy of fourteen years, or maybe fifteen, perhaps, was mounted, and riding along a pleasant country road, upon a little Creole pony, such as boys in Louisiana usually ride when they have nothing better at hand. He had hunted, and carried his gun before him.

It is unpleasant to state that Bertrand was not so depressed as he should have been, in view of recent events that had come about. Within the past week he had been recalled from the college of Grand Coteau to his home, the Bon-Accueil plantation. He had found his father and his grandmother depressed over money matters, awaiting certain legal developments that might result in his permanent withdrawal from school. That very day, directly after the early dinner, the two had driven to town, on this very business, to be absent till the late afternoon. Bertrand, then, had saddled Picayune and gone for a long jaunt, such as his heart delighted in.

He was returning now, and had approached the beginning of the great tangled Cherokee hedge that marked the boundary line of Bon-Accueil, and that twinkled with multiple white roses. The pony started suddenly and violently at something there in the turn of the road, and just under the hedge. It looked like a bundle of rags at first. But it was a tramp, seated upon a broad, flat stone.

Bertrand had no maudlin consideration for tramps as a species; he had only that morning driven from the place one such who was making himself unpleasant at the kitchen window. But this tramp was old and feeble. His beard was long, and as white as new-ginned cotton, and when Bertrand saw him he was engaged in stanching a wound in his bare heel with a fistful of matted grass.

"What's wrong, old man?" asked the boy, kindly.

The tramp looked up at him with a bewildered glance, but did not answer.

"Well," thought Bertrand, "since it's decided that I'm to be a physician someday, I can't begin to practice too early."

He dismounted, and examined the injured foot. It had an ugly gash. Bertrand acted mostly from impulse. Fortunately his impulses were not bad ones. So, nimbly, and as quickly as he could manage it', he had the old man astride Picayune, whilst he himself was leading the pony down the narrow lane.

The dark green hedge towered like a high and solid wall on one side. On the other was a broad, open field, where here and there appeared the flash and gleam of uplifted, polished hoes, that negroes were plying between the even rows of cotton and tender corn.

"This is the State of Louisiana," uttered the tramp, quaveringly.

"Yes, this is Louisiana," returned Bertrand cheerily.

"Yes, I know it is. I've been in all of them since Gettysburg. Sometimes it was too hot, and sometimes it was too cold; and with that bullet in my head…you don't remember? No, you don't remember Gettysburg."

"Well, no, not vividly," laughed Bertrand.

"Is it a hospital? It isn't a factory, is it?" the man questioned.

"Where we 're going? Why, no, it's the Delmandé plantation, Bon-Accueil. Here we are. Wait, I 'll open the gate."

This singular group entered the yard from the rear, and not far from the house. A big black woman, who sat just without a cabin door, picking a pile of rusty-looking moss, called out at sight of them, "W'at's that you's bringin' in this yard, boy? top that hoss?"

She received no reply. Bertrand, indeed, took no notice of her inquiry.

"For a boy w'at goes to school like you does, where's your sense?" she went on, with a fine show of indignation; then, muttering to herself, "Ma'ame Bertrand an' Marse St. Ange ain't goin' stan' that, I knows they ain't. Dah! If he ain't done sat 'im on the gallery, plumb down in his pa's rockin' chair!"

The boy had seated the tramp in a pleasant corner of the veranda, while he went in search of bandages for his wound.

The servants showed high disapproval, the housemaid following Bertrand into his grandmother's room, where he had carried his investigations.

"W'at you tearin' your gra'ma's closet to' pieces that way, boy?" she complained in her high soprano.

"I'm looking for bandages."

"Then why you don't ask for ban'ges, an' leave your gra'ma's closet alone? You want to listen to me; you goin' get shed o' that tramp sittin' there next to the dinin' room! When the silver be missin', 'tain' you w'at goin' grt blame, it's me."

"The silver? Nonsense, 'Cindy; the man's wounded, and can't you see he's out of his head?"

"No more out his head 'an I is. 'T ain' me w'at want to trust 'im with the storeroom key, if he is out his head," she concluded with a disdainful shrug.

But Bertrand's protégé proved so unapproachable in his long-worn rags, that the boy concluded to leave him unmolested till his father's return, and then ask permission to turn the forlorn creature into the bath-house, and array him afterward in clean, fresh garments.

So there the old tramp sat in the veranda corner, stolidly content, when St. Ange Delmandé and his mother returned from town.

St. Ange was a dark, slender man of middle age, with a sensitive face, and a plentiful sprinkle of grey in his thick black hair; his mother, a portly woman, and an active one for her sixty-five years.

They were evidently in a despondent mood. Perhaps it was for the cheer of her sweet presence that they had brought with them from town a little girl, the child of Madame Delmandé's only daughter, who was married, and lived there.

Madame Delmandé and her son were astonished to find so uninviting an intruder in possession. But a few earnest words from Bertrand reassured them, and partly reconciled them to the man's presence; and it was with wholly indifferent though not unkindly glances that they passed him by when they entered. On any large plantation there are always nooks and corners where, for a night or more, even such a man as this tramp may be tolerated and given shelter.

When Bertrand went to bed that night, he lay long awake thinking of the man, and of what he had heard from his lips in the hushed starlight. The boy had heard of the awfulness of Gettysburg, till it was like something he could feel and quiver at.

On that field of battle this man had received a new and tragic birth. For all his existence that went before was a blank to him. There, in the black desolation of war, he was born again, without friends or kindred; without even a name he could know was his own. Then he had gone forth a wanderer; living more than half the time in hospitals; toiling when he could, starving when he had to.

Strangely enough, he had addressed Bertrand as "St. Ange," not once, but every time he had spoken to him. The boy wondered at this. Was it because he had heard Madame Delmandé address her son by that name, and fancied it?

So this nameless wanderer had drifted far down to the plantation of Bon-Accueil, and at last had found a human hand stretched out to him in kindness.

When the family assembled at breakfast on the following morning, the tramp was already settled in the chair, and in the corner which

Bertrand's indulgence had made familiar to him. If he had turned partly around, he would have faced the flower garden, with its gravelled walks and trim parterres, where a tangle of colour and perfume were holding high revelry this April morning; but he liked better to gaze into the back yard, where there was always movement. Men and women coming and going, bearing implements of work; little workers' children in scanty garments, darting here and there, and kicking up the dust in their exuberance. Madame Delmandé could just catch a glimpse of him through the long window that opened to the floor, and near which he sat.

Mr. Delmandé had spoken to the man pleasantly; but he and his mother were wholly absorbed by their trouble, and talked constantly of that, while Bertrand went back and forth ministering to the old man's wants. The boy knew that the servants would have done the office with ill grace, and he chose to be cup-bearer himself to the unfortunate creature for whose presence he alone was responsible.

Once, when Bertrand went out to him with a second cup of coffee, steaming and fragrant, the old man whispered, "What are they saying in there?" pointing over his shoulder to the dining-room.

"Oh, money troubles that will force us to economize for a while," answered the boy. "What father and mé-mère feel worst about is that I shall have to leave college now."

"No, no! St. Ange must go to school. The war's over, the war's over! St. Ange and Florentine must go to school."

"But if there's no money," the boy insisted, smiling like one who humours the vagaries of a child.

"Money! Money!" murmured the tramp. "The war's over... Money! Money!"

His sleepy gaze had swept across the yard into the thick of the orchard beyond, and rested there.

Suddenly he pushed aside the light table that had been set before him, and rose, clutching Bertrand's arm. "St. Ange, you must go to school!" he whispered. "The war's over." Looking furtively around, he said, "Come. Don't let them hear you. Don't let the negroes see us. Get a spade, the little spade that Buck Williams was digging his cistern with."

Still clutching the boy, he dragged him down the steps as he said this, and traversed the yard with long, limping strides, himself leading the way.

From under a shed where such things were to be found, Bertrand selected a spade, since the tramp's whim demanded that he should, and together they entered the orchard.

The grass was thick and tufted here, and wet with the morning dew. In long lines, forming pleasant avenues between, were peach-trees growing, and pear and apple and plum. Close against the fence was the pomegranate hedge, with its waxen blossoms, brick-red. Far down in the centre of the orchard stood a huge pecan-tree, twice the size of any other that was there, seeming to rule like an old-time king.

Here Bertrand and his guide stopped. The tramp had not once hesitated in his movements since grasping the arm of his young companion on the veranda. Now he went and leaned his back against the pecan-tree, where there was a deep knot, and looking steadily before him he took ten paces forward. Turning sharply to the right, he made five additional paces. Then pointing his finger downward, and looking at Bertrand, he commanded, "There, dig. I would do it myself, but for my wounded foot. For I've turned many a spade of earth since Gettysburg. Dig, St. Ange, dig! The war's over and you must go to school."

Is there a boy of fifteen under the sun who would not have dug, even knowing he was following the insane dictates of a demented man? Bertrand entered with all the zest of his years and his spirit into the curious adventure; and he dug and dug, throwing great spadefuls of the rich, fragrant earth from side to side.

The tramp, with body bent, and fingers like claws clasping his bony knees, stood watching with eager eyes, that never unfastened their steady gaze from the boy's rhythmic motions.

"That's it!" he muttered at intervals. "Dig, dig! The war's over. You must go to school, St. Ange."

Deep down in the earth, too deep for any ordinary turning of the soil with spade or plough to have reached it, was a box. It was of tin, apparently, something larger than a cigar box, and bound round and round with twine, rotted now and eaten away in places.

The tramp showed no surprise at seeing it there; he simply knelt upon the ground and lifted it from its long resting place.

Bertrand had let the spade fall from his hands, and was quivering with the awe of the thing he saw. Who could this wizard be that had come to him in the guise of a tramp, that walked in cabalistic paces upon his own father's ground, and pointed his finger like a divining-rod to the spot where boxes, maybe treasures, lay? It was like a page from a wonder-book.

And walking behind this white-haired old man, who was again leading the way, something of childish superstition crept back into Bertrand's heart. It was the same feeling with which he had often sat, long ago, in the weird firelight of some negro's cabin, listening to tales of witches who came in the night to work uncanny spells at their will.

Madame Delmandé had never abandoned the custom of washing her own silver and dainty china. She sat, when the breakfast was over, with a pail of warm suds before her that 'Cindy had brought to her, with an abundance of soft linen cloths. Her little granddaughter stood beside her playing, as babies will, with the bright spoons and forks, and ranging them in rows on the polished mahogany. St. Ange was at the window making entries in a note-book, and frowning gloomily as he did so.

The group in the dining-room were so employed when the old tramp came staggering in, Bertrand close behind him. He went and stood at the foot of the table, opposite to where Madame Delmandé sat, and let fall the box upon it.

The thing in falling shattered, and from its bursting sides gold came, clicking, spinning, gliding, some of it like oil; rolling along the table and off it to the floor, but heaped up, the bulk of it, before the tramp.

"Here's money!" he called out, plunging his old hand in the thick of it. "Who says St. Ange shall not go to school? The war's over. Here's money! St. Ange, my boy," turning to Bertrand and speaking with quick authority, "tell Buck Williams to hitch Black Bess to the buggy, and go bring Judge Parkerson here."

Judge Parkerson, indeed, who had been dead for twenty years and more!

"Tell him that…that…" The hand that was not in the gold went up to the withered forehead, "that…Bertrand Delmandé needs him!"

Madame Delmandé, at sight of the man with his box and his gold, had given a sharp cry, such as might follow the plunge of a knife. She lay now in her son's arms, panting hoarsely.

"Your father, St. Ange,… come back from the dead…your father!"

"Be calm, mother!" the man implored. "You had such sure proof of his death in that terrible battle, this may not be he."

"I know him! I know your father, my son!" and disengaging herself from the arms that held her, she dragged herself as a wounded serpent might to where the old man stood.

His hand was still in the gold, and on his face was yet the flush which had come there when he shouted out the name Bertrand Delmandé.

"Husband," she gasped, "do you know me…your wife?"

The little girl was playing gleefully with the yellow coin.

Bertrand stood, pulseless almost, like a young Actæon cut in marble.

When the old man had looked long into the woman's imploring face, he made a courtly-bow. "Madame," he said. "An old soldier, wounded on the field of Gettysburg, craves for himself and his two little children your kind hospitality."

The Silent Friend

This story has been edited and adapted from Henry W. Shoemaker's Allegheny Episodes, first published in 1922 by the Altoona Tribune Company, based out of Altoona, Pennsylvania. This was one of a series of collections forming the Pennsylvania Folk Lore series.

Everyone who has hunted in the "Seven Brothers'", as the Seven Mountains are called in Central Pennsylvania, has heard of Daniel Karstetter, the famous Nimrod. The Seven Mountains comprise the Path Valley, Short Bald, Thick Head, Sand, Shade and Tussey Mountains. Though three-quarters of a century has passed since he was in his hey-day as a slayer of big game, his fame is undiminished. Anecdotes of his prowess are related in every hunting camp; by one and all he has been acclaimed the greatest hunter that the Seven Brothers ever produced.

The great Nimrod, who lived to a very advanced age, was born in 1818 on the banks of Pine Creek, at the Blue Rock, half a mile below the present town of Coburn. In addition to his hunting prowess, he was interested in psychic experiences, and was as prone to discuss his adventures with supernatural agencies as his conflicts with the wild denizens of the forests. There was a particular ghost story which he loved dearly to relate.

Accompanied by his younger brother Jacob, he had been attending a dance one night across the mountains, in the environs of the town of Milroy, for like all the backwoods boys of his time, he was adept in the art of terpsichore. The long journey was made on horseback, the lads being mounted on stout Conestoga chargers.

The homeward ride was commenced after midnight, the two brothers riding along the dark trail in single file. In the wide flat on the top of the "Big Mountain" Daniel fell into a doze. When he awoke, his mount having stumbled on a stone, Jacob was nowhere to be seen. Thinking that his brother had put his horse to trot and gone on ahead, Daniel dismissed the matter of his absence from his mind.

As he was riding down the steep slope of the mountain, he noticed a horseman waiting for him on the path. When they came abreast the other rider fell in beside him, skilfully guiding his horse so that it did not encounter the dense foliage which lined the narrow way. Daniel supposed the party to be his brother, although the unknown kept his lynx-skin collar turned up, and his felt cap was pulled down level with his eyes. It was pitchy dark, so to make sure, Daniel called out, "Is that you, Jacob?"

His companion did not reply, so the young man repeated his query in still louder tones, but all he heard was the crunching of the horses' hoofs on the pebbly road.

Daniel Karstetter, master slayer of panthers, bears and wolves, was no coward, though on this occasion he felt uneasy. Yet he disliked picking a quarrel with the silent man at his side, who clearly was not his brother, and he feared to put his horse to a gallop on the steep, uneven roadway. The trip home never before seemed of such interminable length. For the greater part of the distance Daniel made no attempt to converse with his unsociable comrade. Finally, he heaved a sigh of relief when he saw a light gleaming in the horse stable at the home farm. When he reached the barnyard gate he dismounted to let down the bars, while the stranger apparently vanished in the gloom.

Daniel led his mount to the horse stable, where he found his brother Jacob sitting by the old tin lantern, fast asleep. He awakened him and asked him when he had gotten home. Jacob stated that his horse had been feeling good, so he let him canter all the way. He had been sleeping, but judged that he had been home at least half an hour. He had met no horseman on the road.

Daniel was convinced that his companion had been a ghost, or, as they are called in the "Seven Brothers," a gshpook. But he made no further comment that night.

A year afterwards, in coming back alone from a dance in Stone Valley, he was again joined by the silent horseman, who followed him to his barnyard gate. He gave up going to dances on that account. At least once a year, or as long as he was able to go out at night, he met the ghostly rider. Sometimes, when tramping along on foot after a hunt, or, in later years, coming back from market at Bellefonte in his Jenny Lind, he would find the silent horseman at his side. After the first experience, he never attempted to speak to the night rider, but he became convinced that it meant him no harm.

As his prowess as a hunter became recognized, he had many jealous rivals among the less successful Nimrods. In those old days threats of all kinds were freely made. He heard on several occasions that certain hunters were setting out to "fix" him. But a man who could wrestle with panthers and bears knew no such thing as fear.

One night, while tramping along in Green's Valley, he was startled by someone in the path ahead of him shouting out in Pennsylvania German, "Hands up!" He was on the point of dropping his rifle, when he heard the rattle of hoof beats back of him. The silent horseman in an instant was by his side, the dark horse pawing the earth with his giant hoofs. There was a crackling of brush in the path ahead, and no more threats of "hend uff".

The ghostly rider followed Daniel to his barn yard gate, but was gone before he could utter a word of thanks. As the result of this adventure, he became imbued with the idea that he possessed a charmed life. It gave him added courage in his many encounters with panthers, the fierce red bears and lynxes.

Apart from his love of hunting the more dangerous animals, Daniel enjoyed the sport of deer-stalking. He maintained several licks, one of them in a patch of low ground over the hill from the entrance to the "dry" part of Penn's Cave. At this spot he constructed a blind, or platform, between the two ancient tupelo trees, about twenty feet from the ground, and many were the huge white-faced stags which fell to his unerring bullets during the rutting season.

One cold night, according to an anecdote frequently related by one of his descendants, while perched in his eyrie overlooking the natural clearing which constituted the lick, and in sight of a path frequented by the fiercer beasts, which led to the opening of the "dry" cave, he saw, about midnight, a huge pantheress, followed by a large male of the same species, come out into the open.

The pantheress strolled from the path, so the story went, and came and laid herself down at the roots of the tupelo trees, while the male panther remained in the path, and seemed to be listening to some noise as yet inaudible to the hunter.

Daniel soon heard a distant roaring; it seemed to come from the very summit of the Brush Mountain, and immediately the pantheress answered it. The panther on the path, his jealousy aroused, commenced to roar with a voice so loud that the frightened hunter almost let go his trusty rifle and held tighter to the railing of his blind, lest he might tumble to the earth. As the voice of the animal that he had heard in the distance gradually approached, the pantheress welcomed him with renewed roarings, and the panther, restless, went and came from the path to his flirtatious flame, as though he wished her to keep silence, as though to say, 'Let him come if he dares; he will find his match'.

In about an hour a panther, with mouse-colour, or grey coat, stepped out of the forest, and stood in the full moonlight on the other side of the cleared place, the moonbeams illuminating his form with a glow like phosphorescence. The pantheress, eyeing him with admiration, raised herself to go to him, but the panther, divining her intent, rushed before her and marched right at his adversary. With measured step and slow, they approached to within a dozen paces of each other, their smooth, round heads high in the air, their bulging yellow eyes gleaming, their long, tufted tails slowly sweeping down the brittle asters that grew about them. They crouched to the earth, a moment's pause, and then they bounded with a hellish scream high in the air and rolled on the ground, locked in their last embrace.

The battle was long and fearful, to the amazed and spellbound witness of this midnight duel. Even if he had so wished, he could not have taken steady enough aim to fire. But he preferred to watch the combat, while the moonlight lasted. The bones of the two combatants cracked under their powerful jaws, their talons painted the frosty ground with blood, and their outcries, now guttural, now sharp and loud, told their rage and agony.

At the beginning of the contest the pantheress crouched herself on her belly, with her eyes fixed upon the gladiators, and all the while the battle raged, manifested by the slow, catlike motion of her tail, the pleasure she felt at the spectacle. When the scene closed, and all was quiet and silent and deathlike on the lick, and the moon had commenced to wane, she cautiously approached the battle-ground and, sniffing the lifeless bodies of her two lovers, walked leisurely to a nearby oak, where she stood on her hind feet, sharpening her fore claws on the bark.

She glared up ferociously at the hunter in the blind, as if she meant to vent her anger by climbing after him. In the moonlight her golden eyes appeared so terrifying that Daniel dropped his rifle, and it fell to the earth with a sickening thud. As he reached after it, the flimsy railing gave way and he fell, literally into the arms of the pantheress. At that moment the rumble of horses' hoofs, like thunder on some distant mountain, was heard. Just as the panther was about to rend the helpless Nimrod to bits, the unknown rider came into view. Scowling at the intruder, mounted on his huge black horse. The brute abandoned its prey and ambled off up the hill in the direction of the dry cave.

Daniel seized his firearm and sent a bullet after her retreating form, but it apparently went wide of its mark. Meanwhile, before he had time to express his gratitude to the strange deliverer, he had vanished.

Daniel was dumbfounded. As soon as he had recovered from the blood-curdling episodes, he built a small fire near the mammoth carcasses, where he warmed his much benumbed hands. Then he examined the dead panthers, but found that their hides were too badly torn to warrant skinning.

Disgusted at not getting his deer, and being even cheated out of the panther pelts, he dragged the ghastly remains of the erstwhile kings of the forest by their tails to the edge of the entrance to the dry cave. There he cut off the long ears in order to collect the bounty, and then shoved the carcasses into the opening. They fell with sickening thuds into the chamber beneath, to the evident horror of the pantheress, which uttered a couple of piercing screams as the horrid remnants of the recent battle royal landed in her vicinity.

Then Jacob shouldered his rifle and started out in search of small game for breakfast. That night he went to another of his licks on Elk Creek, near Fulmer's Sink, where he killed four superb stags, so the story concludes.

But to his dying day he always placed the battle of the panthers first of all his hunting adventures. And his faith in the unknown horseman as his deliverer and good genius became the absorbing, all-pervading influence of his life.

Ezra's Thanksgivin' Out West

This story has been edited and adapted from Eugene Field's book A Little Book of Profitable Tales, first published in 1891 in New York.

Ezra had written a letter to the home folks, and in it he had complained that never before had he spent such a weary, lonesome day as this Thanksgiving day had been. Having finished this letter, he sat for a long time gazing idly into the open fire that snapped cinders all over the hearthstone and sent its red forks dancing up the chimney to join the winds that frolicked and gambolled across the Kansas prairies that raw November night. It had rained hard all day, and was cold; and although the open fire made every honest effort to be cheerful, Ezra, as he sat in front of it in the wooden rocker and looked down into the glowing embers, experienced a dreadful feeling of loneliness and homesickness.

"I'm sick o' Kansas," said Ezra to himself. "Here I 've been in this plaguy country for goin' on a year, and, yes, I'm sick of it, powerful sick of it. What a miser'ble Thanksgivin' this has been! They don't know what Thanksgivin' is out this way. I wish I was back in ol' Mass'chusetts, that's the country for me, and they have the kind o' Thanksgivin' I like!"

Musing in this strain, while the rain went patter-patter on the window-panes, Ezra saw a strange sight in the fireplace, yes, right among the embers and the crackling flames Ezra saw a strange, beautiful picture unfold and spread itself out like a panorama.

"How very wonderful!" murmured the young man. Yet he did not take his eyes away, for the picture soothed him and he loved to look upon it.

"It is a picture of long ago," said Ezra, softly. "I had like to forgot it, but now it comes back to me as nat'ral-like as an ol' friend. An' I seem to be a part of it, an' the feelin' of that time comes back with the picture, too."

Ezra did not stir. His head rested upon his hand, and his eyes were fixed upon the shadows in the firelight.

"It is a picture of the ol' home," said Ezra to himself. "I am back there in Belchertown, with the Holyoke hills up north an' the Berkshire mountains a-loomin' up grey an' misty-like in the western horizon. Seems as if it wuz early mornin'; everything is still, and it is so cold when we boys crawl out o' bed that, if it wuzn't Thanksgivin' mornin', we'd crawl back again an' wait for Mother to call us. But it is Thanksgivin' mornin', an' we're goin' skatin' down on the pond. The squealin' o' the pigs has told us it is five o'clock, and we must hurry; we're goin' to call by for the Dickerson boys an' Hiram Peabody, an' we've got to hyper! Brother Amos gets on 'bout half o' my clothes, an' I get on 'bout half o' his, but it's all the same; they are stout, warm clothes, and they're big enough to fit any of us boys. Mother looked out for that when she made 'em. When we go down-stairs we find the girls there, all bundled up nice an' warm, Mary an' Helen an' Cousin Irene. They're goin' with us, an' we all start out tiptoe and quiet-like so's not to wake up the ol' folks. The ground is frozen hard; we stub our toes on the frozen ruts in the road. When we come to the minister's house, Laura is standin' on the front stoop, a-waitin' for us. Laura is the minister's daughter. She's a friend o' Sister Helen's, pretty as a daguerreotype, an' gentle-like and tender. Laura lets me carry her skates, an' I'm glad of it, although I have my hands full already with the lantern, the hockies, and the rest. Hiram Peabody keeps us waitin', for he has overslept himself, an' when he comes trottin' out at last the girls make fun of him, all except Sister Mary, an' she sort o' sticks up for Hiram, an' we're all so 'cute we kind o' calculate we know the reason why.

"And now," said Ezra, softly, "the picture changes; seems as if I could see the pond. The ice is like a black lookin'-glass, and Hiram Peabody slips up the first thing, an' down he comes lickety-split, an' we all laugh, except Sister Mary, an' she says it is very impolite to laugh at other folks' misfortunes. Ough! How cold it is, and how my fingers ache with the frost when I take off my mittens to strap on Laura's skates! But, oh, how my cheeks burn! And how careful I am not to hurt Laura, an' how I ask her if that's 'tight enough,' an' how she tells me 'just a little tighter,' and how we two keep foolin' along till the others have gone an' we are left alone! An' how quick I get my own skates strapped on, none o' your new-fangled skates with springs an' plates an' clamps an' such, but honest, ol'-fashioned wooden ones with steel runners that curl up over my toes an' have a bright brass button on the end! How I strap 'em and lash 'em and buckle 'em on! An' Laura waits for me an' tells me to be sure to get 'em on tight enough. Why, bless me! After I once got 'em strapped on, if them skates had come off, the feet would ha' come with 'em! An' now away we go, Laura an' me. Around the bend, near the meadow where Si Barker's dog killed a woodchuck last summer, we meet the rest. We forget all about the cold. We run races an' play snap the whip, an' cut all sorts o' didoes, an' we never mind the pick'rel weed that is froze in on the ice an' trips us up every time we cut the outside edge; an' then we boys jump over the airholes, an' the girls stan' by an' scream an' tell us they know we're agoin' to drownd ourselves. So the hours go, an' it is sun-up at last, an' Sister Helen says we must be gettin' home. When we take our skates off, our feet feel as if they were wood. Laura has lost her tippet; I lend her mine, an' she kind o' blushes. The old pond seems glad to have us go, and the fire-hangbird's nest in the willer-tree waves us good-by. Laura promises to come over to our house in the evenin', and so we break up.

"Seems now," continued Ezra, musingly, "seems now as if I could see us all at breakfast. The race on the pond has made us hungry, and Mother says she never knew anybody else's boys that had such capac'ties as hers. It is the Yankee Thanksgivin' breakfast, sausages an' fried potatoes, an' buckwheat cakes an' syrup, maple syrup, mind you, for Father has his own sugar-bush, and there was a big run o' sap last season.

Mother says, 'Ezry an' Amos, won't you never get through eatin'? We want to clear off the table, for there's pies to make, an' nuts to crack, and laws sakes alive! The turkey's got to be stuffed yet!' Then how we all fly round! Mother sends Helen up into the attic to get a squash while Mary's makin' the pie-crust. Amos an' I crack the walnuts, they call 'em hickory nuts out in this pesky country of sage-brush and pastureland. The walnuts are hard, and it's all we can do to crack 'em. Ev'ry once 'n a while one on 'em slips out of our fingers an' goes dancin' over the floor or flies into the pan Helen is squeezin' pumpkin into through the col'nder. Helen says we're shif'less an' good for nothin' but frivollin'; but Mother tells us how to crack the walnuts so's not to let 'em fly all over the room, an' so's not to be all jammed to pieces like the walnuts was down at the party at the Peasleys' last winter.

An' now here comes Tryphena Foster, with her gingham gown an' muslin apron on; her folks have gone up to Amherst for Thanksgivin', an' Tryphena has come over to help our folks get dinner. She thinks a great deal o' Mother, 'cause Mother teaches her Sunday-school class an' says Tryphena oughter marry a missionary. There is bustle everywhere, the rattle of pans an' the clatter of dishes; an' the new kitchen stove begins to warm up an' get red, till Helen loses her wits an' is flustered, an' sez she never could get the hang o' that stove's dampers.

"An' now," murmured Ezra, gently, as a tone of deeper reverence crept into his voice, "I can see Father sittin' all by himself in the parlour. Father's hair is very grey, and there are wrinkles on his honest old face. He is lookin' through the winder at the Holyoke hills over yonder, and I can guess he's thinkin' of the time when he wuz a boy like me an' Amos, an' useter climb over them hills an' kill rattlesnakes an' hunt partridges. Or doesn't his eyes quite reach the Holyoke hills? Do they fall kind o' lovingly but sadly on the little buryin'-ground just beyond the village? Ah, Father knows that spot, an' he loves it, too, for there are treasures there whose memory he wouldn't swap for all the world could give. So, while there is a kind o' mist in Father's eyes, I can see he is dreamin'-like of sweet an' tender things, and communin' with memory, hearin' voices I never heard an' feelin' the touch of hands I never pressed; an' seein' Father's peaceful face I find it hard to think of a Thanksgivin' sweeter than Father's is.

"The picture in the firelight changes now," said Ezra, "an' seems as if I wuz in the old frame meetin'-house. The meetin'-house is on the hill, and meetin' begins at half-pas' ten. Our pew is well up in front, seems as if I could see it now. It has a long red cushion on the seat, and in the hymn-book rack there is a Bible an' a couple of Psalmodies. We walk up the aisle slow, and Mother goes in first; then comes Mary, then me, then Helen, then Amos, and then Father. Father thinks it is just as well to have one o' the girls set in between me an' Amos. The meetin'-house is full, for everybody goes to meetin' Thanksgivin' day. The minister reads the proclamation an' makes a prayer, an' then he gives out a psalm, an' we all stan' up an' turn round an' join the choir. Sam Merritt has come up from Palmer to spend Thanksgivin' with the ol' folks, an' he is singin' tenor today in his ol' place in the choir. Some folks say he sings wonderful well, but I don't like Sam's voice. Laura sings soprano in the choir, and Sam stands next to her an' holds the book.

"Seems as if I could hear the minister's voice, full of earnestness an' melody, comin' from 'way up in his little round pulpit. He is tellin' us why we should be thankful, an', as he quotes Scripture an' Dr. Watts, we boys wonder how anybody can remember so much of the Bible. Then I get nervous and worried. Seems to me the minister was never comin' to lastly, and I find myself wonderin' whether Laura is listenin' to what the preachin' is about, or is writin' notes to Sam Merritt in the back of the tune-book. I get thirsty, too, and I fidget about till Father looks at me, and Mother nudges Helen, and Helen passes it along to me with interest.

"An' then," continues Ezra in his revery, "when the last hymn is given out an' we stan' up ag'in an' join the choir, I am glad to see that Laura is singin' outer the book with Miss Hubbard, the alto.

An' goin' out o' meetin' I kind of edge up to Laura and ask her if I kin have the pleasure of seen' her home.

"An' now we boys all go out on the Common to play ball. The Enfield boys have come over, and, as all the Hampshire county folks know, they are tough fellers to beat. Gorham Polly keeps tally, because he has got the newest jack-knife, oh, how slick it whittles the old broom-handle Gorham picked up in Packard's store an' brought along just to keep tally on! It is a great game of ball; the bats are broad and light, and the ball is small and soft. But the Enfield boys beat us at last; leastwise they make 70 tallies to our 58, when Heman Fitts knocks the ball over into Aunt Dorcas Eastman's yard, and Aunt Dorcas comes out an' picks up the ball an' takes it into the house, an' we have to stop playin'. Then Phineas Owens allows he can flop any boy in Belchertown, an' Moses Baker takes him up, an' they wrassle like two tartars, till at last Moses tuckers Phineas out an' downs him as slick as a whistle.

"Then we all go home, for Thanksgivin' dinner is ready. Two long tables have been made into one, and one of the big tablecloths Gran'ma had when she set up housekeepin' is spread over 'em both. We all sit round, Father, Mother, Aunt Lydia Holbrook, Uncle Jason, Mary, Helen, Tryphena Foster, Amos, and me. How big an' brown the turkey is, and how good it smells! There are bounteous dishes of mashed potato, turnip, an' squash, and the celery is very white and cold, the biscuits are light an' hot, and the stewed cranberries are red as Laura's cheeks. Amos and I get the drumsticks; Mary wants the wish-bone to put over the door for Hiram, but Helen gets it. Poor Mary, she always did have to give up to 'rushin' Helen,' as we call her.

The pies, oh, what pies Mother makes; no dyspepsia in 'em, but good-nature an' good health an' hospitality! Pumpkin pies, mince an' apple too, and then a big dish of pippins an' russets an' bellflowers, an', last of all, walnuts with cider from the Zebrina Dickerson farm! I tell you, there's a Thanksgivin' dinner for you! That's what we get in old Belchertown; an' that's the kind of livin' that makes the Yankees so all-fired good an' smart.

"But the best of all," said Ezra, very softly to himself, "oh, yes, the best scene in all the picture is when evenin' comes, when the lamps are lit in the parlour, when the neighbours come in, and when there is music an' singin' an' games. An' it's this part o' the picture that makes me homesick now and fills my heart with a longin' I never had before; an' yet it sort o' mellows an' comforts me, too. Miss Serena Cadwell, whose beau was killed in the war, plays on the melodeon, and we all sing, all on us, men, women folks, an' children. Sam Merritt is there, an' he sings a tenor song about love. The women sort of whisper round that he's goin' to be married to a Palmer lady nex' spring, an' I think to myself I never heard better singin' than Sam's.

Then we play games, proverbs, buzz, clap-in-clap-out, Copenhagen, fox-an'-geese, button-button-who's-got-the-button, spin-the-platter, go-to-Jerusalem, my-ship's-come-in, and all the rest. The ol' folks play with the young folks just as nat'ral as can be; and we all laugh when Deacon Hosea Cowles has to measure six yards of love ribbon with Miss Hepsy Newton, and cut each yard with a kiss; for the deacon has been sort o' purrin' round Miss Hepsy for goin' on two years.

Then, aft'r a while, when Mary an' Helen bring in the cookies, nut-cakes, cider, an' apples, Mother says, 'I don't b'lieve we're goin' to have enough apples to go round; Ezry, I guess I'll have to get you to go down-cellar for some more.'

Then I says, 'All right, Mother, I'll go, providin' some one'll go along an' hold the candle.' An' when I say this I look right at Laura and she blushes.

Then Helen, just for meanness, says, 'Ezry, I s'pose you ain't willin' to have your fav'rite sister go down-cellar with you an' catch her death o' cold?' But Mary, who has been showin' Hiram Peabody the phot'graph album for more 'n an hour, comes to the rescue an' makes Laura take the candle, and she shows Laura how to hold it so it won't go out.

"The cellar is warm an' dark. There are cobwebs all between the rafters an' everywhere else except on the shelves where Mother keeps the butter an' eggs an' other things that would freeze in the buttery upstairs. The apples are in barrels up against the wall, near the potater-bin. How fresh an' sweet they smell! Laura thinks she sees a mouse, an' she trembles an' wants to jump up on the pork-barrel, but I tell her that there shan't no mouse hurt her while I'm around; and I mean it, too, for the sight of Laura a-tremblin' makes me as strong as one of Father's steers.

'What kind of apples do you like best, Ezry?' asks Laura, 'russets or greenin's or crow-eggs or bell-flowers or Baldwins or pippins?'

'I like the Baldwins best,' says I, "coz they've got red cheeks jest like yours.'

'Why, Ezry Thompson! how you talk!' says Laura. 'You oughter be ashamed of yourself!'

But when I get the dish filled up with apples there ain't a Baldwin in all the lot that can compare with the bright red of Laura's cheeks. An' Laura knows it, too, an' she sees the mouse ag'in, an' screams, and then the candle goes out, and we are in a dreadful stew. But I, bein' almost a man, contrive to bear up under it, and knowin' she is an orph'n, I comfort an' encourage Laura the best I know how, and we are almost up-stairs when Mother comes to the door and wants to know what has kept us so long. Just as if Mother doesn't know! Of course she does; an' when Mother kisses Laura goodbye that night there is in the act a tenderness that speaks more sweetly than even Mother's words.

"It is so like Mother," mused Ezra, "so like her with her gentleness an' clingin' love. Hers is the sweetest picture of all, and hers the best love."

Dream on, Ezra; dream of the old home with its dear ones, its holy influences, and its precious inspiration, mother. Dream on in the far-away firelight; and as the angel hand of memory unfolds these sacred visions, with you and them shall abide, like a Divine comforter, the spirit of thanksgiving.

La Belle Zoraïde

This story has been edited and adapted from Kate Chopin's Bayou Folk, first published in 1894 by the Houghton Mifflin Company of Boston and New York.

The summer night was hot and still; not a ripple of air swept over the marais. Yonder, across Bayou St. John, lights twinkled here and there in the darkness, and in the dark sky above a few stars were blinking. A lugger that had come out of the lake was moving with slow, lazy motion down the bayou. A man in the boat was singing a song.

The notes of the song came faintly to the ears of old Manna Loulou, herself as black as the night, who had gone out upon the gallery to open the shutters wide.

Something in the refrain reminded the woman of an old, half-forgotten Creole romance, and she began to sing it low to herself while she threw the shutters open:

"Lisett' to kité la plaine,

Mo perdi bonhair à moué;

Ziés à moué semblé fontaine,

Dépi mo pa miré toué."

And then this old song, a lover's lament for the loss of his mistress, floating into her memory, brought with it the story she would tell Madame, who lay in her sumptuous mahogany bed, waiting to be fanned and put to sleep to the sound of one of Manna Loulou's stories. The old negress had already bathed her mistress's pretty white feet and kissed them lovingly, one, then the other. She had brushed her mistress's beautiful hair, that was as soft and shining as satin, and was the colour of Madame's wedding-ring. Now, when she re-entered the room, she moved softly toward the bed, and seating herself there began gently to fan Madame Delisle.

Manna Loulou was not always ready with her story, for Madame would hear none but those which were true. But tonight the story was all there in Manna Loulou's head, the story of la belle Zoraïde, and she told it to her mistress in the soft Creole patois, whose music and charm no English words can convey.

La belle Zoraïde had eyes that were so dusky, so beautiful, that any man who gazed too long into their depths was sure to lose his head, and even his heart sometimes. Her soft, smooth skin was the colour of café-au-lait. As for her elegant manners, her svelte and graceful figure, they were the envy of half the ladies who visited her mistress, Madame Delarivière.

No wonder Zoraïde was as charming and as dainty as the finest lady of la rue Royale: from a toddling thing she had been brought up at her mistress's side; her fingers had never done rougher work than sewing a fine muslin seam; and she even had her own little servant to wait upon her. Madame, who was her godmother as well as her mistress, would often say to her, "Remember, Zoraïde, when you are ready to marry, it must be in a way to do honour to your bringing up. It will be at the Cathedral. Your wedding gown, your corbeille, all will be of the best; I shall see to that myself. You know, M'sieur Ambroise is ready whenever you say the word; and his master is willing to do as much for him as I shall do for you. It is a union that will please me in every way."

M'sieur Ambroise was then the body servant of Doctor Langlé. La belle Zoraïde detested the little mulatto, with his shining whiskers and his small eyes, that were cruel and false as a snake's. She would cast down her own mischievous eyes, and say, "Ah, nénaine, I am so happy, so contented here at your side just as I am. I don't want to marry now; next year, perhaps, or the next." And Madame would smile indulgently and remind Zoraïde that a woman's charms are not everlasting.

But the truth of the matter was, Zoraïde had seen le beau Mézor dance the Bamboula in Congo Square. That was a sight to hold one rooted to the ground. Mézor was as straight as a cypress-tree and as proud looking as a king. His body, bare to the waist, was like a column of ebony and it glistened like oil.

Poor Zoraïde's heart grew sick in her bosom with love for le beau Mézor from the moment she saw the fierce gleam of his eye, lighted by the inspiring strains of the Bamboula, and beheld the stately movements of his splendid body swaying and quivering through the figures of the dance.

But when she knew him later, and he came near her to speak with her, all the fierceness was gone out of his eyes, and she saw only kindness in them and heard only gentleness in his voice; for love had taken possession of him also, and Zoraïde was more distracted than ever. When Mézor was not dancing Bamboula in Congo Square, he was hoeing sugar-cane, barefooted and half naked, in his master's field outside of the city. Doctor Langlé was his master as well as M'sieur Ambroise's.

One day, when Zoraïde kneeled before her mistress, drawing on Madame's silken stockings, that were of the finest, she said, "Nénaine, you have spoken to me often of marrying. Now, at last, I have chosen a husband, but it is not M'sieur Ambroise; it is le beau Mézor that I want and no other." And Zoraïde hid her face in her hands when she had said that, for she guessed, rightly enough, that her mistress would be very angry. And, indeed, Madame Delarivière was at first speechless with rage. When she finally spoke it was only to gasp out, exasperated, "That man! That negro! Bon Dieu Seigneur, but this is too much!'

"Am I white, nénaine?" pleaded Zoraïde.

"You white! Malheureuse! You deserve to have the lash laid upon you like any other slave; you have proven yourself no better than the worst."

"I am not white," persisted Zoraïde, respectfully and gently. "Doctor Langlé gives me his slave to marry, but he would not give me his son. Then, since I am not white, let me have from out of my own race the one whom my heart has chosen."

However, you may well believe that Madame would not hear to that. Zoraïde was forbidden to speak to Mézor, and Mézor was cautioned against seeing Zoraïde again.

"But you know how the people are, Ma'zélle Titite," added Manna Loulou, smiling a little sadly.

There is no mistress, no master, no king nor priest who can hinder them from loving when they will. And these two found ways and means.

When months had passed by, Zoraïde, who had grown unlike herself, sober and preoccupied, said again to her mistress, "'Nénaine, you would not let me have Mézor for my husband; but I have disobeyed you, I have sinned. Kill me if you wish, nénaine: forgive me if you will; but when I heard le beau Mézor say to me, 'Zoraïde, mo l'aime toi,' I could have died, but I could not have helped loving him."

This time Madame Delarivière was so actually pained, so wounded at hearing Zoraïde's confession, that there was no place left in her heart for anger. She could utter only confused reproaches. But she was a woman of action rather than of words, and she acted promptly. Her first step was to induce Doctor Langlé to sell Mézor. Doctor Langlé, who was a widower, had long wanted to marry Madame Delarivière, and he would willingly have walked on all fours at noon through the Place d'Armes if she wanted him to. Naturally he lost no time in disposing of le beau Mézor, who was sold away into Georgia, or the Carolinas, or one of those distant countries far away, where he would no longer hear his Creole tongue spoken, nor dance Calinda, nor hold la belle Zoraïde in his arms.

The poor thing was heartbroken when Mézor was sent away from her, but she took comfort and hope in the thought of her baby that she would soon be able to clasp to her breast.

La belle Zoraïde's sorrows had now begun in earnest. Not only sorrows but sufferings, and with the anguish of maternity came the shadow of death. But there is no agony that a mother will not forget when she holds her first-born to her heart, and presses her lips upon the baby flesh that is her own, yet far more precious than her own.

So, instinctively, when Zoraïde came out of the awful shadow she gazed questioningly about her and felt with her trembling hands upon either side of her. "Où li, mo piti a moin? Where is my little one?" she asked imploringly.

Madame who was there and the nurse who was there both told her in turn, "To piti à toi, li mouri'. Your little one is dead", which was a wicked falsehood that must have caused the angels in heaven to weep. For the baby was living and well and strong. It had at once been removed from its mother's side, to be sent away to Madame's plantation, far up the coast.

Zoraïde could only moan in reply, "Li mouri, li mouri," and she turned her face to the wall.

Madame had hoped, in thus depriving Zoraïde of her child, to have her young waiting-maid again at her side free, happy, and beautiful as of old. But there was a more powerful will than Madame's at work, the will of the good God, who had already designed that Zoraïde should grieve with a sorrow that was never more to be lifted in this world. La belle Zoraïde was no more. In her stead was a sad-eyed woman who mourned night and day for her baby. "Li mouri, li mouri," she would sigh over and over again to those about her, and to herself when others grew weary of her complaint.

Yet, in spite of all, M'sieur Ambroise was still in the notion to marry her. A sad wife or a merry one was all the same to him so long as that wife was Zoraïde. And she seemed to consent, or rather submit, to the approaching marriage as though nothing mattered any longer in this world.

One day, a servant entered the room in which Zoraïde sat sewing. With a look of strange and vacuous happiness upon her face, Zoraïde arose hastily. "Hush, hush," she whispered, lifting a warning finger, "my little one is asleep. You must not awaken her."

Upon the bed was a senseless bundle of rags shaped like an infant in swaddling clothes. Over this dummy the woman had drawn the mosquito bar, and she was sitting contentedly beside it. In short, from that day Zoraïde was demented. Night nor day did she lose sight of the doll that lay in her bed or in her arms.

And now Madame was stung with sorrow and remorse at seeing this terrible affliction that had befallen her dear Zoraïde. Consulting with Doctor Langlé, they decided to bring back to the mother the real baby of flesh and blood that was now toddling about, and kicking its heels in the dust yonder upon the plantation.

It was Madame herself who led the pretty, tiny little "griffe" girl to her mother. Zoraïde was sitting upon a stone bench in the courtyard, listening to the soft splashing of the fountain, and watching the fitful shadows of the palm leaves upon the broad, white flagging.

"Here," said Madame, approaching, "here, my poor dear Zoraïde, is your own little child. Keep her. She is yours. No one will ever take her from you again."

Zoraïde looked with sullen suspicion upon her mistress and the child before her. Reaching out a hand she thrust the little one mistrustfully away from her. With the other hand she clasped the rag bundle fiercely to her breast, for she suspected a plot to deprive her of it.

Nor could she ever be induced to let her own child approach her; and finally the little one was sent back to the plantation, where she was never to know the love of mother or father.

And now this is the end of Zoraïde's story. She was never known again as la belle Zoraïde, but ever after as Zoraïde la folle, whom no one ever wanted to marry, not even M'sieur Ambroise. She lived to be an old woman, whom some people pitied and others laughed at, always clasping her bundle of rags, her 'piti'.

"Are you asleep, Ma'zélle Titite?"

"No, I am not asleep; I was thinking. Ah, the poor little one, Manna Loulou, the poor little one! Better had she died!"

The Rooster That Crowed Too Soon

This story has been edited and adapted from Abbie Phillips Walker's The Sandman's Hour, first published in 1917 by Harper & Brothers, London and New York.

Red Rooster felt it was time he showed the new drake that had come to live in the barnyard that he was a very brave rooster, as well as the ruler of the barnyard.

So the next time he saw the drake he said, "I suppose you have been in many battles, and no doubt the home you have just come from will miss your protection as well as your company.'

"No," replied the drake, "I never was in a battle. I do not quarrel with anyone. I believe in living in peace with all around me."

"Oh, well, that is all very well for you, perhaps," said the rooster, "but for me, it is a different matter. I have to protect all the hens and chickens and I also protect myself. I can whip any rooster around here, and no one dares come into my yard."

The drake did not reply, for just then a strange rooster came into the yard, and Red Rooster ran at him with sweeping wings. He pecked at the intruder and spurred him until he was glad to run away.

"There, what did I tell you?" said Red Rooster, coming back to the drake. "I am the greatest fighter around this part of the country. I am not afraid of anything."

"Oh, don't talk so much about it," said the dog from his house nearby. "I think there are a few things even you are afraid of, Mr. Rooster. I guess you would run from a fox."

"I am not afraid of a fox," said Red Rooster. "I can scare him by crowing loudly. Master knows when I make a great noise it is time for him to find the cause. Oh, I am very brave and can take care of myself."

Red Rooster felt so brave that he thought the highest place he could get on the wall would be a good place to talk about his bravery, so he flew up on the wall by the gate, and then to the top of the hen-house.

Madam Pig was in her pen on the other side. "Madam Pig," he said, "did you see me whip that impudent rooster that came through our yard?"

Madam Pig grunted that she did not, as she could not see over the wall.

"You surely missed a great sight," said the rooster, stretching his neck and strutting along the roof. "I am a brave fellow. I never allow anyone to come around here that does not belong here. I have just been telling the new drake about my prowess and bravery.

"Mr. Drake," he called, as the new drake and his family waddled past the hen-house, "if you need protection at any time do not hesitate to call upon me."

A robin perched upon the roof not far from him, and Red Rooster flew at him. "Go away," he said. "I am very fierce and brave, and if you were as large as a cow I should attack you just the same. I am not afraid of anything."

Red Rooster strutted up and down, crowing and thinking how brave he was, and so intent was he upon his greatness that he did not heed the warning cries that came from the fowls in the yard below him.

In a moment more a big hawk swooped down and held Red Rooster in his claws. He started to fly just as the shot from a gun sounded, and Red Rooster fell to the ground. He jumped up and shook himself, and looked in time to see his master pick up the dead hawk.

"I guess that hawk won't show himself around here again," he said. "That was a very hard fight, but I won, even if I did get a tumble."

"Well, if you are not a conceited fellow!" laughed the dog, "but I was not the only one that saw the hawk start off with you, and we all know that if master had not shot it you would not be here to crow tomorrow morning."

"No," piped the robin from a tree, "you were telling me how brave you were, and the hawk was not half as large as a cow. You were not very brave when he came upon you. You did not do a thing. Oh, dear! It was so funny to hear you crowing about your bravery and then to see you caught up so soon by a hawk that is only a little larger than you."

The drake and all his family were listening, and Madam Pig had put her head over the wall to listen. Poor Red Rooster felt that it was no time to crow about his bravery, so he walked away with all the dignity he could muster.

"He crowed too soon," said the drake.

"He crowed too much," said the dog.

"He crowed too loud," said the robin, "or he would have heard the warning cries from the hens and chickens."

Compensations

This story has been edited and adapted from Henry W. Shoemaker's Allegheny Episodes, first published in 1922 by the Altoona Tribune Company, based out of Altoona, Pennsylvania. This was one of a series of collections forming the Pennsylvania Folk Lore series.

It seemed that Andrew McMeans and Oscar Wellendorf were born to be engaged in rivalry, although judging by their antecedents, the former was in a class beyond, McMeans being well-born, of old Scotch-Irish stock, a valuable asset on the Allegheny. Wellendorf, of Pennsylvania Dutch origin, of people coming from one of the eastern counties, was consequently rated much lower socially, had much more to overcome in the way of life's obstacles. The boys were almost of school age; Wellendorf, if anything, was a month or two older. In school in Hickory Valley neither was a brilliant scholar, but they were evenly matched, and although not aspiring to lead their classes, felt a keen rivalry between one another.

When school days were over, and they took to rafting as the most obvious occupation in the locality, their rivalries as to who could run a fleet quickest to Pittsburgh, and come back for another, was the talk of the river. In love it was not different, and despite the talk in McMean's family that he should marry Anna McNamor, daughter of his father's life-long friend, Tabor McNamor, the girl showed an open preference for Oscar Wellendorf.

The old Scotch-Irish families were, as the London Times said in commenting on some of the characteristics of the late Senator Quay (inherited from his mother, born Stanley) "clannish to degree," and Anna's "people" were equally anxious that she marry one of her own stock, and not ally herself with the despised and socially insignificant "Dutch". Old Grandmother McClinton called attention to the fact that the headstrong beauty was not without a strain of "Dutch" blood herself, for her great, great grandmother had been none other than the winsome Madelon Ury, a Swiss-Huguenot girl of Berks County, who, when surprised in the field hoeing corn by a blood-thirsty native warrior, had dropped her hoe and taken to her heels. She ran so fast over the soft ground that she would have escaped her moccasined pursuer had she not taken time to cross a stone fence. This gave the man the chance to throw his tomahawk, striking her in the neck, and she fell face downward over the wall. Just as her foe was overtaking her, Martin McClinton, a sword maker from Lancaster, who was passing along the Shamokin trail en route to deliver a sabre to Colonel Conrad Weiser, at Heidelberg, rushed to her rescue and shot down the warrior, so that he fell dead across his fair victim.

McClinton extricated the tomahawk from her neck, bound up the wound with his own neckerchief and carried her to her parent's home, near the Falling Springs. He remained until the wound healed when he married her. Later the pair migrated west of the Alleghenies.

Madelon McClinton was very dark, with an oval face and aquiline features, possibly having had a strain of Pennsylvania Jewish blood to account for her brunette type of beauty. She always wore a red scarf wrapped about her neck, being proud and sensitive of the ugly long white scar left by her assailant's weapon.

This ancestress, so Grandmother McClinton thought, was responsible for Anna's affinity for the rather prosaic Dutchman Wellendorf. Although the girl was open in her preference for Oscar, she did not make a decision as to matrimony for some time. When Wellendorf was absent, she was nicer to McMeans than anyone else. However, if Oscar appeared on the scene, she had eyes and ears for no other.

On one occasion when the two young men started down the river on their rafts, proudly standing at the steering oars in the rear, for the Allegheny pilots rode at the back of the rafts, whereas those on the Susquehanna were always at the front. Anna was at the water's edge, under a huge buttonwood tree, or, as Wellendorf called it in the breezy vernacular of the Pennsylvania Dutch, a "wasserpitcher", and waved a red kerchief impartially at both.

McMean's raft on this trip was of "pig iron", that is unpeeled hemlock logs, as heavy as lead, and became submerged when he had only gotten as far as the mouth of French Creek. He had to run ashore to try and devise ways and means to save it from sinking altogether, while Wellendorf floated along serenely on his raft of white pine, and was to Pittsburgh and back home before McMeans ever reached the "Smoky City."

John C. French tells us that White Pine (pinus strobus) was King, and his dusky Queen was a beautiful Wild Cherry, lovely as Queen

Aliquippa. Rafting lumber from Warren County began about 1800, and it reached its maximum in the decade, 1830 to 1840. The early history of Warren County abounds in very interesting incidents, along the larger Allegheny River, from rafts of pine lumber assembled to couple up for Pittsburgh fleets.

After the purchase of Louisiana, in 1804, the hardy lumbermen decided to extend their markets for pine beyond Pittsburgh, Wheeling, Cincinnati and Louisville, to go, in fact, to New Orleans with pine and cherry lumber. So large boats were built in the winter of 1805 and 1806 at many mills. Seasoned lumber of the best quality was loaded into the flat boats and they untied on April 1, 1806, for the run of two thousand miles, bordered by forests to the river's edge.

It was in defiance to 'All Fools' Day', but they went through and sold both lumber and boats. For clear pine lumber, $40.00 was the price per one thousand feet received at New Orleans, just double the Pittsburgh price at that date. For three years thereafter the mills of Warren County sent boats to New Orleans loaded with lumber, and the men returned on foot. Joseph Mead, Abraham Davis and John Watt took boats through in 1807, coming back via Philadelphia on coastal sailing ships.

The pilots and men returned by river boats or on foot, as they best could. The markets along the Ohio from Pittsburgh to St. Louis soon took all the lumber from the Allegheny mills, and the longer trips were gladly discontinued.

It was in 1850 that there came the first lumber famine at Pittsburgh. Owing to the low price of lumber and an unfavourable winter for the forest work, few rafts of lumber and board timber went down the Allegheny on the spring freshets, but the November floods brought one hundred rafts that sold for more favourable prices than had previously prevailed. Clear pine lumber sold readily for $18.00 and common pine lumber for $9.00 per one thousand feet.

The renown of these prices stimulated lumbering on the Allegheny headwaters and the larger creeks. So the demand for lumber was supplied and the railroads soon began to bring lumber from many sawmills. The board timber was hewed on four sides, so there were only five inches of wane on each of the four corners. These rafts of round-square timber were sold by square feet to Pittsburgh sawmills.

Rafts of pine boards at headwater mills were made up of platforms, 16 feet square and from 18 to 25 courses thick, 9 pins or "grubs" holding boards in place as rafted. Four or five platforms were coupled in tandem with 3 feet "cribs" at each joint, making an elastic piece 73 feet or 92 feet long for a 4 or 5 platform piece as the case might be, 10 feet wide.

At Larrabee or at Millgrove four of these pieces were coupled into a Warren fleet, 32 feet wide, 149 feet or 187 feet long.

Four Warren pieces or fleets were put together at Warren to make up a Pittsburgh fleet. At Pittsburgh four or more Pittsburgh fleets were coupled to make an Ohio River fleet. Some became very large, often covering nearly two acres of surface, containing about 1,500,000 feet of lumber at Cincinnati or at Louisville. They each had a hut for sheltering the men and for cooking their food. They often ran all night on the Ohio. To find where the shore was on a very dark night, the men would throw potatoes, judging from the sound how far away the riverbank was and of their safe or dangerous position. These men were of rugged bodies and of daring minds.

A small piece, in headwaters and creeks, had an oar or sweep at each end of the piece to steer the raft with. Each oar usually had two men to pull it. An oar-stem was from 28 to 35 feet long, 8″ by 8″, and tapered to 4″ by 4″, shaved to round hand-hold near the end toward centre of raft. The oar blade was 12′, 14′ or 16′ long, and 18″ to 20″ wide, a pine plank, 4″ thick at the oar-stem socket, and 1″ thick at the out-end, tapered its whole length.

There were other sizes of stem and blade, but the above indicates the power that guided a raft of lumber along the flood-tides, crooked streams, and over a dozen mill dams to the broader river below.

From the Allegheny boats or scows, 30 feet long and 11 feet wide, carried loads of baled hay, butter, eggs and other farm produce to the oil fields of Venango County in the '60's, sold there and took oil in barrels to the refinery at Pittsburgh. Then sold the scows to carry coal or goods down the Ohio.

Mr. Westerman built five boats at Roulette about 1870, 40 feet long and 12 feet wide, loaded them with lumber and shingles and started for Pittsburgh, but the boats were too long for the dams and broke up at Burtville, the first dam.

Much of the pine timber of the west half of Potter county was cut in sawlogs and sent to mills at Millgrove and Weston's in log drives down the river and Oswayo Creek into the State of New York. The lumber was shipped via the Genesee Valley Canal to Albany and New York City and other points on the Hudson River.

The first steamboat to steam up the river from Warren was in 1830. It was built by Archibald Tanner, Warren's first merchant, and

David Dick and others of Meadville. It was built in Pittsburgh; the steamer was called Allegheny. It went to Olean, returned and went out of commission.

While the steamer was passing a reservation, some twenty odd miles above Warren, the famous chief, Cornplanter, paddled his canoe out to the vessel and actually paddled his small craft up stream and around the Allegheny, the old chief giving a vigorous war hoop as he accomplished the proud feat.

Chief Cornplanter, alias John O'Bail, first took his young men to Clarion County, about 1795, to learn the method of lumbering, and in 1796 he built a sawmill on Jenneseedaga Creek, later named Cornplanter Run, in Warren County, and rafted lumber down the Allegheny to Pittsburgh for many years.

Many tributary streams, such as Clarion, Tionesta and Oswayo, contributed rafts each year to make up the fleets that descended the Allegheny River from 1796 to 1874, in our story's rafting days.

We must mention the Hotel Boyer, on the Duquesne Way, on the Allegheny River bank, near the "Point" at Pittsburgh, where the raftsmen and the lumbermen foregathered, traded, ate and drank together, after each trip. Natives were good pilots, but must be kept sober on the rafts. 'Bootleggers' along the river often ran boats out to the rafts and relieved the droughty crews by dispensing bottles of 'red-eye' from the long tops of the boots they wore."

Of the big trees in the Allegheny country, Dr. J. T. Rothrock, "Father of Pennsylvania Forestry," has said, "About 1860, when I was with a crew surveying the line for the Sunbury & Erie Railroad, we had some difficulty in getting away from a certain location. A preliminary line came in conflict with an enormous original white pine tree, and the transitman shouted 'cut down that tree'. After it was felled another nearby was found to be in the way, and was ordered out. The stump of the first tree, four feet above the ground measured 6 feet, 3 inches in diameter; of the second tree a trifle over 6 feet. Such was the wastefulness of the day."

As soon as Oscar returned he saw Anna forthwith. She was in a particularly pliant mood, and in response to his direct question if she would marry him, replied she would, and the couple boarded the train at Warren for Buffalo City, where they were married.

When Andrew McMeans came back from his protracted expedition they were already home from their honeymoon, and residing with the elder McNamors in the big brick house, overlooking the Bend. Andrew McMeans felt his jilting deeply; it was the first time that any real disappointment had come in the twenty-one years of his life; he had imagined that, despite her predilection for Wellendorf, he would yet win her, and his pride as well as his heart was lacerated. Outwardly he revealed little, but inwardly a peculiar melancholy such as he had never felt before overcame him, and like Lincoln, after the death of Ann Rutledge, he realized that he must either "die or get better."

Anna seemed happy enough in her new life, and liked to flaunt her devotion to Oscar whenever her rejected lover was about. Ordinarily this might have wounded him still deeper, but he was absorbing fresh anxieties, reading Herbert Spencer, whose abominable agnosticism soon wrecked his faith, and bereft of love and the solace of immortality, he became the most wretched of men.

It was five years after Anna's elopement, and when she was twenty-one years old, that one morning she started for Endeavour to get the mail and make some purchases at the country store. It was a cold, raw day in the early spring, and the wild pigeons were flying. The beechwoods on both sides of the road were alive with gunners, old and young. Someone fired a shot which hurtled close to the nose of the old roan family horse, a track horse in his day, and he took the bit in his teeth and ran away madly, with the buggy careening after him. Anna, standing up in the vehicle, was sawing on the lines until he crashed into a big ash tree and fractured the poor girl's skull. She was picked up by some of the hunters and carried home unconscious. The next thing was to get the news to her husband. Oscar at that time had just finished a raft on West Hickory Creek, while his old time rival, McMeans, was completing one on East Hickory, which stream flowed into "The Beautiful River", almost directly opposite to the West Hickory Run.

About the moment that Anna received her cruel death stroke, the two rafts were being launched simultaneously, with much cheering on both banks, for partisanship ran high among dwellers on either side of the river. Members of the family hurried to the river side to watch for the Wellendorf raft, to "head him off" before it was too late. It was several hours after the accident when the two rival rafts, with the stalwart young pilots at the sterns, swept around the Bend, traveling "nip and tuck". It promised to be an evenly matched race, barring accidents, clear to Pittsburgh. The skippers of the contending yachts for the American Cup could not have been more enthused for their races than were Andrew McMeans and Oscar Wellendorf.

In front of the McNamor homestead several women were to be seen running up and down the grassy sward, frantically waving red and green shawls. What could they mean? They were so vehement that Oscar divined something was wrong, and steered ashore, followed by McMeans, who, noting the absence of Anna from the signalling party, feared that a mishap had befallen her.

Both young men jumped ashore almost simultaneously, leaving their rafts to their helpers. The worst had happened. Anna was in the house with a fractured skull, and the doctors said she could not live the night. If anything, McMeans turned the paler of the two. The men said little as they followed the women up the boardwalk to the house.

That night McMeans, who asked to be allowed to remain until the outcome of the case, for the river had lost its attractions, was sitting in the kitchen with Grandmother McClinton. The raw air had blown itself into a gale after sundown, and during the night the fierce wind beat about the eaves and corners of the house like an avenging fury. The tall old clock, made years before by John Vanderslice, of Reading, on top of which was a stuffed Colishay, or grey fox, with an uncommonly fine brush, was striking twelve. Amid the storm a wailing voice joined in the din, incessantly, so that there was no mistaking it, the Warning of the McClintons.

The old grandmother watched McMeans' face until she saw that he understood. Then she nodded to him. "It is strange how that thing has followed the McClinton family for hundreds of years. In Scotland it was their 'Caointeach', in Ireland their 'Banshee', in Pennsylvania their 'Token' or 'Warning'. It never fails."

As McMeans listened to the terrible shrieks of anguish, which sometimes drowned the storm, he shivered with pity for the lost soul out there in the cold, giving the death message, so melancholy and sad, and perhaps unwillingly. Anna lay upstairs in her room, facing the river, or windward side of the house, and the Warning was evidently somewhere below her window, where the water in waves like the sea, was over-running the banks.

On a kitchen chair still lay a red Paisley shawl that had been used to signal to Wellendorf earlier in the day. It seemed ample and warm. Picking it up, McMeans went to the kitchen door, which he opened with some effort in the force of the gale, and, walking around the house, laid it on one of the benches at the front door, saying, "Put on this shawl, and come around to the leeward side of the house."

When he returned, he said to Grandmother McClinton, "That Token's voice touched me somehow tonight. Something tells me she hated her task, is cold and miserable. I left the shawl on the front porch and told her to come out of the wind."

After that they both noticed that the unhappy wailings ceased, there was nothing that vied with the storm.

"Perhaps you have laid her," said Grandmother McClinton. "Anna may now pull through."

But these words were barely out of her mouth, when Oscar Wellendorf, pale as a ghost, appeared in the kitchen to say that Anna had just passed away. Andrew felt her death keenly, but he was also satisfied that perhaps he had by an act of kindness, removed the Warning of the McClintons. He was more convinced when a year later Anna's father joined the majority, then her mother, with no visits from the mournful-voiced Warning.

Five years more rolled around, and Andrew McMeans, still unmarried, and cherishing steadfastly the memory of his beloved Anna, embarked his fleet for Pittsburgh. It was a morning in the early spring, the air was soft and warm, and the shad flies were flitting about. He arrived in safety, but was some time collecting his money, as he was dealing with a scamp, and meanwhile put up at a boarding house on the river front, near the Hotel Boyer. The afternoon after his arrival he was sitting on the porch of his lodgings, gazing out at the rushing, swirling river, which ran bank full, on a bench similar in all ways to the one on which he had laid the shawl to warm the freezing back of the Warning of the McClintons. Somehow he fell to thinking about that ghost, and its disappearance, and of Anna McNamor, and how much he would give if only he could see her again.

He recalled how the old grandmother had told him that some families married out of the Warning, while others married into it, much as he had heard was the case with the Assembly Ball in Philadelphia. The McClinton Warning had evidently clung to the female line, as it had been very much in evidence when Anna McNamor's time had come.

Something made him look up the street. Coming slowly towards him was a slender schoolgirl, with a little green hat perched on her head, the living image of Anna, dead for five years! He almost fell off the bench in surprise, to note the same slim oval face, the aquiline features, and hazel eyes that he had known and loved so well. She paused for a moment in front of the house next door, holding her schoolbooks in her arms, while she looked out at the raging river. The spring breezes blowing her short skirts showed her slim legs encased in light brown worsted stockings. Then she went indoors.

It did not take him long to seek his landlady and learn that she was a flesh and blood, sure enough girl, Anna Harbord by name, whose mother, widow of Mike Harbord, an old time riverman, also ran a boarding house. It was not many days before some errand brought the girl to the house where McMeans was stopping, and matters fortuitously adjusted themselves so that he met her.

He was struck by her similarity to the dead girl, even the tones of her voice, and it seemed strange she should have such a counterpart. She appeared friendly disposed towards him from the start, and it was like a compensation sent after all his years of disappointment and loneliness. She was then sixteen years old, and must have been eleven when her "double" passed away.

As their acquaintance grew into love, and all seemed so serene, as if it was to be, Andrew McMeans gradually regaining his faith, human and divine, felt he owed his happiness to the Warning of the McClintons', whose misery he had appeased by taking the cloak out to her, while engaged in her disagreeable duty of foretelling the coming dissolution of the unfortunate girl.

McMeans and Anna Harbord married. They decided to remain in Pittsburgh, and he became in a few years a successful and respected businessman.

If few persons had been kind to ghosts, certainly he had profited by his interest in the welfare of the "Warning of the McClintons". The girl's mother informed him that in the early spring, about five years before, her daughter had been seized with a cataleptic attack, had laid for days unconscious, and when she came out of it, her entire personality, even the colour of her eyes, had changed. Could it have been, the young husband often thought, as he sat gazing at his bride with undisguised admiration, some act of the grateful

"Warning," in sending Anna McNamor's soul to enter the body of this girl in Pittsburgh, and reserving her for him, safe and sound from Wellendorf and all harm, until his travels brought her across his path! Human personality, he reasoned, is merely a means to an end. The unfinished life of Anna McNamor could not go on, like a flower unfolding, until her fragrance had been spent on the one who needed it most. Then he would shudder at the idea that if the schoolgirl, who stopped to look at the flooded river, had started on again, passing him by, never to see her again. He would feel that he had been dreaming perhaps, until, touching his wife's soft creamy cheeks, would realize that she was actually there, and his.

Through her his soul took on new light, and from a vigorous young woodsman, he was slowly but surely passing into an intellectual existence. He had been strangely favoured by the mainsprings of destiny, and why should he not give the world all that was best in him. Life, ruthless though it seems, has always compensations, and if we live rightly and truly, the debt will be owing us, whereas most of us through mistakes and misdeeds, have a great volume of retribution coming in an inevitable sequence.

Death's Valley, Or, The Golden Boulder

This story has been edited and adapted from May Wentworth's Fairy Tales From Gold Lands, first published in 1868 by A. Roman and Company.

Years ago, even before what Californians understand to be the "early days," Dick Fielding was promoted to a captaincy in the United States Army.

Merry days were those, while he was stationed near the metropolitan city. Good pay, little work, brilliant parties to attend, and beautiful women to make love to. Love making seemed the natural element of the gay young captain, and thanks to his handsome face and shining epaulettes, he was very successful.

In this world our dear delights are but fleeting as the smiles of an April day, so thought poor Dick as he sat one morning about eleven o'clock at his luxurious breakfast, reading a dispatch from head-quarters that doomed him to the wilderness of Fort Tejon, far below the quaint old Spanish town of Los Angelos.

'Twas a sad day for the gallant young captain, but all his sighs and regrets were unavailing. There was no reprieve and orders must be obeyed. Fortunately Dick was of an elastic temperament, and the love of adventure and the charm of novelty which the new country possessed for him soon returned to him that zest for life which youth and health seldom entirely lose.

Southern California has a most generous climate, producing in the valleys the luxurious vegetation of the tropics, and on the hills and mountains the hardier products of the temperate zone.

Dick was a favourite among the officers, social and joyous in his disposition, and he became the life of the garrison. He was a fine horseman, and often he would join a party of the Mexican rangers in their excursions, and ride for days over the beautiful country round Fort Tejon.

He could shoot an arrow very handsomely, and by his easy good nature he was soon on friendly terms with the native tribes, who in that part of the country are so mixed with the native Californians or Mexicans that it is difficult to distinguish the races.

He became an expert in all the athletic sports of the country, but with all he could do, the monotony of a life at Fort Tejon was very wearisome to him; so when he found a beautiful young girl among the local tribes, he plunged recklessly into his old habit of love making, and in a few weeks he was domesticated in a little adobe house near the fort with his pretty bride, who amused him for the time like any other novelty of the country.

She, poor simple child of the wild-wood, worshiped her handsome, blue-eyed husband, and thought his hair and beard had stolen their golden beauty from the glowing sunshine.

After a time a little one came to the cottage, and the young mother was very happy in loving the father and child who made the wilderness a heaven for her.

Weeks, months, and years passed by, and Captain Fielding longed intensely to visit the bright city world again. He had grown weary of his wife, and his son in his eyes was only a young papoose, of whom he was very much ashamed.

At length the order came for his reprieve. He was summoned to return to the Atlantic States; but of this he said nothing to his wife. One bright spring morning he left her looking out after him from the door of the little adobe, holding her three-year old boy in her arms, smiling and telling him in her own soft language that dear papa would come back at evening.

The burning fingers of remorse pressed heavily upon the father's heart as he looked upon the pretty picture, but only for a moment. He turned away, saying with a sigh of relief, "She'll soon forget me, for some Chief, perhaps," and was gone from her sight out into the distance, on toward the great busy world.

Night came on with its damps and darkness, wrapping the heart of the young wife in its shroud of shadows, never to be lifted till the brightness of the spirit land made glad morning shine about her.

Day by day she watched the shadows lengthen, hoping when the sun went down in the crimson west that he would return; but the golden moonlight found her watching in vain, swaying her sleeping boy to and fro in her arms, and drearily singing the song of her heart, in a voice from which the gladness of hope was fast dying out.

She called him Dick, for his father, and with a perseverance which only deep love could give her, talked his father's language to him in her pretty, imperfect way.

The little one grew to be a strong, handsome boy, with a dark Spanish face, and eyes full of fire, or love as his mood moved them. In some things he was like his father; exciting and dashing, and attractive in his disposition, he became a great favourite with the officers at Fort Tejon, who taught him to read and write and many other things, much to the delight of his mother, who would say with tears in her dark eyes, "If his father lives to return he will thank you better than I can."

In the spring she would say, "Before the orange-flowers ripen to golden fruit he will return," and in the autumn, "before the fair buds gladden the green hillsides he will be here!"

But springs and autumns passed, till the broken spirit, hopeless and weary with waiting, passed into the unknown future, and they buried her where the first rays of the morning sun fell upon the graveyard flowers.

Dick loved his mother fondly, and after she died he grew wilder and daring than ever, but with the undercurrent of his nature flowed all the subtle instinct of the native warrior.

Often at Fort Tejon he heard of the great world far beyond the wilderness, and he learned that gold was the talisman that opened the gates of earthly paradise. So he said in his heart, "I will have gold!"

Young as he was and wild in his nature, he saw a witching paradise in the soft blue eyes and sunny curls of the Colonel's young daughter Madeline, but no one knew that he worshiped her, no one but God and his own heart.

Among the native and Spanish boys Dick was chief. To the lowliest he was gentle, to the proudest, superior, and by a wonderful magnetic power in one so young he bowed them all to his will. No one among them thought to question his bidding; he was the ruler, and without a thought they obeyed him. He could ride fearlessly the wildest horse, send the truest arrow from the bow, and laughed carelessly at danger as though he bore a charmed life.

One evening he lay upon the green grass before a native encampment, looking dreamily up at the great golden moon as it sailed along through the clear summer sky, surrounded by the paler light of the modest stars, and thinking how Madeline was like the moon, queen of all maidens.

The rest were beautiful, but in comparison with the sweet Madeline were but attendant lights. Then he thought of the great world where one day Madeline would shine fairest of the fair, and that before he could enter the charmed circle he must win the talisman that would give him everything, but best of all, sweet Madeline.

Near him youths and maidens had gathered round an old man of their tribe, who was telling them the legend of the "Golden Boulder."

"Yes," said the old man, "white men would risk their lives for it, if they could only find the valley, but even our people, except for one tribe who make war upon all others, have lost trace of it; but there in the centre rises a great round boulder, yellow as the full moon, all gold, pure gold!"

"Where?" cried Dick, springing with one bound into the circle. Then for the first time he listened to the old tradition of the Golden Boulder in Death's Valley.

"Far to the south," said the old storyteller, "lies a country rich in gold and precious stones. The tribe who inhabits that region makes war with all who dare to cross the boundaries of their hunting-grounds. In some way they have become possessed of guns from which they shoot golden bullets with unerring precision.

"The country is shut in by mountains, and the great Colorado pours its waters through it. Far into the interior, deep down in the shadows, lies Death's Valley, and in its centre rises the great Golden Boulder, and round it are scattered innumerable precious stones, whose brightness pierces the dusky shadows with their shining light."

The tradition came from an old man of the hostile tribe who many years ago was taken prisoner. Many adventurous Mexicans and Spaniards had sought Death's Valley, but none had ever returned from its shroud of shadows.

Dick listened to the story with deep attention. For days the thought of it pursued him, and at night when he closed his eyes the great round boulder of gold rose before him, and the glittering stones made the night shining as the day.

He could learn nothing more from the tribes folk than the old tradition, but every day he became more resolved, at any hazard, to win the great talisman, gold, which alone could open the door of happiness and greatness for him; even if he were obliged to seek it among the shadows in Death's Valley, he would win it.

It was the early days of February, which in Lower California is the springtime of the year. Golden oranges still hung upon the trees amid the shining leaves and snow-white flowers, the buds of promise for the coming year, while everywhere gorgeous flowers brightened the fragrant hillsides and dewy valleys.

Without a word of farewell to anyone, Dick started out into the trackless wilderness alone, with only his rifle and a small hatchet to blaze the trees now and then. Guided by a native and unerring instinct, he reached the Colorado, as strong and vigorous as when he left the neighbourhood of Fort Tejon.

He had wanted for nothing; his trusty gun had supplied him with game, and the fruits of the wild-wood had furnished him dessert. Thus alone in the luxuriance of that sunny clime he wandered for days, but still no trace of the valley, or the Golden Boulder; but he was not disheartened.

Day and night, the gorgeous imagery that decked the future, gathered round him. As the reward of all this toil and lonely wanderings, he saw his golden hopes fulfilled, and the sunny curls of the Colonel's daughter resting upon his bosom. For this hope more than all others he laboured on.

It was the close of an excessively hot day. The dewy coolness of evening was delightful to the weary gold-seeker, and he threw himself down upon his couch of leaves, under the shadow of the forest trees, thinking the way was long and weary, and feeling the desolation of the solitary wilderness, casting its long shadows upon his heart.

But toil, is the mother of forgetfulness, and sleep was casting its drowsy mantle over his saddened musings, when his quick ear, detected a sound like a light, but rapid, footstep among the dried leaves. Nearer and nearer it came, snapping the brittle twigs that covered the ground. He hastily concealed himself, and waited in almost breathless stillness the approach of wild beasts, or wilder night-time raiders.

A moment more, and a young native girl appeared, bearing upon her head a birchen bucket. Light and graceful, with the freedom of the woods, she walked along until she came to a clear spring, and bending over, she filled her bucket with the pure fresh water.

Just then, a rare cluster of flowers attracted her eye, and with a maiden's love of the beautiful, she stopped to gather it, then poising her bucket upon her head, she would have started for the encampment, but she was fastened spell-bound to the spot, by an unconquerable terror.

Just opposite, and crouched ready to spring upon her, she saw a huge panther, his large eyes, like great balls of fire, glaring out from the intense shadow, already devoured her. She was paralyzed by an intense terror. The fearful eyes fascinated and bewildered her. In them she saw the frail bridge, that separated her from the spirit land.

She could not move, or utter a sound. The panther crouched lower among the tangled grass. A moment more, and he would spring upon her. The stream was drawing nearer, the bridge was shorter, from those fearful eyes, she could see the gleaming of the lights of spirit land, then a flash! A sharp report of the rifle, and the panther sprang into the air, and fell at the feet of the affrighted maiden!

She lived! But the waters of the spring were glowing red and warm with the lifeblood of the terrible beast. His glowing eyes grew dim and sightless, in the river of death, and in its place, to her sight appeared the handsome young gold-seeker.

With all her intense emotion, she was calm, as only a native maiden could be, but a deep glowing flush burned through the darkness of her cheek, as with timid grace, she gave her hand to her deliverer, and through the dusk of evening led him to the encampment, and to the chieftain, her father.

There was great excitement in the encampment when they saw the young girl returning with a stranger. Fiercely the people of the hostile tribe gathered round them, for the girl clung tremblingly to his hand, and by the fitful firelight he saw the dark scowls of passion gathering upon their faces, yet a thrill of joy filled his heart, for he now knew he was by the camp-fire of the wild tribe of whom nothing was known, save their uncompromising cruelty, and that with them rested the secret of Death's Valley, the great Golden Boulder, and the glittering stones.

He had saved their chieftain's daughter, and they would not harm him, for well he knew the power of gratitude upon the wild heart. Calm and resolute he stood among them, without the shadow of a fear darkening his face, until he saw the fierce fires of cruelty that shot from their wild eyes soften into the kindly light of gratitude and friendship, as the young girl told her story with all the pathos and ardour which the almost miraculous escape, had awakened in her heart.

The old chief loved his daughter with a savage intensity. She was all the Great Spirit had left him, of many sons and daughters, and he felt that he would be ready to battle with death itself, but he could not give up his only child.

There was a mist over his fierce eyes, and a trembling about his cruel heart, as he bade the stranger a kindly welcome, who but for his good fortune in saving the girl, would have been condemned to a torturing death, unheard of.

So it was at last by this unforeseen accident, that the young gold-seeker slept peacefully by the smouldering camp-fire of the most cruel, relentless, tribe of the Colorado, and dreamed of his blue-eyed darling, far away over the desert waste, safely sheltered in Fort Tejon.

The morning dawned rich with the glowing warmth of a Southern climate, and though our young hero woke early, he was wearied from long travel, and lay for some time with half-closed eyes, lazily watching the tribe folk they busied themselves about the encampment.

He was thinking how he should turn the advantage he had gained to the furtherance of his plans, when suddenly he felt, more than saw, that dark, jealous eyes were upon him. He feigned to be sleeping, while by a stolen glance he understood everything.

The tall, stalwart, young man, who bent over him with dark, knitted brows and flashing eyes, loved the girl whom he had saved, and was already his enemy, and one not to be scorned, as his proud bearing, and the deference shown him by others attested. That he was in danger, Dick realized; yet he rose with a free and careless manner, greeting the young men with a smile, which was returned.

"Worse than I supposed," he said to himself. "Treachery! But they shall not find me unprepared!"

The old chief and his daughter treated him with marked kindness, and he, by his modesty and pleasantry, tried to make friends among the young men.

After breakfast preparations were made for a hunt, and Dick was furnished with a fresh horse, and invited to join the company.

The day was warm and sultry, and, toward evening, the hunters, in starting for the camp, became scattered, and, on entering the shadows of a deep ravine, Dick found himself surrounded by five of the strongest young men, and, prominent among them, his enemy.

In an instant of time his hands were pinioned, and he was ordered to prepare for death. Looking calmly upon the dark, scowling faces around him, he said, "I am ready, only I would make one request of Tolume, my foe. It's this; that if in his wanderings he should ever reach Fort Tejon, he would bear a message for me to the woman I love."

The face of Tolume brightened, and he ordered the prisoner unbound, and leading him to a mossy stone, listened to the story of his love for the fair, blue-eyed maiden of Fort Tejon, and of all his hopes and plans, till the sun went down and the silver moon looked into the ravine.

Tolume was jealous no longer; so they became friends, and after listening to the story of Death's Valley and the great Golden Boulder, he promised to go with Dick in search of it.

Nothing was said on their return to the camp of the closing event of the day's hunt, but Dick saw with great satisfaction, that his new friend and the dark-eyed girl he had saved from death, were again mutually happy.

The tribes generally care but little for gold, but this tribe had mingled enough with the Spaniards to know something of its value; so the young Indian was very ready to accompany Dick in his adventures, and to accede to all his proposals, for he soon learned to look upon our hero as a superior being.

"Tonight," whispered Dick, as he passed carelessly by the young man, "when the moon rises above the mountain-tops, we will start."

The warrior bowed assent, and looked fondly upon the young girl he must leave, and whom he loved with all the fierceness of his wild nature.

During the afternoon he told her he was going away for a short time, but would return bringing her beautiful feathers, embroidered moccasins, strings of shining beads, and all that the heart of a pretty girl could desire. Then they parted, as all lovers part, with mingled hopes and fears.

When the moon rose clear and bright, casting its soft, mellow light over the glowing landscape, the young men met silently upon the brow of the hill, and started upon their journey.

They were well equipped with guns and ammunition. Each had a good horse, and as much food as they could carry; the only thing they had to fear was lack of water and hostiles.

For two days they travelled on without encountering any difficulty; but on the third they entered a dry, waste tract of country entirely destitute of vegetation. The ground was covered with a formation of salt and soda, and when the wind blew it nearly suffocated them.

"This must be Death's Valley," said Dick, as they rode on, talking cheerfully, looking carefully for any signs of gold. By noon they began to feel very thirsty, but there was no water, no cooling spring in all the vast desert spread out before them.

The burning rays of the noontide sun seemed to dry up their blood, and their tongues were parched and feverish, but there was no shelter; no water. Heat, thirst, and travel began to tell upon their horses, so they dismounted, and led them by the bridle, till night came on, finding them weary and faint, and, above all, perishing with thirst. Their fevered tongues began to swell, and it seemed as though the salt dust permeated their whole bodies; but they dare not stop, even for a moment, they were dying of thirst, and there was no water.

At last the clear, full moon rose over the desert waste of Death's Valley and over the wayworn prospectors. They thought no more of gold, only of water, clear, cool, bubbling water. It seemed to Dick as though he could hear the murmuring of the brook that rippled by the cottage of his childhood home, near Fort Tejon.

He walked along, every moment growing more hopeless, when suddenly he saw something bright and shining on the ground. It was a curious bow and quiver ornamented with little bells of silver and gold.

"Someone has been here, and only a short time ago, or the wind would have swept away the track," said Dick, as he bent down and examined a footprint upon the ground. "'Tis too small for a man," he said. "'Tis very strange."

Then he gave a loud shout, and they both listened eagerly, till they heard a low faint voice in reply, and, looking around, they saw by the clear moonlight an odd little figure trying in vain to rise from the ground. The young men hastened to his assistance, and found a queer little dwarf, with a long grey beard reaching nearly to his feet.

"Give me water!" said the man. "My horse has thrown me, and all day long I have lain here in the burning sun, too weak to move, for I am dying of thirst! Oh give me water, only a drop of water!"

"No water! No water!" cried Dick, in despair. "We, too, are famishing for want of it! We must on, we have not a moment to lose, or we shall die here in the desert."

"Do not leave me," cried the little man. "I can show you water, but I cannot move!" So they placed him upon one of the horses, and he pointed out the way.

Dick would have thrown aside the bow and quiver, but as he looked at the curious little being beside him, quaint old traditions came to his mind.

"This bow may serve me yet," he said, as he secured it to his leather belt. "Who knows but it belongs to one of the dwarf treasure-guard of the valley."

All night they travelled on and till nearly noon the next day, when a little green spot in the desert's sand met their sight. The horses snuffed the refreshing smell of water, and horses and men, faint, weary, and famishing, exerting all their strength started on the full run for the blessed Eden before them, and soon sank down upon the soft green grass by the side of a clear, bubbling spring.

"Now I will leave you," said the little man. "Give me my bow and quiver. We are even, I showed you the water, and you brought me to it."

"Not quite so fast, my little friend," said Dick. "Before I give you the bow and quiver, or permit you to leave us, you must lead us to the treasure of the valley, then furnish us with a guide, two good mules, and as much of the treasure as we can carry away."

"I accede to your proposition on one condition! Never attempt to point out the treasure to anyone, or to return to it yourself. If you do, death will swiftly follow, and the treasure you shall carry away will be lost to you and your family for ever."

So they gave the promise he required, and as they were very tired they concluded to wait till morning and made their frugal supper under the trees, drinking plentifully of the clear, delicious water; and slept peacefully till morning.

The little grey man woke them early. "Come," he said. "The sun is rising, we must away." So they arose, and taking a drink of water and eating a tortilla, started. For some hours they travelled on in the pleasant morning air, and just as the sun was beginning to be scorching in its heat they entered a deep ravine, and there they saw the wonderful Golden Boulder, and countless precious stones, and nuggets of bright yellow gold scattered round it upon the shining sand.

Dick and his companions were bewildered by the glittering spectacle, and a thousand glowing visions filled their minds. The little grey man blew a shrill whistle. Another little grey man appeared, and bowing low, said humbly, "What is the will of the master?"

"Food and drink!" answered the master.

The slave prepared a more comfortable meal than the young men had enjoyed since they left the encampment, and they ate heartily while the slave served them. When they had eaten, the chief ordered the slave to lade the mules with treasure and conduct the young men to the confines of the valley.

Then Dick returned the bow and quiver to the grey chief, and bid him goodbye.

"Never forget your promise, or beware!" said the grey man, as they turned away, and looking back they saw in the distance the last of the little man with up-raised fingers.

"He is saying again beware!" said Dick, laughing. How they went, neither of the young men could tell, but in a wonderfully short time they were out of Death's Valley. The warrior returned to his tribe, but Dick, with a happy heart, started for Fort Tejon, and after a speedy and safe journey he reached his early home.

It soon became rumoured about, that he was the richest young man in the whole country. In a short time, poor Dick, the half-breed, was forgotten, but everyone courted Don Richard Fielding, the rich and elegant Spanish gentleman.

There was a great feast made at the fort, when Don Richard was united in the "holy bonds of matrimony" with the Colonel's lovely daughter, and never was man happier than he, when he led his golden-haired bride through the halls of his pleasant mansion.

"We will travel by-and-by, love," he whispered. "But first we will rest and be happy in our own dear home!"

A Misunderstanding

This story has been edited and adapted from Henry W. Shoemaker's Allegheny Episodes, first published in 1922 by the Altoona Tribune Company, based out of Altoona, Pennsylvania. This was one of a series of collections forming the Pennsylvania Folk Lore series.

It was the night before Christmas in the little mountain church near Wolfe's Store. The small, low-roofed, raftered chapel was illumined as brightly as coal oil lamps in the early stage of their development could do it; a hemlock tree, decked out with candles and tinsel stood to one side of the altar, an almost red-hot ten-plate stove on the other, while the chancel and rafters were twined and garlanded with ground pine and ilex, or winter berries. In one of the rear pews sat a very good looking young couple, a former schoolteacher revisiting the valley, and his favourite pupil. Lambert Girtin and Elsie Vanneman were their names.

The young man, who was a veteran of the Civil War, possessed the right to wear the Congressional medal, and while teaching at the little red schoolhouse on the pike near the road leading to Gramley's Gap, had noticed and admired the fair Elsie, so different from the rest of his flock. She was the daughter of a prosperous lumberman, a jobber in hardwoods, and her mother was above the average in intelligence and breeding, yet Elsie in all ways transcended even her parents.

She had seemed like a mere child when he left her at the close of the term the previous Christmas, but he could not evict her image from his soul. It was mainly to see her, though he would have admitted this to no one, that induced him to revisit the remote valley during the following holiday season. The long drive in the stage through drifted roads had seemed nothing to him, he was so elated at the thought of reviving old memories at the sight of this most beloved of pupils.

In order not to arouse any one's suspicions, he did no more than to inquire how she was at the general store and boarding house where he stopped.

"You would never know her," exclaimed old Mother Wolfe, the landlady. "Why, she's a regular young lady, grown a head taller," making a gesture with her hand to denote her increased stature.

On Christmas Eve there was to be the usual entertainment at the Union Church, and Lambert Girtin posted himself outside the entrance to wait for the object of his dreams. The snow was drifted deep, and it was bitterly cold, yet social events were so rare in the mountains that almost everyone braved the icy blasts to be present. It was not long before he was rewarded by a sight of Elsie Vanneman. It was remarkable how tall she'd grown! As he expressed it to himself, "An opening bud became a rose full-blown" in one short year!

She of course recognized him, and greeted him warmly, and they entered the church together. Inside by the lamplight he had a better chance to study her appearance more in detail than by the cold starlight on the church steps. She had grown until she was above the middle height, yet had literally taken her figure and her grace with her. She was slender, yet shapely, dainty and graceful in the extreme. Her violet eyes were even more deeply pensive than of yore, her cheeks were pink and white, her lips red and slightly full. Her hair was a golden or coppery brown, and shone like those precious metals in the reflected light of the lamps and the stove; the slight upward turn of her nose still remained.

How demure, earnest and sincere she was! In the intervening year he had never seen her like in Bellefonte, Altoona or Pittsburgh. She seemed to be happy to be with him again, minus the restraint existing between a pupil and teacher. Instinctively their fingers touched, and they held hands during most of the evening.

Towards the end of the sermon, which was long and loud, and gave the young couple plenty of opportunity to advance their love making unnoticed, Girtin whispered to her, "Have you an escort home, dear Elsie?"

The answer was a hesitating "Yes."

The young man felt his heart give a jolt, then almost stop throbbing, and an instant hatred of some unknown rival made his blood boil furiously. How could she act that way? She had, even as his pupil, been indifferent to all of the opposite sex except him, and during the period of their separation her sprightly letters had borne evidence of tender sentiments, to the utter exclusion of all others. Had he not believed in her, he would not have taken that long journey back into the mountains, that many might have been glad to quit for good. Her beauty and her grace had haunted him, and he had determined to wed her, until this sign of duplicity had been sprung on him. Of course she did not know he was coming, and had made the fatal arrangements before; yet, if she cared for him as he did for her, she would not be making engagements with the boys, especially at her tender age.

He tried to console himself by noticing a shade of regret flit over her blushing face after she said the fateful words, but until the close of services he was ill at ease and scarcely opened his mouth. At the benediction he managed to stammer "Good evening," and was out of the church in the frosty starlight night before anyone else.

With long strides he walked up the snowy road ahead of the crowd who had followed him. The sky was very clear, and the North Star, "The Three Kings," or Jacob's Rake, Job's Coffin, and other familiar constellations, were glimmering on the drifted snow. Instead of observing the stars, had he looked back he would have seen that the "escort" she referred to was none other than a girl friend, Katie Moyer, and both, Elsie in particular, would have been only too happy to have a sturdy male companion to see them through the snowbanks.

As a result of his disappearance, Elsie was as unhappy and silent as Girtin had been, as she floundered about in the drifts. Despite her gentle, sunny nature, she was decidedly out of sorts when she reached home at the big white house near the Salt Spring. She gave monosyllabic answers to her parents in response to their queries as to how she had enjoyed the long-looked for Christmas entertainment. She did not sleep at all that night, but tossed about the bed, keeping her friend awake, and on Christmas Day was in a rebellious mood. Her mother reminded her how ungrateful she was to be so tearful and sullen in the face of so many blessings and gifts.

There was no stage or sleigh out of the valley on Christmas Day, else Girtin would have departed. He moped about all day, telling those who asked the matter that he was ill. Elsie, knowing that he was still in the valley, hoped up to bedtime that he would at least come to pay her a brief Christmas call, but supper over, and no signs of him, she was uncivil to her mother to such a degree that her friend openly said that she was ashamed of her.

Though Katie and she were rooming together, it did not deter her mother, goaded by the remarks of the younger children to visit her room while they were undressing, saying "that she deserved a good dose of the gad," and, ordering her to lay face downward on the bed, administered a good, old-fashioned spanking with the flax-paddle. After this humiliating chastisement in the presence of her friend, the unhappy girl cried and sobbed until morning.

It was a wretched ending for what might have been a memorable Christmas for Lambert Girtin and Elsie Vanneman.

The next morning the young man managed to hire a cutter and was driven to Bellefonte, leaving the valley with deep regrets. Through friends in the valley he learned afterwards that Elsie had gone as a missionary to China.

Life ran smoothly in some ways for Lambert Girtin, for he became uniformly successful as a businessman. The oil excitement was at its height, and he was sent by a large general supply house in Pittsburgh to open a store in Pithole City, "the Magic City," to the success of which he contributed so much that he was given an interest in the concern.

At heart he was not happy. He could never focus his attentions on any woman for long, as in the background he always saw the slender form, the blushing face, the pansy-like eyes and the copper-brown, wavy hair of his mountain sweetheart, Elsie Vanneman. Her loveliness haunted him, and all others paled beside her. He was in easy circumstances to marry; friends less opulent were taking wives and building showy homes with Mansard roofs, along the outskirts of the muddy main thoroughfare of Pithole City, where landscape gardening often consisted of charred, blackened pine stumps and abandoned oil derricks.

Sometimes, in his spiritual loneliness, he betook himself to strange companions. One of these was a Chinese laundryman, a prototype of Bret Harte's then popular "Heathen Chinee," who seemed to be a learned individual, despite his odd appearance. Girtin, who had read of the exploits of the Fox sisters and other exponents of early spiritualism, was unprepared for the learning and insight possessed by this undistinguished Celestial.

Drawn to him at first because he could possibly tell about conditions in China, where Elsie was supposed to be, he became gradually more and more absorbed by the laundryman's philosophic speculations. The fellow confided at length that he was married, and had five children at Tien-Tsin, to whom he was deeply attached. He would have died of a broken heart to be so far away from them but for the power he had developed by concentrating on the image of his native mountains, which yearning was reciprocated, and at night he claimed that his spirit was drawn out of his body and "hopped" half the span of the globe to the side of his loved ones. There must be something after all in the old Scotch quotation, "Oh, for my strength, once more to see the hills."

Girtin expressed a strong desire to be initiated into these compelling mysteries. In order to cultivate his psychic sense, the

Chinaman induced him to smoke opium, which, while repellent to Girtin, he undertook in order to reach his desired object. If he had been a man of any mental equilibrium, he would have secured a leave of absence from business and gone to China and claimed the fair Elsie, if she was still unmarried. He would not do that because he was still tortured by the memory of her preferring another at the moment when his hopes had been highest, yet he wanted to see her, hoping that he could do so without her knowing it.

The results attained were beyond his expectations. He quickly mastered his soul and "hopped" to the interior of China. Elsie was there, surrounded by her classes; at twenty-one more wondrously lovely and beautiful than when he had parted from her that frosty night, with the Dipper and Jacob's Rake shining so clearly in the heavens.

Though there were many missionaries and foreign officials who would have courted her, her dignity and quiet reserve were impenetrable. Was she so because of the love for the youth who was to escort her home from church that night, or did she cherish the memory of her whilom schoolmaster admirer? These were the thoughts that annoyed him by day, the "hang over" of his spiritual adventures at night.

The opium and the intense mental concentration were taking a lot out of him. He became sallow and irritable, and neglected many business opportunities. One of the head partners of the firm in Pittsburgh was going to Pithole City "to have it out with him," as the mountain folks would say. Before he could reach the scene word was telegraphed that Lambert Girtin, frightfully altered in appearance, was found dead one morning in a bunk back of the Charley Wah Laundry at Pithole.

He had no relatives in the town, and his sisters, who could not come on, telegraphed to bury him in the new Mount Moriah Cemetery, now all overgrown and abandoned, like Pithole itself! There could be no doubt as to his death, as Bill Brewer, just coming into fame as the "Hick Preacher," officiated at the obsequies. So Lambert Girtin was quickly forgotten in most all quarters. If he was remembered for a time, it was in the remote valley in which he had taught school, and where news of his early demise occasioned profound regret.

Years passed, and Elsie Vanneman, after giving some of the best years of her life to missionary activities in various parts of China, resigned her position, in consequence of a shattered nervous system, caused by overwork during a great earthquake, where she ministered to thousands of refugees, and started for home. Her parents had died while she was in the "Celestial Kingdom," but she had a number of brothers and sisters who were glad to welcome her, and with whom she planned a round of visits.

She was only thirty when she returned, a trifle paler and a few small lines around her mouth, but otherwise a picture of saintliness and loveliness. One of the first bits of news she heard on reaching the valley was of the ignominious end of Lambert Girtin in a Chinese laundryman's shack–"a promising career cut short," all allowed.

It was shocking to Elsie, as she had dreamed of this young man nearly every night from a certain period of her stay in China. She was on the street during the great quake, and as the earth cracked and swallowed countless victims, she fancied she saw a European, the counterpart of Girtin, plunged into the deadly abyss. She had come home with the intention of learning definite news of him, and if he was not the earthquake victim, and still lived, perhaps to renew their old-time interests.

She had been so upset by his failure to call, or even to write, after the Christmas eve at the little country church, that she had never communicated with him again. Her dreams had been most vividly realistic, as if he had been really near to her in China, and she could not make herself believe that he was dead in Pithole City, Pennsylvania.

Owing to this piece of bad news, she did not remain as long in the valley as she had planned, and almost from the day of her arrival had pined to be back in the Far East. The valley seemed dull, anyway; saw-mills were making it as treeless as China; she hated to see Luther Guisewhite destroy those giant original white pines, which reared their black-topped spiral heads along the foot of the mountains on the winter side; the wild pigeons no longer darkened the sky with their impressive flights, the flying squirrels were being shot out in Fulmer's Sink, near her old home; her parents were gone and everything was different.

Unsettled and dissatisfied, especially after a visit to the girl who had accompanied her home on the eventful Christmas Eve, now the mother of eight handsome children, she decided to return to China. The vast herds of buffaloes that had impeded the progress of her train on her first journey westward were gone. The Native Americans, who occasionally furnished a touch of colour to the prairie landscape, likewise had disappeared. Civilization was spreading through the Great West.

She timed her arrival in San Francisco so as to be there shortly after the arrival of a ship from China, so as to go back on its return journey. She would have several days to wait in the City of the

Golden Gate but it was quaint and picturesque, the time would pass quickly.

One evening, for she was not afraid, as she knew the language and customs of the Celestials, she decided to take a stroll through the famous Chinese Quarter. As she was walking along, her head down, her mind abstracted and noticing little, someone touched her on the arm. Looking around, as if to resent a familiarity, to her bewilderment she beheld her long-lost friend, Lambert Girtin.

"Lambert Girtin!" she said, in amazed tones.

"Elsie Vanneman. It is surely you?" he replied.

"Of all people, after all these years! I had been hearing that you died five years ago in the oil regions somewhere; what are you doing?"

The ex-schoolmaster took hold of both of her hands, there in the crowded, moving throngs of Chinatown, saying, "I came in from China today, after what I thought was a hopeless search for you. Years ago, after our separation, a Chinaman showed me how to visit China in my dreams, and be close to you. It took a whole lot of mental concentration, and it was pulling me down physically. I kept it up too long, for one night I dreamed I was in a terrible earthquake. It was so vivid that my physical as well as my spiritual being was translated to China, and I found myself there penniless. But, search as I may, I could not find you. If I died in the oil regions, it must have been another physical self, shed as a snake does his skin, for the Lambert Girtin who stands before you is fully alive, and resolved never to part from you again."

Old memories came to Elsie Vanneman, conquering her fears, and her face flushed as in schoolgirl days, "You speak of our 'separation'. Pray, tell me more about it; why did you leave me so abruptly and run away that Christmas Eve after meeting? I could never understand why you did not even come to wish me a 'Merry Christmas' the next day. Why didn't you ever write me a line? What did I do to merit such neglect?"

"What did *you* do?" replied Girtin, drawing her aside from the passing stream of pig-tailed humanity into a shadowy doorway. "It doesn't seem very serious now, but it hurt me a whole lot at the time. You told me you had an engagement with someone to see you in from church, and I was angry and jealous, for I had been imagining that your thoughts had only been of me, that you cared for no one else."

"I had an engagement with someone, that is true, but only a girl friend, Katie Moyer, who came and spent the night with me" replied the girl with alacrity.

Girtin turned as pale as death; his sufferings, mental and physical, his wanderings, physical and actual, his wasted years, all had been caused by a misunderstanding. He was at a loss for words for some time, but he held on to Elsie's hands, looking into her beautiful, ethereal face, the vari-coloured light of a Chinese lantern shining down on her coppery-gold hair.

"Do you care for me at all, now?" he said, at length.

"Yes, I think I do; I must, or I would not have come back all the way from China to hunt you," she answered.

"Then we have both suffered," he said, sadly.

"What shall we do now?" "she said.

"Let us return to the Pennsylvania mountains; it is home" she said.

"That's where I want to go," he replied, "if I can ever live down that dying story in Pithole City."

"Of course you can" said Elsie. "There was a case in our valley of a soldier reported as killed at Gettysburg; they sent his body home, began paying his widow a pension; she married a former sweetheart, and then, worse than 'Enoch Arden,' he appeared as if from the grave. He had no explanations to make, and our mountain people asked no questions, all having faith in supernatural things. Neither will I ask any of you. I have seen too much in the east to make me disbelieve anything, or that we can die two or three times under stress of circumstances, shedding our physical selves, to use your words, as snakes do their skins. I am only happy I did not marry someone else, as I was tempted to do when I imagined you were engulfed in the earthquake."

That night in Chinatown for once a misunderstanding ended happily.

Legends Of The Province-House – Howe's Masquerade

This story has been edited and adapted from Nathaniel Hawthorne's Twice Told Tales, first published in 1889 by David McKay, Publisher, Philadelphia.

At one of the entertainments given at the province-house during the latter part of the siege of Boston there passed a scene which has never yet been satisfactorily explained. The officers of the British army and the loyal gentry of the province, most of whom were collected within the beleaguered town, had been invited to a masqued ball, for it was the policy for Sir William Howe to hide the distress and danger of the period and the desperate aspect of the siege under an ostentation of festivity. The spectacle of this evening, if the oldest members of the provincial court circle might be believed, was the most gay and gorgeous affair that had occurred in the annals of the government. The brilliantly-lighted apartments were thronged with figures that seemed to have stepped from the dark canvas of historic portraits or to have flitted forth from the magic pages of romance, or at least to have flown here from one of the London theatres without a change of garments.

Steeled knights of the Conquest, bearded statesmen of Queen Elizabeth and high-ruffed ladies of her court were mingled with characters of comedy, such as a parti-coloured Merry Andrew jingling his cap and bells, a Falstaff almost as provocative of laughter as his prototype, and a Don Quixote with a bean-pole for a lance and a pot-lid for a shield.

But the broadest merriment was excited by a group of figures ridiculously dressed in old regimentals which seemed to have been purchased at a military rag-fair or pilfered from some receptacle of the cast-off clothes of both the French and British armies. Portions of their attire had probably been worn at the siege of Louisburg, and the coats of most recent cut might have been rent and tattered by sword, ball or bayonet as long ago as Wolfe's victory. One of these worthies, a tall, lank figure brandishing a rusty sword of immense longitude, purported to be no less a personage than General George Washington, and the other principal officers of the American army, such as Gates, Lee, Putnam, Schuyler, Ward and Heath, were represented by similar scarecrows. An interview in the mock-heroic style between the rebel warriors and the British commander-in-chief was received with immense applause, which came loudest of all from the loyalists of the colony.

There was one of the guests, however, who stood apart, eying these antics sternly and scornfully at once with a frown and a bitter smile. It was an old man formerly of high station and great repute in the province, and who had been a very famous soldier in his day. Some surprise had been expressed that a person of Colonel Joliffe's known Whig principles, though now too old to take an active part in the contest, should have remained in Boston during the siege, and especially that he should consent to show himself in the mansion of Sir William Howe. But there he had come with a fair granddaughter under his arm, and there, amid all the mirth and buffoonery, stood this stern old figure, the best-sustained character in the masquerade, because so well representing the antique spirit of his native land. The other guests affirmed that Colonel Joliffe's black puritanical scowl threw a shadow round about him, although, in spite of his sombre influence, their gayety continued to blaze higher, like, in an ominous comparison, the flickering brilliancy of a lamp which has but a little while to burn.

Eleven strokes full half an hour ago had pealed from the clock of the Old South, when a rumour was circulated among the company that some new spectacle or pageant was about to be exhibited which should put a fitting close to the splendid festivities of the night.

"What new jest has Your Excellency in hand?" asked the Reverend Mather Byles, whose Presbyterian scruples had not kept him from the entertainment. "Trust me, sir, I have already laughed more than beseems my cloth at your Homeric confabulation with yonder ragamuffin general of the rebels. One other such fit of merriment, and I must throw off my clerical wig and band."

"Not so, good Dr. Byles," answered Sir William Howe, "if mirth were a crime, you would never have gained your doctorate in divinity. As to this new foolery, I know no more about it than yourself, perhaps not so much. Honestly, now, doctor, have you not stirred up the sober brains of some of your countrymen to enact a scene in our masquerade?"

"Perhaps," slyly remarked the granddaughter of Colonel Joliffe, whose high spirit had been stung by many taunts against New England. "Perhaps we are to have a masque of allegorical figures, Victory with trophies from Lexington and Bunker Hill, Plenty with her overflowing horn to typify the present abundance in this good town, and Glory with a wreath for His Excellency's brow."

Sir William Howe smiled at words which he would have answered with one of his darkest frowns had they been uttered by lips that wore a beard. He was spared the necessity of a retort by a singular interruption. A sound of music was heard without the house, as if proceeding from a full band of military instruments stationed in the street, playing, not such a festal strain as was suited to the occasion, but a slow funeral-march. The drums appeared to be muffled, and the trumpets poured forth a wailing breath which at once hushed the merriment of the auditors, filling all with wonder and some with apprehension. The idea occurred to many that either the funeral procession of some great personage had halted in front of the province-house, or that a corpse in a velvet-covered and gorgeously-decorated coffin was about to be borne from the portal. After listening a moment, Sir William Howe called in a stern voice to the leader of the musicians, who had hereto enlivened the entertainment with gay and lightsome melodies. The man was drum-major to one of the British regiments.

"Dighton," demanded the general, "what means this foolery? Bid your band silence that dead march, or, by my word, they shall have sufficient cause for their lugubrious strains. Silence it, sirrah!"

"Please, Your Honour," answered the drum-major, whose rubicund visage had lost all its colour, "the fault is none of mine. I and my band are all here together, and I question whether there be a man of us that could play that march without book. I never heard it but once before, and that was at the funeral of his late Majesty, King George II."

"Well, well!" said Sir William Howe, recovering his composure, "it is the prelude to some masquerading antic. Let it pass."

A figure now presented itself, but among the many fantastic masks that were dispersed through the apartments none could tell precisely from where it came. It was a man in an old-fashioned dress of black serge and having the aspect of a steward or principal domestic in the household of a nobleman or great English landholder. This figure advanced to the outer door of the mansion, and, throwing both its leaves wide open, withdrew a little to one side and looked back toward the grand staircase, as if expecting some person to descend. At the same time, the music in the street sounded a loud and doleful summons. The eyes of Sir William Howe and his guests being directed to the staircase, there appeared on the uppermost landing-place, that was discernible from the bottom, several personages descending toward the door. The foremost was a man of stern visage, wearing a steeple-crowned hat and a skull-cap beneath it, a dark cloak and huge wrinkled boots that came halfway up his legs. Under his arm was a rolled-up banner which seemed to be the banner of England, but strangely rent and torn; he had a sword in his right hand and grasped a Bible in his left. The next figure was of milder aspect, yet full of dignity, wearing a broad ruff, over which descended a beard, a gown of wrought velvet and a doublet and hose of black satin; he carried a roll of manuscript in his hand. Close behind these two came a young man of very striking countenance and demeanour with deep thought and contemplation on his brow, and perhaps a flash of enthusiasm in his eye; his garb, like that of his predecessors, was of an antique fashion, and there was a stain of blood upon his ruff. In the same group with these were three or four others, all men of dignity and evident command, and bearing themselves like personages who were accustomed to the gaze of the multitude. It was the idea of the beholders that these figures went to join the mysterious funeral that had halted in front of the province-house, yet that supposition seemed to be contradicted by the air of triumph with which they waved their hands as they crossed the threshold and vanished through the portal.

"In the devil's name, what is this?" muttered Sir William Howe to a gentleman beside him. "A procession of the regicide judges of King Charles the martyr?"

"These," said Colonel Joliffe, breaking silence almost for the first time that evening, "these, if I interpret them aright, are the Puritan governors, the rulers of the old original democracy of Massachusetts, Endicott with the banner from which he had torn the symbol of subjection, and Winthrop and Sir Henry Vane and Dudley, Haynes, Bellingham and Leverett."

"Why had that young man a stain of blood upon his ruff?" asked Miss Joliffe.

"Because in after-years," answered her grandfather, "he laid down the wisest head in England upon the block for the principles of liberty."

"Will not Your Excellency order out the guard?" whispered Lord Percy, who, with other British officers, had now assembled round the general. "There may be a plot under this mummery."

"Tush! we have nothing to fear," carelessly replied Sir William Howe. "There can be no worse treason in the matter than a jest, and that somewhat of the dullest. Even were it a sharp and bitter one, our best policy would be to laugh it off. See! here come more of these gentry."

Another group of characters had now partly descended the staircase. The first was a venerable and white-bearded patriarch who cautiously felt his way downward with a staff. Treading hastily behind him, and stretching forth his gauntleted hand as if to grasp the old man's shoulder, came a tall soldier-like figure equipped with a plumed cap of steel, a bright breastplate and a long sword, which rattled against the stairs. Next was seen a stout man dressed in rich and courtly attire, but not of courtly demeanour; his gait had the swinging motion of a seaman's walk, and, chancing to stumble on the staircase, he suddenly grew wrathful and was heard to mutter an oath. He was followed by a noble-looking personage in a curled wig such as are represented in the portraits of Queen Anne's time and earlier, and the breast of his coat was decorated with an embroidered star. While advancing to the door he bowed to the right hand and to the left in a very gracious and insinuating style, but as he crossed the threshold, unlike the early Puritan governors, he seemed to wring his hands with sorrow.

"Prithee, play the part of a chorus, good Dr. Byles," said Sir William Howe. "What worthies are these?"

"If it please Your Excellency, they lived somewhat before my day," answered the doctor, "but doubtless our friend the colonel has been hand and glove with them."

"Their living faces I never looked upon," said Colonel Joliffe, gravely, "although I have spoken face to face with many rulers of this land, and shall greet yet another with an old man's blessing before I die. But we talk of these figures. I take the venerable patriarch to be Bradstreet, the last of the Puritans, who was governor at ninety or thereabouts. The next is Sir Edmund Andros, a tyrant, as any New England schoolboy will tell you, and therefore the people cast him down from his high seat into a dungeon. Then comes Sir William Phipps, shepherd, cooper, sea-captain and governor. May many of his countrymen rise as high from as low an origin! Lastly, you saw the gracious earl of Bellamont, who ruled us under King William."

"But what is the meaning of it all?" asked Lord Percy.

"Now, were I a rebel," said Miss Joliffe, half aloud, "I might fancy that the ghosts of these ancient governors had been summoned to form the funeral procession of royal authority in New England."

Several other figures were now seen at the turn of the staircase. The one in advance had a thoughtful, anxious and somewhat crafty expression of face, and in spite of his loftiness of manner, which was evidently the result both of an ambitious spirit and of long continuance in high stations, he seemed not incapable of cringing to a greater than himself. A few steps behind came an officer in a scarlet and embroidered uniform cut in a fashion old enough to have been worn by the duke of Marlborough. His nose had a rubicund tinge, which, together with the twinkle of his eye, might have marked him as a lover of the wine-cup and good-fellowship; notwithstanding which tokens, he appeared ill at ease, and often glanced around him as if apprehensive of some secret mischief. Next came a portly gentleman wearing a coat of shaggy cloth lined with silken velvet; he had sense, shrewdness and humour in his face and a folio volume under his arm, but his aspect was that of a man vexed and tormented beyond all patience and harassed almost to death. He went hastily down, and was followed by a dignified person dressed in a purple velvet suit with very rich embroidery; his demeanour would have possessed much stateliness, only that a grievous fit of the gout compelled him to hobble from stair to stair with contortions of face and body. When Dr. Byles beheld this figure on the staircase, he shivered as with an ague, but continued to watch him steadfastly until the gouty gentleman had reached the threshold, made a gesture of anguish and despair and vanished into the outer gloom, where the funeral music summoned him.

"Governor Belcher, my old patron, in his very shape and dress!" gasped Dr. Byles. "This is an awful mockery."

"A tedious foolery, rather," said Sir William Howe, with an air of indifference. "But who were the three that preceded him?"

"Governor Dudley, a cunning politician; yet his craft once brought him to a prison," replied Colonel Joliffe. "Governor Shute, formerly a colonel under Marlborough, and whom the people frightened out of the province, and learned Governor Burnett, whom the legislature tormented into a mortal fever."

"I think they were miserable men, these royal governors of Massachusetts," observed Miss Joliffe. "Heavens! How dim the light grows!"

It was certainly a fact that the large lamp which illuminated the staircase now burned dim and duskily; so that several figures which passed hastily down the stairs and went forth from the porch appeared rather like shadows than persons of fleshly substance.

Sir William Howe and his guests stood at the doors of the contiguous apartments watching the progress of this singular pageant with various emotions of anger, contempt or half-acknowledged fear, but still with an anxious curiosity. The shapes which now seemed hastening to join the mysterious procession were recognized rather by striking peculiarities of dress or broad characteristics of manner than by any perceptible resemblance of features to their prototypes. Their faces, indeed, were invariably kept in deep shadow, but Dr. Byles and other gentlemen who had long been familiar with the successive rulers of the province were heard to whisper the names of Shirley, of Pownall, of Sir Francis Bernard and of the well-remembered Hutchinson, thereby confessing that the actors, whoever they might be, in this spectral march of governors had succeeded in putting on some distant portraiture of the real personages. As they vanished from the door, still did these shadows toss their arms into the gloom of night with a dread expression of woe. Following the mimic representative of Hutchinson came a military figure holding before his face the cocked hat which he had taken from his powdered head, but his epaulettes and other insignia of rank were those of a general officer, and something in his mien reminded the beholders of one who had recently been master of the province-house and chief of all the land.

"The shape of Gage, as true as in a looking-glass!" exclaimed Lord Percy, turning pale.

"No, surely," cried Miss Joliffe, laughing hysterically, "it could not be Gage, or Sir William would have greeted his old comrade in arms. Perhaps he will not suffer the next to pass unchallenged."

"Of that be assured, young lady," answered Sir William Howe, fixing his eyes with a very marked expression upon the immovable visage of her grandfather. "I have long enough delayed to pay the ceremonies of a host to these departing guests; the next that takes his leave shall receive due courtesy."

A wild and dreary burst of music came through the open door. It seemed as it the procession, which had been gradually filling up its ranks, were now about to move, and that this loud peal of the wailing trumpets and roll of the muffled drums were a call to some loiterer to make haste. Many eyes, by an irresistible impulse, were turned upon Sir William Howe, as if it were he whom the dreary music summoned to the funeral of departed power.

"See! Here comes the last," whispered Miss Joliffe, pointing her tremulous finger to the staircase.

A figure had come into view as if descending the stairs, although so dusky was the region from where it emerged that some of the spectators fancied that they had seen this human shape suddenly moulding itself amid the gloom. Downward the figure came with a stately and martial tread, and, reaching the lowest stair, was observed to be a tall man booted and wrapped in a military cloak, which was drawn up around the face so as to meet the napped brim of a laced hat; the features, therefore, were completely hidden. But the British officers deemed that they had seen that military cloak before, and even recognized the frayed embroidery on the collar, as well as the gilded scabbard of a sword which protruded from the folds of the cloak and glittered in a vivid gleam of light. Apart from these trifling particulars there were characteristics of gait and bearing which impelled the wondering guests to glance from the shrouded figure to Sir William Howe, as if to satisfy themselves that their host had not suddenly vanished from the midst of them. With a dark flush of wrath upon his brow, they saw the general draw his sword and advance to meet the figure in the cloak before the latter had stepped one pace upon the floor.

"Villain, unmuffle yourself!" cried he. "You pass no farther."

The figure, without blenching a hair's-breadth from the sword, which was pointed at his breast, made a solemn pause and lowered the cape of the cloak from about his face, yet not sufficiently for the spectators to catch a glimpse of it. But Sir William Howe had evidently seen enough. The sternness of his countenance gave place to a look of wild amazement, if not horror, while he recoiled several steps from the figure and let fall his sword upon the floor. The martial shape again drew the cloak about his features and passed on, but, reaching the threshold with his back toward the spectators, he was seen to stamp his foot and shake his clenched hands in the air. It was afterward affirmed that Sir William Howe had repeated that self-same gesture of rage and sorrow when for the last time, and as the last royal governor, he passed through the portal of the province-house.

"Hark! The procession moves," said Miss Joliffe.

The music was dying away along the street, and its dismal strains were mingled with the knell of midnight from the steeple of the Old South and with the roar of artillery which announced that the beleaguered army of Washington had intrenched itself upon a nearer height than before. As the deep boom of the cannon smote upon his ear Colonel Joliffe raised himself to the full height of his aged form and smiled sternly on the British general.

"Would Your Excellency inquire further into the mystery of the pageant?" said he.

"Take care of your grey head!" cried Sir William Howe, fiercely, though with a quivering lip. "It has stood too long on a traitor's shoulders."

"You must make haste to chop it off, then," calmly replied the colonel, "for a few hours longer, and not all the power of Sir William Howe, nor of his master, shall cause one of these grey hairs to fall. The empire of Britain in this ancient province is at its last gasp tonight; almost while I speak it is a dead corpse, and I think the shadows of the old governors are fit mourners at its funeral."

With these words Colonel Joliffe threw on his cloak, and, drawing his granddaughter's arm within his own, retired from the last festival that a British ruler ever held in the old province of Massachusetts Bay. It was supposed that the colonel and the young lady possessed some secret intelligence in regard to the mysterious pageant of that night. However this might be, such knowledge has never become general. The actors in the scene have vanished into deeper obscurity than even that wild band who scattered the cargoes of the tea-ships on the waves and gained a place in history, yet left no names. But superstition, among other legends of this mansion, repeats the wondrous tale that on the anniversary night of Britain's discomfiture the ghosts of the ancient governors of Massachusetts still glide through the portal of the Province House. And last of all comes a figure shrouded in a military cloak, tossing his clenched hands into the air and stamping his iron-shod boots upon the broad freestone steps with a semblance of feverish despair, but without the sound of a foot-tramp.

Legends Of The Province-House – Edward Randolph's Portrait

This story has been edited and adapted from Nathaniel Hawthorne's Twice Told Tales, first published in 1889 by David McKay, Publisher, Philadelphia.

In one of the apartments of the province-house there was long preserved an ancient picture the frame of which was as black as ebony, and the canvas itself so dark with age, damp and smoke that not a touch of the painter's art could be discerned. Time had thrown an impenetrable veil over it and left to tradition and fable and conjecture to say what had once been there portrayed. During the rule of many successive governors it had hung, by prescriptive and undisputed right, over the mantel piece of the same chamber, and it still kept its place when Lieutenant-governor Hutchinson assumed the administration of the province on the departure of Sir Francis Bernard.

The lieutenant-governor sat one afternoon resting his head against the carved back of his stately arm-chair and gazing up thoughtfully at the void blackness of the picture. It was scarcely a time for such inactive musing, when affairs of the deepest moment required the ruler's decision; for within that very hour Hutchinson had received intelligence of the arrival of a British fleet bringing three regiments from Halifax to overawe the insubordination of the people. These troops awaited his permission to occupy the fortress of Castle William and the town itself, yet, instead of affixing his signature to an official order, there sat the lieutenant-governor so carefully scrutinizing the black waste of canvas that his demeanour attracted the notice of two young persons who attended him. One, wearing a military dress of buff, was his kinsman, Francis Lincoln, the provincial captain of Castle William; the other, who sat on a low stool beside his chair, was Alice Vane, his favourite niece. She was clad entirely in white, a pale, ethereal creature who, though a native of New England, had been educated abroad and seemed not merely a stranger from another clime, but almost a being from another world. For several years, until left an orphan, she had dwelt with her father in sunny Italy, and there had acquired a taste and enthusiasm for sculpture and painting which she found few opportunities of gratifying in the undecorated dwellings of the colonial gentry. It was said that the early productions of her own pencil exhibited no inferior genius, though perhaps the rude atmosphere of New England had cramped her hand and dimmed the glowing colours of her fancy. But, observing her uncle's steadfast gaze, which appeared to search through the mist of years to discover the subject of the picture, her curiosity was excited.

"Is it known, my dear uncle," inquired she, "what this old picture once represented? Possibly, could it be made visible, it might prove a masterpiece of some great artist; else why has it so long held such a conspicuous place?"

As her uncle, contrary to his usual custom, for he was as attentive to all the humours and caprices of Alice as if she had been his own best-beloved child, did not immediately reply, the young captain of Castle William took that office upon himself.

"This dark old square of canvas, my fair cousin," said he, "has been an heirloom in the province-house from time immemorial. As to the painter, I can tell you nothing; but if half the stories told of it be true, not one of the great Italian masters has ever produced so marvellous a piece of work as that before you."

Captain Lincoln proceeded to relate some of the strange fables and fantasies which, as it was impossible to refute them by ocular demonstration, had grown to be articles of popular belief in reference to this old picture. One of the wildest, and at the same time the best-accredited, accounts stated it to be an original and authentic portrait of the evil one, taken at a witch-meeting near Salem, and that its strong and terrible resemblance had been confirmed by several of the confessing wizards and witches at their trial in open court. It was likewise affirmed that a familiar spirit or demon abode behind the blackness of the picture, and had shown himself at seasons of public calamity to more than one of the royal governors. Shirley, for instance, had beheld this ominous apparition on the eve of General Abercrombie's shameful and bloody defeat under the walls of Ticonderoga. Many of the servants of the province-house had caught glimpses of a visage frowning down upon them at morning or evening twilight, or in the depths of night while raking up the fire that glimmered on the hearth beneath, although if any were bold enough to hold a torch before the picture, it would appear as black and undistinguishable as ever. The oldest inhabitant of Boston recollected that his father, in whose days the portrait had not wholly faded out of sight, had once looked upon it, but would never suffer himself to be questioned as to the face which was there represented. In connection with such stories, it was remarkable that over the top of the frame there were some ragged remnants of black silk, indicating that a veil had formerly hung down before the picture until the duskiness of time had so effectually concealed it. But, after all, it was the most singular part of the affair that so many of the pompous governors of Massachusetts had allowed the obliterated picture to remain in the state-chamber of the province-house.

"Some of these fables are really awful," observed Alice Vane, who had occasionally shuddered as well as smiled while her cousin spoke. "It would be almost worthwhile to wipe away the black surface of the canvas, since the original picture can hardly be so formidable as those which fancy paints instead of it."

"But would it be possible," inquired her cousin," to restore this dark picture to its pristine hues?"

"Such arts are known in Italy," said Alice.

The lieutenant-governor had roused himself from his abstracted mood, and listened with a smile to the conversation of his young relatives. Yet his voice had something peculiar in its tones when he undertook the explanation of the mystery.

"I am sorry, Alice, to destroy your faith in the legends of which you are so fond," remarked he, "but my antiquarian researches have long since made me acquainted with the subject of this picture, if picture it can be called, which is no more visible, nor ever will be, than the face of the long-buried man whom it once represented. It was the portrait of Edward Randolph, the founder of this house, a person famous in the history of New England."

"Of that Edward Randolph," exclaimed Captain Lincoln, "who obtained the repeal of the first provincial charter, under which our forefathers had enjoyed almost democratic privileges, he that was styled the arch-enemy of New England, and whose memory is still held in detestation as the destroyer of our liberties?"

"It was the same Randolph," answered Hutchinson, moving uneasily in his chair. "It was his lot to taste the bitterness of popular odium."

"Our annals tell us," continued the captain of Castle William, "that the curse of the people followed this Randolph where he went and wrought evil in all the subsequent events of his life, and that its effect was seen, likewise, in the manner of his death. They say, too, that the inward misery of that curse worked itself outward and was visible on the wretched man's countenance, making it too horrible to be looked upon. If so, and if this picture truly represented his aspect, it was in mercy that the cloud of blackness has gathered over it."

"These traditions are folly to one who has proved, as I have, how little of historic truth lies at the bottom," said the lieutenant-governor. "As regards the life and character of Edward Randolph, too implicit credence has been given to Dr. Cotton Mather, who, I must say it, though some of his blood runs in my veins, has filled our early history with old women's tales as fanciful and extravagant as those of Greece or Rome."

"And yet," whispered Alice Vane, "may not such fables have a moral? And I think, if the visage of this portrait be so dreadful, it is not without a cause that it has hung so long in a chamber of the province-house. When the rulers feel themselves irresponsible, it were well that they should be reminded of the awful weight of a people's curse."

The lieutenant-governor started and gazed for a moment at his niece, as if her girlish fantasies had struck upon some feeling in his own breast which all his policy or principles could not entirely subdue. He knew, indeed, that Alice, in spite of her foreign education, retained the native sympathies of a New England girl.

"Peace, silly child!" cried he, at last, more harshly than he had ever before addressed the gentle Alice. "The rebuke of a king is more to be dreaded than the clamour of a wild, misguided multitude. Captain Lincoln, it is decided: the fortress of Castle William must be occupied by the royal troops. The two remaining regiments shall be billeted in the town or encamped upon the Common. It is time, after years of tumult, and almost rebellion, that His Majesty's government should have a wall of strength about it."

"Trust, sir, trust yet a while to the loyalty of the people," said Captain Lincoln, "nor teach them that they can ever be on other terms with British soldiers than those of brotherhood, as when they fought side by side through the French war. Do not convert the streets of your native town into a camp. Think twice before you give up old Castle William, the key of the province, into other keeping than that of true-born New Englanders."

"Young man, it is decided," repeated Hutchinson, rising from his chair. "A British officer will be in attendance this evening to receive the necessary instructions for the disposal of the troops. Your presence also will be required. Till then, farewell."

With these words the lieutenant-governor hastily left the room, while Alice and her cousin more slowly followed, whispering together, and once pausing to glance back at the mysterious picture. The captain of Castle William fancied that the girl's air and mien were such as might have belonged to one of those spirits of fable, fairies or creatures of a more antique mythology, who sometimes mingled their agency with mortal affairs, half in caprice, yet with a sensibility to human weal or woe. As he held the door for her to pass Alice beckoned to the picture and smiled. "Come forth, dark and evil shape!" cried she. "It is your hour."

In the evening Lieutenant-governor Hutchinson sat in the same chamber where the foregoing scene had occurred, surrounded by several persons whose various interests had summoned them together. There were the selectmen of Boston, plain patriarchal fathers of the people, excellent representatives of the old puritanical founders whose sombre strength had stamped so deep an impress upon the New England character. Contrasting with these were one or two members of council, richly dressed in the white wigs, the embroidered waistcoats and other magnificence of the time, and making a somewhat ostentatious display of courtier-like ceremonial. In attendance, likewise, was a major of the British army, awaiting the lieutenant-governor's orders for the landing of the troops, which still remained on board the transports. The captain of Castle William stood beside Hutchinson's chair, with folded arms, glancing rather haughtily at the British officer by whom he was soon to be superseded in his command. On a table in the centre of the chamber stood a branched silver candlestick, throwing down the glow of half a dozen wax lights upon a paper apparently ready for the lieutenant-governor's signature.

Partly shrouded in the voluminous folds of one of the window-curtains, which fell from the ceiling to the floor, was seen the white drapery of a lady's robe. It may appear strange that Alice Vane should have been there at such a time, but there was something so childlike, so wayward, in her singular character, so apart from ordinary rules, that her presence did not surprise the few who noticed it. Meantime, the chairman of the selectmen was addressing to the lieutenant-governor a long and solemn protest against the reception of the British troops into the town.

"And if Your Honour," concluded this excellent but somewhat prosy old gentleman, "shall see fit to persist in bringing these mercenary sworders and musketeers into our quiet streets, not on our heads be the responsibility. Think, sir, while there is yet time, that if one drop of blood be shed, that blood shall be an eternal stain upon Your Honour's memory. You, sir, have written with an able pen the deeds of our forefathers; the more to be desired is it, therefore, that yourself should deserve honourable mention as a true patriot and upright ruler when your own doings shall be written down in history."

"I am not insensible, my good sir, to the natural desire to stand well in the annals of my country," replied Hutchinson, controlling his impatience into courtesy, "nor know I any better method of attaining that end than by withstanding the merely temporary spirit of mischief which, with your pardon, seems to have infected older men than myself. Would you have me wait till the mob shall sack the province-house as they did my private mansion? Trust me, sir, the time may come when you will be glad to flee for protection to the king's banner, the raising of which is now so distasteful to you."

"Yes," said the British major, who was impatiently expecting the lieutenant-governor's orders. "The demagogues of this province have raised the devil, and cannot lay him again. We will exorcise him in God's name and the king's."

"If you meddle with the devil, take care of his claws," answered the captain of Castle William, stirred by the taunt against his countrymen.

"Craving your pardon, young sir," said the venerable selectman, "let not an evil spirit enter into your words. We will strive against the oppressor with prayer and fasting, as our forefathers would have done. Like them, moreover, we will submit to whatever lot a wise Providence may send us, always after our own best exertions to amend it."

"And there peep forth the devil's claws!" muttered Hutchinson, who well understood the nature of Puritan submission. "This matter shall be expedited forthwith. When there shall be a sentinel at every corner and a court of guard before the town-house, a loyal gentleman may venture to walk abroad. What to me is the outcry of a mob in this remote province of the realm? The king is my master, and England is my country; upheld by their armed strength, I set my foot upon the rabble and defy them."

He snatched a pen and was about to affix his signature to the paper that lay on the table, when the captain of Castle William placed his hand upon his shoulder. The freedom of the action, so contrary to the ceremonious respect, which was then considered due to rank and dignity, awakened general surprise, and in none more than in the lieutenant-governor himself. Looking angrily up, he perceived that his young relative was pointing his finger to the opposite wall. Hutchinson's eye followed the signal, and he saw what had hereto been unobserved, that a black silk curtain was suspended before the mysterious picture, so as completely to conceal it. His thoughts immediately recurred to the scene of the preceding afternoon, and in his surprise, confused by indistinct emotions, yet sensible that his niece must have had an agency in this phenomenon, he called loudly upon her, "Alice! Come here, Alice!"

No sooner had he spoken than Alice Vane glided from her station, and, pressing one hand across her eyes, with the other snatched away the sable curtain that concealed the portrait. An exclamation of surprise burst from every beholder, but the lieutenant-governor's voice had a tone of horror.

"By Heaven!" said he, in a low inward murmur, speaking rather to himself than to those around him, "if the spirit of Edward Randolph were to appear among us from the place of torment, he could not wear more of the terrors of hell upon his face."

"For some wise end," said the aged selectman, solemnly, "has Providence scattered away the mist of years that had so long hid this dreadful effigy. Until this hour no living man has seen what we behold."

Within the antique frame which so recently had enclosed a sable waste of canvas now appeared a visible picture, still dark, indeed, in its hues and shadings, but thrown forward in strong relief. It was a half-length figure of a gentleman in a rich but very old-fashioned dress of embroidered velvet, with a broad ruff and a beard, and wearing a hat the brim of which overshadowed his forehead. Beneath this cloud the eyes had a peculiar glare which was almost lifelike. The whole portrait started so distinctly out of the background that it had the effect of a person looking down from the wall at the astonished and awe-stricken spectators. The expression of the face, if any words can convey an idea of it, was that of a wretch detected in some hideous guilt and exposed to the bitter hatred and laughter and withering scorn of a vast surrounding multitude. There was the struggle of defiance, beaten down and overwhelmed by the crushing weight of ignominy. The torture of the soul had come forth upon the countenance. It seemed as if the picture, while hidden behind the cloud of immemorial years, had been all the time acquiring a more intense depth and darkness of expression, till now it gloomed forth again and threw its evil omen over the present hour. Such, if the wild legend may be credited, was the portrait of Edward Randolph as he appeared when a people's curse had wrought its influence upon his nature.

"'Twould drive me mad, that awful face," said Hutchinson, who seemed fascinated by the contemplation of it.

"Be warned, then," whispered Alice. "He trampled on a people's rights. Behold his punishment, and avoid a crime like his."

The lieutenant-governor actually trembled for an instant, but, exerting his energy, which was not, however, his most characteristic feature, he strove to shake off the spell of Randolph's countenance.

"Girl," cried he, laughing bitterly, as he turned to Alice, "have you brought here your painter's art, your Italian spirit of intrigue, your tricks of stage-effect, and think to influence the councils of rulers and the affairs of nations by such shallow contrivances? See here!"

"Stay yet a while," said the selectman as Hutchinson again snatched the pen, "for if ever mortal man received a warning from a tormented soul, Your Honour is that man."

"Away!" answered Hutchinson, fiercely. "Though yonder senseless picture cried 'Forbear!' It should not move me!"

Casting a scowl of defiance at the pictured face, which seemed at that moment to intensify the horror of its miserable and wicked look, he scrawled on the paper, in characters that betokened it a deed of desperation, the name of Thomas Hutchinson. Then, it is said, he shuddered, as if that signature had granted away his salvation.

"It is done," said he, and placed his hand upon his brow.

"May Heaven forgive the deed!" said the soft, sad accents of Alice Vane, like the voice of a good spirit flitting away.

When morning came, there was a stifled whisper through the household, and spreading from there about the town, that the dark mysterious picture had started from the wall and spoken face to face with Lieutenant-governor Hutchinson. If such a miracle had been wrought, however, no traces of it remained behind; for within the antique frame nothing could be discerned save the impenetrable cloud which had covered the canvas since the memory of man. If the figure had, indeed, stepped forth, it had fled back, spirit-like, at the day-dawn, and hidden itself behind a century's obscurity.

The truth probably was that Alice Vane's secret for restoring the hues of the picture had merely effected a temporary renovation. But those who in that brief interval had beheld the awful visage of Edward Randolph desired no second glance, and ever afterward trembled at the recollection of the scene, as if an evil spirit had appeared visibly among them. And, as for Hutchinson, when, far over the ocean, his dying-hour drew on, he gasped for breath and complained that he was choking with the blood of the Boston Massacre, and Francis Lincoln, the former captain of Castle William, who was standing at his bedside, perceived a likeness in his frenzied look to that of Edward Randolph. Did his broken spirit feel at that dread hour the tremendous burden of a people's curse?

Legends Of The Province-House – Lady Eleanore's Mantle

This story has been edited and adapted from Nathaniel Hawthorne's Twice Told Tales, first published in 1889 by David McKay, Publisher, Philadelphia.

Not long after Colonel Shute had assumed the government of Massachusetts Bay - now nearly a hundred and twenty years ago - a young lady of rank and fortune arrived from England to claim his protection as her guardian. He was her distant relative, but the nearest who had survived the gradual extinction of her family; so that no more eligible shelter could be found for the rich and high-born Lady Eleanore Rochcliffe than within the province-house of a Transatlantic colony. The consort of Governor Shute, moreover, had been as a mother to her childhood, and was now anxious to receive her in the hope that a beautiful young woman would be exposed to infinitely less peril from the primitive society of New England than amid the artifices and corruptions of a court. If either the governor or his lady had especially consulted their own comfort, they would probably have sought to devolve the responsibility on other hands, since with some noble and splendid traits of character Lady Eleanore was remarkable for a harsh, unyielding pride, a haughty consciousness of her hereditary and personal advantages, which made her almost incapable of control. Judging from many traditionary anecdotes, this peculiar temper was hardly less than a monomania; or if the acts which it inspired were those of a sane person, it seemed due from Providence that pride so sinful should be followed by as severe a retribution. That tinge of the marvellous which is thrown over so many of these half-forgotten legends has probably imparted an additional wildness to the strange story of Lady Eleanore Rochcliffe.

The ship in which she came passenger had arrived at Newport, from where Lady Eleanore was conveyed to Boston in the governor's coach, attended by a small escort of gentlemen on horseback. The ponderous equipage, with its four black horses, attracted much notice as it rumbled through Cornhill surrounded by the prancing steeds of half a dozen cavaliers with swords dangling to their stirrups and pistols at their holsters. Through the large glass windows of the coach, as it rolled along, the people could discern the figure of Lady Eleanore, strangely combining an almost queenly stateliness with the grace and beauty of a maiden in her teens. A singular tale had gone abroad among the ladies of the province that their fair rival was indebted for much of the irresistible charm of her appearance to a certain article of dress, an embroidered mantle, which had been wrought by the most skilful artist in London, and possessed even magical properties of adornment. On the present occasion, however, she owed nothing to the witchery of dress, being clad in a riding-habit of velvet which would have appeared stiff and ungraceful on any other form.

The coachman reined in his four black steeds, and the whole cavalcade came to a pause in front of the contorted iron balustrade that fenced the province-house from the public street. It was an awkward coincidence that the bell of the Old South was just then tolling for a funeral; so that, instead of a gladsome peal with which it was customary to announce the arrival of distinguished strangers, Lady Eleanore Rochcliffe was ushered by a doleful clang, as if calamity had come embodied in her beautiful person.

"A very great disrespect!" exclaimed Captain Langford, an English officer who had recently brought despatches to Governor Shute. "The funeral should have been deferred lest Lady Eleanore's spirits be affected by such a dismal welcome."

"With your pardon, sir," replied Dr. Clarke, a physician and a famous champion of the popular party, "whatever the heralds may pretend, a dead beggar must have precedence of a living queen. King Death confers high privileges."

These remarks-were interchanged while the speakers waited a passage through the crowd which had gathered on each side of the gateway, leaving an open avenue to the portal of the province-house. A black slave in livery now leaped from behind the coach and threw open the door, while at the same moment Governor Shute descended the flight of steps from his mansion to assist Lady Eleanore in alighting. But the governor's stately approach was anticipated in a manner that excited general astonishment. A pale young man with his black hair all in disorder rushed from the throng and prostrated himself beside the coach, thus offering his person as a footstool for Lady Eleanore Rochcliffe to tread upon. She held back an instant, yet with an expression as if doubting whether the young man were worthy to bear the weight of her footstep rather than dissatisfied to receive such awful reverence from a fellow-mortal.

"Up, sir!" said the governor, sternly, at the same time lifting his cane over the intruder. "What means the Bedlamite by this freak?"

"Nay," answered Lady Eleanore, playfully, but with more scorn than pity in her tone, "Your Excellency shall not strike him. When men seek only to be trampled upon, it were a pity to deny them a favour so easily granted, and so well deserved!" Then, though as lightly as a sunbeam on a cloud, she placed her foot upon the cowering form and extended her hand to meet that of the governor.

There was a brief interval during which Lady Eleanore retained this attitude, and never, surely, was there a more apt emblem of aristocracy and hereditary pride trampling on human sympathies and the kindred of nature than these two figures presented at that moment. Yet the spectators were so smitten with her beauty, and so essential did pride seem to the existence of such a creature, that they gave a simultaneous acclamation of applause.

"Who is this insolent young fellow?" inquired Captain Langford, who still remained beside Dr. Clarke. "If he be in his senses, his impertinence demands the bastinado; if mad, Lady Eleanore should be secured from further inconvenience by his confinement."

"His name is Jervase Helwyse," answered the doctor, "a youth of no birth or fortune, or other advantages save the mind and soul that nature gave him; and, being secretary to our colonial agent in London, it was his misfortune to meet this Lady Eleanore Rochcliffe. He loved her, and her scorn has driven him mad."

"He was mad so to aspire," observed the English officer.

"It may be so," said Dr. Clarke, frowning as he spoke, "but I tell you, sir, I could wellnigh doubt the justice of the Heaven above us if no signal humiliation overtake this lady who now treads so haughtily into yonder mansion. She seeks to place herself above the sympathies of our common nature, which envelops all human souls; see if that nature do not assert its claim over her in some mode that shall bring her level with the lowest."

"Never!" cried Captain Langford, indignantly. "Neither in life nor when they lay her with her ancestors."

Not many days afterward the governor gave a ball in honour of Lady Eleanore Rochcliffe. The principal gentry of the colony received invitations, which were distributed to their residences by messengers on horseback bearing missives sealed with all the formality of official despatches. In obedience to the summons, there was a general gathering of rank, wealth and beauty, and the wide door of the province-house had seldom given admittance to more numerous and honourable guests than on the evening of Lady Eleanore's ball. Without much extravagance of eulogy, the spectacle might even be termed splendid, for, according to the fashion of the times, the ladies shone in rich silks and satins outspread over wide-projecting hoops, and the gentlemen glittered in gold embroidery laid unsparingly upon the purple or scarlet or sky-blue velvet which was the material of their coats and waistcoats. The latter article of dress was of great importance, since it enveloped the wearer's body nearly to the knees and was perhaps bedizened with the amount of his whole year's income in golden flowers and foliage. The altered taste of the present day, a taste symbolic of a deep change in the whole system of society, would look upon almost any of those gorgeous figures as ridiculous, although that evening the guests sought their reflections in the pier-glasses and rejoiced to catch their own glitter amid the glittering crowd. What a pity that one of the stately mirrors has not preserved a picture of the scene which by the very traits that were so transitory might have taught us much that would be worth knowing and remembering!

Would, at least, that either painter or mirror could convey to us some faint idea of a garment already noticed in this legend, the Lady Eleanore's embroidered mantle, which the gossips whispered was invested with magic properties, so as to lend a new and untried grace to her figure each time that she put it on! Idle fancy as it is, this mysterious mantle has thrown an awe around my image of her, partly from its fabled virtues and partly because it was the handiwork of a dying woman, and perchance owed the fantastic grace of its conception to the delirium of approaching death.

After the ceremonial greetings had been paid, Lady Eleanore Rochcliffe stood apart from the mob of guests, insulating herself within a small and distinguished circle to whom she accorded a more cordial favour than to the general throng. The waxen torches threw their radiance vividly over the scene, bringing out its brilliant points in strong relief, but she gazed carelessly, and with now and then an expression of weariness or scorn tempered with such feminine grace that her auditors scarcely perceived the moral deformity of which it was the utterance. She beheld the spectacle not with vulgar ridicule, as disdaining to be pleased with the provincial mockery of a court-festival, but with the deeper scorn of one whose spirit held itself too high to participate in the enjoyment of other human souls. Whether or not the recollections of those who saw her that evening were influenced by the strange events with which she was subsequently connected, so it was that her figure ever after recurred to them as marked by something wild and unnatural, although at the time the general whisper was of her exceeding beauty and of the indescribable charm which her mantle threw around her. Some close observers, indeed, detected a feverish flush and alternate paleness of countenance, with a corresponding flow and revulsion of spirits, and once or twice a painful and helpless betrayal of lassitude, as if she were on the point of sinking to the ground. Then, with a nervous shudder, she seemed to arouse her energies, and threw some bright and playful yet half-wicked sarcasm into the conversation. There was so strange a characteristic in her manners and sentiments that it astonished every right-minded listener, till, looking in her face, a lurking and incomprehensible glance and smile perplexed them with doubts both as to her seriousness and sanity. Gradually, Lady Eleanore Rochcliffe's circle grew smaller, till only four gentlemen remained in it. These were Captain Langford, the English officer before mentioned; a Virginian planter who had come to Massachusetts on some political errand; a young Episcopal clergyman, the grandson of a British earl; and, lastly, the private secretary of Governor Shute, whose obsequiousness had won a sort of tolerance from Lady Eleanore.

At different periods of the evening the liveried servants of the province-house passed among the guests bearing huge trays of refreshments and French and Spanish wines. Lady Eleanore Rochcliffe, who refused to wet her beautiful lips even with a bubble of champagne, had sunk back into a large damask chair, apparently overwearied either with the excitement of the scene or its tedium; and while, for an instant, she was unconscious of voices, laughter and music, a young man stole forward and knelt down at her feet. He bore a salver in his hand on which was a chased silver goblet filled to the brim with wine, which he offered as reverentially as to a crowned queen, or, rather, with the awful devotion of a priest doing sacrifice to his idol. Conscious that someone touched her robe, Lady Eleanore started, and unclosed her eyes upon the pale, wild features and dishevelled hair of Jervase Helwyse.

"Why do you haunt me thus?" said she, in a languid tone, but with a kindlier feeling than she ordinarily permitted herself to express. "They tell me that I have done you harm."

"Heaven knows if that be so," replied the young man, solemnly. "But, Lady Eleanore, in requital of that harm, if such there be, and for your own earthly and heavenly welfare, I pray you to take one sip of this holy wine and then to pass the goblet round among the guests. And this shall be a symbol that you have not sought to withdraw yourself from the chain of human sympathies, which whoso would shake off must keep company with fallen angels."

"Where has this mad fellow stolen that sacramental vessel?" exclaimed the Episcopal clergyman.

This question drew the notice of the guests to the silver cup, which was recognized as appertaining to the communion-plate of the Old South Church, and, for aught that could be known, it was brimming over with the consecrated wine.

"Perhaps it is poisoned," half whispered the governor's secretary.

"Pour it down the villain's throat!" cried the Virginian, fiercely.

"Turn him out of the house!" cried Captain Langford, seizing Jervase Helwyse so roughly by the shoulder that the sacramental cup was overturned and its contents sprinkled upon Lady Eleanore's mantle. "Whether knave, fool or Bedlamite, it is intolerable that the fellow should go at large."

"Pray, gentlemen, do my poor admirer no harm," said Lady Eleanore, with a faint and weary smile. "Take him out of my sight, if such be your pleasure, for I can find in my heart to do nothing but laugh at him, whereas, in all decency and conscience, it would become me to weep for the mischief I have wrought."

But while the bystanders were attempting to lead away the unfortunate young man he broke from them and with a wild, impassioned earnestness offered a new and equally strange petition to Lady Eleanore. It was no other than that she should throw off the mantle, which while he pressed the silver cup of wine upon her she had drawn more closely around her form, so as almost to shroud herself within it.

"Cast it from you," exclaimed Jervase Helwyse, clasping his hands in an agony of entreaty. "It may not yet be too late. Give the accursed garment to the flames."

But Lady Eleanore, with a laugh of scorn, drew the rich folds of the embroidered mantle over her head in such a fashion as to give a completely new aspect to her beautiful face, which, half hidden, half revealed, seemed to belong to some being of mysterious character and purposes.

"Farewell, Jervase Helwyse!" said she. "Keep my image in your remembrance as you behold it now."

"Alas, lady!" he replied, in a tone no longer wild, but sad as a funeral-bell, "we must meet shortly when your face may wear another aspect, and that shall be the image that must abide within me." He made no more resistance to the violent efforts of the gentlemen and servants who almost dragged him out of the apartment and dismissed him roughly from the iron gate of the province-house.

Captain Langford, who had been very active in this affair, was returning to the presence of Lady Eleanore Rochcliffe, when he encountered the physician, Dr. Clarke, with whom he had held some casual talk on the day of her arrival. The doctor stood apart, separated from Lady Eleanore by the width of the room, but eying her with such keen sagacity that Captain Langford involuntarily gave him credit for the discovery of some deep secret.

"You appear to be smitten, after all, with the charms of this queenly maiden," said he, hoping thus to draw forth the physician's hidden knowledge.

"God forbid!" answered Dr. Clarke, with a grave smile, "and if you be wise, you will put up the same prayer for yourself. Woe to those who shall be smitten by this beautiful Lady Eleanore! But yonder stands the governor, and I have a word or two for his private ear. Good-night!"

He accordingly advanced to Governor Shute and addressed him in so low a tone that none of the bystanders could catch a word of what he said, although the sudden change of His Excellency's hereto cheerful visage betokened that the communication could be of no agreeable import. A very few moments afterward it was announced to the guests that an unforeseen circumstance rendered it necessary to put a premature close to the festival.

The ball at the province-house supplied a topic of conversation for the colonial metropolis for some days after its occurrence, and might still longer have been the general theme, only that a subject of all-engrossing interest thrust it for a time from the public recollection. This was the appearance of a dreadful epidemic which in that age, and long before and afterward, was wont to slay its hundreds and thousands on both sides of the Atlantic. On the occasion of which we speak it was distinguished by a peculiar virulence, insomuch that it has left its traces, its pit marks, to use an appropriate figure, on the history of the country, the affairs of which were thrown into confusion by its ravages. At first, unlike its ordinary course, the disease seemed to confine itself to the higher circles of society, selecting its victims from among the proud, the well-born and the wealthy, entering unabashed into stately chambers and lying down with the slumberers in silken beds. Some of the most distinguished guests of the province-house, even those whom the haughty Lady Eleanore Rochcliffe had deemed not unworthy of her favour, were stricken by this fatal scourge. It was noticed with an ungenerous bitterness of feeling that the four gentlemen, the Virginian, the British officer, the young clergyman and the governor's secretary, who had been her most devoted attendants on the evening of the ball were the foremost on whom the plague-stroke fell. But the disease, pursuing its onward progress, soon ceased to be exclusively a prerogative of aristocracy. Its red brand was no longer conferred like a noble's star or an order of knighthood. It threaded its way through the narrow and crooked streets, and entered the low, mean, darksome dwellings and laid its hand of death upon the artisans and labouring classes of the town. It compelled rich and poor to feel themselves brethren then, and stalking to and fro across the Three Hills with a fierceness which made it almost a new pestilence, there was that mighty conqueror, that scourge and horror of our forefathers, the small-pox.

We cannot estimate the affright which this plague inspired of yore by contemplating it as the fangless monster of the present day. We must remember, rather, with what awe we watched the gigantic footsteps of the Asiatic cholera striding from shore to shore of the Atlantic and marching like Destiny upon cities far remote which flight had already half depopulated. There is no other fear so horrible and dehumanizing as that which makes man dread to breathe heaven's vital air lest it be poison, or to grasp the hand of a brother or friend lest the grip of the pestilence should clutch him. Such was the dismay that now followed in the track of the disease or ran before it throughout the town. Graves were hastily dug and the pestilential relics as hastily covered, because the dead were enemies of the living and strove to draw them headlong, as it were, into their own dismal pit. The public councils were suspended, as if mortal wisdom might relinquish its devices now that an unearthly usurper had found his way into the ruler's mansion. Had an enemy's fleet been hovering on the coast or his armies trampling on our soil, the people would probably have committed their defence to that same direful conqueror who had wrought their own calamity and would permit no interference with his sway. This conqueror had a symbol of his triumphs: it was a blood-red flag that fluttered in the tainted air over the door of every dwelling into which the small-pox had entered.

Such a banner was long since waving over the portal of the province-house, for from there, as was proved by tracking its footsteps back, had all this dreadful mischief issued. It had been traced back to a lady's luxurious chamber, to the proudest of the proud, to her that was so delicate and hardly owned herself of earthly mould, to the haughty one who took her stand above human sympathies, to Lady Eleanore. There remained no room for doubt that the contagion had lurked in that gorgeous mantle which threw so strange a grace around her at the festival. Its fantastic splendour had been conceived in the delirious brain of a woman on her death-bed and was the last toil of her stiffening fingers, which had interwoven fate and misery with its golden threads. This dark tale, whispered at first, was now bruited far and wide. The people raved against the Lady Eleanore and cried out that her pride and scorn had evoked a fiend, and that between them both this monstrous evil had been born. At times their rage and despair took the semblance of grinning mirth; and whenever the red flag of the pestilence was hoisted over another and yet another door, they clapped their hands and shouted through the streets in bitter mockery, "Behold a new triumph for the Lady Eleanore!"

One day in the midst of these dismal times a wild figure approached the portal of the province-house, and, folding his arms, stood contemplating the scarlet banner, which a passing breeze shook fitfully, as if to fling abroad the contagion that it typified. At length, climbing one of the pillars by means of the iron balustrade, he took down the flag, and entered the mansion waving it above his head. At the foot of the staircase he met the governor, booted and spurred, with his cloak drawn around him, evidently on the point of setting forth upon a journey.

"Wretched lunatic, what do you seek here?" exclaimed Shute, extending his cane to guard himself from contact. "There is nothing here but Death; back, or you will meet him."

"Death will not touch me, the banner-bearer of the pestilence," cried Jervase Helwyse, shaking the red flag aloft. "Death and the pestilence, who wears the aspect of the Lady Eleanore, will walk through the streets tonight, and I must march before them with this banner."

"Why do I waste words on the fellow?" muttered the governor, drawing his cloak across his mouth. "What matters his miserable life, when none of us are sure of twelve hours' breath? - On, fool, to your own destruction!"

He made way for Jervase Helwyse, who immediately ascended the staircase, but on the first landing-place was arrested by the firm grasp of a hand upon his shoulder. Looking fiercely up with a madman's impulse to struggle with and rend asunder his opponent, he found himself powerless beneath a calm, stern eye which possessed the mysterious property of quelling frenzy at its height. The person whom he had now encountered was the physician, Dr. Clarke, the duties of whose sad profession had led him to the province-house, where he was an infrequent guest in more prosperous times.

"Young man, what is your purpose?" demanded he.

"I seek the Lady Eleanore," answered Jervase Helwyse, submissively.

"All have fled from her," said the physician. "Why do you seek her now? I tell you, youth, her nurse fell death-stricken on the threshold of that fatal chamber. Do you not realise that never came such a curse to our shores as this lovely Lady Eleanore, that her breath has filled the air with poison, that she has shaken pestilence and death upon the land from the folds of her accursed mantle?"

"Let me look upon her," rejoined the mad youth, more wildly. "Let me behold her in her awful beauty, clad in the regal garments of the pestilence. She and Death sit on a throne together; let me kneel down before them."

"Poor youth!" said Dr. Clarke, and, moved by a deep sense of human weakness, a smile of caustic humour curled his lip even then. "Will you still worship the destroyer and surround her image with fantasies the more magnificent the more evil she has wrought? Thus man does ever to his tyrants. Approach, then. Madness, as I have noted, has that good efficacy that it will guard you from contagion, and perhaps its own cure may be found in yonder chamber." Ascending another flight of stairs, he threw open a door and signed to Jervase Helwyse that he should enter.

The poor lunatic, it seems probable, had cherished a delusion that his haughty mistress sat in state, unharmed herself by the pestilential influence which as by enchantment she scattered round about her. He dreamed, no doubt, that her beauty was not dimmed, but brightened into superhuman splendour. With such anticipations he stole reverentially to the door at which the physician stood, but paused upon the threshold, gazing fearfully into the gloom of the darkened chamber.

"Where is the Lady Eleanore?" whispered he.

"Call her," replied the physician.

"Lady Eleanore! Princess! Queen of Death!" cried Jervase Helwyse, advancing three steps into the chamber. "She is not here. There, on yonder table, I behold the sparkle of a diamond which once she wore upon her bosom. There...", and he shuddered, "there hangs her mantle, on which a dead woman embroidered a spell of dreadful potency. But where is the Lady Eleanore?"

Something stirred within the silken curtains of a canopied bed and a low moan was uttered, which, listening intently, Jervase Helwyse began to distinguish as a woman's voice complaining dolefully of thirst. He fancied, even, that he recognized its tones.

"My throat! My throat is scorched," murmured the voice. "A drop of water!"

"What thing are you?" said the brain-stricken youth, drawing near the bed and tearing asunder its curtains. "Whose voice have you stolen for your murmurs and miserable petitions, as if Lady Eleanore could be conscious of mortal infirmity? Fie! Heap of diseased mortality, why do you lurk in my lady's chamber?"

"Oh, Jervase Helwyse," said the voice, and as it spoke the figure contorted itself, struggling to hide its blasted face, "look not now on the woman you once loved. The curse of Heaven has stricken me because I would not call man my brother nor woman sister. I wrapped myself in pride as in a mantle and scorned the sympathies of nature, and therefore has Nature made this wretched body the medium of a dreadful sympathy. You are avenged, they are all avenged, Nature is avenged; for I am Eleanore Rochcliffe."

The malice of his mental disease, the bitterness lurking at the bottom of his heart, mad as he was, for a blighted and ruined life and love that had been paid with cruel scorn, awoke within the breast of Jervase Helwyse. He shook his finger at the wretched girl, and the chamber echoed, the curtains of the bed were shaken, with his outburst of insane merriment.

"Another triumph for the Lady Eleanore!" he cried. "All have been her victims; who so worthy to be the final victim as herself?" Impelled by some new fantasy of his crazed intellect, he snatched the fatal mantle and rushed from the chamber and the house.

That night a procession passed by torchlight through the streets, bearing in the midst the figure of a woman enveloped with a richly-embroidered mantle, while in advance stalked Jervase Helwyse waving the red flag of the pestilence. Arriving opposite the province-house, the mob burned the effigy, and a strong wind came and swept away the ashes. It was said that from that very hour the pestilence abated, as if its sway had some mysterious connection, from the first plague-stroke to the last, with Lady Elcanore's mantle. A remarkable uncertainty broods over that unhappy lady's fate. There is a belief, however, that in a certain chamber of this mansion a female form may sometimes be duskily discerned shrinking into the darkest corner and muffling her face within an embroidered mantle. Supposing the legend true, can this be other than the once proud Lady Eleanore?

Legends Of The Province-House – Old Esther Dudley

This story has been edited and adapted from Nathaniel Hawthorne's Twice Told Tales, first published in 1889 by David McKay, Publisher, Philadelphia.

The hour had come, the hour of defeat and humiliation, when Sir William Howe was to pass over the threshold of the province-house and embark, with no such triumphal ceremonies as he once promised himself, on board the British fleet. He bade his servants and military attendants go before him, and lingered a moment in the loneliness of the mansion to quell the fierce emotions that struggled in his bosom as with a death-throb. Preferable then would he have deemed his fate had a warrior's death left him a claim to the narrow territory of a grave within the soil which the king had given him to defend. With an ominous perception that as his departing footsteps echoed adown the staircase the sway of Britain was passing for ever from New England, he smote his clenched hand on his brow and cursed the destiny that had flung the shame of a dismembered empire upon him.

"Would to God," cried he, hardly repressing his tears of rage, "that the rebels were even now at the doorstep! A blood-stain upon the floor should then bear testimony that the last British ruler was faithful to his trust."

The tremulous voice of a woman replied to his exclamation. "Heaven's cause and the king's are one," it said. "Go forth, Sir William Howe, and trust in Heaven to bring back a royal governor in triumph."

Subduing at once the passion to which he had yielded only in the faith that it was unwitnessed, Sir William Howe became conscious that an aged woman leaning on a gold-headed staff was standing betwixt him and the door. It was old Esther Dudley, who had dwelt almost immemorial years in this mansion, until her presence seemed as inseparable from it as the recollections of its history. She was the daughter of an ancient and once eminent family which had fallen into poverty and decay and left its last descendant no resource save the bounty of the king, nor any shelter except within the walls of the province-house. An office in the household with merely nominal duties had been assigned to her as a pretext for the payment of a small pension, the greater part of which she expended in adorning herself with an antique magnificence of attire. The claims of Esther Dudley's gentle blood were acknowledged by all the successive governors, and they treated her with the punctilious courtesy which it was her foible to demand, not always with success, from a neglectful world. The only actual share which she assumed in the business of the mansion was to glide through its passages and public chambers late at night to see that the servants had dropped no fire from their flaring torches nor left embers crackling and blazing on the hearths. Perhaps it was this invariable custom of walking her rounds in the hush of midnight that caused the superstition of the times to invest the old woman with attributes of awe and mystery, fabling that she had entered the portal of the province-house, none knew from where, in the train of the first royal governor, and that it was her fate to dwell there till the last should have departed.

But Sir William Howe, if he ever heard this legend, had forgotten it. "Mistress Dudley, why are you loitering here?" asked he, with some severity of tone. "It is my pleasure to be the last in this mansion of the king."

"Not so, if it please Your Excellency," answered the time-stricken woman. "This roof has sheltered me long; I will not pass from it until they bear me to the tomb of my forefathers. What other shelter is there for old Esther Dudley save the province-house or the grave?"

"Now, Heaven forgive me!" said Sir William Howe to himself. "I was about to leave this wretched old creature to starve or beg. Take this, good Mistress Dudley," he added, putting a purse into her hands. "King George's head on these golden guineas is sterling yet, and will continue so, I warrant you, even should the rebels crown John Hancock their king. That purse will buy a better shelter than the province-house can now afford."

"While the burden of life remains upon me I will have no other shelter than this roof," persisted Esther Dudley, striking her staff upon the floor with a gesture that expressed immovable resolve, "and when Your Excellency returns in triumph, I will totter into the porch to welcome you."

"My poor old friend!" answered the British general, and all his manly and martial pride could no longer restrain a gush of bitter tears. "This is an evil hour for you and me. The province which the king entrusted to my charge is lost. I go from here in misfortune, perchance in disgrace, to return no more. And you, whose present being is incorporated with the past, who have seen governor after governor in stately pageantry ascend these steps, whose whole life has been an observance of majestic ceremonies and a worship of the king, how will you endure the change? Come with us; bid farewell to a land that has shaken off its allegiance, and live still under a royal government at Halifax."

"Never! never!" said the pertinacious old dame. "Here will I abide, and King George shall still have one true subject in his disloyal province."

"Beshrew the old fool!" muttered Sir William Howe, growing impatient of her obstinacy and ashamed of the emotion into which he had been betrayed. "She is the very moral of old-fashioned prejudice, and could exist nowhere but in this musty edifice. Well, then, Mistress Dudley, since you will needs tarry, I give the province-house in charge to you. Take this key, and keep it safe until myself or some other royal governor shall demand it of you." Smiling bitterly at himself and her, he took the heavy key of the province-house, and, delivering it into the old lady's hands, drew his cloak around him for departure.

As the general glanced back at Esther Dudley's antique figure he deemed her well fitted for such a charge, as being so perfect a representative of the decayed past, of an age gone by, with its manners, opinions, faith and feelings all fallen into oblivion or scorn, of what had once been a reality, but was now merely a vision of faded magnificence. Then Sir William Howe strode forth, smiting his clenched hands together in the fierce anguish of his spirit, and old Esther Dudley was left to keep watch in the lonely province-house, dwelling there with Memory; and if Hope ever seemed to flit around her, still it was Memory in disguise.

The total change of affairs that ensued on the departure of the British troops did not drive the venerable lady from her stronghold. There was not for many years afterward a governor of Massachusetts, and the magistrates who had charge of such matters saw no objection to Esther Dudley's residence in the province-house, especially as they must otherwise have paid a hireling for taking care of the premises, which with her was a labour of love; and so they left her the undisturbed mistress of the old historic edifice. Many and strange were the fables which the gossips whispered about her in all the chimney-corners of the town.

Among the time-worn articles of furniture that had been left in the mansion, there was a tall antique mirror which was well worthy of a tale by itself, and perhaps may hereafter be the theme of one. The gold of its heavily-wrought frame was tarnished, and its surface so blurred that the old woman's figure, whenever she paused before it, looked indistinct and ghostlike. But it was the general belief that Esther could cause the governors of the overthrown dynasty, with the beautiful ladies who had once adorned their festivals, the native chiefs who had come up to the province-house to hold council or swear allegiance, the grim provincial warriors, the severe clergymen, in short, all the pageantry of gone days, all the figures that ever swept across the broad-plate of glass in former times, she could cause the whole to reappear and people the inner world of the mirror with shadows of old life. Such legends as these, together with the singularity of her isolated existence, her age and the infirmity that each added winter flung upon her, made Mistress Dudley the object both of fear and pity, and it was partly the result of either sentiment that, amid all the angry license of the times, neither wrong nor insult ever fell upon her unprotected head. Indeed, there was so much haughtiness in her demeanour toward intruders, among whom she reckoned all persons acting under the new authorities, that it was really an affair of no small nerve to look her in the face. And, to do the people justice, stern republicans as they had now become, they were well content that the old gentlewoman, in her hoop-petticoat and faded embroidery, should still haunt the palace of ruined pride and overthrown power, the symbol of a departed system, embodying a history in her person. So Esther Dudley dwelt year after year in the province-house, still reverencing all that others had flung aside, still faithful to her king, who, so long as the venerable dame yet held her post, might be said to retain one true subject in New England and one spot of the empire that had been wrested from him.

And did she dwell there in utter loneliness? Rumour said, "Not so." Whenever her chill and withered heart desired warmth, she was wont to summon a black slave of Governor Shirley's from the blurred mirror and send him in search of guests who had long ago been familiar in those deserted chambers. Forth went the sable messenger, with the starlight or the moonshine gleaming through him, and did his errand in the burial-grounds, knocking at the iron doors of tombs or upon the marble slabs that covered them, and whispering to those within, "My mistress, old Esther Dudley, bids you to the province-house at midnight," and punctually as the clock of the Old South told twelve came the shadows of the Olivers, the Hutchinsons, the Dudleys, all the grandees of a bygone generation, gliding beneath the portal into the well-known mansion, where Esther mingled with them as if she likewise were a shade. Without vouching for the truth of such traditions, it is certain that Mistress Dudley sometimes assembled a few of the stanch though crestfallen old Tories who had lingered in the rebel town during those days of wrath and tribulation. Out of a cobwebbed bottle containing liquor that a royal governor might have smacked his lips over they quaffed healths to the king and babbled treason to the republic, feeling as if the protecting shadow of the throne were still flung around them. But, draining the last drops of their liquor, they stole timorously homeward, and answered not again if the rude mob reviled them in the street.

Yet Esther Dudley's most frequent and favoured guests were the children of the town. Toward them she was never stern. A kindly and loving nature hindered elsewhere from its free course by a thousand rocky prejudices lavished itself upon these little ones. By bribes of gingerbread of her own making, stamped with a royal crown, she tempted their sunny sportiveness beneath the gloomy portal of the province-house, and would often beguile them to spend a whole play-day there, sitting in a circle round the verge of her hoop-petticoat, greedily attentive to her stories of a dead world.

And when these little boys and girls stole forth again from the dark, mysterious mansion, they went bewildered, full of old feelings that graver people had long ago forgotten, rubbing their eyes at the world around them as if they had gone astray into ancient times and become children of the past. At home, when their parents asked where they had loitered such a weary while and with whom they had been at play, the children would talk of all the departed worthies of the province as far back as Governor Belcher and the haughty dame of Sir William Phipps. It would seem as though they had been sitting on the knees of these famous personages, whom the grave had hidden for half a century, and had toyed with the embroidery of their rich waistcoats or roguishly pulled the long curls of their flowing wigs.

"But Governor Belcher has been dead this many a year," would the mother say to her little boy. "And did you really see him at the province-house?"

"Oh yes, dear mother, yes!" the half-dreaming child would answer. "But when old Esther had done speaking about him, he faded away out of his chair."

Thus, without affrighting her little guests, she led them by the hand into the chambers of her own desolate heart and made childhood's fancy discern the ghosts that haunted there.

Living so continually in her own circle of ideas, and never regulating her mind by a proper reference to present things, Esther Dudley appears to have grown partially crazed. It was found that she had no right sense of the progress and true state of the Revolutionary war, but held a constant faith that the armies of Britain were victorious on every field and destined to be ultimately triumphant. Whenever the town rejoiced for a battle won by Washington or Gates or Morgan or Greene, the news, in passing through the door of the province-house as through the ivory gate of dreams, became metamorphosed into a strange tale of the prowess of Howe, Clinton or Cornwallis. Sooner or later, it was her invincible belief, the colonies would be prostrate at the footstool of the king. Sometimes she seemed to take for granted that such was already the case. On one occasion she startled the townspeople by a brilliant illumination of the province-house with candles at every pane of glass and a transparency of the king's initials and a crown of light in the great balcony-window. The figure of the aged woman in the most gorgeous of her mildewed velvets and brocades was seen passing from casement to casement, until she paused before the balcony and flourished a huge key above her head. Her wrinkled visage actually gleamed with triumph, as if the soul within her were a festal lamp.

"What means this blaze of light? What does old Esther's joy portend?" whispered a spectator. "It is frightful to see her gliding about the chambers and rejoicing there without a soul to bear her company."

"It is as if she were making merry in a tomb," said another.

"Pshaw! It is no such mystery," observed an old man, after some brief exercise of memory. "Mistress Dudley is keeping jubilee for the king of England's birthday."

Then the people laughed aloud, and would have thrown mud against the blazing transparency of the king's crown and initials, only that they pitied the poor old dame who was so dismally triumphant amid the wreck and ruin of the system to which she appertained.

Oftentimes it was her custom to climb the weary staircase that wound upward to the cupola, and from there strain her dimmed eyesight seaward and country-ward, watching for a British fleet or for the march of a grand procession with the king's banner floating over it.

The passengers in the street below would discern her anxious visage and send up a shout, "When the golden warrior on the province-house shall shoot his arrow, and when the cock on the Old South spire shall crow, then look for a royal governor again!" for this had grown a by-word through the town.

And at last, after long, long years, old Esther Dudley knew, or perchance she only dreamed, that a royal governor was on the eve of returning to the province-house to receive the heavy key which

Sir William Howe had committed to her charge. Now, it was the fact that intelligence bearing some faint analogy to Esther's version of it was current among the townspeople. She set the mansion in the best order that her means allowed, and, arraying herself in silks and tarnished gold, stood long before the blurred mirror to admire her own magnificence. As she gazed the grey and withered lady moved her ashen lips, murmuring half aloud, talking to shapes that she saw within the mirror, to shadows of her own fantasies, to the household friends of memory, and bidding them rejoice with her and come forth to meet the governor. And while absorbed in this communion Mistress Dudley heard the tramp of many footsteps in the street, and, looking out at the window, beheld what she construed as the royal governor's arrival.

"Oh, happy day! Oh, blessed, blessed hour!" she exclaimed. "Let me but bid him welcome within the portal, and my task in the province-house and on earth is done." Then, with tottering feet which age and tremulous joy caused to tread amiss, she hurried down the grand staircase, her silks sweeping and rustling as she went; so that the sound was as if a train of special courtiers were thronging from the dim mirror.

And Esther Dudley fancied that as soon as the wide door should be flung open all the pomp and splendour of bygone times would pace majestically into the province-house and the gilded tapestry of the past would be brightened by the sunshine of the present. She turned the key, withdrew it from the lock, unclosed the door and stepped across the threshold. Advancing up the court-yard appeared a person of most dignified mien, with tokens, as Esther interpreted them, of gentle blood, high rank and long-accustomed authority even in his walk and every gesture. He was richly dressed, but wore a gouty shoe, which, however, did not lessen the stateliness of his gait. Around and behind him were people in plain civic dresses and two or three war-worn veterans, evidently officers of rank, arrayed in a uniform of blue and buff. But Esther Dudley, firm in the belief that had fastened its roots about her heart, beheld only the principal personage, and never doubted that this was the long-looked-for governor to whom she was to surrender up her charge. As he approached she involuntarily sank down on her knees and tremblingly held forth the heavy key.

"Receive my trust! Take it quickly," cried she, "for I think Death is striving to snatch away my triumph. But he comes too late. Thank Heaven for this blessed hour! God save King George!"

"That, madam, is a strange prayer to be offered up at such a moment," replied the unknown guest of the province-house, and, courteously removing his hat, he offered his arm to raise the aged woman. "Yet, in reverence for your grey hairs and long-kept faith, Heaven forbid that any here should say you nay. Over the realms which still acknowledge his sceptre, God save King George!"

Esther Dudley started to her feet, and, hastily clutching back the key, gazed with fearful earnestness at the stranger, and dimly and doubtfully, as if suddenly awakened from a dream, her bewildered eyes half recognized his face. Years ago she had known him among the gentry of the province, but the ban of the king had fallen upon him. How, then, came the doomed victim here? Proscribed, excluded from mercy, the monarch's most dreaded and hated foe, this New England merchant had stood triumphantly against a kingdom's strength, and his foot now trod upon humbled royalty as he ascended the steps of the province-house, the people's chosen governor of Massachusetts.

"Wretch, wretch that I am!" muttered the old woman, with such a heartbroken expression that tears gushed from the stranger's eyes. "Have I bidden a traitor welcome? Come, Death! Come quickly!"

"Alas, venerable lady!" said Governor Hancock, lending her his support with all the reverence that a courtier would have shown to a queen, "your life has been prolonged until the world has changed around you. You have treasured up all that time has rendered worthless, the principles, feelings, manners, modes of being and acting which another generation has flung aside, and you are a symbol of the past. And I and these around me, we represent a new race of men, living no longer in the past, scarcely in the present, but projecting our lives forward into the future. Ceasing to model ourselves on ancestral superstitions, it is our faith and principle to press onward, onward. Yet," continued he, turning to his attendants, "let us reverence for the last time the stately and gorgeous prejudices of the tottering past."

While the republican governor spoke he had continued to support the helpless form of Esther Dudley; her weight grew heavier against his arm, but at last, with a sudden effort to free herself, the ancient woman sank down beside one of the pillars of the portal. The key of the province-house fell from her grasp and clanked against the stone.

"I have been faithful unto death," murmured she. "God save the king!"

"She has done her office," said Hancock, solemnly. "We will follow her reverently to the tomb of her ancestors, and then, my fellow-citizens, onward, onward. We are no longer children of the past."

Historical Notes

This section contains some brief biographical notes about the original collectors and their books featured in this collection. These notes have been adapted from those primarily on Wikipedia along with other supporting sources and notes.

Kate Chopin

Kate Chopin (February 1850 – August 1904) was an American author of short stories and novels based in Louisiana. She is considered by scholars to have been a forerunner of American 20th-century feminist authors of Southern or Catholic background, such as Zelda Fitzgerald, and is one of the most frequently read and recognized writers of Louisiana Creole heritage.

Of maternal French and paternal Irish descent, Chopin was born in St. Louis, Missouri. She married and moved with her husband to New Orleans. They later lived in the country in Cloutierville, Louisiana. From 1892 to 1895, Chopin wrote short stories for both children and adults that were published in such national magazines as *Atlantic Monthly, Vogue, The Century Magazine*, and *The Youth's Companion*. Her stories aroused controversy because of her subjects and her approach; they were condemned as immoral by some critics.

Her major works were two short story collections: *Bayou Folk* (1894) and *A Night in Acadie* (1897). Her important short stories included *Désirée's Baby* (1893), a tale of miscegenation in antebellum Louisiana, *The Story of an Hour* (1894), and *The Storm* (1898).

Chopin also wrote two novels: *At Fault* (1890) and *The Awakening* (1899), which are set in New Orleans and Grand Isle, respectively. The characters in her stories are usually residents of Louisiana, and many are Creoles of various ethnic or racial backgrounds. Many of her works are set in Natchitoches in north-central Louisiana, a region where she lived.

Within a decade of her death, Chopin was widely recognized as one of the leading writers of her time. In 1915, Fred Lewis Pattee wrote, "some of her work is equal to the best that has been produced in France or even in America."

Henry W. Shoemaker

Henry Wharton Shoemaker (February 1880 – July 1958) was a prominent American folklorist, historian, diplomat, writer, publisher, and conservationist.

Praised for drawing attention in his creative writing to the traditions of the Pennsylvania "mountaineers", Shoemaker nonetheless drew criticism for his alteration and occasional fabrication of legends. His goal, he announced, was to show the legacy of legends for landscape features such as trees, animals, caves and caverns, rivers, and mountains; by making people realising the spiritual narratives associated with the environment he hoped to make them more respectful and conservation-minded.

An example is his publication of the legend of Princess Nit-a-Nee, supposedly connected to the Nittany Mountains in Centre County; the legend has been perpetuated in many tourist brochures for sites to the present day such as Penn's Cavern and the Pennsylvania State University.

Shoemaker's humanistic interests in his creative writing also showed in his campaign to have artists use local folklore as a resource for literature, poetry, art, and music. A prolific writer, he produced more than 100 books and pamphlets and hundreds of articles. In addition to his books of legends such as *Susquehanna Legends, In the Seven Mountains, Penn's Grandest Cavern, Tales of the Bald Eagle Mountains, Allegheny Episodes, Juniata Memories, North Mountain Mementos, South Mountain Sketches, Black Forest Souvenirs*, for which he is best known, he published more ethnographic field collections of songs and ballads (*Mountain Minstrelsy of Pennsylvania*, 1931), folk speech (*Scotch-Irish and English Proverbs and Sayings of the West Branch Valley of Central Pennsylvania*, 1927), and crafts (*Early Potters of Clinton County*, 1916). He also wrote some of the earliest accounts of hunting and animal lore, such as *Pennsylvania Deer and Their Horns* (1915), *Pennsylvania Lion or Panther* (1914), *Wolf Days in Pennsylvania* (1914), and *Stories of Great Pennsylvania Hunters* (1913).

Charles F. Lummis

Charles Fletcher Lummis (March 1859 – November 1928) was a United States journalist, and an activist for native rights and historic preservation. A traveller in the American Southwest, he settled in Los Angeles, California, where he also became known as an historian, photographer, ethnographer, archaeologist, poet, and librarian

He lost his mother at age 2 and was home-schooled by his father, who was a schoolmaster. Lummis enrolled in Harvard for college and was a classmate of Theodore Roosevelt's, but dropped out during his senior year. While at Harvard he worked during the summer as a printer and published his first work, *Birch Bark Poems*. This small volume was printed on paper-thin sheets of birch bark; he won acclaim from *Life* magazine and recognition from some of the day's leading poets. He sold the books by subscription and used the money to pay for college. A poem from this work, *My Cigarette*, highlighted tobacco as one of his life's obsessions.

In 1880, at the age of 21, Lummis married Dorothea Rhodes of Cincinnati, Ohio.

In 1884, Lummis was working for a newspaper in Cincinnati and was offered a job with the *Los Angeles Times*. At that time, Los Angeles had a population of only 12,000. Lummis decided to make the 3,507-mile journey from Cincinnati to Los Angeles on foot, taking 143 days, all the while sending weekly dispatches to the paper chronicling his trip. One of his dispatches chronicled his meeting and interview with famed outlaw Frank James. The trip began in September and lasted through the winter. Lummis suffered a broken arm and struggled in the heavy winter snows of New Mexico. He became enamoured with the American Southwest, and its Spanish and Native American inhabitants. Several years later, he published his account of this journey in *A Tramp Across the Continent* (1892).

Upon his arrival, Lummis was offered the job of the first City Editor of the *Los Angeles Times*. He covered a multitude of interesting stories from the new and growing community. Work was hard and demanding under the pace set by publisher Harrison

Gray Otis. Lummis was happy until he suffered from a mild stroke that left his left side paralyzed.

In 1888, Lummis moved to San Mateo, New Mexico to recuperate from his paralysis. He rode on the Plains while holding a rifle in one good hand and shooting jack rabbits. Here, he began a new career as a prolific freelance writer, writing on everything that was particularly special about the Southwest and native cultures. His articles about corrupt bosses committing murders in San Mateo drew threats on his life, so he moved to a new location in the Pueblo village of Isleta, New Mexico, on the Rio Grande.

Somewhat recovered from his paralysis, Lummis was able to win over the confidence of the Pueblo natives, a Tiwa people, by his outgoing and generous nature. But a hit man from San Mateo was sent up to Isleta, where he shot Lummis but failed to kill him.

In Isleta, Lummis divorced his first wife and married Eva Douglas, who lived in the village and was the sister-in-law of an English trader. Somehow he convinced Eva to stay with Dorothea in Los Angeles until the divorce went through. In the meantime, Lummis became entangled in fights with the U.S. government agents over native education. In this period, the government was pushing assimilation and had established Indian boarding schools. It charged its agents with recruiting Native American children for the schools, where they were usually forced to give up traditional clothing and hair styles, and prevented from speaking their own languages or using their own customs. They were often prohibited from returning home during holidays or vacation periods, or their families were too poor to afford such travel. Lummis persuaded the government to allow 36 children from the Albuquerque Indian School to return to their homes.

Jane Pentzer Myers

Jane Pentzer Myers published only one book, a collection of twelve children's fantasies, *Stories of Enchantment* (Chicago: A.C. McClurg & Co., 1901), illustrated by Harriet Roosevelt Richards. Several of the stories contain Native American elements, like *The Ghost Flower* and *The Corn Fairy*.

Very little is known of the author. She was born Jane Pentzer Hamlin in south-eastern Wisconsin in September 1847; her father, Alanson Hamlin (1815/20-c.1855), was from Connecticut, her mother, Elizabeth J. Bassett (1824-after 1860), from England. She was the third child of five or six, having two older brothers, one younger sister and one younger brother. By 1860 she and her siblings were living with a family surnamed Kent - presumably relations (possibly the Elizabeth J. Kent listed is their remarried mother) - near Oran, in Fayette County in north-eastern Iowa. On 3 July 1866, in Fairbanks, Iowa (in Buchanan County, the next county to the south of Fayette), she married William D. Myers (1846-1921), and they settled in Humboldt County, in the northern central part of Iowa - first in Livermore, and then in Springvale (which was later renamed Humboldt). In 1880 they were running a restaurant, but by 1900 William was working as a general agent for machinery, and in 1910 he gave his occupation as gardener. They had four children, three sons and one daughter. According to the 1920 Census, enumerated on January 19th, they were living in Oswego, in Labette County in south-eastern Kansas, joined by one of their widowed sons, William E. Myers.

Reprinted with kind permission from Douglas A. Anderson's blog at: https://desturmobed.blogspot.com/2012/08/jane-pentzer-myers.html

Bret Harte

Bret Harte (born Francis Brett Hart; August 1836 – May 1902) was an American short story writer and poet, best remembered for his short fiction featuring miners, gamblers, and other romantic figures of the California Gold Rush. In a career spanning more than four decades, he wrote poetry, plays, lectures, book reviews, editorials, and magazine sketches in addition to fiction. As he moved from California to the eastern U.S. to Europe, he incorporated new subjects and characters into his stories, but his Gold Rush tales have been the works most often reprinted, adapted, and admired.

Nathaniel Hawthorne

Nathaniel Hawthorne (July 1804 – May 1864) was an American novelist, dark romantic, and short story writer. His works often focus on history, morality, and religion.

He was born in Salem, Massachusetts, to Nathaniel Hathorne and the former Elizabeth Clarke Manning. His ancestors include John Hathorne, the only judge from the Salem witch trials who never repented his involvement. He entered Bowdoin College in 1821, was elected to Phi Beta Kappa in 1824, and graduated in 1825. He published his first work in 1828, the novel *Fanshawe*; he later tried to suppress it, feeling that it was not equal to the standard of his later work. He published several short stories in periodicals, which he collected in 1837 as *Twice-Told Tales*. The next year, he became engaged to Sophia Peabody. He worked at the Boston Custom House and joined Brook Farm, a transcendentalist community, before marrying Peabody in 1842. The couple moved to The Old Manse in Concord, Massachusetts, later moving to Salem, the Berkshires, then to The Wayside in Concord. *The Scarlet Letter* was published in 1850, followed by a succession of other novels. A political appointment as consul took Hawthorne and family to Europe before their return to Concord in 1860. Hawthorne died on May 19, 1864, and was survived by his wife and their three children.

Much of Hawthorne's writing centres on New England, many works featuring moral metaphors with an anti-Puritan inspiration. His fiction works are considered part of the Romantic movement and, more specifically, dark romanticism. His themes often centre on the inherent evil and sin of humanity, and his works often have moral messages and deep psychological complexity. His published works include novels, short stories, and a biography of his college friend Franklin Pierce, the 14th President of the United States.

Eugene Field

Eugene Field Sr. (September 1850 – November 1895) was an American writer, best known for his children's poetry and humorous essays. He was known as the "poet of childhood".

Field set to work as a journalist for the *St. Joseph Gazette* in Saint Joseph, Missouri, in 1875. That same year he married Julia Comstock, with whom he had eight children. For the rest of his life he arranged for all the money he earned to be sent to his wife, saying that he had no head for money himself.

Field soon rose to city editor of the Gazette.

He became known for his light, humorous articles written in a gossipy style, some of which were reprinted by other newspapers around the country. It was during this time that he wrote the famous poem *Lovers Lane* about a street in St. Joseph, Missouri.

From 1876 through 1880, Field lived in St. Louis, first as an editorial writer for the *Morning Journal* and subsequently for the

Times-Journal. After a brief stint as managing editor of the *Kansas City Times*, he worked for two years as editor of the *Denver Tribune*.

In 1883, Field moved to Chicago where he wrote a humorous newspaper column called *Sharps and Flats* for the *Chicago Daily News*. His home in Chicago was near the intersection of N. Clarendon and W. Hutchinson in the neighbourhood now known as Buena Park.

Field first started publishing poetry in 1879, when his poem *Christmas Treasures* appeared in *A Little Book of Western Verse*. Over a dozen volumes of poetry followed and he became well known for his light-hearted poems for children, among the most famous of which are *Wynken, Blynken, and Nod* and *The Duel* (which is perhaps better known as *The Gingham Dog and the Calico Cat*). Equally famous is his poem about the death of a child, *Little Boy Blue*. Field also published a number of short stories, including *The Holy Cross* and *Daniel and the Devil*.

Field died in Chicago of a heart attack at the age of 45. He is buried at the Church of the Holy Comforter in Kenilworth, Illinois. Slason Thompson's 1901 biography of Field states that he was originally buried in Graceland Cemetery in Chicago, but his son-in-law, Senior Warden of the Church of the Holy Comforter, had him reinterred on March 7, 1926.

H. C. Bunner

Henry Cuyler Bunner (August 1855 – May 1896) was an American novelist and poet, known mainly for *Tower of Babel*.

He was born in Oswego, New York to Rudolph Bunner, Jr. (1813–1875) and Ruth Keating Tuckerman (1821–1896) and was educated in New York City. His paternal grandparents were

Rudolph Bunner (1779–1837) and Elizabeth Church (1783–1867), the daughter of John Barker Church (1748–1818) and Angelica Schuyler (1756–1814).

In 1886, he published a novel, *The Midge*, followed in 1887 by *The Story of a New York House*. But his best efforts in fiction were his short stories and sketches *Short Sixes* (1891), *More Short Sixes* (1894), *Made in France* (1893), *Zadoc Pine and Other Stories* (1891), *Love in Old Clothes and Other Stories* (1896), and *Jersey Street and Jersey Lane* (1896). His verses A*irs from Arcady and Elsewhere* (1884), containing the well-known poem, *The Way to A ready; Rowen* (1892); and *Poems* (1896), edited by his friend Brander Matthews, displaying a light play of imagination and a delicate workmanship. He also wrote clever vers de société and parodies. One of his several plays (usually written in collaboration), was *The Tower of Babel* (1883).

His short story *Zenobia's Infidelity* was made into a feature film called *Zenobia* starring Harry Langdon and Oliver Hardy by the Hal Roach Studio in 1939.

About The Editor

I was born in 1962 into a predominantly sporting household – Dad being a good footballer, playing senior amateur and lower league professional football in England, as well as running a series of private businesses in partnership with mum, herself an accomplished and medal winning dancer.

I obtained a degree in History from Leeds University before wandering rather haphazardly into the emerging world of business computing in the late nineteen-eighties.

I followed a succession of amateur writing paths alongside my career in technology, including working as a freelance journalist and book reviewer, my one claim to fame being a by-line in a national newspaper in the UK, The Sunday people.

I also spent 10 years treading the boards, appearing all over the south of the UK in pantos and plays, in village halls and occasionally on the stage of a professional theatre or two.

Following the sporting theme I worked on live TV broadcasts for the BBC, ITV, TVNZ, EuroSport and others as a rugby "Stato", covering Heineken Cups, Six Nations, IRB World Sevens and IRB World Cups in the late '90's and early '00's.

You can find out more at: www.clivegilson.com

I have edited Clive Gilson's books for over a decade now – he's prolific and can turn his hand to many genres - poetry, short fiction, contemporary novels, folklore and science fiction – and the common theme is that none of them ever fails to take my breath away. There's something in each story that is either memorably poignant, hauntingly unnerving or sidesplittingly funny.

Lorna Howarth, *The Write Factor*

Tales From The World's Firesides is a grand project. I've collected thousands of traditional texts as part of other projects, and while many of the original texts are available through channels like Project Gutenberg, some of the narratives can be hard to read for modern audiences, & so the Fireside project was born. Put simply, I collect, collate & adapt traditional tales from around the world & publish them as a modern archive. This book is the 6th and final piece in *Part 2 – North America*, following on from the titles in *Part 1* covering a host of nations & regions across Europe. I'm not laying any claim to insight or specialist knowledge, but these collections are born out of my love of story-telling & I hope that you'll share my affection for traditional tales, myths & legends.

Images by Clker-Free-Vector-Images & Jim Cooper from Pixabay